WHAT WE LEAVE BEHIND

WHAT WE LEAVE BEHIND

Also by Sue Halpern

Summer Hours at the Robbers Library
The Book of Hard Things
Introducing . . . Sasha Abramowitz
Can't Remember What I Forgot
A Dog Walks into a Nursing Home
Migrations to Solitude
Four Wings and a Prayer

WHAT WE LEAVE
BEHIND

A Novel

SUE HALPERN

HARPER ⬤ PERENNIAL

NEW YORK • LONDON • TORONTO • SYDNEY • NEW DELHI • AUCKLAND

HARPER ● PERENNIAL

HarperCollins books may be purchased for educational, business, or sales promotional use. For information, please email the Special Markets Department at SPsales@harpercollins.com.

FIRST EDITION

Designed by Jamie Lynn Kerner

Library of Congress Cataloging-in-Publication Data

Names: Halpern, Sue, author.
Title: What we leave behind: a novel / Sue Halpern.
Description: First edition. | New York, NY: HarperPerennial, 2025.
Identifiers: LCCN 2024035537 | ISBN 9780063415386 (trade paperback) | ISBN 9780063415393 (ebook)
Subjects: LCGFT: Domestic fiction. | Novels.
Classification: LCC PS3608.A549 W47 2025 | DDC 813/.6—dc23/eng/20240802
LC record available at https://lccn.loc.gov/2024035537.

ISBN 978-0-06-341538-6 (pbk.)

25 26 27 28 29 LBC 5 4 3 2 1

To my family, of course

WHAT WE LEAVE BEHIND

WHAT WE LEAVE BEHIND

CHAPTER ONE

Melody Marcus pulled a piece of paper from the pocket of her skirt and smoothed out its creases on the lectern in front of her. She looked down at her shoes—the black Doc Martens her mother, Delia, said looked like combat boots, "which is fine, if that's the look you're going for," which was clearly not an endorsement—then trained her eyes on the pink-and-purple gladiolus at the back of the room so it seemed as though she was looking at the crowd, which, to a person, had grown perfectly still when she rose from her chair and walked up to the microphone. The place was packed, with neighbors and relatives who had flown in the night before or driven up from the city, and friends of her parents and two rows of her father's employees, her friend, Karolina, and some other kids from school who ordinarily would not have acknowledged her existence, the mean girls and the dopey boys in their thrall, and strangers, so many strangers. It was a good crowd, her mother would have said if she'd been there, but she was not, because she was dead—two days dead already. "Jews like to get theirs in the ground right away," she'd heard a woman somewhere behind her whisper before the service began, though Delia would not be going into the ground, not that way. There was no casket, no need for a phalanx of solemn men to shoulder her body, permanently sequestered in a pine box, no need for a hearse to deliver it to a hole that had been dug that morning. Delia had been reduced to ash, and her cremains, as the funeral director, Mr. Mason, called them, were packed into a terra-cotta urn resting on a table to the left of the lectern where Melody stood, feeling the hectic drumbeat of her heart. To remind everyone that Delia had been a real, live person just two days before, Mr. Mason had set up a digital picture frame next to the urn, broadcasting pictures of her mother, whose face, more often than not, was obscured by the big-brimmed hats she wore to shield her face from the sun because, she said, she didn't want to end up a wrinkled old woman. What was it that people said? Be careful what you wish for? Well, Delia Marcus would neither grow old nor get wrinkled.

Melody was in shock. That's what everyone kept telling her—Mr. Mason, the police, the women who materialized on their doorstep with casseroles and deli platters—so she guessed she was. Two days ago, she was in her room with the door closed with Mumford & Sons playing through the tinny speakers of her laptop, ostensibly studying for the SAT but mostly scrolling aimlessly through the internet. She was a senior, and a good enough student, and the last thing she wanted to do on the weekends was sit in yet another classroom listening to some Harvard graduate—who, for some reason, was working for the Princeton Review and not Goldman Sachs—explain all the tricks that got him ten points shy of a perfect score. The deal was that she'd study on her own, and if her scores weren't high enough, she'd take the class. Her father, Eddie, was at the club, palling around with his regular crew. ("Bag man," they called him, because he was the CEO of the biggest, and most lucrative, paper bag company in the country. "Even if you've got flying cars and people living on Mars, you're always going to need paper bags. They're evergreen," he'd say, laughing at his own joke. Eddie, gregarious and affable, was a man of many jokes.) It had been a crazy-wet summer, and the ground had finally dried out enough to play the full eighteen holes. Delia was off on a shopping expedition—something about sniffing out a sample sale somewhere. Hunting and gathering was her favorite pastime, though earlier in her life, before Melody, she'd been a lawyer at a firm in Manhattan, a litigator.

Melody didn't hear the doorbell. Didn't hear the knocking. And then, suddenly, their next-door neighbor, Mrs. Schein, was standing outside her bedroom, frantically calling her name. "Come!" she commanded, when Melody opened the door.

She followed the woman down the stairs, where two uniformed state troopers, a man and a woman, were standing with their arms folded across their chests as if they were cold.

They asked Melody to state her name. She told them. They asked her to tell them her age. "Seventeen," she said.

They asked her to sit down and pointed to the staircase. "Am I in trouble?" she asked. Had they found weed in her school locker? She didn't think she would have been so stupid, but she'd heard stories of the police planting drugs on people.

The officers looked at each other and then back at her. "What? No," the man said. He seemed flustered.

The woman took a step toward her and squatted down so they were eye to eye. "There's been an accident," she said, and put her hand on Melody's knee. "When your mom was on the Saw Mill Parkway," she began, and Melody could see the whole thing: the narrow, twisty road, her mother's tendency to take the corners too fast.

The male cop cleared his throat. "It was the rain," he said, which confused her. It was a perfect, blue-sky day.

The female cop looked up at him and shook her head. "There's no easy way to say this," she said, tightening her grip on Melody's knee. The look of concern on the cop's face, the hand on her knee, the scripted words, reminded Melody of an after-school TV movie. She almost said so, too, almost laughed—was that shock?

"A rock—a boulder, actually—fell from the ledge above the road and crashed through the roof of her car," the cop continued.

Mrs. Schein took a quick, deep breath and let out a strange guttural sound. Melody shut her eyes, but there was no unseeing: the car, pancaked; Delia, squished like a bug.

"Is she dead?" Melody asked, even though she knew the answer.

"She didn't know what hit her," the male cop said.

Out of nowhere, Melody felt a bolt of anger rip through her body. "Why do people always say that?" she said. "Maybe she didn't know what hit her, but she definitely knew *something* hit her. She definitely knew that!"

The female cop rubbed her knee. Melody didn't remember who said it first, but someone told her she was in shock. Maybe it was Mrs. Schein, but she didn't think so, not yet. She could hear sirens coming closer. An ambulance, with Delia in it? But that made no sense: Delia was dead.

"That's going to be your father," the female cop said, which also made no sense. How would they know where to find him?

"I told them that I saw him put his golf clubs in the Porsche," Mrs. Schein volunteered, answering a question Melody hadn't actually asked. But it wasn't her father, it was more police, two local guys who heard about the accident on their scanner. Eddie Marcus was a generous donor to their annual Christmas toy drive.

Later—though Melody couldn't say how much later, since time was no longer marked in regular increments but, instead, by a before and an after—the house was filled with people. Her father was there, parked at the kitchen table with his head mostly in his hands, surrounded by his golfing buddies and their wives, like linebackers protecting their quarterback. Neighbors she knew only by sight and who didn't know one another milled around the living room, passing plates of cookies and telling stories about

Delia—how she always waved when she saw them on the street, how she'd just gotten that red Audi—trying to claim their bona fides. Her mother's hairdresser, Jeffrey, had shown up, and so had Stephen, Delia's personal trainer, though she'd fallen off that wagon a few months earlier when she'd gotten tendonitis in her right elbow playing tennis. Both were talking to a woman in a pale-green caftan whose blond hair flowed past her waist, who was somehow connected to Delia's brother, who had, theoretically, renounced all worldly things, including his family, after he'd followed a celebrity yogi to India years before.

Their housekeeper, Maria, who'd taken a livery cab from Mount Vernon when she'd heard the news, was buzzing around with a Marcus paper bag in her hand, tossing in used Solo cups and empty wine bottles that had also somehow materialized in the house. Before Melody retreated to her bedroom, she heard someone say that the accident was all over the news, and that one of the TV stations had obtained dashcam footage of the boulder hurtling toward Delia's car, but not the moment it hit. "It was like a meteor," they said. And someone else said, "Like the dinosaurs." She closed the door and lay on her bed and looked up at the glow-in-the-dark stars her parents had stuck to the ceiling when she was small and waited for the tears to come.

Melody ran her fingers through her hair. Her mother was right—had been right—she needed a haircut. The dirty-blond corkscrew curls that had been cute when she was a child had blossomed into an unruly light-brown mess that, as Delia would sometimes remind her, made her look like their old poodle mutt, Rowdy—also dead—when he needed to go to the groomer's. She adjusted the microphone, tapped it twice, and listened to the sound ricochet around the room. It roused her father, who raised his bowed head and looked straight at her, but vacantly, as if he didn't know where he was or who she was, even though it was his idea that she eulogize her mother because, he said, he had "no words." And it did seem so. He'd hardly uttered a complete sentence since he'd found out, unless the word "why" counted as both subject and object. The rent-a-rabbi was fine leading the prayers, but he didn't know Delia and wasn't in a position to say anything meaningful, although standing there, Melody wasn't sure she was, either. Her right leg, shielded by both the lectern and the below-the-knee black godet skirt she'd found in Delia's closet that fit like Cinderella's slipper, was shaking from nerves. She tried to stop it, but it seemed to have a life of its own.

"Good morning," she said, when it was no longer possible to keep stalling. It wasn't good, obviously. How could it be? Maybe if they'd been Christian and believed Delia was now in a better place, but they weren't, and she wasn't, and everyone knew that. She took a deep breath and gripped the sides of the lectern as if they were gunwales on a rocking boat and began. "Delia Danziger Marcus," she said slowly, carefully enunciating each syllable, "was not my mother." She heard someone gasp.

"Let me clarify that," she said. "Delia Danziger Marcus was not my *biological* mother." She paused to let this sink in, though, she figured, most of the people gathered there knew this already. "If it were not for her, and for my dad"—she nodded in the direction of her father—"I don't know what my life would be like right now. But I do know that I would not be standing up here, telling you about this amazing woman who rescued me from foster care when I was just about three."

As she heard her own words, she realized she was stating the obvious: Of course she wouldn't be standing there talking about her adoptive mother if she hadn't been adopted by her. She imagined her brilliant friend Lily, a Cardinal scholar at Stanford, who she'd known since they met at "adoption" day camp when she was five and Lily not yet seven, wagging her finger and say-ing "Department of Redundancy Department" and letting out a delighted giggle. Melody plowed ahead. The one thing she knew about eulogies from the cursory research she'd done online was that they should verbally photoshop the deceased and cast their story as a hero's journey.

"To be honest," Melody continued, "I don't remember much, except that when the social worker told me I'd be getting a new mummy, apparently I burst out crying because I thought mum-mies were dead people." There was faint, polite laughter, and she was suddenly aware that she probably should not have made a dead mother joke. But the thing was, Delia liked to tell that story, and when she did, it made people chuckle—but of course, Delia was alive when she said it. And it could have been apocryphal. What almost-three-year-old knew about mummies?

Melody remembered little of life before the Marcuses. She was called Jane then, a name given to her by someone, though she did not know who. It was generic, as if the person who be-stowed it didn't want to imprint themselves on her. But Delia had other ideas. "We named you Melody because once you arrived, our family was finally complete and we were living in harmony," she explained. The funny thing was that in adoption-world, Mel-ody was damaged goods. People wanted babies. Newborns. She was well past that when she moved in with Delia and Eddie, and big for her age, and already "had a mouth." But Delia, the litigator, was used to verbal contests and felt confident that a toddler would be no match for her. For his part, Eddie claimed he was happy to be getting a child who wouldn't have to resort to crying when she was hungry or tired or needed something she couldn't articulate. "There are fewer surprises with the older ones," Delia said when they picked Rowdy, who was already housebroken—like her!—out of an online album of available dogs. It wasn't lost on Melody, when she thought about it a few years later, that maybe that was how her parents had approached adopting a child, too, though the mast cell tumors Rowdy got four years after they rescued him definitely caught them unawares. Melody was thirteen then, and attached to the dog, and there was no way she was going to let the good boy die. "What's money for?" she said to her parents when the vet explained how much the surgery would cost, repeating back to them the very words they'd exclaim when flying first class or heading out to dinner at the Four Seasons. Rowdy got the surgery. "The kid's going to be a lawyer, just like her mother," Eddie told his friends.

"Let me tell you about Delia," Melody said. "She was, as we say now, fashion forward, which would have shocked anyone who knew her in college, when she lived in a pair of overalls—though I suppose since she had denim overalls, brown corduroy overalls, cornflower-blue overalls, quilted overalls, flannel-lined overalls, and train-engineer-striped overalls, the seeds of her fashionability"—she paused, wondered for a second if that was even a word, smiled in case it wasn't so they'd think she knew it wasn't, just in case— "were there all along. She was a graduate of Columbia Law School, but she gave up the law to raise me." (This was an outright lie: Delia had already left her firm.) "She told me once that she fell in love with Eddie—back when he had hair, by the way, so obviously a long time ago—because she once saw him slip a twenty-dollar bill to a homeless man when he thought she wasn't looking. But she was looking, and when she called him out on it because she was sure the guy was going to turn around and buy drugs or alcohol, he told her he wasn't the vice squad, and that you could never really know what someone else was going through, which made her realize that, unlike most of the men she had dated, he was a mensch, and a mensch was a better bet for the long run." (What

Melody didn't say was that this was not long after Alan Marcus, Eddie's older brother, who had schizophrenia, died of exposure on a Cambridge street near MIT, where he'd gone to school before he got sick. What she also didn't say, because no one ever told her outright, was that what Eddie called Alan's "condition" was the reason, he told Delia soon after they met, that he was happy not to have biological children. He'd rather roll the dice with someone else's genetic material.)

Melody looked over at her father, whose chin was resting on his chest. If Delia had been there, she would have whispered to him to sit up straight. She was a stickler for good posture, especially in the worst circumstances. What Melody saw, too late, was that if he were to look up, the photos of Delia would be in his line of sight, and it was too much. He loved his wife, but now he didn't have a wife, and those pictures proved it. He had been proud of her—proud of her Columbia degree, proud that she threw herself into the civic life of their suburban town (zoning board, planning board, ethics commission), proud that she "took care of herself" even if it was expensive—or maybe because it was expensive, proud that she didn't have to work a drudge job, or any job, unless she wanted to, and proud of himself for making that happen, though he'd never say so. He was a balding guy with a bit of a belly, happy to let his wife choose his clothes and needle him about joining a gym, a well-respected captain of industry who never forgot what it was like to be a private. Marcus Bags was a multimillion-dollar company with factories around the country and a supply chain that stretched from the Carolinas to China. On Eddie's desk was a bronze paperweight that said THE BUCK STOPS HERE, in an office as cramped and cluttered as their five-bedroom home (with a view of the Hudson from the oversized tub in the master bath) was spacious and refined. When Melody was old enough to sound out words, she pointed to the paperweight and said, "Is that why we're rich?" because as far as she knew, a buck was a dollar, and if all the bucks stopped with Eddie, then. . . . Eddie had laughed.

"It means I'm responsible for everything that happens here," he said. (Was this the first time Delia told her that they weren't rich, they were wealthy, as if there was a distinction?) At work he was the boss, no question about it. But at home the boss was definitely Delia, and he deferred to her, not out of weakness or disinterest but, again, out of pride. And now?

"What more is there to say?" Melody asked rhetorically, wrapping up after a series of anecdotes that she hoped captured Delia's spirit. "Everything—and nothing. Thank you, Mom." She lifted the pieces of paper from the lectern and refolded them, and as she was sticking them back in her pocket, someone began to clap. It was just one person at first, but then, as she was walking back to her seat, a few others joined in, and then the whole room erupted in applause. *Did people clap at funerals?* Melody wondered. She'd only been to a few, and she didn't remember that happening.

She turned and walked back to the microphone, and the clapping stopped, and she was relieved. "I forgot to say that you are all invited back to our house for a"—she caught herself before saying "party"—"reception," and sat down again. The rabbi came up, thanked her, said a few words in Hebrew, and it was over.

But nobody moved. It dawned on Melody that they were waiting for her and her father to leave first, so she tapped him on the shoulder and led him out the back exit, so they wouldn't have to walk down the long aisle, exposed. There was a black town car waiting to drive them the seven miles to Cornell Drive—all the neighboring streets were named after Ivies, too. The driver opened the car door, and Eddie, who was dabbing his eyes with one of the monogrammed handkerchiefs Delia had gotten for him a few years before, got in first.

"Miss, miss!" It was Mr. Mason, the funeral director, jogging toward her, carrying what looked like a football under his arm. "You forgot this!" And handed her the urn with what was left of her mother.

CHAPTER TWO

The first time Melody saw the house at 58 Cornell Drive, she was certain it was a palace. "Is that where a king and queen live?" she was supposed to have said—of course she had no memory of looking up at the brick facade strung with ivy that had been strategically placed to make the house seem older than it was.

Her room, on the second floor, with its own bathroom, was stocked with stuffed animals and two American Girl dolls (Felicity and Josefina), like a Toys"R"Us. They were piled high on a canopy bed, with drawers underneath filled with Hanna Andersson pajamas and J.Crew separates. The black trash bag that held the remnants of her first three years went straight to the town dump before it could contaminate the message Delia wanted to convey: that those years, the Jane years, did not exist. This was where Melody's life began.

And now, nearly fifteen years later, she was standing in the grand entrance to that house—under the Georg Jensen chandelier, on the Italian tile Delia had shipped from Siena after seeing something similar in a church, of all places—greeting guests, thanking them for coming, and directing them to a spread the caterers had laid out on the cherry-wood dining room table that could seat sixteen, fully extended, under another Jensen light fixture. "I'm so sorry," they said, almost to a person, and "You were so lucky to have her as your mother," which Melody couldn't help but hear as "You're so lucky to have landed in this 5,600-square-foot house in this upscale neighborhood with such generous people as your parents."

Someone—maybe one of Eddie's business associates—came up behind her and told her that they'd run out of ice, and she wanted to ask him what he wanted her to do about it, because why, all of a sudden, was that her responsibility? But he was saying, "So why don't I run over to the 7-Eleven and get some," and left before she could say anything, even "thanks."

"You look good, hon, despite everything." It was Marcia Yandel, Delia's doubles partner, good friend, and sometimes rival, though neither would admit that. She gave Melody's arm a squeeze. "How are you holding up?"

But before Melody could answer with the obligatory "fine under the circumstances," Marcia let out a small squeal because her son, Daniel, "the genius," who was studying ethnomusicology at Wellesley, or maybe Wesleyan, Melody couldn't keep straight which one was the women's college, was walking up the driveway. ("If he's such a genius, then why is he majoring in people banging on drums?" Delia would say, but never to Marcia.)

Danny Yandel was taller than Melody remembered, and thinner, and he'd ditched the unsightly dreadlocks, which Marcia was certain he'd grown just to embarrass her. Instead he had a buzz cut, almost down to the scalp, as if he had just reported for boot camp, or had lice, or cancer—though if it were cancer, she was sure she'd have heard about it. Danny was Marcia's favorite topic of conversation. "The Russians could drop a nuclear bomb, and Marcia would still be chattering about Danny," Delia had said more than once, even though she, too, admired him. (Hackley valedictorian; Harvard book prize; stem cell research intern at Rockefeller when he was in tenth grade.) After high school, the boy had spent time in Ghana, where, much to his mother's dismay, his interest shifted from medicine to indigenous instrumentation.

Now he was a college senior with not a single premed course on his transcript, and the life his mother had envisioned for him was in shambles.

As he got closer, Melody could see that Danny was wearing a black-and-gray dashiki under a navy-blue blazer, chinos, and red high-tops with red-and-white laces striped like candy canes. And he had an earring, just one, a turquoise stud in the shape of a butterfly, in his left ear. She suppressed a laugh, imagining what Delia would say about his "look." Something that sounded like a compliment but wasn't. She was good at that.

Danny was checking her out, too. "Nice shoes," he said as he approached. She could feel Marcia grimace on behalf of Delia. Complaining about their children's sartorial choices was one of their favorite topics.

"Nice earring," she said.

"It's a blue morpho," he said. "They're not really blue, I mean this one is, obviously, but in the wild they're not. They only look blue, which is a cool metaphor," though he didn't say for what.

"It was good of you to come," Melody said, "all the way from"—she took a guess—"Connecticut." She was pretty sure that's where Wesleyan, if that's where he went to school, was.

"We're on break," he said.

"But he would have come in any case," Marcia interjected.

"Yeah," he said, "your mom was great. It sucks. The way she died," he added.

That's one way of putting it, Melody thought but did not say. People were obtuse. Even geniuses.

He gave her a polite hug and moved on, stepping into the foyer, followed by Marcia, who'd had her share of tragedies: a surgeon husband in his prime who had a stroke while running on a treadmill but didn't die for another couple of years, and another son, Danny's older brother, Seth, who went to Israel junior year, stayed there, became Hasidic, changed his name to Gedaliah, and now had five children he would not let her visit. Still, in the unstated scorekeeping that dominated her friendship with Delia, Delia had just won for all time by getting obliterated by a stray chunk of schist.

A short woman whose thin face was framed by a puff of white hair came over and took both of Melody's hands in hers. "You did a beautiful job, dear. Delia would have loved your eulogy."

"Thank you," Melody said, unsure who she was or how she could have known what Delia would have thought. Someone's cousin, or someone's cousin's great-aunt, maybe. From what she could tell, funerals brought relatives out of the woodwork the way a rainstorm drew worms from the soil.

"I'm sure Dad would love to see you," Melody said, though she was fairly certain that he wouldn't. Since they'd gotten home, Eddie had been parked in the Eames chair Delia had gotten him for his fiftieth birthday, a year ago. His socked feet were resting on the ottoman—Delia had trained him well: he had taken his shoes off as soon as he got home—so no one could sit there. Guests came over to talk anyway, standing over him, or squatting if they had the knees for it. They would touch his arm, and he'd smile wanly, and pretend to be listening to whatever they had to say about his wife, but he didn't want to hear it. He just wanted to roll back the tape to two days ago, before he had left for his golf game, and before Delia had pulled her red Audi out of the garage. If he had told her not to go, she would be here now, and all these people would not. If he had told her not to go—but when, ever, did he do that?

Melody's phone buzzed in her pocket. She'd set it to vibrate when she got home, knowing that the only person who might call was the one person she cared about who could not be there, her friend Lily, in California. They'd talked the night before, when

Melody was struggling with the eulogy, when she was waiting for the tears to come, when she felt, she said, "encased in numbness." The image that came to mind was a fossil, preserved in amber, though she didn't know if she was the fossil or the amber.

"Grief is weird," Lily said. "I don't think it's supposed to be linear. You're grieving."

"Am I? I could hear Eddie wailing last night. It was awful. He sounded like one of those elephants that watch their babies get shot by poachers. But I can't seem to cry. It's like I don't know how to. It doesn't make sense."

"It's not supposed to make sense," Lily said. "I mean, it doesn't make sense, right? In what world does what happened to your mom make sense?"

Melody pulled out her phone and read what her friend had written.

LILY: I heard that your eulogy killed!

And then a smiley-face emoji. Only Lily could get away with a joke like that. Before Melody could answer, she saw that Lily was still typing.

LILY: Couldn't help myself. Srsly, how are you?????
MELODY: OK, I guess. This is all just so strange. Call later?

"Mother's not even in the ground and she's on her phone already," Melody heard someone say. A woman, who clearly wanted her to hear.

"Figures." A man's voice.

"No kidding," the woman said.

"Hey," a third voice, this one whispering. "Don't listen to them. They're idiots." It was Danny, drink in hand, who seemed to have come from nowhere. Danny, who had been her babysitter when she was little and let her play with his *Toy Story* action figures but since then had all but disappeared from her life. "Come with me," he said, and grabbed her elbow, and began guiding her in the direction of the kitchen. He let go when they crossed the transom so they could thread their way through the random collection of women, some wearing Delia's aprons, some from the catering company, slicing cake and transferring canapés onto serving platters, who, as if on cue, stopped talking when she and Danny entered the room.

"Carry on!" Danny said jauntily, downing his drink in a single gulp and leaving the glass on the counter as the two of them made their way to the side door, which he opened for her, waving his hand like a maître d' showing her to her table.

"Where are we going?" Melody said when they were outside.

"You'll see," he said. "Follow me." And then, when they were out of earshot of the men gathered on the deck, ties loosened, pint glasses in hand, he said, "I've got some really excellent weed. Jamaican. Smooth. It will take the edge off."

Was there an edge? What did that even mean? If there was an edge, would she fall off? But she followed along—because why not?—until they got to her old swing set, an architectural wonder with a spiral slide and a rope ladder like the ones in army recruitment videos, and a turreted playhouse with a cedar shake roof. They hoisted themselves inside, crawling so they wouldn't hit their heads, and sat down, knees touching, because that's all the space there was. "I don't remember the last time I was in here," Melody said as Danny reached into his blazer pocket, feeling around for matches and the blunt. "It might have been with you."

The swing set predated her by a few days. When they knew they'd be bringing her home, Delia and Eddie had it shipped express from Canada and built just in time for her arrival. It was magical—she did remember that. Remembered swirling down the slide, over and over again, remembered Delia snapping photographs and worrying she'd get too dizzy—or maybe it was too dirty. It occurred to her, crammed in there with Danny, that Delia, who oversaw the landscapers who oversaw the property, didn't have the swing set taken down when Melody had outgrown it because it was some sort of symbol, an announcement that a child lived there, a declaration that—like Melody's name itself—they were a real family. But this thought drifted away as soon as Danny released the smoke from his first hit, punctuated by a rough cough that blasted the vapor into her face. He handed her the joint. She watched it burn for a second, then put it in her mouth, took a draw, and was passing it back to Danny when he said, "Take another one," so she did. A piece of ash fell on the floor, and she—suddenly high and a little paranoid—said, "Delia will kill us if we start a fire."

After a while she said, "I wonder how long it will take."

"To burn it down?" Danny asked.

"No. To get used to, you know, the past tense."

"Oh," he said. And then, brightly: "I guess you'll find out." And inexplicably, they both started laughing.

"Welcome to the club," he said, and inhaled deeply. He held his breath and stared at her.

"What club?" she said, taking the joint from his outstretched hand.

Danny exhaled loudly, aiming the smoke at her. He rolled his eyes. "What club?" he repeated.

Melody was confused—and then she wasn't. "Oh, *that* club!"

she said, and they both started giggling again, till tears began running down Melody's cheeks.

"Come here," Danny said and patted the floor next to him.

"No," she said, petulantly. She was embarrassed. "I wasn't crying, just so you know," she said, wiping her eyes. "I was laughing. When I laugh, it looks like I'm crying. Just so you know," she said again.

"Cool," he said. They were quiet for a while. "I'm really wasted," he said, breaking the silence.

Melody appeared to consider this. "What's it like?" she said.

"Haven't you ever been high before?" he asked. "I mean, I'm sorry if—"

She cut him off. "No. Of course I have. I meant what's it like"—she hesitated—"after your parent dies."

"Ohhh!" he said. "Sorry. My bad. Hmm. Well, I was pretty young. I remember that at first I was really confused. I mean, I guess I knew about death. Our cat got run over and we had a funeral, and my brother, Seth—that was his name then—who is five years older, was the rabbi, which in retrospect was either the spark that put him on the path to becoming an Orthodox Jew, or it was in him already. Anyhow, it was really confusing. I kept forgetting that Dad was dead, but I also kept remembering. For a while I was convinced that it was my fault, which the shrink said was normal. But nothing was normal. Marcia fell apart, and when she got put back together again she was different. Fiercer. More protective. Kept telling people I was going to be a doctor like my dad. Said it so much I was convinced it was true. Like it was my destiny. And it was, till it wasn't, and it's been like killing my dad all over again."

"But you didn't kill him," Melody said.

"Not the first time," he said. "I guess the short answer to your question is that you miss them, and you miss the life you were living, and you wonder how things would have been if it didn't happen, and you get mad sometimes, and sometimes you get really sad, and sometimes—probably most of the time now—you don't think about it, and when you realize you're not thinking about it, you feel like crap. Ow!" He blew on his fingers where the rolling paper had singed them. "I was so busy regaling you with my tale of woe that I let this thing burn down," he said, repositioning his fingers and taking another hit.

"What's with the hair?" Melody asked, and reached over and touched the stubble sticking out of his scalp.

He closed his eyes, exhaled, and said, "So I took this course. It was called The White Man's Burden, which was ironic because you know, who is more privileged than white men—"

"Like you," she interrupted.

"Exactly," he said. He opened his eyes. "The class was all about colonialism. Africa. Europe. The Americas." He stopped speaking. "I'm really high," he said. "What was I saying?"

"You were saying that you shaved your head because you took some class."

"Right. The point was, I was doing the same thing with my hair. It was cultural appropriation. I was a white guy with dreads. It was wrong."

"I'm sure Marcia was thrilled," Melody said. "She was not a fan."

"Marcia thinks I'm gay," he said. "That's what she tells people, I think so they will assure her that I'm not. She tells me that her hairdresser and her decorator are both gay, as if to prove she's not homophobic, or because she is. Hard to tell."

Melody considered this. "She wasn't too happy about that girl you hooked up with in Ghana," she said after a bit. "You've got to wonder, though, in Marcia's world, which is worse—being gay or having a Black African girlfriend?"

Danny shook his head. "Now there's a question," he said.

They sat peaceably for a few minutes, listening to the squirrels scampering across the roof overhead, and the chickadees in the nearby trees.

"The thing is," Danny said, breaking the silence, then stopped. "The thing is," he started again, "sexuality is a social construct."

"I think you mean gender," Melody said. This had been a unit in health class, until some of the parents protested.

"Do I?" he said, and she couldn't tell if he was agreeing with her or challenging her. He stubbed out the roach on the bottom of his sneaker, which didn't seem safe to Melody, since it was rubber, but she said nothing. Instead she stared at him, taking in his practiced movements, his long fingers, the possibility that he might be balding. *When you're high*, she thought, *you can see people for who they really are*. It was like one of those solvents that art restorers use to reveal the painting underneath the painting. Danny Yandel, she could see, was a tangle of confusions.

"Don't you have to do a college tour?" he said suddenly. "You should look at Wesleyan."

"Way to kill the buzz, soldier," she said. *Soldier*—where did that come from? The college tour was a rite of passage: a road trip with Mom or Dad or both, to all the places whose decals they'd be happy to stick on the back of their Suburban. Delia had been looking forward to it, wondering if it would jinx Melody's chances at Tufts or Northwestern or Columbia if they bought the sweatshirt before she'd even applied. They were going to do it in the summer, but then Delia read that it made more sense to go when there were students on campus, so it hadn't happened yet.

"So," he said, adopting the singsong inflection of their parents'

friends, "where do you want to go to college?" It was a natural pro-
gression. When they were little kids, the adults wanted to know
what they wanted to be when they grew up, and when they were
teenagers, they wanted to know where they wanted to go to school,
as if wanting and going were the same thing.

"I'm thinking of taking a gap year," Melody said. The thought
had just popped up in her brain.

"Cool," he said. "That's what I did. Went to Africa and it
changed my life."

"I'll probably bag groceries at ShopRite. Trader Joe's if I'm
lucky."

"That's genius," Danny said. "College admissions officers love
that shit."

CHAPTER THREE

Candace was driving home from work when she heard the news about the woman who had been crushed to death by a stray boulder a few days earlier. Most of the time she listened to the classical station, not because she loved classical music but because the disc jockeys, if that's what they were called on public radio, didn't yell, or dole out unsolicited relationship advice, or yammer on about this or that celebrity breakup. But they were in the midst of their fund drive, begging listeners to be the one hundredth caller and promising a cloth tote bag for fifty dollars and a dog leash branded with the station's call numbers for seventy-five. As soon as she heard the phones ringing in the background and the station manager thanking "Jeremy in Riverdale" for his support, she switched to the all-news-all-the-time station, where the newscaster—or maybe the right term was news anchor, as if the whole enterprise was a ship that needed to be stabilized, which, she guessed, given the sorry state of journalism, it was—was asking a geology professor from Vassar if she thought the boulder dislodged because of global warming. The professor was hedging, saying that they couldn't be sure, but that all the rain they'd been having—which she said was predicted by all the climate models— could have caused erosion, which could have unmoored the rock.

"We'll probably never know," the professor said, which struck Candace as ridiculous: Why waste everyone's time if the so-called expert didn't have a clue? Why even raise the question?

Candace knew that stretch of road. Back when she lived in the city, after her company relocated to Stamford she'd take the Saw Mill for a more scenic drive when she didn't want to take the train. It never occurred to her to look up in case a huge boulder was barreling toward her. Who would?

Now she lived in Connecticut, in an updated Craftsman bungalow she'd bought not long after her company moved and her human resources job turned into a vice presidency, with a substantial salary that she, a single woman, felt she could not refuse. For a while she'd reverse commuted, getting on the train in Grand Central as everyone else was getting off, only driving when she needed to stay late or meet a colleague for drinks. This also let her take a tax deduction for keeping the car garaged in Manhattan—a cost that could cover rent for a family of four in most other cities. But after a woman who lived in her building was mugged (though not in the building or on their Chelsea block), and after she grew tired of stepping over homeless men sleeping on the steam grates near the 28th Street subway, and after she admitted to herself that she was married to her job, she decided to quit New York City and move to the suburbs. She envisioned a house on the Long Island Sound, or close enough to it to take early morning walks along the beach or sit on a jetty sipping coffee. She imagined being lulled to sleep by the sound of waves washing the sand, instead of sirens and car alarms and cabbies honking their horns.

The bungalow, as it turned out, was nowhere near the beach. It was tucked into the woods, not far from a spring-fed pond. The real estate listing described it as "your own private Walden," which Candace found a bit redundant—was there such a thing as a nonprivate Walden? But to her surprise, she also found the idea attractive. She dealt with people and their problems all day: someone who needed to take emergency leave because their kid had fallen off their skateboard and was in the hospital with a head injury (she had to stop herself from asking if he had been wearing a helmet), reviewing the corporate sexual harassment policy with a "handsy" department head, mediating personality conflicts between employees who either cared too much or cared too little, advocating for more women's bathrooms after advocating for the company to hire more women. When Candace was asked what she did as HR vice president, she'd say, "Hiring, firing, and everything in between." It was the "everything in between" that led her to pay cash for the house. Even though the pond was a quarter mile down a dirt track, she could imagine herself shedding her work clothes at the end of the day and sinking into the water, cleansing herself of the mental detritus of the office, and then retreating to the house, where she'd sit by the fireplace, glass of Chardonnay in hand, reading a British murder mystery or watching Helen Mirren solve one on TV.

"Won't you be lonely?" her friend Angela had asked when Candace showed her the listing. Angela, her best friend at work, lived in a four-bedroom duplex in Jersey City with her disabled husband, three teenage boys, and their Doberman, Abe Lincoln. (The boys didn't seem to notice she wasn't one of them—"Which says something about the state of sex ed!" Angela joked.)

Their place was a hive of activity, a three-card monte of shifting alliances and grievances that Angela had learned to ignore unless there was blood. The noise-canceling headphones Candace gave her one Christmas also helped. Work, for Angela, was a balm. Just sitting for hours on end, looking at spreadsheets, was meditative. But still, she couldn't imagine coming home to an empty house that looked like it had been air-dropped into a forest. "The quiet would creep me out," she told Candace. "Also, how are you going to meet anyone there?"

By "anyone," Angela meant men, and what she worried about

most, she told Candace, was not that she wouldn't meet someone, but that she *would*, on Match or eHarmony or some other dating app, and they'd go back to her place "in the middle of nowhere, and no one will hear you scream when he turns out to be a serial killer. Or just a killer. I mean, serial killers have to start somewhere."

"I'm only half kidding," Angela had said when she brought it up again, but Candace just laughed.

"I'm not worried," she'd said, though it wasn't clear if she meant she wasn't worried about getting murdered, or wasn't worried about not meeting anyone. Home ownership appealed to her. She was a single woman in her forties, and what better way to declare her independence? (But to whom—the real estate agent?) Her parents' marriage had been a good model for what not to do: they were always at each other's throats. It was a mistake she was not going to repeat. And she did meet men; men were attracted to her. The grays hadn't yet started to infiltrate her dusty blond curls, she was athletic looking—strong, but not too strong (an ideal type, according to *Allure*)—and a little aloof. No one was going to confuse her for the clingy type, which was good, since some of the men she met were married and not looking for anything more than a few fun nights at this or that conference, though sometimes they'd call if they were in the city on business, and they'd meet for dinner and pretend they had something to say to each other. For the most part, it was the ones who weren't married who were the dangerous ones. They were the ones who wanted more—wanted to leave a few shirts in her dresser, wanted her to put their phone number on speed dial. They were the ones who felt used when she told them "sometimes a cigar is just a cigar" as she moved on.

"Men are overrated," Candace told Angela, realizing after the words had come out of her mouth that she was talking to a woman whose only female ally in her immediate family was a ninety-six-pound dog. "I mean most men," Candace said. "Not yours, of course."

Angela's husband, Nick, was at home watching the Giants game with a buddy of his, while she, the boys, and Abe Lincoln had driven up to spend the day at Candace's. The boys had played Marco Polo in the pond as the dog patrolled the shore and, when they tired of that, searched for green sticks among a stand of beech and birch trees, which the two younger ones, ten-year-old twins Andy and Drew, presented to their fourteen-year-old brother, Liam, an aspiring Eagle Scout who wore a pocketknife clipped to his jeans "just in case." Liam whittled the ends of each stick to a sharp point and, when they got back to the house, made a fire in the backyard firepit. They roasted hot dogs, and then marshmallows for s'mores.

"This is nice," Angela admitted as she and Candace sat on the patio, watching the boys. There was a slight chill in the air, and as the sun set, it seemed to favor the tops of the swamp maples, which were just turning red. "I can see why you like it here."

"I know, right?" Candace said. And, after a while, listening to the sound of the boys' voices as darkness gathered around them, "They're such good guys. You're lucky." She hoped this made up for what she'd said earlier.

Angela laughed but said nothing. It was clear that she thought so, too—most days. It was also clear that just as she was waiting for them to grow up, she was waiting for Candace to get serious, find a partner, and settle down. Same coin, different sides. "Some of the time, love is right in front of you," the way it was with her and Nick, she'd tell Candace, "and sometimes it requires a bit of searching." And, as much as she believed in serendipity— the chance meeting of two people both cashing paychecks at the bank on a Friday afternoon, or seated next to each other on an airplane—Angela also believed that those encounters were meant to happen, and that God had a plan for everyone.

"What if God's plan for me is exactly what I'm doing?" Candace teased her. "I mean, if God has a plan for me, how could I possibly be doing anything else?"

But Candace got it. She'd probably feel the same way if the love of her life, who she'd met in second grade and married when she was in college and he was at the Police Academy, was wasting away from some disease he might have gotten from working at Ground Zero after the planes incinerated the Twin Towers and half his unit. One minute he was a robust, strong guy who could carry all three sons at the same time, and the next he had to hold on to them to shuffle from the bedroom to the kitchen. Better to believe that God had a plan, because the alternative was unbearable. Candace wondered what Angela would say about the woman who'd been crushed by the boulder, but her friend didn't mention it, and Candace thought better than to bring it up.

Candace hung her keys on the hook by the front door, kicked off her knockoff Louboutins, poured a glass of wine, and settled in on the sectional in front of a TV that took up most of the living room wall. The television was her first purchase after the closing, when she worried that she'd made a mistake, a big one, moving out of the city—where there were mocha lattes on every block and all of humanity jostling to get on the 2 train and every kind of takeout when she didn't feel like cooking—to all this nothingness. She liked her own company, but did she like it enough? So she got a TV so large that everyone was life-size and she could turn it on for easy companionship, watching the news after work and unwinding by listening to problems no one was asking her to solve: a war in Yemen, hurricanes in Haiti, a woman dead on the highway because a rock fell from the sky.

"I'm sure many of you have driven on that highway. I know I have," the newscaster, Bradley Bailey, said with a shudder in his voice, as if the boulder had narrowly missed him. The accident had happened a few days before, but the channel was milking it for ratings. He turned to his coanchor a stylish Black woman in a shimmering light-blue sleeveless dress that could have been an advertisement for her perfectly toned triceps and who was clearly bound for bigger and better. "So, Maya," he said, "I've heard people wondering"—he paused—"if this wouldn't have been so bad if the car wasn't a convertible."

"Oh, come on, Bradley!" Candace yelled at the TV. Maya didn't lose her bright smile while staring him down with an "are you an idiot? Yes, you're an idiot" look—"You go, girl!" Candace yelled.

"Well, Bradley," Maya said, "we'll never know, will we? I mean, the top wasn't down."

"Well, let's be grateful that more people weren't hurt," said Bradley Bailey.

"Oh, come on!" Candace shouted again. "Listen to yourself. Do you think her family is grateful it didn't hurt more people?" She laughed at herself for yelling at the screen, then got up and went into the kitchen to make dinner. She'd picked up a salmon steak at the grocery store, thinking that the omega-3s, or maybe it was 6s, would be good for her, but standing in front of the open refrigerator, eyeing the brown butcher paper, folded neatly and secured with a piece of masking tape, she thought better of it. Too much trouble. She closed the door and took a bag of microwave popcorn from the pantry, then waited as the smell of popping corn and fake butter filled the room.

Now the *News at Seven on Seven* remote team was standing at a makeshift memorial of flowers and teddy bears lining each side of a long driveway blocked off by traffic cones. The reporter, who wore a somber expression, was interviewing neighbors, who were saying the things neighbors always said at times like these: "She was a nice lady." "I just saw her drive down the street last week. I knew it was her because it was a red Audi." "I didn't know her well. She kept to herself." Candace knew what they were going to say before they said it, but still, she couldn't look away. The screen split, and the reporter was now sharing its real estate with a photograph of a balding man wearing a green polo shirt, one arm around a girl whose age was indeterminate because her face was fuzzed out, and the other around a woman almost as tall as he, wearing what looked to be a gray Eileen Fisher caftan and a floppy brimmed hat that all but obscured her face. Candace laughed, imagining the producer frantically searching for a better photo. The chyron read, "Delia Danziger Marcus, 1967–2015."

The popcorn was greasy and satisfying. Apparently, Delia Danziger Marcus had been on her way to a sample sale at Neiman Marcus—no relation—at the Central Avenue Mall. Candace had been to that mall. She'd been to that Neiman Marcus. She wondered if they'd ever bumped shoulders going in and out of the fitting rooms. When was she there last? Maybe eight months ago. Did she buy anything? Candace couldn't remember. She picked up the remote and began scrolling through the channels, finally stopping on a documentary about big-wave surfing. She had no interest in surfing—though the men who weren't wearing wetsuits had pretty bodies—but she was mesmerized by the waves, which seemed to be cresting and crashing and rolling into her living room. Candace turned out the lights and turned off the sound and watched the ocean rise up and come straight at her, then pull back, and come at her again, over and over, and before long she was asleep, still in her work clothes. It had been a long day. They were all long days. That's what she signed up for.

CHAPTER FOUR

Eight days after the boulder accident, the news shows had moved on and the story of the lady killed by a random hunk of schist had come and gone. The weekend had not arrived too soon. Candace was cocooned in her bed under a comforter topped by a weighted blanket, and even though she heard the crunch of tires on gravel, she made no effort to get up. She knew it was her friend Paul, the man she called her "nonresident husband," who came most Sundays bearing fresh bagels from the city, walking into her house without knocking and going straight to the kitchen, where he'd brew fresh coffee and put the bagels in the toaster and know that the twin aromas would, soon enough, lure her to the breakfast table.

"Hey, gorgeous," he said when she finally emerged. It had become a joke between them, since she usually had a bad case of bed head and pillow wrinkles on her cheeks, and she hadn't yet showered.

"Back at you," she yawned. She was wearing sweats with the word "Michigan" running down the left leg, which she'd taken from the lost and found at the gym where Paul used to work and where, years before, he'd been her trainer, and a T-shirt from a 5K race the two of them had run together in Central Park around the same time.

"Those were the days," he said when he saw it. Neither of

them ran much now, though Candace kept telling herself she was going to start again, soon.

"How are the ladies?" she said, sitting down. After he'd been laid off from the gym during the financial crisis, and after a couple of months moping on his couch eating ice cream by the pint and potato chips (and still not getting fat, she complained to him), he'd started his own personal training business. It was doing so well that he drove a BMW with a GT RIPT vanity plate and had a waiting list that never seemed to shrink. Most days found him on the Upper East Side or the tonier Westchester suburbs, putting stay-at-home moms through rigorous workouts designed to sculpt their arms, plump their glutes, flatten their tummies, and strengthen their core.

Women loved him. He was handsome. He believed in them. He was gay. That was his superpower.

"They're delightful. Of course," Paul said, handing her a cup of coffee, then rubbing his thumb and next two fingers together—the universal sign for money, lots of it. "I had this revelation," he said. Paul was often having revelations and insights. It was one of the things Candace loved about him. He was so earnest. He believed in the power of positive thinking and a person's ability to manifest what they wanted. ("It works. Exhibit A: I've always wanted a Beemer.")

"Do tell," she said.

"So," he said, "I realized that the reason men ditch their wives after twenty or thirty years of marriage is not only because they find younger women more attractive. I mean, that's part of it, right? But it's only part. I think the other part is that they don't think they are old. When they look in the mirror, they don't see that they've gotten jowls and a triple chin. They see their younger selves. I mean, don't we all? But when they turn around and look at their wives, they think, 'Why am I, this young, virile dude—'"

"Viagra notwithstanding," Candace said, buttering a bagel.

Paul ignored her. "'—with this old woman? I should be with someone my own age.' See?"

"So they dump the mother of their children, the woman who put them through med school or business school? Are you sure they don't have dementia?" Candace said.

"It's not dementia. It's perception. Also, did you know that feeling younger than you are helps you stay healthier and live longer? There are studies." He put down his mug on the table as if it were punctuation.

"I'll remember to explain it that way to the next fifty-five-year-old whose husband is in Cancún with his way-too-personal assistant," Candace said.

"It's just a theory," he said. And then, smiling, "But a good one, I think."

Paul, on the other hand, with his carapace of perfect abs, pecs, and traps and his flawless bronzed skin, seemed destined never to age. Candace could do a lifetime of planks and bridges, and gravity would still get the better of her. It already had, if she was being honest.

"Gravity is a bitch," she said out loud.

"Speaking of which," he said between bites of his bagel, slathered with raspberry jam, savoring each one. (Sunday was his one day of carbs.) "I passed the place where that boulder fell. You know my friend Jayson? From Equinox." He didn't wait for her to answer. "His friend Philip works with a guy at Planet Fitness who used to work with Stephen Tuttle." He rubbed his hands on his coffee cup as if they were cold and gave her a knowing look.

"Stephen who? Or what?"

"Oh, sorry, I thought everyone knew. He was her trainer. The lady who died. He was quoted in all the articles."

Candace leaned over and brushed away a crumb stuck to the corner of his mouth.

"So that makes us, what, five degrees of separation from that poor woman?" She was being sarcastic, but he didn't notice.

"Actually," he said, "I'm four and you're five. Anyway, they finally opened the road. Last week that lane was closed, but now they've put netting all the way up the cliff. Everyone was speeding up when they went by, though, just in case. And someone put up a cross, the way people do."

"I think I read that she was Jewish."

Paul shrugged. "I don't think it matters," he said, then brightened and rubbed his hands together. "Okay, ready?" and without waiting for an answer, pulled a folded copy of *The New York Times* from his messenger bag and opened it. Candace sipped her coffee and looked on, amused. Paul scanned the page. "This is a good one," he said, and started reading. "Cordelia Rinehart Rappaport, who goes by Corky, was seven years old the first time she met George John Thaddeus Adams, and it didn't go well. Ms. Rappaport was the flower girl for her cousin Marjorie Tyler-Hamilton, daughter of former ambassador Theodore Hamilton, while Mr. Adams—"

Candace cut him off. "Let me guess," she said. "While Mr. Adams, a distant relative of the second and sixth presidents of the United States, was the ring bearer."

"Not quite," Paul said, continuing. "While Mr. Adams, a distant relative of the second and sixth presidents of the United States, who was then thirteen, was his father's best man. 'He dropped the ring,' Ms. Rappaport remembered, 'and it rolled to where I was standing and I didn't know what to do, and I guess he didn't, either, because we just stood there, looking at each other. It was awkward.' Ten years later, the two met again at—" Paul stopped.

"Harvard," she said without missing a beat.

And he went on, "When she was visiting a friend from—"

"I don't know," she said, "Brearley? Miss Porter's? The Darien Yacht Club? Too many choices."

"Nice try," he said, "but you will not be going home with the grand prize today."

"I'm already home," she said, biting off a piece of the bagel.

"When she was visiting a friend from summer camp who was locked out of her room. 'I was a resident tutor in Winthrop House,' Mr. Adams explained. 'And our knight in shining armor,' Ms. Rappaport added. 'Quite literally. He was on his way to a Renaissance Faire.'" Paul stopped reading. "Should I go on, or move on?" he asked.

"If you only read the Vows column, you'd think that everyone in the world went to Harvard for college and wintered in Palm Beach."

"Los Cabos," he corrected her. "According to my clients," he added. He picked up the paper again. "What about these two? They didn't go to Harvard, they went to . . . ?"

"Princeton," she said.

"Bingo!"

"When did 'winter' become a verb?" she said to no one. Then, to Paul, "This is too easy. These people are too predictable."

"That's what makes it fun," Paul said. "Anyway, it's good to have rituals, don't you think? And this one is ours."

"Did you know they call the Vows column the sports page for women," Candace said.

Paul looked at her, annoyed. "So you've said."

"I mean, it is fun," she said. "So many Corkys and Mumsies and men with numbers after their names."

"How the other half lives," he said, stabbing his knife into the tub of cream cheese.

"Definitely the other half," she said.

"Oh, here's a good one," and began to read out loud again.

If someone were to ask them, as they had asked each other, when this ritual of reading the wedding announcements in the Sunday *Times* began, neither could say. It just evolved, as their friendship evolved, and as they realized that despite their obvious differences—man-woman, gay-straight, parochial school–public school, gregarious-reserved—they were more alike than not. New York could be a lonely place, yet for the longest time Candace felt immune to its loneliness, happy to be swallowed up by the anonymous horde, and then she met Paul, and he insinuated himself into her life. At least, that's what she told herself, though if she were being truthful, it was the other way around. Paul was the honey that attracted flies, and somehow, in spite of herself, she had become one of those winged creatures.

She intimidated him at first. "You were so obedient, and so, so, what's the word, 'imperious,'" he said, years later, when they were comfortable enough with each other to talk about it.

She punched him gently in the arm. "I was not imperious," she protested. "I was businesslike."

"In my business, we engage with our clients," he said.

"Mine, too," she said. "The gym was a refuge. A place where I didn't have to do that. Until you broke me," she said.

"Just doing my job," he said as a big smile spread across his face like an advancing tide.

When Candace first met Paul, back in their Planet Fitness days, he was the only trainer who didn't sound like he was praising a puppy for not peeing in the house. He wasn't tough, exactly, but only doled out encouragement when he thought it was warranted, which appealed to Candace, who found the words "nice job" annoying. She had a job, and this wasn't it. She couldn't remember precisely when her status changed from client to friend. It was a gradual transition. She was still paying him, so she thought that maybe theirs was just one of those friendly transactional relationships that existed only as long as there were transactions to be made, which was fine with her. Friendship did not come naturally to her. She'd never had a sleepover when she was growing up, never invited anyone home from college. Her father—the bane of her mother's existence—was one of those hail-fellow-well-met friends to everyone he met at the bar, and the polar opposite of her mother, who spent twenty-seven years berating herself for succumbing to his boozy, glad-handing charm. She didn't have to say it. Candace got the message: the closer people got, the more disappointing they were, so keep your distance.

But it turned out, somewhat ironically, that Paul lived in her neighborhood, and they would see each other on the street and at Jamba Juice, and they just fell into it, the way people do in New York. He invited her to walk along with him at the 8th Avenue street fair. They went together to the Union Square Greenmarket. At first, it was parallel play, but before long, their lives began to enmesh. They watched *Clueless* on her VCR, and old *Seinfeld* episodes on his. He invited her to a Friendsgiving. Somewhere along the line they found out they were birthday twins, born on the same day, two years apart. Angela called him her "Latin lover," even after Candace explained that Angela was only half right. "His mother is from Argentina, but his father is from Jersey," Candace told her. "And he's gay. Paul, not his father."

What she didn't tell her friend was that they had tried—almost. It was the third summer of their friendship, and she was his date at a cousin's wedding on the Jersey Shore. They were tipsy from the sun and the cocktails and a night of dancing and so many of his relatives telling them that they made such a beautiful couple. Her rational brain knew this was wishful thinking on their part; they loved their "beautiful Paulie," who they wanted so badly not to be who he was. And maybe, for that night, neither did either of them. It was like a game of truth or dare, and they chose dare—until the truth was undeniable.

"I had sex with girls in high school," he told her as he swiped the key card to the room they were sharing. "It's not that I don't know how to do it."

"Good to know," she said, lying stiffly on the motel bed closest to the door, suddenly sober enough to know that they were tottering on the precipice of a big mistake. He shed his jacket, tie, and shirt, then sat down at the edge of the other bed, facing the wall, and bent over, peeling off his socks. As he did, she couldn't help but admire his back, a tanned topographical map of muscles Candace had no idea existed. And then, all of a sudden, his shoulders started jerking up and down. Was he crying?

"I'm sorry," she said, and as she did he flung himself onto the bed like a backstroke swimmer at the start of a race, and she was aware once again how lovely his body was, and though it was inches away, how out of reach it would always be. He was holding his hands over his eyes, and his chest was heaving.

"Must have been those vodka shots!" he said, and she realized he was laughing.

"Thank God," she said, "I thought you were crying."

"Laughing," he said. "I was laughing." He folded his hands on his chest and craned his neck to look at her. "Not at you," he said. If there was one thing he understood about women, it was how even the most beautiful were insecure about their bodies.

"At who, then?" she said.

"Oh, you know, the world. Us," he said. "Not you, specifically," he clarified. "It's just that when I'm with my family, I know how much they don't want me to be gay, and when I'm with them I don't want to be, either. But it's no use, obviously.

"This isn't going to be weird," he declared. "We are going to go to sleep, and when we wake up, we are going to do ten push-ups as penance."

"As penance for what?"

"I'm not sure, but there must be something. Indulge me. I'm a graduate of Saint Mary's of Metuchen High School."

So that's what they did. Ten push-ups before breakfast on the stained motel carpet.

"Let's not pretend we didn't, you know, talk about doing it," he said, effortlessly lowering his body to the floor and raising it up again before his chest grazed the pile. "Repression isn't good for the soul."

"It's always worked for me," she said, gritting her teeth as her arms began to wobble.

"Are you sure?" he said. And then, "Breathe through it."

She was sure. Repression was her friend. It kept her feelings at bay. It was something she learned, watching her mother, who couldn't hide hers. Candace would have said that the disappointment her mother felt colored everything, but in fact it rendered the woman colorless. Even the food she cooked—begrudgingly— was bland. What was that saying? "Let it all hang out"? Candace saw what happened when you let it all hang out, and she wanted nothing to do with it. Keep your own counsel. Hold your cards close to your vest. Never let them see you cry. Repression is your friend. These were her mantras, and they had gotten her to where she was. Paul was the exception that proved the rule.

Candace pulled a second bagel from the bag, which was followed by a spray of poppy seeds.

"Oh, here's a good one," Paul said, lowering the paper. "These two ladies have gotten hitched. *The Times* is calling them both wives."

"What else would they call them?"

"Good question," he said, "but it just feels so, I don't know, old fashioned. Also, and this will blow the minds of every homophobe who reads the Vows column—"

"Which is probably zero," she said.

"True. Okay," he said, amending his statement, "this will blow the minds of guys who go for all that girl-on-girl action—"

"With women who look like *Sports Illustrated* swimsuit models," she added.

"The women wore identical strapless Vera Wang wedding dresses," he read. "None of that butch tuxedo stuff. Translation: two nice, almost normal, girls."

Candace considered this: Was *The Times* trying to sugarcoat gay marriage, or were they trying to normalize it? As her friend Angela liked to say whenever her oldest boy confronted another hurdle of puberty, "It's a brave new world." It was a new world, for sure, but unlike the inevitabilities of the body, it took a lot of bravery to get there.

"Oh God," Paul said suddenly. "I almost forgot to tell you. My father, God bless him—not really—has been telling all the relatives and probably anyone else who will listen that he did not contribute to my DNA! Because, you know, there was no way his sperm could have made a ho-mo-sex-u-al," he said, pulling the word apart, like taffy.

"Do tell," she said.

"So," he said, taking a deep breath. "You know my mom is from Argentina, right? Did you know that after she met my dad and they got engaged, she went back to Argentina to wait for her green card or something? You know I was born there, right?"

"You've got an interesting way of telling a story," Candace said. "And I don't mean that as a compliment."

"Hush, girl," he said. "She goes back, finds out she's pregnant, and stays there to have the baby—me—and comes back to the States when I'm, like, some months old. Not sure. It's a little fuzzy. They get an apartment in Paterson and settle into family life. Which should be the end of the story, right?"

"I'm guessing it's not," Candace said.

"What do you know about the Dirty War?" he asked.

She thought for a moment. "Not much. I saw *Evita*. The one with Madonna."

"Okay," he said. "So Evita's in power, right, but she gets pushed out, the military takes over, and eventually it starts rounding up people it doesn't like—which is putting it mildly. I mean, they start killing lots of folks, throwing them out of helicopters, torturing them—that sort of thing. Lots of them just disappear without a trace. There's this group, the Mothers of the Disappeared, who start protesting, and some of them are 'disappeared' themselves.

"I'm giving you the SparkNotes version," he said. "Well, actually, the Wikipedia version. Anyway, one of the things that happened during that time was that babies born to some of the women who were abducted were given to people who supported the bad guys. But those kids had no idea. They were handed over as soon as they were born." He paused and took a sip of his coffee, which by then had grown cold. "Not good," he said, and Candace wasn't sure if he meant the coffee or the abductions. "And now my father is telling everyone that I'm one of those."

Candace was puzzled. "You're one of those what?" she said.

"One of those kids. Of the disappeared. That the whole story that my mother was pregnant with his child was a ruse to get him to marry her, because the most macho thing a guy like him can do, apparently, is knock a girl up. But she wasn't pregnant." He looked at Candace, whose head was cocked to one side, like a dog trying to decipher the words of its owner.

"And he knows this how?"

"My mom. She told him."

"Let me get this straight," she began and saw him smirk. "Let me rephrase that," she started again. "After decades of marriage, she tells him this?"

"Best day of his life, apparently," Paul said. "It's perfect. After he found out I was gay, he started giving my mother a hard time, telling her that there is no effing way that his genes made a faggot, says the bad seed must have come from her, blah blah blah. And he hounds my mom so much that she eventually tells him this story—which is what he's wanted to hear all my life. Or, all my life that he's known I'm gay. And—icing on the cake—she even tells him that my real parents are Jewish. Which makes me as unrelated to my good Catholic parents as it is possible to be, which was the point."

He got up, took a glass from the cupboard over the sink, and filled it with water. "You really should filter this, you know," he said, taking a swig. "Heavy metals.

"Honestly," he said, "I wish it was true. I mean, look at me! I never fit in. It would explain so much if I'm a queer Jew! Maybe I should just embrace the lie and start going to temple!"

"But you're not religious!" She knew it was a ridiculous thing to say, even as she said it.

"Did it ever occur to you that I am not religious because I was never supposed to pray on my knees."

"No," she said. "Not for a second. And for your information, it's well water and I had it tested before I bought the house."

CHAPTER FIVE

After the meal train organized by Eddie's employees stopped delivering dinner every evening, and after there were no more empty casserole dishes on the back deck waiting to be picked up, Melody found herself rattling around the big house, heard Eddie rattling around, too, and it struck her how, until that moment, she assumed that was just a description you'd find in a novel: "The widower and his daughter rattled around the empty house, hollowed out by the death of the matriarch," or some such thing. But now she could hear it: the unsettled quiet, interrupted now and then by footfalls on the polished plank hallway floor, the flush of a toilet, a door in need of oiling—the faint, intermittent broadcast that life went on.

Despite the mac and cheeses, the lasagnas, the glutinous pasta Alfredos, her father was losing weight. Once she noticed, she realized he had just been pushing food around his plate like a little kid, hoping no one would notice he was not eating the liver and waiting till his mother turned her back so he could slip it to the dog. But they didn't have a dog. After Rowdy died, Delia decided she was allergic. But Melody wondered if what Delia was allergic to was a dog walking on the white Berber carpet in the living room and scratching the wood floors upstairs.

When the meal train had been running, every night Melody would heat up that night's offering in the microwave and yell up to her father that it was suppertime, and he'd show up dutifully, like she had when her mother summoned her. But she wasn't his mother, obviously, though she supposed that at seventeen she could be someone's mother, sitting there with spoon in hand, urging them to take one more bite. *No wonder there is an obesity epidemic*, she thought. Everyone was just listening to the adults in their life, telling them to take another bite and then another. Except for Eddie, who appeared to be shrinking. His face was gaunt. His pants were cinched with a belt that would soon need an extra hole or two to hold them up.

Most nights they sat in silence, listening to each other chew and swallow. Eating was a chore, like brushing and flossing, or filling up the car with gas. Melody knew better than to bring her phone to the table and text with friends—not that Eddie would notice—because the voice in her head, her mother's voice, was telling her it was rude, and how could she push back at a disembodied voice? It was like pushing on air. Her mother was air. No, she was something less than air.

When Eddie did speak, his sentences almost always included the words "your mother," as in, "Your mother was thinking of going back to work," which was news to her. Delia hadn't worked for years—or, Melody corrected herself, hadn't worked outside of the home in years, which is how Delia would have put it.

"Where?" she asked him, to no response. At another time in her life, Melody would have insisted, would have asked him again, louder, demanding to be acknowledged, but not anymore. The voluble and solicitous Eddie, the father she adored, was as gone as his brainy, regal, tough-minded, loving wife. In his place was a man surviving on nothing more, it seemed to Melody, than reminiscence and regret.

Melody had her own regrets, of course. How could she not? She had only recently emerged from what Delia had taken to calling "the eye-rolling years," when Delia could do nothing right, try as she did. Melody had no interest—none—in going on a mother-daughter spa weekend at Canyon Ranch, didn't want to spend a Saturday shopping for shoes, didn't want to go into the city for sushi and a matinee, something she'd loved doing when she was younger. They'd get hot chestnuts from a street vendor and peel them, fingers burning, as they walked to the theater, and, after the show, pop into the M&M's store on Broadway so Melody could assemble a bag of candy, piece by piece, that she'd present to Eddie when they got home, then detour to the Magnolia Bakery in the bowels of Grand Central for a red velvet cupcake to eat on the train, devouring the buttercream before taking bites around the cakey perimeter as if it were an apple or an ear of corn, trying to make the whole thing last until the conductor called their stop.

"I get it. I was the same way when I was your age," Delia said when Melody blew her off yet again. "I remember being thirteen."

Melody was incensed. "I'm fourteen," she said sharply, but that wasn't what irked her. It was feeling like her feelings weren't her own, like she was following a script she hadn't written, like her life wasn't hers. She used to love being compared to her mother, especially when people would say that she was the spitting image of Delia, who just smiled and made no effort to correct them. Loved the matching Lanz nightgowns Eddie got them when Melody was nine, and again when she was eleven. Loved the fact that both she and Delia always put red pepper flakes on their pizza, and loved that Eddie declared them both "barbaric" when they did.

When did that change? Melody couldn't remember. Did she just wake up one day between 1,500-thread-count Egyptian cotton sheets and feel that everything Delia did (like buying those sheets) rubbed her the wrong way? Breakfast was on the table, but she didn't want French toast, and why did Delia assume she did? Her hair was a mess, but it was her hair and her mess. She could remember Delia's face then: more hurt than angry. The anger, the butting of heads, that would come later.

But it was Delia's expression that Melody was remembering—her eyes, startled, her mouth, pained—as if she'd accidentally touched a hot stove. She remembered, too, how powerful it made her feel then, which now made her feel ashamed.

"You could be nicer to your mother," Eddie would say every once in a while. Not "should" but "could," as if giving her a choice. She rarely took it.

Melody would like to believe that the eye-rolling years had ended well before her mother died, and to a large extent they had, but she worried that they had ended because Delia had given up. She hoped she had been nice to Delia the morning she died, and was pretty sure she'd been nice enough, which in retrospect was probably not as nice—as Eddie might have said—as she could have been.

"My father says that regret is part of the grieving process," Lily told her after Melody asked, for the ninth time, if she thought Melody was a good person.

"I should have gone with her," Melody said.

"You couldn't have stopped the rock, Mel. The best person in the world could not have stopped the rock."

Five weeks after what they obliquely called "the accident," if they called it anything at all, Melody was startled to find Eddie in the kitchen, grinding beans for coffee, when she rushed in before school to grab a granola bar. He was clean shaven, what was left of his hair was neatly combed, and he was wearing a charcoal-gray pinstripe suit she had never seen before and a pale-pink spread collar shirt, which was also new to her.

"What do you think?" he said, slowly turning around to give her the 360-degree view. "Your mom had it made for me almost twenty years ago on Savile Row in London. The shirt, too. She knew they wouldn't fit me. You know how she was always telling me I should lose a few pounds. Well, I guess she figured these beautiful and, I may add, ungodly expensive garments would motivate me. And now look!" He twirled again.

So many inappropriate thoughts went through Melody's head—she imagined an infomercial for the dead-wife diet, with before and after photos—but she restrained herself. The suit fit him well, the pink offset his pallor, and he no longer looked like he'd just woken up from a long, fitful nap. Eddie put the freshly ground beans into Nespresso pods, then watched the rich, brown liquid drip into a Marcus Bags to-go cup.

"I have a lot of work to catch up on, so I'll be home late," he told her. It was so normal that it was weird.

Melody had gone back to school two weeks earlier. After a while it just seemed like a better option than sitting at home, watching blooper videos on YouTube and texting with her friend Karolina, especially after Karolina had her phone confiscated for using it during math class. Danny wrote a few times, to "check in," he said.

MELODY: It's like he thinks we're friends :-(

She texted Karolina before Karolina was separated from her phone. Karolina wrote back.

KAROLINA: Some people like to be associated with tragedy. Makes them feel better about themselves, or important.

Karolina was planning on becoming a therapist; she liked to try out her analyses on her classmates.

Melody decided to go back to school on a Thursday, to ease into it. Walking into the building—a modernist, cement-block structure that, kids said, was an exact replica of a medium-security prison in Iowa—she didn't take off the oversize dark glasses her mother liked to wear (but not *that* day, when she must have forgotten them), and hadn't gone more than five steps in the direction of her locker when the hall monitor told her to remove them. She kept going, pretending not to hear. Maybe he'd think she had an eye problem and therefore didn't hear well, either. She'd seen people shouting at blind people, as if not being able to see meant they couldn't hear, either.

"School rules," he said, following her. "It's in the dress code." He was a short man with a bushy black mustache who patrolled the halls with a walkie-talkie holstered on his hip like a gun, and a hefty ring of keys that bounced loudly against his thigh when he walked. His name tag said MR. BLANCHARD, but in all the years Melody had been at that school, she only ever heard him called "the CO." She reached her locker and began spinning the combination. Blanchard stood nearby, tapping his foot conspicuously, waiting for her to follow his order. She didn't.

In the vice principal's office, Melody's mind wandered as the man flipped through the Board of Education's dress code handbook, looking for the section that prohibited students from wearing dark glasses indoors. "Okay, yes," he said when he found it, then read it to himself as Melody looked on. "Right," he said when he finished. And then to her, "The only exception is for medical purposes."

He stood up, but instead of dismissing her, began to shuffle the papers on his desk. Not sure if she was free to go, Melody stood, too, but didn't leave. When he looked up, he seemed startled to find that she was still there. "I'm sorry about your— I'm sorry about what happened," he said, and began scribbling something. "Here," he said, holding out a hall pass. "You'll need this."

The whole time she had been in the office, she hadn't removed her mother's sunglasses. They were still on when she walked out, and no one stopped her. If she couldn't avoid everyone's stares, at least she could pretend not to see them.

It was a Tuesday. It was a Friday. It was a Wednesday. It was a day not unlike the day before it. Melody woke up at 7:15, put on the pair of ripped jeans Delia hated, splashed water on her face, and pulled a brush through her unruly hair, which could still use a trim, but getting her an appointment with Jeffrey, or one of his assistants, was, as her father liked to say—past tense—"Delia's department."

In the kitchen she found a note on the table, the same one Eddie had left the day before, and the one before that, written in black Sharpie on the back of an envelope from the phone company. "Nice job recycling," Melody said to the empty room, not bothering to read "Home late. Have a nice day." Delia had been dead for seven weeks, and now he wanted her to have a nice day? (Was he having a nice day? Grief was so strange.)

Outside it *was* nice—sunny, with only a wisp of wind. (Didn't it *know*?) She had a car, the silver Lexus her parents hadn't traded in when they bought the red Audi, a sixteenth birthday present that was waiting for her when she passed her driving test. She could go anywhere. The key fob was in her pocket. She could go anywhere, even not to school, which had become unbearable now that she was "that girl."

Melody went back upstairs and walked into her parents' bedroom. Her father had not made the bed—apparently that was Delia's department, too—and the mauve duvet was in a haphazard pile where Eddie had kicked it off. She walked into her mother's

closet, knowing what she was searching for but suddenly mesmerized by the ordinariness of the skirts and blouses suspended from
padded hangers, and the shoes, boots, and sandals lined up underneath as if waiting to be slipped into and walked away. There was
the emerald-green kimono Eddie had brought back from a business trip to Japan, and the Laura Ashley robe that, Melody knew,
possessed the unmistakable scent of her mother—a cocktail of
Chanel No. 5 and Pantene hair spray.

Delia liked to shop, no doubt about it. A muted pink Kate
Spade blazer hung next to a brown suede Tom Ford blazer, both
with their tags still on, which seemed unbearably sad to her.
Standing there, she found herself nostalgic for the arguments
they'd had, when Melody asked her mother why she needed a
two-thousand-dollar Burberry tote when there were homeless
people living on the street (though not their street, or any other
street in their town, to be fair), and Delia wanted to know why
Melody wanted to pay two hundred dollars for a pair of jeans
intentionally torn across the thighs that, in her day, most people
would have patched or thrown in the garbage unless they didn't
have a choice, and the blowup when Delia bought an Italian
leather jacket—because, cows—during the brief moment when
Melody was vegan, which tore through their household like bad
weather and then was gone. There it was, hanging with the other
jackets, this thing that had caused them all such, as Eddie would
say, *tsuris*. Melody hesitated, then reached into a pocket. She felt
a few stray coins and what she assumed was a handkerchief. She
took it off the hanger and slipped her arms through the sleeves,
feeling them slide in easily along the silk lining. She admired
herself in the mirror. For a moment she forgot what she'd come
for, then remembered, and started looking in earnest till she
found it, resting on the floor behind a row of dresses organized by
color: the old L.L.Bean duffel they used when she was small and

she and Delia would spend the afternoon at the Rye beach and Eddie would join them after work and they'd picnic there. She pulled it out and looked inside, half expecting to find sand at the bottom, but there was no evidence that it, or they, had ever gone anywhere.

Back in her room, Melody opened the dresser drawers, one at a time, and extracted underwear, socks, and a couple of shirts, dropping them into the duffel in no particular order. She put in a pair of black jeans, then swapped them for a pair of rust-colored Carhartt's instead. She'd wear the leather jacket. In the bathroom, she removed her toothbrush from its charger, thought about taking the charger, too, decided against it, rooted around for the small tube of Crest she was sure was there, found it, gave herself a mental high five, skipped the salicylic acid face wash (she didn't have acne; Delia was sure that bathing her face in this stuff was why), and grabbed a hairbrush and two hotel-size bottles of Aveda shampoo and conditioner that, if she remembered correctly, she had taken from one of their trips to Bermuda. Floss, yes, the waxed kind. Tampons, of course.

Downstairs again, she found the Sharpie Eddie had used to write his note and drew a line on the envelope to separate his words from hers. She wrote in all caps, to get his attention:

DAD,
FORGOT TO TELL YOU I HAVE A COLLEGE TOUR THIS
WEEK. YOU KNOW HOW TO REACH ME.
XOXO,
MEL

She hoisted the duffel on one shoulder and slung her knapsack, full of the detritus of her high school life—MacBook, phone, chargers, *Thomas' Calculus*, *Middlemarch*, five-subject spiral notebook, lip gloss, wallet—on the other. She took a quick look around the kitchen, grabbed a Granny Smith apple from a fruit basket someone had sent belatedly, and walked out the door.

"This was your idea," she said when Danny opened the door. It was just after one in the afternoon, and Danny Yandel was standing in the doorway in a faded Wesleyan T-shirt and red plaid boxers, rubbing his eyes. His hair—which had grown in a bit—was tamped down, like grass in a field where an animal had spent the night, and a small line of dried drool extended from the corner of his mouth before getting lost in the poor excuse for a beard shading his chin.

Danny looked at her dumbly, as if he couldn't quite place her, and Melody felt like an idiot—small, and young, and foolish. Two guys walking by, one with a Frisbee under his arm, nodded and gave a thumbs-up without breaking stride. Unfamiliar music—maybe reggaeton, she thought, but really had no idea—wafted down the long corridor like an aroma escaping an oven. A door swung open across the hall and a girl (who was probably a few years older than she was and who she knew she was not supposed to call a girl, because this was college) emerged, her hair wet, a towel cinched around her waist and nothing on top.

"Hey D," she said, breasts bouncing as she lifted an arm to wave.

"Hey," he said. That seemed to wake him up.

Turning his attention back to Melody, he said, "I don't have classes on Wednesdays. But don't you?"

Melody shrugged.

One of the Frisbee guys came trotting back down the hall, and as he passed said, "Forgot something," and "You're supposed to invite her in, Yandel," and was gone in a flash.

Danny said nothing but stepped aside. Melody picked up the duffel that she'd dropped on the floor and crossed the threshold.

Danny's room was surprisingly neat. The Levi's he wasn't wearing were folded tidily on a chair, and a row of different-colored binders were lined up on the desk, bookended by stacks of library books.

"Cool picture," Melody said, standing in front of a signed photo that said, *To Daniel, Yes we did!* signed by Barack Obama.

"I worked on his campaigns," Danny said.

Of course you did, Melody thought.

He took his jeans from the chair and motioned for her to sit. A look of embarrassment crossed his face, as if he realized for the first time that he wasn't wearing any pants.

"Sorry," he said. "That was awkward."

She didn't know if he meant the pants situation or that he'd opened the door and found her there, or that it was well after noon and she had woken him up.

"Sorry I didn't text," she said. "It was a spur-of-the-moment thing. Honestly, when I left the house this morning, I wasn't exactly sure where I was going."

If she were completely honest, she would have told him that when she Googled directions to his college, it routed her through Massachusetts, because once again she'd confused Wellesley, a women's college outside of Boston, with Wesleyan, a coed college not far from Yale, and when she realized her mistake, she wondered why, if Danny was such a genius, he didn't end up there.

His phone rang. "Hi, Mom!" he said and rolled his eyes. She could hear Marcia chirping away, and finally, when she paused, Danny said, "Hey, Mom, I have to go, Melody Marcus just got here." Marcia must have said something, because he said, "College tour. Yes, I know. I will," and hung up.

"My mother says I should take you to lunch," he said.

"What did she say when you said, 'I know'?" Melody asked. She knew it was rude. She also knew Danny would tell her.

He hesitated a moment, turning to excavate his socks from the sheets. "Um, she said that it was sad that you had to do the whole college tour thing without your mother, and I should be nice to you." He reached into the bed, patted around and pulled out one sock, then the other, and sat down to put them on.

"You should lose the jacket," he said, not looking at her.

"What? Why?"

"People here won't appreciate that you're wearing a dead animal."

"Do people here wear shoes?" she said. *Could she sound more like Delia?*

"I don't make the rules," Danny said, shrugging.

"Well, that's a relief," Melody said, and made no move to take it off.

"We have lots of options," Danny said as they made their way across the campus, stepping on chalk messages written into the sidewalk. TAKE BACK THE NIGHT; KNOW JUSTICE, KNOW PEACE; WOMYN4WOMYN; CARDINAL PRIDE; and some she couldn't decipher that had been smudged by the rain or erased by foot traffic. "We could go to Usdan, but a lot of classes got out recently, so it may be really crowded, or maybe the Pi Café."

"There's a whole café just for pie?" she asked. "Who wouldn't want to go to school here?"

Danny laughed. "It's pi, as in 3.1415926—I can't remember the rest. It's in the science building. Let's just go to Usdan. It's got everything," and proceeded to run down the list as if he were a waiter reeling off the day's specials, though they weren't specials, they were just what students here were offered every day. "There's also a frozen yogurt machine, and a freezer full of Ben and Jerry's, and a sundae bar with lots of toppings, like M&M's and hot fudge sauce." No wonder this college was hard to get into.

She followed him up a broad set of stairs, into a building that looked like a fortress. The place was enormous, with a circular stairway in the middle, and it was loud, very loud.

"Just take what you want," Danny said, handing her a tray. She watched him disappear into a crowd of students wearing identical Wesleyan sweatshirts, in the direction of a sign that said PANINIS.

She spun around and saw a sign for pizza and another for waffles, and one that said DAILY SPECIALS, though she'd have to get closer to see what they were, and there were too many people in her way. She was closest to the bank of waffle irons, where a tall, skinny boy with a long, dirty-blond ponytail was watching batter seep out from the side of one of them, so she pretended to be interested, too. The light turned from red to green, and he opened the top and speared a golden-brown waffle with a fork and delivered it to a plate. He turned around and saw her standing there, tray in hand. "Do you want this one?" he asked, and before she could say she didn't, he had put the plate on her tray.

Where was Danny? Melody stood in the middle of the cafeteria, scanning the tables, confused and a little angry. She felt exposed. Like everyone was looking at her, even though she could see that they were focused on their food and on one another or, headphones on, doing their schoolwork.

"You look lost." It was the guy with the ponytail. "Come with me," he said, and led her through the room, past tables of chattering students, all of whom seemed to belong—to one another, to this school—to a table at the far end of the room, away from the din.

His name was Connor, he was from Colorado, his mother was a physical therapist, his father was a banker, that's how they met (which confused her—did they meet because his father needed

PT or because his mother needed a loan or something—until it became clear that they met as students at Wesleyan), he hadn't cut his hair since he was eleven and read about Locks of Love and was planning on donating his hair so it could be made into a wig for a cancer patient, he played Ultimate Frisbee (of course) and the double bass in a New Orleans–style jazz band, and was double majoring in interdisciplinary studies and dance.

"I've never seen you here before. What's your story?" he asked. "Nice jacket, by the way." Then, before she could answer, he stood up, said he'd be right back, and headed into the fray. She watched him move swiftly across the room, ponytail swishing across his back, nodding greetings as he went.

What *was* her story? For the first time since Delia's death, she was talking to someone who had no idea what it was. She could invent a narrative, the story of who she wished she was (but who was that?), or who it would be fun to be (the daughter of diplomats, who had grown up in the Seychelles or Belize, two places her family had gone on vacation, so she could at least paint a reasonable picture). Alternatively, she could tell him the truth. They'd never see each other again, so why not? But where to begin? Foster care, getting adopted by the Marcuses, Delia's death, how she'd died? It would be interesting, watching the reaction of someone who knew none of this.

"Here!" he said triumphantly, depositing a bowl of fresh strawberries on the table between them. "They're perfect on waffles, and good for you, too." He dumped half the bowl on his waffle, which was already drenched in maple syrup and covered with whipped cream. Connor was an enthusiast—she had to give him that.

"When are you going to cut your hair?" Melody asked.

"Not sure," he said, dragging a piece of waffle around the

plate to sop up excess syrup. "My mom asks me that every time she calls."

"Sorry," Melody said.

"No apology necessary," Connor said, grinning. He had a snaggletooth and a lopsided smile that Melody found surprisingly endearing. He was a type: she imagined that a lot of the shirts in his dresser were tie-dye, and that the only shoes he owned were Birkenstocks and hiking boots, though she supposed he also had a pair of sneakers or cleats, since he played Ultimate, unless he was one of those barefoot runners. "I mean, it's a legit question. I just don't have an answer. I guess I've become attached to it. It's like part of my identity by now. It would be strange to look in a mirror and not recognize yourself, wouldn't it? These strawberries are really good." He pushed the bowl toward her.

"So," he said, "what about you?"

Where was Danny? Was he looking for her, or did he intentionally lose her in this raucous, cavernous place? Did she care?

Melody hesitated, looked away from Connor's large, blue-gray eyes and his unusually long eyelashes, scanned the room for a second or two, and said, "College tour," and when she did, he banged the table so hard that their plates and silverware jumped up and crashed back down.

"I knew it!" Connor said. "Perfect! You know how some people have gaydar—like they know if someone is gay, even if they themselves don't know—I have prospie-dar!"

"Prospie-dar?"

"Yes," he said, though she didn't understand. "I mean, I can spot prospective students a mile away."

"Is that because we're the only ones not wearing Wesleyan sweatshirts?" Melody asked between bites.

Connor smiled his crooked smiled. "It's my job," he said. "Sort of. I'm an official tour guide. You know, one of those people who walk backward while pointing out all the great things about the college and all the cool people who went here. Like, did you know that Hannah Arendt taught here?"

"I don't know who that is," Melody admitted.

"OK," he said. "Bill Belichick?"

"Who is . . . ?"

"Who *is*?" he said indignantly. "Only the coach of the New England Patriots! You have heard of the NFL, right?"

"Very funny," she said. "I went to a Super Bowl party once."

"Oh, yeah? Who was playing?"

"Lots of very large men," she said.

"Ha ha," he said. "So are you signed up for the afternoon tour? Don't go if you are. Let me show you around. It's like my favorite thing. That's not creepy, right?" Before she could answer—this was becoming a pattern—he said, "Wait for me outside the library. I've got a class till 3:30. Better yet, you should come to class with me. That's really the best way to get a sense of the place. It's a pretty big room. The professor won't even know you are there. Not that he'd care. It's called Body, Soul, and Rock 'n' Roll. The professor is a neurophilosopher. You may have heard of him. Tenzin Bobak-Jones."

As Connor spoke, Melody followed his Adam's apple yo-yoing up and down his long neck. It reminded her of the red-and-white bobbers Eddie had tied to their lines when they'd go fishing, before she told him it was animal abuse to skewer a live worm in order to hook a live fish, and he asked her where she thought their food came from, an argument he was sure he was going to win, which was when she declared that she was vegan. Not that that lasted long. But no more fishing.

"There you are!" Having spied her, Danny rushed over to the

table and shook his head. "Wow! Jeez. I couldn't figure out where you'd gone. Mom would have killed me."

"You could have texted," Melody said, not bothering to hide her annoyance.

"I would have, if I hadn't left my phone in my room," he said. "Hi, Connor."

Connor looked from Danny to Melody and back to Danny. "Is this your sister?" he asked.

Danny shook his head.

"Family friend," Melody said, preempting him.

"Yeah," Danny said. "Our moms are good friends. Were," he corrected himself.

Melody glared at him.

Connor, who was loading the contents of her tray onto his, didn't notice. "You coming?" he said to Melody.

She turned to Danny. "I'm going to class with him. Then he's going to show me around."

"Cool," Danny said, and turned to walk away.

"I'll text you later," she said as he retreated.

The man striding across the auditorium stage—clomping, really, in black lace-up motorcycle boots—looked nothing like what Melody assumed a college professor would look like. For one thing, he wasn't old or wearing a tweed sport jacket with leather elbow patches like the professors she was used to seeing on television. For another, when he removed his jean jacket—which he dropped on the floor with a studied air of casual indifference—she saw that not only was he wearing a Radiohead T-shirt, but his arms were marbled with words and images that, at a distance, she couldn't quite make out.

"His sleeves are amazing, aren't they," Connor whispered.

"I guess so," she whispered back, not wanting to tell him that they were tattoos, not shirt sleeves.

Bobak-Jones powered up his laptop, and as he did, music filled the lecture hall. "For those who don't know, though I can't imagine who you are"—Bobak-Jones spoke into a microphone looped over one ear that snaked around to his mouth—"this is 'Should I Stay or Should I Go,' which is one of the great questions of the twenty-first century, a pure representation of privilege if there ever was one. Everyone up. Up. I want to see you all moving!"

On cue, everyone stood up and started bouncing in place. Melody thought it looked stupid, but she stood up, too, and made some obligatory swaying movements as Connor, next to her, was jumping up and making pretend dunks and fake dribbling, as if he were Michael Jordan.

"This is the best!" he shouted in Melody's direction, and then, just as suddenly as the music started, it stopped, and everyone collapsed into their seats, and two brain scans appeared on a screen behind the professor. They were similar—Melody could see that—and colorful, especially the one on the left. Bobak-Jones trained his laser pointer on that one. And then he pointed to the one on the right.

"Where, and what?" he said. Before anyone answered, he pointed to the middle of the brain on the left, and then what looked like the same place on the right.

"Wernicke's area!" someone behind Melody called out.

"Correct," Bobak-Jones said. "And why is that?"

"Because it comprehends written and spoken language," most of the class shouted in unison.

"I see that my work here is done," Bobak-Jones said, and pretended to walk off the stage as the class erupted in laughter. He waited for them to settle down, then projected two more images on the screen. "These are scans of the same woman. She has Alzheimer's, unfortunately," he said. "Does anyone know why the one on the left looks so different, so much more alive, than the one on the right?"

"Because she was listening to the Clash?" a boy with a backward-facing Red Sox cap offered. More laughter.

Bobak-Jones motioned for them to quiet down. Melody thought he seemed like the sort of guy who only liked it when people laughed at his own jokes.

"Not exactly," the professor said. "Actually, she was listening to the Clash, but that's the image on the right. On the left, she was hearing this." For a moment there was silence, and then a few piano chords and a woman's rich contralto singing the words "Just a closer walk with thee . . ."

"What's the difference?" Bobak-Jones asked again.

"One's a hymn," someone called out.

"True," the professor said. "But what's the difference *to her?*"

"She was religious?" a student in the front row ventured.

"Maybe."

"She sang in a choir?" he tried again.

"Possibly," Bobak-Jones repeated.

Connor raised his hand. "Because it's soul music?" he said hopefully.

Melody shook her head and made a face.

"You—" the professor said, pointing to Melody. "Go!"

"But she's a prospie!" Connor protested.

Was he trying to protect her, or was he afraid of being upstaged?

"Better still," Bobak-Jones said. "What's your name?"

Melody hesitated, knowing what was about to happen. "Um, Melody," she said.

The whole class started laughing, even Bobak-Jones. "Okay, Melody," he said, drawing out each syllable. "What did you think of Connor's answer?"

Her heart was thrumming in her ears, and her hands were clammy. Everyone was looking at her, waiting to see what would happen next. She took a deep breath and focused on the screen. "I mean, I guess it's soul music, or gospel music, actually, but that's just a name." She paused, and Bobak-Jones prompted her to continue. "I guess what I mean is that if it was called rock 'n' roll or punk rock or whatever, it would still have the same effect."

"And why is that?" the professor asked. Others in the class raised their hands, but he warned them off. "No," he said, "let's allow our prospie to finish her thought." He waited a beat or two, then addressed Melody. "Why doesn't it matter what genre it is?" he asked her.

"You've got this," Connor whispered.

She knew it, too. "Because she wouldn't have cared, or wouldn't have known, because she had Alzheimer's."

"Keep going," Bobak-Jones said. "You're almost there. So tell us, Melody, what *would* she have known?"

"The song," Melody said. "She knew that song, but not the other."

"Bingo," Bobak-Jones said. "Well done! The woman had no memory associated with the Clash, but she knew this gospel hymn, probably from the time she was a small child. It was encoded in the architecture of her brain. Even when she could no longer read or know what to do with a fork, she could remember this song."

The guy with the backward Red Sox cap raised his hand. "But why? Surely she'd used a fork a million more times than she listened to this song?"

Bobak-Jones snapped his fingers. "That's an excellent observation," he said, then pointed to the clock on the wall to his right. "We'll take that up next time, and if our prospective student is still with us then, I hope she will join us. Now, let's talk about the tegmentum." For the next forty minutes, Bobak-Jones marched back and forth across the stage, talking about arousal and sleep-wake cycles and homeostatic pathways as the class dutifully wrote down what he was saying.

No one was taking notes by hand, Melody noticed. Laptops were banned at her high school after it was brought to the attention of the administration that students pretending to take notes were actually playing video games or watching YouTube with the sound muted. In college it seemed that no one cared, one way or the other. Connor, she noticed, wasn't taking notes at all. His laptop was closed, his elbows were flanking it, and his head was resting on his upturned hands as he watched Bobak-Jones intently. He reminded her of Rowdy when she had a treat in her hands.

"Why aren't you taking notes?" she whispered.

"It's an experiment I'm doing," he whispered back. "I'm trying to train my brain to have perfect recall."

Bobak-Jones stopped in midsentence and looked up in their direction. He was quiet for a beat or two, as if contemplating something serious, then clapped his hands together and smiled. "I'm pleased that our prospie is so engaged in the material. It gives me hope for the future." He gave a small nod in Melody's direction, picked up his jacket, and strode off the stage.

Connor was beaming as they shuffled out of the class and emerged into the bright sunlight. "You're famous!" he exclaimed. "You've got the Bobak-Jones stamp of approval. How great is that?"

Being famous, even among strangers, was exactly what Melody did not want to be. As she followed Connor around campus, he walking backward, she facing him, they kept running into people who now knew her name.

"This is weird," she said. "I doubt this many kids in my high school know who I am." But of course, that wasn't true. Everyone, even the assistant football coach, who'd left a message on the funeral home's online guestbook, knew who she was.

As they walked, Connor continued to toss out facts that had no meaning for her, and she continued to obsess about that class, which in retrospect seemed kind of silly to her. That guy, Bobak-Jones, seemed like a performer, not a teacher, though maybe that's what made professors different from high school teachers, who probably didn't have the energy to dance around a stage, or the incentive. It wasn't as if the kids in her chemistry class or AP English had any choice but to be there if they wanted to go to college.

And then they'd get to college, this mythical place, to be entertained by their professors. Though, to be fair, she'd been to exactly one college class, and maybe Bobak-Jones was just a singular weirdo. As her AP Statistics teacher junior year kept saying, "N's matter"—in other words, the sample size can determine the outcome. Melody smiled to herself. *At least I learned something in that class*, she thought.

As they approached the library steps, the official afternoon tour group was coming down them, led by a petite Asian woman in a Wesleyan sweatshirt, brown corduroy skirt, fishnet tights, and hiking boots. She waved to Connor, and he called up to her, "Private tour," whereupon the disparate gaggle of high schoolers turned as one to get a better look at her, and their anxious parents began whispering among themselves, wondering what it took to get a private college tour, and speculating who Melody's famous parents were. She heard "Springsteen" and "Gates" as the two tours crossed paths, and suppressed a desire to correct them with the words "paper bag king," but they were hustling away. She imagined some of them would be texting their college counselors, the ones they started paying when their kids were in ninth grade so all the boxes were ticked by application time (foreign service trip, check; menial after-school job, check; original research project, possibly resulting in a patent, an Intel prize, or a paper in a prestigious journal, check), to find out how to get a private tour when they visited Amherst or Stanford or, God forbid, Villanova.

"You know you don't have to babysit me," Melody said when they had looked around the library and were on their way out.

"I'm not babysitting you," Connor said, feigning hurt. "This is good practice for me. But, speaking of practice, I've got Ultimate pretty soon. You could come, if you want. We're pretty good. Which is actually an understatement." He looked at her expectantly, and as he did, she realized why he seemed so familiar to her. He was like her neighbors', the Scheins', old golden retriever, Willy—short for Wilhemina—friendly, eager, and always hopeful someone would play ball.

"I should get going," Melody said. She patted her knapsack. "I've got homework I should do."

Connor pulled his phone from his back pocket and handed it to her. "Write your number," he said. "I'll text you so you have mine if you end up going here next year. Though I'm probably going to take some time off to WWOOF." *Definitely a golden retriever!*

"Woof? As in bark?"

He laughed. "WWOOFing. Worldwide Opportunities on Organic Farms! It's the best. You give them your labor in exchange for room and board. Like all over the world. Costa Rica, France, Croatia. Lots of kids do it. It's a great way to travel and really learn about a place. Get your hands dirty, so to speak. I'm thinking western Massachusetts, Vermont, or maybe Sonoma. Or Italy. Not sure."

They had paused at the bottom step, and Melody watched as students in white shirts and black pants began to walk past them and assemble on the steps.

"It's a cappella tryouts next week, so every day a different group does a little concert out here to kind of show off," Connor said as singers broke into a Coldplay song that had been popular when Melody was in elementary school.

"They really enunciate, don't they?" Connor said.

Melody nodded. She hadn't ever listened closely to the lyrics before, hadn't heard:

When you lose something you can't replace
When you love someone but it goes to waste
Could it be worse?"

Or maybe she had and they had just been words that, strung together, had no meaning for her.

"I've got to go," she said, and took off before he could see the tears welling in her eyes.

"You know Connor's a player, right?" Danny said. They were walking through the college garden, which was mostly dormant now, a tangle of dried cornstalks and raspberry brambles scattered on the ground like fallen soldiers left behind when their platoon retreated.

"He invited me to his Ultimate practice, if that's what you mean," she said.

"You know it's not," Danny said.

"I don't know," Melody said. "He seemed like a big puppy dog to me. Sweet."

"Yeah," Danny said. "That's his MO."

They were walking between rows of what had been beefsteak and Big Boy tomato plants, according to small plastic signs stuck in the dirt. "These are like grave markers," he said, and then, in a deep, stentorian voice, "Here lies Barry Beefsteak"—then stopped midsentence. "Sorry," he said. "I'm an idiot."

"It's fine," she said. "Don't worry about it." And then, to lighten the mood, said, "We're thinking of scattering her ashes in the women's shoe department at Bloomingdale's."

But he didn't laugh. "I'm serious about Connor," he said.

"Well, I'm not. First of all, I don't go here. And even if I did, he's probably taking next year off to go WWOOFing." She smiled, imagining Connor as a golden retriever, ponytail wagging, howling at the moon.

"Of course he's going to WWOOF," Danny said, disgusted. "It's like the agricultural Peace Corps for rich kids."

Melody was confused. "I thought it was free. You have to be rich? It costs money to work for free?"

"Only indirectly," Danny said. "You don't get paid, so only people who don't need to make money can do it."

"Well, good for Connor," Melody said, and kicked a partially deflated pumpkin.

He took her to a different dining hall for dinner, one where, she suspected, they wouldn't run into Connor, and sat with some of Danny's friends from the radio station, where he hosted a weekly music show called *Fantasy Foosball*, though no one could remember why it was called that.

"I think it may have been sophomore year, when we were doing mushrooms," said a girl with what looked like a safety pin attached to her eyebrow.

"Which time?" Danny said, and they all laughed.

"So where are you applying to college?" the girl with the pierced eyebrow, whose chosen name was Lark, wanted to know.

"No clue," Melody said. She looked at Danny, sitting opposite her. "Actually, I'm thinking of WWOOFing." They all—except Danny—nodded approvingly.

"Sweet," Lark said.

CHAPTER SIX

What Candace liked most about work—about working—was how orderly it was. By now her weekday routine was entwined with her DNA: up at 6:30, a brisk seven-minute workout, shower, French roast (black), almond butter on wheat berry toast (seven-grain if the store was out or if it was day old), dry hair, a dab of blush, concealer if she didn't sleep well, step into some variation of the power suit (loosely defined), and out the door by 7:45. At the office there were meetings—so many meetings, so much coffee—and it wasn't unusual for her to play mediator, inserting herself between warring colleagues and leading them to some sort of détente— until the next time. "This happens more often than you can imagine," she told Paul. He had never worked in an office, and never intended to, and found it crazy that people cared about their jobs so much they'd go to war with each other. "It's about identity. And getting credit," she explained. "People want to feel valued."

"That's hilarious," he said.

"I'm just telling you what I know," she replied.

The sexual harassment complaints, though, were tricky. The goal, above all, was to avoid litigation. Litigation was expensive. And it could embarrass the company. Stories about food drives for hungry children were good. Stories about revenge porn and work trips where bosses tried to bed the interns were bad. Yes, she had the crisis PR firm on speed dial, but the objective was never to call it. DataStream was a company ripe for takeover, which meant it was a company ripe for exploitation by pissed-off employees who didn't own equity shares and felt a payoff was their due, too. Not that Candace had equity, herself. She wasn't employee number sixteen, like Angela. By the time Candace got to the company, no one was bothering to count.

DataStream was one of those unlikely start-up successes that was hatched not in someone's garage or dorm room, but—or so the origin story went—in the shower. "No, no, I did not build it in the shower!" the CEO, Vivek Banerjee, would say whenever someone, usually a novice business reporter, brought it up. All the veterans had heard the tale of the fifteen-year-old watching the water cascade from the showerhead one morning and had the bright idea of trademarking the name "DataStream," though it wasn't until he was at Virginia Tech that he came up with a product to match it, an app that sorted and indexed information in real time. The first product led to others, and to a high enough valuation that companies and private equity firms had been sniffing around for a while. Banerjee, at thirty-eight, was still CEO, but his real devotion had migrated elsewhere, to Hollywood, where there was interest in his life story—he'd survived polio when he was a young boy, and that, along with his reputation as a high-flying digital disruptor, had a couple of producers talking biopic— and to Newport, Rhode Island, where he'd taken up competitive sailing and moored his X-Treme32 racing yacht. He liked to say that the company ran itself, a conceit that not one of his now 279 employees shared.

As jobs went, hers was a good one. No two days were alike, she was well compensated, and in the hierarchy of the office she wasn't at the peak of the pyramid, but she wasn't stuck in the middle, either. She had responsibilities, but was not, when all was said and done, responsible, capital R. The only person she reported to was Rodney Nguyen Smythe (no hyphen), the COO, and he left her alone for the most part because, Candace realized after a while, he thought of human resources as women's work.

Stamford wasn't Manhattan, but it, too, had its good points. On a slow day, she could take her lunch break at the shore, and there was always a table available at the Barcelona Wine Bar, a Friday-night indulgence she shared now and then with Angela, or where she'd sometimes meet her "dates," if they were willing to take the train from the city with only the possibility of a night at the Delamar, in Greenwich, where she was partial to the water-front rooms with the big soaking tubs.

While the women's magazines Candace picked up at her hair salon extolled the "work-life balance," she was of the opinion that balance was overrated.

"You've got to love your job or you won't want to get out of bed in the morning, and if you don't get out of bed you'll be late, and if you're late you'll be letting down the members of your team," she told prospective new hires, carefully watching their reactions. It was like truth serum, and it made her life easier in the long run. She only wanted to hire people who weren't going to complain when they had to work long hours or get called in on weekends. She only wanted people proud to wear the company logo on their fleece vests and carry it on a reusable canvas bag as they wandered through the supermarket.

She had her mother to thank for instilling this idea—this *belief*—that hard work was everything. That there was no time to get in trouble if you were always working.

"Case in point," her mother would say, "all those drug-addled, drug-addicted, overdosed children of the mega-rich, who had everything handed to them on a silver platter. No, a silver platter encrusted with diamonds!" whereupon she'd bring up Bobby Kennedy, Jr., and his heroin addiction. Maybe this was a way to assuage her own guilt for the long hours she spent at the insurance firm where she'd worked her way up from receptionist to head claims adjuster, a realization Candace only had later, after her mother's dementia had rendered her speechless. There was another revelation, too: all that work was the drug she took to try to anesthetize the pain of her perpetually failing marriage and the sole responsibilities of raising a child and maintaining a home because her husband made it clear he was good at neither of these. (He was good at drinking, so good it eventually killed him.) They weren't poor, but what Candace only realized long after the fact was that there might have been an undercurrent of worry bringing all those bromides and lectures about hard work and self-sufficiency to the surface. But it was too late. Candace had already internalized them.

Yet while her mother extolled the virtues of hard work, she was, at the same time, wary of ambition. To her it was another trap, a way to buy into other people owning you. "If they know you're hungry, they'll dangle the food just out of reach" was a favorite expression of hers. But the takeaway for Candace was that she should always pretend to be sated no matter how hungry she was. At Williams, courtesy of the Coca-Cola Scholars Foundation, it seemed that everyone else came from money, and she got to see, up close, what money could buy: spring break in Saint Barts (or was it Saint Barth?), $400 jeans from Rag & Bone, a string of pearls worn with cool indifference atop a strategically ripped cashmere sweater. If her sweaters had holes, they were not there on purpose. Candace hunkered down, studying these people like an anthropologist would. She might not be of them, but she quickly learned that the rich just assumed everyone around them was rich, too.

The recruiters started coming to campus in October. She'd be walking along and see men in three-piece suits, their black wing tips shiny as a teacher's apple, portfolios tucked under their arms, striding toward the career center, and young men, some she recognized from class, dressed in identical Brooks Brothers suits, rushing in the same direction, their ties flapping and their hands nervously raking their hair if they weren't burdened by textbooks or the monogrammed briefcases they'd gotten for high school graduation. In they'd go, and out they'd come with offers from McKinsey or Bain for summer internships that paid a thousand dollars a week, and the presumption of a job after graduation with a salary that guaranteed that nothing would interrupt the lifestyle to which they'd grown accustomed. Ten grand for a summer's work would prove to her mother that this four-year liberal arts sojourn in the middle of nowhere was not frivolous. For the time being she'd keep her campus job, checking people in and out of the fitness center, and she'd spend breaks temping at her mother's insurance agency, but come sophomore autumn, she'd be stepping into her one good dress, borrowing a roommate's pearls, and attending those interviews herself. Bridgewater or Boston Consulting Group or Bain, it didn't matter which.

And it worked. "Do well this summer and you'll be invited back next summer, too, and after that, who knows?" a partner at the Lucentum Group (not quite top tier, but striving) told her class of summer hires. (Williams, Amherst, Penn, two Yales, three Dartmouths, and four Harvards.) But they all knew. This was the ticket.

Candace looked around. Everyone was white, like her, and, except for her, expensively turned out. She had splurged on a Banana Republic blazer, but everyone else, it seemed, including the other two women, had shopped at Barneys or J. Press. She imagined that details like this mattered, especially when the jackets would be slung over the mesh backs of their Aeron chairs, labels exposed. By next summer, she told herself, she would improve her wardrobe, dropping a few thousand of those Lucentum dollars at Nordstrom Rack on a shopping spree that would give her a taste of what it would be like to have what her economics textbooks called "disposable income."

"How can a nineteen-year-old"—meaning her, Candace knew—"be a business consultant? What does a nineteen-year-old know about business?" her mother wanted to know. It was a reasonable question, one that Candace asked herself that first day, when she sat in the glass-paneled conference room at Lucentum during orientation.

Her welcome packet was on the table in front of her. Everyone else had slipped their company IDs over their heads like first-place ribbons, which she guessed they were.

She fished hers out of the otherwise empty accordion file she'd been handed that morning, turned it around so that her name and title—"summer associate," written in red ink (black was for second-years)—were visible, and dropped the lanyard around her neck. It announced to the world that she, Candace Milton, was among the chosen.

But chosen to do what? Everything at Lucentum seemed to be a test. How good she was at regression analysis. How well she knew econometrics. How strategically she handled clients. How many ways she could demonstrate her loyalty to Lucentum and to its partners. She was assigned to a team tasked with reducing costs at an aerospace company. The company made uncrewed military drones, and not just for the US military. "Is it untoward that one of our clients is selling weapons to countries with terrible human rights violations?" one of the Harvard boys asked at the weekly summer associates' lunch (lobster rolls flown in from Maine).

"Untoward"? What did that even mean? Still, Candace

squirmed in her seat. Even posing the concern as a question, she thought, was potentially dangerous, a way of signaling that you were a prospective thorn-in-side kind of troublemaker. But that, apparently, was not how this world worked.

"You bring up a good and important point," the partner on the project told them, beaming at the Harvard boy, who beamed back, knowing he'd just bested all the other associates. (Everything was a competition.) "Lucentum has a strict code of ethics," the partner said gravely, pausing to make eye contact with each one of them. "We do not take on clients who will misuse our expertise in any way. That is a hard-and-fast rule. Anyone who works with us is required to agree to our ethical standards. This is central to our core mission. If you are going to work here, you need to understand that."

Later, when Candace thought about this exchange, she realized it was a setup. Someone, probably from the apparently very prestigious Porcellian Club, which the Harvard guys seemed always to be casually bringing up (and which she'd never heard of till that summer and at first thought had something to do with expensive china), must have tipped off that first-year that the partners loved to be "challenged" in this way. It made them feel good about themselves. (They had standards! They were good people!) Live and learn.

The junior partner, Kelvin Moore, who, rumor had it, was on the fast track to make full partner, pulled Candace aside. It was the second week of her second summer, after she'd made it through what was called plebe year, even though it was only ten weeks long and even though she'd been paid handsomely and taken to the best restaurants (where, of course, they were being evaluated for their compatibility with company culture). Plebe year was all about triage. Summer associates were expected to work long hours—everyone knew that when extra tickets to Yankees games or Broadway shows were on offer you did not take them—but the real tests were more subtle.

Everyone thought they were being judged on the quality of their work, but like in calculus class, where you were graded on how you derived the answer to the problem, the higher-ups were looking for facile minds, so the journey was just as important as, and maybe more important than, the destination. And somehow, Candace had made the cut. And now Kelvin Moore, the rare Black junior partner, wanted her on his team for the summer.

"Why me?" she asked. They were sitting at the small round table in his office, away from the warren of cubicles where the associates sat. It wasn't a corner office—that would come next— but it was an office with a door and, from a certain angle, a partial view of the East River. A glass wall separated Moore's office from what everyone called "the bullpen," as if the summer associates and recent hires were pitchers waiting to be called into the game. And now she had been.

Moore smiled. He had perfect teeth, Candace saw, and wondered if his parents had paid good money for that smile or if he was genetically gifted. He was wearing a bright-blue bow tie, and his crisp white oxford shirt had the initials KSM discreetly embroidered on the French cuffs, which were fastened by a pair of US Navy cuff links.

He tapped a pen on the table. "I hope you won't mind me saying so," he began, "but you remind me of me." Then, before she could ask him what he meant, he said, "A bit of a fish out of water."

Candace laughed. "So you noticed," she said. "But I mean, you—you went to the Naval Academy, you were a SEAL, you went to Harvard Business School, you were a White House fellow"— she tried to remember the bullet points on his company profile. "You seem like a pretty big tuna to me."

Moore frowned. "Don't be naive," he said coolly.

"Right," she said, feeling her face color. They both knew she'd been disingenuous. There was only one full partner who was Black, and he'd been an assistant secretary of the Treasury before being lured by Lucentum to rejoin the private sector. Moore was likely to be the second.

The start of the second-year's summer at Lucentum was run like a TV dating show. Having observed the associates during plebe year, partners would tap the ones they wanted to have work with them, and then it was up to the summer associate to choose among them if they'd gotten multiple offers. She'd heard that the senior partners put money on who would match with who. Candace didn't wait to see if anyone but Kelvin Moore wanted her. It would be too humiliating if no one else did, and since he did, she said yes on the spot.

It was a good summer. Moore was a reasonable boss, shooing her out of the office if she was there past nine, even if he was staying. The work was interesting: Moore's expertise was supply chain management. "Sounds dull, but if the supply chain is interrupted, all hell breaks loose," he told her. "Our job is to rationalize supply chains, make them work more smoothly and efficiently. We have to find the burps and glitches and come up with workarounds for our clients. It's always a race against time. That's what makes it exciting." So Candace memorized shipping routes, became adept at anticipating port congestion and finding redundant suppliers that could be called upon when a cyclone or a public health emergency interrupted the flow of materials. "It's counterintuitive," Moore told her, "but in this business, efficiency often comes from addition, not subtraction." Around her, the other summer associates studied pharmaceutical research, pored over maps of rare earth mineral deposits, cajoled IP lawyers, and deciphered patent applications. They were all swimming in the deep end of the pool, the water was over their heads, and somehow it did not matter.

On the last day of the summer, they were all at their desks, pretending to work, as if at this late date anything they did mattered—if it ever had. Soon they would be summoned, one by one, to the managing partner's oak-paneled office on the twenty-first floor to learn their fate. Would they be getting invited back the next summer, with a six-figure postgraduation job offer as part of the deal, or would they be thanked for their service, as if they were being decommissioned with a vaguely honorable discharge? The whole experience—the eighty-hour workweeks, the frisson of competition—had begun to seem to Candace like an elaborate, though lucrative, hazing ritual. And any minute now she'd find out if she was being invited to join this fraternity.

At 8:17 a.m. the light on her phone console lit up. She looked around, hoping no one noticed, girded herself, and answered it.

"Candace Milton," she said. "How may I help you?" It sounded dumb, but it was the first thing that came to mind.

"Milton, Moore." She turned around in the direction of his office. The blinds were drawn, but she could make out that he was inside, leaning back in his chair with his ridiculously expensive Italian loafers propped on his desk. Was he looking at her, too? She couldn't tell. "Look," he said. "You're going to be fine."

Under the circumstances, this was not encouraging. In her experience, people told you that you were going to be fine after a painful breakup ("I never liked him anyway—you'll be fine without him") or a college rejection ("You'll do great at Podunk College. Brown is overrated").

Then, before she could ask him what he meant, he said,

"That's all I can say. But I want you to understand one thing: No one here is your friend. On the surface, yes. But when push comes to shove, it's every man for himself. And yes, I mean man. Just keep your eyes on the prize."

"Which is?" she said.

He sighed. "Don't be naive, Milton," and hung up.

CHAPTER SEVEN

When Melody had knocked on Danny's door earlier in the day, she hadn't realized how awkward it would be to knock on it again that night. It never occurred to her that he would care where she went or who she went there with. It never occurred to her that he would care about her at all. But he was so weird about Connor, who seemed like a good guy, though of course you could never really tell—not at first, anyway. But he didn't seem like the stalker type, though, again, you could never tell. When they'd parted, she'd stuck out her hand to shake his, and as he grabbed it, he pulled her into a hug—just a quick friend hug, but still, it was nothing that she would have initiated.

After dinner with Danny and his friends, she wandered around for a while, watching the college students as they went about their business, which seemed mostly to be smoking cigarettes or looking at their phones. She found an empty carrel in the library and parked herself down and pulled out her math homework. Everywhere she looked, people were reading, heads down, notebooks out, pens and mechanical pencils gliding over paper, making little more noise than snow falling. Someone had left a stack of books written in Japanese in the carrel, and as she flipped through one, the undecipherable characters reminded her of the arguments she'd had with Eddie, and especially Delia, when she told them she would not be learning Hebrew, because she would not be having a bat mitzvah, because it was a joke, because the kids only did it for the money they'd collect and the parents only did it to show off the money they could afford to blow on this very special day.

"What's wrong with a little party?" Eddie wanted to know, but it wouldn't be little, that was certain, and the truth was, Melody did not want to be the center of attention, did not want to stand up in front of everyone and give a speech that they would all expect would be a big thank-you to her parents for rescuing her from a life of deprivation and who knows what other horrors. She was thankful, and she did, sometimes, obsess about the life she wasn't living, especially when she was talking with Lily, who had been left in a box on a bridge in Chengdu swaddled in a thin blanket when she was no more than a day old.

"I've decided that the blanket meant that they loved me and wanted me to have something of theirs, but they just couldn't keep me because of the whole one-child law," Lily told her. She also said that she felt guilty, some of the time, because she knew that despite everything, being left on that bridge was the best thing that ever happened to her. Her adoptive parents were both doctors. Dr. Shapiro, Peter, was a psychiatrist. Dr. Horowitz, Nina, delivered babies, a specialty chosen before she found out she couldn't have her own. They lived in a suburb chosen because there would be other Asian kids in her grade, so that their Chinese child would not feel like a freak, but then they sent her to private school anyway.

"If I have siblings, they're probably working on some factory assembly line, soldering chips or something. Sometimes I wonder if they made my phone, or my computer. Like if I dusted for fingerprints, I'd find theirs," she said. "Not that I'd know it was theirs."

"I think the people who work in those factories wear gloves," Melody said. "I think I saw that on some propaganda documentary we had to watch in social studies. I don't remember the point, though."

"Could've been me," Lily said. "If I was lucky and didn't have to work in a rice paddy. Which isn't a stereotype, FYI."

Melody hadn't been left on a bridge—she knew that much. But those years before the Marcuses claimed her were largely lost to her. She remembered images so fleeting—a stuffed bear with a bell in its ear; the white bars of her crib—that she didn't know if they were real or imagined.

She'd asked Delia, more than once, why she hadn't been adopted when she was a baby, and the explanations were never satisfying: "because you were waiting for us!" she said when Melody was around six; and "because there was a problem with the paperwork," when Melody was around ten.

All Melody knew was that she was supposed to have been adopted as a newborn, maybe even the day she was born; maybe those other parents were in the room when she popped out (though maybe she'd been cut out), but then something happened, and that adoption didn't go through, or was in limbo, and she ended up in foster care while the paperwork, or whatever it was, was sorted out, and that couple had moved on.

"If I hadn't been adopted, I could be married off by now. A child bride. It's legal in, I don't know, at least seven states," Melody told Lily. "I could be a meth addict. I could be living in a cardboard box." This was how they amused themselves, trying to one-up each other with the worst what-ifs.

"You could also turn out to be Joni Mitchell's daughter," Lily said, "which could never happen to me."

"First of all, if Joni was my birth mother, I'd be like fifty years old. Second of all, you suck."

"It's open," Danny said, when she knocked. He was sitting at his desk, and turned to greet her when she walked in. He was wearing wire-frame glasses and a flannel shirt, its sleeves rolled up to his elbows. He had nice forearms, she noticed, and then wondered if that was a thing, noticing someone's forearms and thinking they were nice.

"I went to the library," she said, before he could ask.

"Cool, cool," he said and turned back to his laptop.

Either he was angry with her or had no social skills, or possibly both, she thought. She sat down on his roommate's minimally made bed, opened her backpack, pulled out a book, and pretended to read. It was a trick she'd learned from Delia. If you feigned indifference, the other person would eventually come around.

"So how was Connor?" he said after a while, not looking away from the computer screen.

"You'd have to ask him" she said. "Like I said, I was at the library."

For some reason, Danny seemed to be annoyed about Connor, which made no sense, but one thing she was learning about boys and, she suspected, men, was that even the ones who claimed to be feminists seemed to have an innate belief that they could lay claim to you. It wasn't explicit. No one was saying "I own you," not directly, but they acted like they had rights when you turned your attention to someone else, even if they weren't interested in you, as her mother might have said, "that way."

Melody went back to her book, and this time started reading it for real. The dorm was surprisingly quiet. Every so often she'd hear the bathroom door open and shut, and footsteps in the hall, and snippets of conversation. Danny's keyboard clattered—he was a fast typist—and while she was curious to know what he was writing, she didn't want to ask and—as her mother also would have said—give him the wrong idea.

"I'm going to go outside for a smoke, if you know what I mean," Danny said, closing his laptop, stretching, and walking toward the door. "Wanna come?"

"No thanks," she said.

"It's that good stuff," he tried.

She shook her head. He took the book out of her hands and looked at the cover. "*Middlemarch*," he said. "We had to read this in high school, too," handed it back, and left the room.

Melody put down the book and checked her phone. There was a text from Eddie, and one from Danny's mother, and she dispatched them together with a cursory:

MELODY: All's well, Danny is an excellent host.

She wrote to Lily:

MELODY: Thinking college might be a big scam

She waited a minute to see if she'd write back. When she didn't, she wrote the same thing to Karolina, who texted back right away.

KAROLINA: How's the boy wonder?
MELODY: Ugh.
KAROLINA: Epic bomb scare today. They brought in dogs. so cute.
MELODY: Did they find a bomb?
KAROLINA: No. Better. They found Mr. Martel's stash.

Martel had been their drivers' ed teacher the year before. There were rumors that he was lighting up in the parking lot.

KAROLINA: Big drama. Ms. Karcher was crying. seems like they've been hooking up.
MELODY: Whaaatt?
KAROLINA: For real. They put him in the police car. Everyone saw.
MELODY: Cool.

Just then, Danny walked back in, his eyes rimmed red. "Whoa," he said as he nearly tripped on the threshold.

MELODY: Gotta go. Keep me posted.

Danny sat down on his bed. Then he lay down with his shoes still on his feet. Melody's first instinct was to tell him to take them off, but she checked herself: What was that about? She wasn't his mother.

"I got a text from your mom," Melody said.

"Nice," he said. "You know what I want to know?" he said after a while. If it was possible to sound dreamy and aggressive at the same time, he had just accomplished that. "What I want to know is, why weren't we friends back in high school?" His hands were laced behind his head, and he was looking up at the ceiling.

"Well, let's see," Melody said. "I was in middle school when you were graduating from high school. I had purple-and-black braces."

"Oh, right," he said. "That was around the time of your bat mitzvah kerfuffle."

"Who uses the word 'kerfuffle'?" she said, and "How did you know about that?"

"Mothers," he said, and grew so quiet that she would have thought he was asleep if his eyes weren't open.

She picked up her book again and was about to start reading when he said, "Do you ever think about her?"

"Who? Delia? How could I not?"

"No, not her. The other one. The one who gave you away."

Now there was a question. Until Delia died, that was the question people, strangers even, asked or wanted to ask her. At adoption camp, they counseled the kids to answer it directly, to just say "I know she had good reasons" and leave it at that.

But that was easier said than done. It was no more satisfying to them than it was to her, so she took another tack. "No," she'd say—actually, "Nope," and stare at them until they walked away. But, of course, she did think about her. She wondered if her birth mother had given her her untamable hair. She wondered about her khaki-green eyes: green was a recessive gene. She wondered about every body part that she liked, and every part that she did not. Mother? Father? Both? She imagined her birth mother was a teenager who had "made a mistake," and then Melody had to convince herself that she herself was not the mistake. She imagined that the girl had gone on to graduate from high school and go to college and move away, far away, maybe to a foreign country. Or maybe after high school she'd joined the military and died in Iraq or Afghanistan. That would explain her permanent radio silence. In her darker moments, Melody wondered if she'd been the product of rape, but as Lily told her more than once, if that were true, she might not have been born at all. "Unless her parents or her church made her," Melody countered, but secretly she was happy that her birth mother cared enough about her not to vacuum away all evidence of her future existence.

"Why does everyone focus on the birth mother?" Melody said to Danny. "What about the birth father? Why doesn't anyone ever ask about him?"

Danny seemed to consider this. "Valid point," he said lazily.

"The reason, I guess, is that the baby has come from the mother's body," Melody said, answering her own question. "I guess that if you carry a baby for nine months, it's yours to give away." She, too, was guilty as charged. She almost never thought about the man who'd supplied half her genes. He was a cipher, a wraith lurking in the background, and most of the time she forgot he was there at all.

"Did you know that in Ghana, when a woman is giving birth, they smear okra on her private place to speed up delivery?" he said.

"Private place? Seriously?"

But he was, all of a sudden, asleep.

Melody turned off the lights, put on her pajamas, and slipped into the other bed. Danny's computer was lighting the room, so she burrowed under the pillow.

"Oww! Shit!" she cried out.

Danny jumped up. "What, what?"

"Apparently your roommate likes to be prepared." She waved a small foil package in the air. "This just stabbed me in the cheek."

He sat up, reached over, and closed his laptop. The room was very dark now, too dark to see him take off his shoes, though she heard them hitting the floor, one, then the other, heard him un-zip his jeans and toss them in the direction of his desk chair, and then his flannel shirt, heard him slide under the covers, heard him sigh, slowly, like a deflating air mattress.

"You know!" he said, suddenly perking up. "You could proba-bly find her if you did one of those DNA tests."

"No, thank you," Melody said brusquely.

"But it could be so cool."

"Not interested. End of story." But that was not precisely true. She had thought about it, even clicked on ads for Ancestry and 23andMe, then kept getting those ads every time she logged on to Facebook or surfed the web and couldn't avoid the stories of people who found long-lost relatives or discovered that their mysterious medical condition was shared by a distant cousin in Sydney. Then there were the other stories, of the mother who wanted nothing to do with her biological son who had spent years searching for her, of the families that fell apart when buried secrets were unearthed for the whole world to see. It was too much risk for too little reward. So what if she found the woman or the man who "gave her up"? Did it really matter why? She could imagine how knowing this might help others satisfy their curiosity, but not how it would help her.

The sound of someone's stereo seeped into the room, and after a while Danny said, "Chick Corea." Melody stayed quiet, trying to practice the breathing techniques the internet said would make her fall asleep. Until Delia died, she'd been an excellent sleeper, but sleep had proved elusive after Delia's death. She'd close her eyes and see that boulder slip from its mooring, close her eyes and see it flatten the car, close her eyes and try to remember that day and what she could have done to keep her mother at home for just a few minutes more, though she wondered if that meant the boulder would have fallen on someone else, someone who would now have a daughter who couldn't sleep and a husband crying in the next room. "Insomnia is an expression of grief," she read, also on the internet, "and of the fear of falling asleep and joining the deceased in their permanent slumber." It was true that the randomness of Delia's death unsettled her.

"When you think about it, we're just sacks of water waiting to be squished," she told Lily during one of their calls.

"What about bones," Lily said. "The whole exoskeleton thing."

"Endo," Melody said. "I can't believe you of all people don't know that. Endoskeleton. Definitely overrated."

Truth be told, Melody was relieved that her insomnia was an expression of bereavement. She had heard about the five stages of grief before the rent-a-rabbi enumerated them at Delia's funeral, and after the horror of how her mother died had subsided a bit—though it would always make her shudder and wonder if, like people kept telling her, it was a blessing that Delia didn't know what hit her, or if they were wrong and Delia's final conscious thought was understanding exactly what did—she realized she'd catapulted past denial, anger, bargaining, and depression, and landed squarely on acceptance. The woman who had chosen her (the way she might have picked a bookcase from a Pottery Barn catalog, taking her measure to see how Melody would fit into the architecture of Delia and Eddie's life) was gone. It was undeniable, full stop.

"Hey, are you asleep?" Danny asked quietly.

She rolled over to face the wall and considered not answering. "Am not. Wish I was," she said after a while. "Or were. I can never remember when to use 'were' instead of 'was.'"

"Yeah," he said. "Like 'who' and 'whom,'" though she suspected he knew precisely when to use one and not the other. She was about to say something snarky about him being a boy wonder when he said, softly, "I'm really sorry this is happening to you."

Melody felt a welt of anger begin to rise. "It didn't happen to me," she said sharply, hoping her tone would shut him up.

It didn't. "You know what I mean," Danny said. "I can't imagine losing my mom—"

Melody cut him off. "I didn't lose her. She wasn't a pair of glasses or, I don't know, a set of keys. She was killed. As you know. Did you forget that you quote, unquote 'lost' your dad?"

"I get that you're angry," Danny said. "It's only natural." (Clearly he knew about Kübler-Ross, too.) "I mean, you're probably angry at your mother, too. Like I told you, I was mad at my father. Still am, probably."

"That's, I don't know, ridiculous. Why would I be angry at her?"

"Why would you be angry at her?" Danny repeated, as if the answer was so obvious that the question was irrelevant. "Because she left you—"

Melody cut him off. "She didn't leave me. It wasn't personal. It had nothing to do with me!"

"Because she left you," Danny said again, "and it probably brings up memories of being abandoned by your birth mother. At least, that's what my therapist suggested."

"You talked to your therapist about me? Why would you do that?" Her anger now felt incendiary, like her whole body was on fire.

"I guess," he said carefully, "because you're here?"

"So, what—now I'm Mount Everest?"

"Huh?"

"You know, what that mountain guy said when he was asked why he climbed Mount Everest. Because it was there."

"Oh, you mean Mallory," he said.

"Whatever," she said. And then, "So what did you tell him?"

"I told him about your mom and all that."

"And all that?"

"Yeah," he said, and yawned. "He said that your loss was opening my old wound."

Now that her eyes had adjusted to the darkness, she could make out Danny, lying in his bed, wrapped in his comforter as if it were a cocoon or—she couldn't help herself—a body bag. Then he moved, and whatever morbid spell had been cast was broken and she could see his feet sticking out, and that the back of his head was again resting on his laced fingers as if he were about to do a sit-up or was stargazing. Her anger was receding, carried out of her by waves of curiosity. She was mad—what right did he have?—it was a violation, but she also wanted to know what the therapist said. She'd resisted Eddie's half-hearted attempts to get her to see the same grief professional his friends were urging him to see, though if that woman was anything like the therapist at adoption camp, she wouldn't say much, just wait for Melody to spill her guts—which she never did. ("Highly defended," she heard the social worker tell her parents as Melody sat in the hall outside her office while Delia and Eddie had their annual one-on-one with her.)

"And the verdict was?" she said, trying not to sound too interested.

"There was no verdict. There never is," Danny said. "He just said it might take you a long time to come to terms with what happened."

"Brilliant," she said.

"You asked," Danny said. "Seriously, he's a good guy."

They were quiet again. Melody guessed it was well after midnight, the time she could usually catch Lily in her room in California, but she was too tired to reach for her phone and start typing. She heard Danny's breathing grow regular, and she thought he might be asleep, but then he coughed, sat up, and took a drink from a water bottle next to his bed. "Allergies," he said.

"Why do you still see a shrink?" Melody asked him. "Aren't you the boy wonder?"

It came out meaner than she meant it and was about to apologize when he laughed and said, "I rest my case."

Danny had already left for class when Melody woke up, so she lay in bed, scrolling through her phone. There was a cryptic text from Lily—a question mark and a heart emoji—and a thumbs-up from Eddie, which surprised her: apparently he'd learned a new skill. There was also an email from Perry, her guidance counselor, scolding her for "failing to inform the office that you'd be out this week." He had attached a permission slip that, he said, needed to be signed by one of her parents or else she'd be suspended. (She was not sure how being suspended from school and not showing up for school were different.) Then there was a second email from him, apologizing for writing "one of your parents," explaining that that language was boilerplate and they'd be revisiting it, and declaring that "in this office we are sensitive to triggers and micro-aggressions," and that under the circumstances Melody would not be suspended, but he hoped to see her the following week.

She considered what she would write, then typed, "Thanks for being so understanding. And yes, that reference stung." It hadn't really, but best to have him think so. It might come in handy later.

Danny was at his Spanish poetry class, and then he had something called Sex and the City, which apparently had nothing to do with the TV show but was about the dominion of patriarchal power, whatever that meant. He'd left a copy of his schedule taped to the door so she couldn't miss it, and a Post-it note that said he'd text her later. In the bathroom Melody was surprised to see a sleepy-looking boy brushing his teeth and another who was bare-chested with a towel around his waist, shaving. "Oh God, am I in the wrong bathroom?" she said, feeling her face redden. The boy brushing his teeth spit into the sink. "Our bathrooms are gender neutral," he said, wiping his mouth with the back of his hand and wiping his hand on his jeans before grabbing his things and walking out, leaving her with the half-dressed—or, as she knew she'd write to Lily, or Karolina, or both, the "half-undressed"—guy. Melody pretended she didn't have to pee, threw some water on her face, and walked out. She felt foolish, but she wasn't ready for this aspect of college life and went in search of if not a gendered bathroom, then a male-less one.

As Melody wandered across campus, it occurred to her that the place looked like the set of one of the romantic comedies Delia liked so much. It had been an unseasonably wet summer, and now it was an unseasonably warm fall, and though the leaves were mostly off the trees, the lawn was still green and soft, and a curly-haired guy she thought she recognized from Body and Soul was sitting on the grass, fingering a banjo, while not five feet away a girl sitting under a beech tree strummed a guitar. In the meet-cute Melody was imagining, the two would spontaneously begin to play the same song, realize it was fate, and live together happily ever after—or at least until the credits rolled. A big black dog was rooting through someone's unattended backpack, until from halfway across the quad she heard a voice shout, "Rufus, cut that out!" though Rufus didn't. Melody recognized that voice, and in a second Connor appeared by her side.

"That's Rufus," he said, as the dog trotted off carrying a bagel wrapped in a paper napkin. "Darn! There goes my second break-fast." He picked up the knapsack—which, she realized, was iden-tical to hers—looked inside, and pulled out a sandwich of some kind, also wrapped in a napkin. "Phew!" Connor said. "At least he didn't get lunch."

"Aren't there, like, dining halls all over this place?" Melody said.

"Come with me, and I will explain," he said, grabbing on to her elbow and steering her in the direction of the science build-ing. "Okay," he said after a while. "It was such a beautiful day, I decided to dine al fresco," he said.

She noticed his feet. He was wearing sturdy leather hiking boots. "Were you planning on climbing a mountain?"

He laughed. "Have you been to Connecticut before? It's al-ways mud season. Always be prepared."

They crossed a road, walked between two buildings wrapped in scaffolding, and emerged into another quad, this one small and cavernous.

"Stay right here," he said, and ran to the other side and stopped. "You can hear me, right?" he said in a whisper.

"That's so strange," Melody said.

"I know. We're having a conversation, but we're nowhere near each other." He motioned her to join him. "It's some weird physics thing," he said as she got closer. "Okay, let's go."

"My parents always told me not to go off with strange men," she said.

"In general, that's sound advice," he said as he led her around a corner and down a short alley, "but in the particular, if you were to follow it, you'd miss this. Ta-da!" He didn't have to point. In front of them was a massive re-creation of a dinosaur, a T. rex, she thought, made out of concrete and wire, and before Melody could read the plaque at its base, Connor had pulled himself up and was sitting on the tail. "Come on up!" he said.

"I don't think so."

"It's not scary."

"Easy for you to say. What is it about boys and dinosaurs, anyway?" Her phone buzzed. She took it from her pocket and saw there was a message from Marcia Yandel.

MARCIA: Nice that you've connected with Daniel.
Just so you know, dear, he is easily distracted.

She deleted the text and put the phone back in her pocket. No wonder Danny was in therapy.

Connor was leaning over and extending his hand. "It's not hard," he said. "Take my hand, put your left foot over there, your right foot here"—he pointed to what might have been a dinosaur heel spur—"and I'll hoist you up." When she hesitated, he said, "I may be skinny, but I'm strong," and she grabbed hold and some-how—it wasn't pretty—ended up astride the dinosaur's tail, too.

"That wasn't so bad, was it?" he said, unzipping the backpack and pulling out the sandwich. "You hungry?" he said, holding it out to her.

"I am not letting go."

"That wasn't the question," he said, extending his arm and waving the sandwich not far from her nose. Melody was not amused.

"I'm not hungry," she said petulantly, making it clear, she hoped, that she was not enjoying this. It was a lie. She was starving.

"Come on, humor me," he said, moving closer. He tore off a piece of the sandwich.

"Fine," Melody said, and opened her mouth.

"It's good, right," Connor said as she was chewing. "Almond butter and honey is reliably delish. Just ask Rufus."

When they were back on firm ground, and before Melody could thank him and say goodbye, Connor jumped in front of her, started walking backward, and said, "What can I show you now? What about the natatorium? That's fancy for swimming pool."

"Don't you have to, you know, go to school?" Melody said.

"It's Thursday. I don't have classes on Thursday."

"Must be nice," she said.

"College: The more you pay, the less you go. I don't have classes on Friday, either."

As they entered the main quad, Rufus came trotting up and Connor took a dog biscuit from the back pocket of his jeans and, without missing a step, tossed it to the dog, who caught it on the fly.

"We have an understanding," Connor said. "Well, he understands that whenever he sees me, I'll give him a treat. I buy them in bulk at Costco. I mean, my mom does."

"What?" he said when he saw Melody frown. "Did I say the wrong thing? You think it's dumb that my mom sends me

Milk-Bones from the other side of the country. The carbon footprint, right?" He looked at her expectantly.

"Not at all," she said. "It's sweet."

"But you're frowning," Connor said.

"Sorry," Melody said. "I'm tired. I need to get going. But this has been great." In her mind she was already walking away, going back to Danny's, grabbing her stuff, and driving away. In her mind she was wondering about Delia. When she was in college, would Delia send her dog biscuits, or chocolate chip cookies, or jars of the expensive bodywash they both loved? Of course not, because she was dead.

"I know about your mother," Connor said. They were walking side by side now, and she could feel him stealing glances at her. Before she could ask how, or simply take off running, he said, "Danny told me last night. He texted me. Told me to be careful."

"To be careful," Melody repeated.

"Yeah," he said. His hands were deep in his pockets, and his shoulders were hunched, as if he was waiting for a blow.

Melody stopped and turned to face him, holding out her hand. "Give it to me," she said.

He looked at her dumbly. She was suddenly surprised by how blue his eyes were today. The word "oceanic" came to mind. "Your phone," she said.

"Not necessary," Connor said and made no move to pull it out of his pocket. A young woman Melody had seen out of the corner of her eye was moving purposefully toward them, and when she got closer, Melody could see that her hoodie said WOMYNSAFE and her earrings looked like repurposed railroad spikes. Her hair was spiky, too, and three shades of pink.

"Is he bothering you?" she asked Melody as she glared at Connor, who looked stricken.

"I—" he began.

"I wasn't talking to you, Connor," she said, and turned to Melody. She did feel bothered, but not in the way the spiky-haired woman was implying.

"It's fine," Melody said. "We're friends." It was a bit of a stretch, since they hardly knew each other, but it seemed like the most expedient thing to say to make her go away.

The WomynSafe woman was unmoved. "Did you know that seventy-three percent of campus sexual harassment incidents and assaults here occur between people who know each other?"

Melody, who had gotten an A in that Advanced Placement Statistics class, suppressed a smile. This college had fewer students than her high school, so wouldn't most people here know each other?

"I'm Tonya, by the way," the young woman said to Melody, reaching into her sweatshirt and pulling a red string over her head, which turned out to have a whistle attached to it. "Here," she said, grabbing Melody's right hand and putting it in her palm. "You might need this."

"Thanks," Melody said, sticking it in the outside pocket of her knapsack.

"It's more effective if you wear it," Tonya said.

"She's a prospie," Connor said.

"Shut up, Connor," Tonya said. She gave Melody's shoulder a squeeze, then walked away, up the stairs and into the library.

As soon as she was gone, Melody held out her hand. "Give it," she said, and without a word, Connor surrendered his phone.

Read one way, the messages Danny sent to Connor were endearing. Read another, they felt violating. They said:

DANNY: Don't be a dick.
DANNY: Melody's mother died recently under tragic circumstances. Repeat: don't be a dick.

She handed back the phone. "Is that why you took me to climb the dinosaur? Were you stalking me, waiting till I left Danny's dorm?"

"I was trying not to be a dick," he said. And then, more softly, "I know what it's like to lose someone close to you under—"

Melody cut him off. "I did not lose her! She was not a pair of glasses or a library book! Why does everyone say that?"

He looked at her thoughtfully, as if she'd meant the question to be answered. "Well, it felt like a loss to me," he said. "Not like she was a pair of glasses or the sock that disappears when you do laundry, but like a crevasse had opened up and there was a big hole in the ground and when you peered inside there was nothing. Just black nothingness."

"She?" Melody said, her voice no longer strident.

"Lucy Chambers, my high school girlfriend. Drunk driver. She was sixteen. She should be here, not me."

"Were you in the car?"

"No, no," Connor said. "I just mean that she was so smart and would have crushed the whole college admissions process. After she died, they gave her a posthumous National Merit Scholarship. It was like one of those medals they give to soldiers after they die."

"That's awful," Melody said. It was not lost on her that the tables had turned and in the face of someone else's grief, there was nothing, really, to say.

"Yeah," he said. "It was three days before my sixteenth birthday, which I spent curled up in my bed. I only got out to go to the funeral because my parents made me. All these people were wearing these white-and-yellow ribbons, pretending that they knew Lucy. If they knew her, they'd have known that she hated yellow. It made me really angry."

"What happened to the guy?" Melody asked.

"What guy?"

"The drunk driver?"

"That's the thing. It wasn't a guy. It was her mother. She died, too."

"Oh God."

"Yeah." He put his thumb in his mouth and absently started biting the nail. "The crazy thing is that it was almost six years ago. It's so weird. Sometimes I forget it happened."

Melody shuddered. Would she forget, someday, that Delia had been killed? Would Delia mostly fade away, so that six or seven years in the future she'd say something similar? It seemed unlikely, but then everything seemed unlikely. Her mother's death, her father's strange revival, sitting here on the library steps with this boy she hardly knew.

"Anyways," Connor said after a while.

"Yeah," she said, standing up. "I guess I should be going."

"The thing is," Connor said, as if he hadn't heard her. "The thing is," he said again, "I wasn't stalking you or anything." Melody sat back down. "I just remembered what it was like when your world has been shredded to bits while everything around you seems so normal and unaffected."

Classes had let out, and the walkways around the quad suddenly filled with students rushing to their dorms or to the dining halls, like a flash flood barreling down a slot canyon. Neither had to say it: this was exactly what Connor was talking about.

"It must be even worse," he said, "when it's your mother."

"I guess," she said. And then, "I'm adopted."

"Huh," he said, nothing more.

Now what? She had ventured into uncomfortable territory, one toe in, and instead of a response she got a one-syllable grunt and now she felt embarrassed and exposed. It had never before occurred to her that in the give-and-take of a conversation, one could give and feel taken. She made a motion to leave again just as one of Connor's Ultimate buddies came bounding up the stairs.

"Captain, my captain," he said, coming closer. He was wearing grass-stained sweatpants and a red fleece with a white cardinal stitched in the left corner where a breast pocket might have been. A pair of cleats hung around his neck, banging into his shoulders as he ran. He nodded briefly at Melody. "C-man, what time does the Trinity bus leave? The email said 2:30 and the text said 2:15."

Connor turned to Melody. "We have a game," he said, then turned back to his teammate. "Sorry, Robbie. My bad. The bus leaves at 2:30 sharp. Be there by 2:15."

"Got it," Robbie said, and took off down the stairs sideways, like he was doing crossovers on a skating rink.

"I really should go," Melody said.

"You were adopted," Connor said, picking up a conversation they hadn't been having. "I guess that would make all this"—he hesitated, searching for the right words—"much harder. No, what I mean is, does that make all this harder?"

Melody frowned. "How would I know?" she said.

"Yeah, right," he said. "Duh."

CHAPTER EIGHT

The more Candace thought about the story Paul's father was telling about his son, the more it seemed like the flip side of the wishful narrative Paul, or she, or anyone who grew up feeling like they were in the wrong family might tell themselves: that they were switched at birth, that they had been abandoned outside a fire station, that they were adopted by people who didn't want them to know they were adopted. And this, in the face of irrefutable physical evidence—a family nose passed from generation to generation, or a distinctive gait, or, like Paul, an unusual eye color shared by father and son, a cornflower blue more typically found in meadows from Maine to California. Children who felt out of place in their families were always searching for a way to understand how they ended up there. Or, in the case of Paul's father, looking for an explanation, however far-fetched, of how a child of his was not.

As Candace mulled this over on the elliptical machine Paul had scored for her when his old gym was upgrading its equipment, and at work, when she was supposed to be reading through a stack of employee self-evaluations (the men all thought they deserved more money, and the women wanted more responsibility), she came to the conclusion that sometimes the combination of nature and nurture created its own mutation: marines whose parents had taken them to antiwar protests growing up, for example. But being gay was different—the scientific consensus seemed to be that homosexuality was just how you were made, which is why Paul's mother needed to come up with a story that would, essentially, disown him.

In her own life, Candace hadn't needed to disown her family, the family had just dissipated over time, like air from a tire. It was better that way. She admired Angela, with her sick husband, three kids, and an aging, periodically incontinent dog, but it was nothing that she wanted for herself.

"My family is my ballast," Angela told her. "Without them, I'd probably float away. They're my tribe. People need to belong to something. Even you, Candace. You just don't know it yet."

What tribe did she belong to? The tribe of unattached women? The tribe of people who lived alone in the woods? The tribe of people who can decide to eat a pint of ice cream for dinner? The tribe of the voluntarily dispossessed? Was that even a thing?

"What are we doing for Thanksgiving?" Paul asked in early November. The trees were mostly bare, though a few withered leaves still hung on, waving a seasonal farewell when the wind blew. He pointed in the direction of the bay window in Candace's living room, a window that in most houses would need to be "dressed," but here, with no neighbors, was always exposed. "That looks very Eliot Porter-ish," he said. "Those naked birch trees. By the way, did you know that his brother was Fairfield Porter, the painter? Also, he went to Harvard Medical School."

"Who went to Harvard Medical School?" One thing that Candace loved about her friend was that he was a fount of information gleaned from the internet.

"Eliot. Also, he was really into birds. You should get a feeder. Maybe I'll get you a feeder for Christmas! What about Thanksgiving?"

That was another thing she loved about him. He was a master

of the circuitous conversation, a verbal puppy, so full of enthusiasms he couldn't talk in a straight line.

"Why don't we do what we always do?" she said. They were eating their Sunday bagels, which were warm and filled the kitchen with a welcoming, yeasty fragrance. He reached over and flicked a stray sesame seed from the corner of her mouth.

Sometimes, she thought, they were like an old married couple—her kind of married couple, the kind that didn't live together and weren't married.

What they always did on Thanksgiving was gather with friends at Paul's one-bedroom apartment in Chelsea. The galley kitchen was a tight fit for more than two people at a time, but no one seemed to mind. Someone was in charge of bringing the turkey, there were copious amounts of alcohol, and Paul's downstairs neighbor, a real estate lawyer who harbored a not-so-secret desire to become a pastry chef, began making pies a week in advance.

"We could," Paul said. "But I was thinking that we should do it here?" He looked at her expectantly.

"Here?" She frowned. Just the thought of lots of people in her house—inside her carapace—put her on edge.

"Precisely," he said. "It's bigger than my place. It's prettier."

"Not in November, it's not," Candace said. "Also, it could snow. And it's kind of a haul from the city."

He was unmoved. "It would be a great change of scenery."

"No one wants to traipse out to the middle of nowhere. Also, I don't think the trains run that day."

"First of all, have you ever heard of the automobile? Second, of course the trains run. How would people without cars get to their Thanksgivings?"

"You know I'm not a very good cook," Candace said. This was not exactly true. She could cook. She just thought that it was mostly a waste of time. Her contribution to past Thanksgivings had been a case of red and a case of white, delivered the day before from Astor Wines & Spirits.

"No worries," Paul said. "We've got this covered."

"We?" She was annoyed. "I just said—" she started.

"No," he said, smiling shyly. "Not you. There's this guy. It's very new." He was blushing. That was new, too. One of the things they had always shared was their professed, though actually unstated, singleness. He had been her plus-one for so long she had settled into it like a favorite easy chair.

"At first I thought it was just a fling, but we really hit it off. He's a doctor. A Jewish doctor, I should add."

"How long have you known him?" Candace asked. This was key. Paul went through men the way other people went through bags of potato chips.

"Not long. I didn't tell you because I wasn't sure it was anything. We met this summer, but then Noah had to fly to California to give grand rounds at UCLA, and we didn't get together again for a couple of weeks. I thought he was out there seeing patients, like on some humanitarian mission, but it turns out that 'grand rounds' just means giving lectures." He stopped, took a drink of coffee, and smiled sheepishly. "Listen to me, 'just' giving lectures. Anyway, he likes to cook, and I really like him, and I want to impress him with your shiny, underutilized Viking oven."

"So essentially, you are asking me to pimp for you?" She laughed, but not happily.

"Is that so bad?" he said.

The guests, laden with bags from Whole Foods and Trader Joe's, started to arrive just after eleven, handsome young men Candace saw once a year whose names she had trouble keeping straight. Was Chad the one with the piercing yellow-green eyes, or was that Nate? Or was Nate actually Christof? And what about Charlie? In past years she knew him by his blond shag and the tic he'd developed to keep it out of his eyes, but this Charlie was wearing a blue knit beanie from which no hair escaped, and his eyes were rimmed by dark circles. Just as she was running through possible scenarios—cancer? HIV?—one of the others clapped him on the back and said, "Way to go!" and Charlie said thanks, and someone else high-fived him, and she was doubly confused. Had he finished chemo and beaten cancer, even though he looked like hell? Candace couldn't think what else to do, so she gave him a hug. Was she feeling an IV port sticking out of his chest? It seemed rude to ask.

"Sounds like you're doing well," she said. "I didn't realize you were sick."

Charlie laughed. "Wow! Empirical evidence that method acting works!"

Then everyone except Candace laughed, and Charlie said, "I'm prepping for a part in a new daytime TV show. Apparently I'll be dying soon, so you will still be able to find me tending bar at the Soho Grand."

Candace sighed audibly. "I thought—" she began, and he cut her off.

"Everyone does. I've been getting a lot of sympathy, mostly from strangers, especially on the subway. It kind of restores your belief in humanity."

"You all should head into the living room, which is also the dining room," Candace said, pointing the way. A rental company had dropped off an extra table and chairs the day before, and the florist had delivered so many arrangements of irises and lilies and tulips and daisies and baby's breath that someone might have thought there was a death in the family. People were milling about, examining the art on the wall—prints from MoMA, for the most part—or sitting on folding chairs because the couches had been pushed into a corner to make room for a table that could seat sixteen, drinking and chatting and looking more comfortable than Candace felt.

"You look mahvelous, darling!" Paul said, spying her as he slid a cooler the size of a bathtub through the front door. He gave her a big squeeze, then stepped back and looked her over. "Fabulous!" he said, running a hand down her sleeve. "Bendel?"

Candace laughed. "Chinatown. Real silk and hand embroidered. Theoretically they are pajamas, but I don't know why anyone would want to hide them under the covers."

"The red suits you," he said, and then, realizing he'd forgotten something, grabbed the arm of the tall, slight man with skin that was either tanned or naturally bronzed standing next to him, and presented him to Candace.

"Candace, Noah, Noah, Candace." Candace stuck out her hand, and Noah took it in both of his.

"Paul has told me so much about you," he said warmly. She was struck by his eyes, a luminous almond brown that were magnified by his rimless glasses. She wondered if it was true. Paul had told her so little about him, which meant either that whatever was going on between them was not very serious, or it was.

"OK," he said, turning to Noah, "let's haul this big boy into the kitchen." To Candace he said, "It's a cornucopia! Just wait and see."

As the two men walked past her, Candace noticed that Noah, who was wearing a tweed sport coat over a chest-hugging blue cashmere sweater and tailored wool trousers, had what looked to be a wedding ring on the fourth finger of his right hand. *What was that about*, she wondered. She'd have to ask her friend as soon as she got the chance.

Candace followed them into the kitchen. Paul unlatched the cooler, reached in, and hauled out the turkey, wrapped in alumi-

num foil and resting in a roasting pan. "Just look at this volup-
tuous butterball!" he said. "Eighteen pounds of deliciousness."

"You cooked this?" Candace said. "That's a first. I'm impressed."

"You should be," he said. "With Noah. It's his baby, so to
speak," and started to turn the knobs on the oven. "He even
brined it."

"So how did you two meet?" Candace said, trying to seem
casual about it.

Noah, who was re-tenting the turkey, laughed. "Where else
do two gay men meet?" he said. "At the gym. He corrected my
form when I was doing crunches. Unsolicited, I might add." He
smiled at Paul.

"What can I say? I couldn't help myself. Also, he was very
cute. And that was before I knew he was a famous neurologist."

"Not famous," Noah said. She could tell he was embarrassed—
and pleased. "You've got a beautiful home," he said. "What I've
seen of it."

"Come on," Paul said, grabbing his hand. "I'll show you
around. You're going to love the wainscoting above the Eliot Porter window." And then, over his shoulder, "Set the timer for thirty
minutes. It's cooked, just needs to get warmed up. Right, hon?"

Somehow, miraculously, the table had been set, the flowers arranged, the sweet potatoes, pearled onions, and green beans
heated and laid out, wine was being poured, and Noah, jacket off
and sleeves rolled, was carving the turkey with almost frightening
precision. Someone's sister—Marco's?—was apologizing for the
lumpy gravy, and the lawyer with aspirations to be a pastry chef
was explaining the best way to make a roux—"For next time," he
said, and it occurred to Candace that they were already thinking
about the next time, probably right here, and she was not sure how

she felt about it. Paul clinked his glass, raised it, waited for the chatter to cease. "A toast. To our host—ess!" he said, and everyone said "brava" or "hurrah" or "here, here." As he sat down, he waved in her direction, and suddenly all eyes were on her.

"Well," Candace said, surveying the table and the guests gathered around it, "thank you all for coming. Look at this spread! You guys are amazing." Was this her tribe? Did she want it to be?

Candace took a sip of wine, and Paul said, "Let the feast commence!" as he did every year, and just like that, dishes were being passed around with the enthusiasm and determination of a bucket brigade bailing a flood.

Cool jazz was playing in the background along with the timpani of knives and forks, and Candace could just catch snippets of conversation breaking through.

"Two-bedroom in Park Slope . . ."

"The best sushi . . ."

"Forty-five days sober . . ."

"Please pass the rolls. And the butter."

After she filled her plate, Candace pushed back her chair and stood up. "Forgot the . . ." she said to no one and everyone, walking away before she finished the sentence. In fact, she had forgotten nothing, except maybe how to be in her own space, when her own space had been transformed into something she hardly recognized. It seemed so unnatural—and, to her surprise, not terrible. In the kitchen, she rooted around in the refrigerator to find something to bring back to the table, though she doubted anyone would notice one way or the other.

"You okay?" Candace jumped and turned quickly to find Noah leaning in the doorway. He really was tall.

Candace was flustered. "Did you play basketball?" she said. She was embarrassed at how dopey it sounded. And then, "Does everyone ask you that?"

"Yes, and yes. Paid for college."

"Nice ring," Candace said. She couldn't help herself. Had he been married? Did his spouse die? Was it a man or a woman? She'd heard of people doing that—putting a wedding ring on the right hand when a spouse died.

Noah held up his hand. "This was my grandmother's. I had to have it resized, of course. She was a Holocaust survivor and then she was a Freedom Rider. You know, in the sixties. She left it to me when she died. She knew I was gay, so maybe she was giving me her blessing to marry whomever I choose to marry, since she married a Black man when it was still illegal in a lot of places, or maybe she just wanted me to have it to remember her. Long answer. Sorry."

"No," Candace said, "don't apologize."

"Don't apologize for what?" Paul said, coming up behind Noah and looking confused. "You're not conspiring behind my back, are you?"

"Believe it or not, not everything is about you," Candace said, handing him a stick of butter. "Bring this to the table, will you?"

Like their past Thanksgiving dinners, this one went on for a long time. "There are so many sides," someone said, and it was not a complaint.

"This is my favorite holiday," she heard Noah say to Paul, and she didn't know if he meant Thanksgiving in general or this Thanksgiving specifically. She hoped it was the latter, for her friend's sake. She saw him reach over and give Noah a kiss on his cheek and saw a look of contentment spread across Noah's face and felt a pang of jealousy that caught her by surprise. She'd met Paul's boyfriends before, but they always seemed ornamental, and fleeting. This one felt different. Angela always said that when you knew, you knew, to explain how she ended up marrying her grade school crush, and Candace wondered if that kind of knowledge was transferable—wondered if she could know before Paul and Noah knew, though it was possible that they did know and were keeping it to themselves, or even from each other.

The pies were passed, and then they were passed again, and before they could make a third trip around the table, Charlie—who wouldn't take one bite, "to preserve my ghoulish figure," he explained—proposed a jaunt outside "to walk it all off."

"There's a lake down the road," Paul said. "We can go there."

"It's a pond," Candace corrected him.

"Whatever," he said.

Noah asked what it was called and she said, "Dedam Pond, according to the maps, but the locals call it Dead Man's Pond, but no one seems to know why."

"Spooky," Charlie said. "I love it."

Candace made a quick detour to her bedroom to change into jeans and a turtleneck, and, catching a glimpse of herself in the dresser mirror, was surprised to see herself smiling. Maybe this was her tribe after all, even if she had trouble keeping their names straight.

The road to the pond was largely untraveled, so they walked in twos and threes, Paul leading the way, Candace not far behind, fielding questions about country versus city real estate prices. In her experience, New Yorkers loved to talk about real estate—complain about it, or brag about it, or fantasize about it. No one could believe that her three-bedroom, three-bath, twenty-five-hundred-square-foot house cost less than a six-hundred-square-foot Upper West Side condo that had been rejiggered into a one-bedroom, with a communal washing machine in the basement.

"But you pay for it in other ways," Paul called back.

"Or it pays you back," Noah said, "like having a pond, and clean air, and solitude."

"I could never do it," said the short, buff one she now knew was Christof. "Give me car alarms and subway rats any day."

"I don't know," Nate said. "It's pretty tempting. I think I'd want to be married first, though."

"Good luck with that," Christof said. It hadn't even been six months since gay marriage was legalized nationwide. "I know a couple who is already getting a divorce."

"Why did you leave the city?" Marco's sister—Beth—asked Candace.

So Candace told her about DataStream, and how it had moved to Stamford, and how she had reverse commuted for a while, and then got the idea to live near the water—"And here we are."

Dedam Pond was ringed by swamp maples that stood a few feet back from a dirt track that followed along its contours. "It takes about half an hour to walk around the whole thing," she told them. It had been unseasonably cold all week, dropping below zero at night for the first time all year, and the water had frozen in a flash, so that the skin of ice atop the pond was a crystalline window to the goings-on below.

"Look!" Christof called, "there's a turtle! It's huge!"

"And kind of scary looking," Nate said. "Prehistoric."

They all stopped and edged close to the lip of the ice. The snapper was meandering along the bottom, like it was out for a stroll.

"Ate too much at Thanksgiving," Charlie said.

Trout were swimming around, and some kind of little fish that might have been baby catfish, and tadpoles paddling frantically with their stubby legs. "They look like they're in a spin class," Paul said, taking a step onto the ice, which cracked underneath.

"Shit!" he called out and jumped back to dry land. "My shoes!" He pointed to the water stain on his Blundstone's. "I just got these. Jeez. Country living."

"OK," Candace said, "how about no one do what he just did. The pond just froze."

"Now you tell us," Paul said. She couldn't tell if he was actually annoyed or being dramatic. She looked over at Noah to see if he was sympathetic to his boyfriend or thought he was being a jerk, but as she did, he pivoted and started running, fast, away from them, shedding his jacket and then his sweater and shirt as he went. He was saying something, too, yelling and pointing, and suddenly, as if they were a single organism, all of them were running after him, Candace at the rear, picking up Noah's clothes as she went.

It felt like it took a few minutes, but was probably seconds, for Candace to see what he'd seen. A dog was skittering on the ice at the far end of the pond, and the man who had gone after him was flailing in the water, the ice breaking each time he tried to climb out, taking him farther and farther from shore. What was it that she'd read once? That you had maybe ten minutes in frigid water before your muscles failed and you went under? But maybe that was the ocean. Dedam Pond couldn't be more than ten feet deep.

"Oh, God," Paul shouted as they watched Noah toss off his shoes and splash into the water. "Someone call 911!" As if it was choreographed, they all pulled out their phones.

"I don't have any service!" Beth said frantically. "Who has service? Does anyone have service?"

"Fuck T-Mobile," Christof said.

"And AT&T," Nate said.

"I've got it," Candace said, punching in the numbers. "Dedam Pond," she said. "No, no *a*. D-e-d-a-m. It's at the end of Thatcher

Road. No, I don't have a street number. It's a pond. Someone fell through the ice. Thank you.

"This could take a while," Candace said, but no one was listening. All eyes were on Noah, who had reached the man, who seemed to be fighting him off. Candace knew, from watching all those big wave shows, that the man might already be hypothermic. How soon before Noah was, too? Paul was in the water now, and in a second he had the man draped over his shoulder, fireman's carry, when Noah, who was behind them, sank from view. They were all screaming now. Screaming at Paul to turn around. Shouting for Noah, who suddenly popped up, waved, and went down again. Candace felt something nudging the back of her leg and turned around. It was the dog, a fluffy golden retriever, who had gotten off the ice on his own.

"You!" she said, and grabbed onto his collar and checked his tags. His name was Winston. She quickly made a leash from her scarf, pulled out her phone, and dialed the number on the dog's ID. While it was ringing, she looked up to see that Charlie had waded in and was now hauling the man out as Paul went back for Noah. "He has no body fat," she said to herself as the phone went to voicemail.

Charlie delivered the man to Christof and Marco, who dragged him up the bank, away from the water.

"Fergus!" Candace said to the man, who had somehow lost his jacket. His lips were blue and he was shivering uncontrollably.

"You know him?" Marco said.

Candace ignored him. "Fergus," she said again. "You're going to be okay." And then, to Marco, "It was the name on the voicemail. We need to get his wet clothes off to warm him up."

Marco got to work, peeling off the clothes. His sister, Beth, took off her jacket.

Candace took off hers. "Wrap him up and hug him. Your body

heat will help." (Something else she remembered from the surfing episode when they were—stupidly, she thought—catching big
waves off Nova Scotia during a hurricane.)

"Here—" she said, handing over the dog. His body heat
should help, too. Noah and Paul were out of the water now, too.
Both were shivering like crazy, jumping up and down as they
awkwardly pulled on their clothes with hands so cold they were
crabbed.

"You're an idiot!" Paul was shouting at Noah. "Which is why
I love you! Let's do twenty jumping jacks. Get the blood flowing."

Candace couldn't hear what Noah said to Paul. She hoped he
said he loved Paul, too.

Fergus was starting to rally. "Oh my God," he said, the words
coming out shaky, through his chattering teeth. "If you guys
hadn't . . ."

"No worries," Beth said.

And then suddenly, as if remembering something he'd forgotten, he said, "Winston!" and tried to stand up.

"He's right here," Beth said. On hearing his name, Winston, who had been resting against his owner's back, stood up,
stretched, and came around, tail wagging, and licked the man's
face.

"I think he's apologizing," Beth said.

They could hear a siren coming closer and closer, and then it
stopped. "Over here!" Candace called to the EMTs, who had left
their ambulance at the end of the road and were standing at the
far end of the pond. "Hurry."

"Well, that was not what I was expecting when I suggested we do
Thanksgiving here," Paul said.

"Suggested?" Candace rolled her eyes. She and Paul and
Noah were arrayed on the sofa, sipping Macallan. The guests

had finally gone home. After their adventure at the pond, none of them seemed eager to depart. She thought they might have been distressed by what had happened, but by the time they had gotten back to the house, they were already retelling the story and feeling proud of themselves.

"We saved a life today!" Charlie said. "Three cheers for us." He had made what he was calling the Soho Grand toddy, though there were no limes in the house, or bitters or maple syrup.

"L'chaim!" Paul said, looking at Noah. And then, like a newly minted bar mitzvah boy, said, "It means 'to life'!"

"Dude, we've all seen the movie," Marco said. And then, "To Dead Man's Pond—*not!*" and they all repeated his words and knocked back their drinks.

Now it was just the three of them—and Winston, who was sleeping peacefully in front of the fire. The man, whose name turned out to be Tom—Fergus, the dog's owner, was his son-in-law—had to leave the dog behind when the EMTs insisted on taking him to the hospital. Before Candace could point out that she didn't know the first thing about dogs, Paul said, "Don't worry, we"—meaning Candace—"will take him."

"It's just overnight," Paul told Candace as they watched the ambulance lights recede. "Tom will get him tomorrow."

"What if he doesn't," Candace said. Winston still had her scarf looped through his collar. His leash had been in Tom's jacket pocket, and the jacket was now at the bottom of the pond with Tom's wallet and phone.

"The guy nearly lost his life for this dog," Paul said. "He'll be back. Don't you worry."

Back at the house, Candace put down a bowl of water and another filled with turkey, considered adding leftover mashed potatoes and green beans, and then thought better of it. Winston scarfed down the turkey, drank noisily, and wandered into the living room and plopped down by the woodstove and promptly went to sleep. Even Paul's "l'chaim" and Marco's Dead Man's Pond joke didn't rouse him.

"He's a good sleeper," Candace said, when the house was so empty they could hear the dog snoring and the logs crackling.

"I'm sorry I called you an idiot," Paul said to Noah.

"You are forgiven," Noah said.

"It's just that I was really scared," Paul said. And then, more quietly, "That I'd lose you."

It was a tender moment that made Candace feel out of place in her own home. "How are your fingers," she said, deliberately trying to break the mood.

"They're fine," Noah said, holding up his hands.

Candace gasped. "Your ring!" she said. "It must have fallen off in the water!"

Noah chuckled.

"Why is that funny?" she said.

"It's not," he said. "Not at all. You just reminded me that I put it in my pants pocket before I went into the water. For some reason, I had the presence of mind to realize it might come off in the water. Because it was so cold."

Candace sighed. "Thank goodness," she said. "Something else to be thankful for," and then she grew quiet, and listened to the hot air being sucked up the chimney, and Winston breathing heavily, every so often letting out a small, high-pitched yip.

He knows, she thought. He knows how tenuous it all is—this life, the warm fire, food in his belly. And she thought, too, to the conversation she'd had with Paul when Noah was in the shower.

"I like him," she told him. "A lot."

"I know, right? He's a keeper."

"So don't fuck it up," she said.

They were in the kitchen. Paul was rooting around in the

apple pie for the filling. He didn't have to say it: fewer carbs. "But that's what I'm worried about. What if he thinks I'm boring. Not as interesting as his doctor friends."

"Maybe his doctor friends are boring. Maybe at the end of the day he doesn't want to talk about doctor things."

Paul considered this. "I don't know. Maybe. But he went to med school, and then more med school and even more med school to become a brain surgeon. I went to the three-month personal training course at Equinox."

"Both useful in their own way," Candace countered. "Anyway, you went to college. You read books."

"Yeah, I went to Rutgers and majored in exploring my sexuality and perfecting my dance moves. Also, sleeping."

"This was the best Thanksgiving I've been to in a long time," Noah said as he walked into the kitchen. "Most Thanksgivings I'm on call and have hospital cafeteria turkey with fake mashed potatoes and gravy from a can."

"Poor baby," Paul said. "Maybe you just can't help saving lives on Thanksgiving."

CHAPTER NINE

Melody arrived home to a house that was dark, with the blinds drawn. Her father's car, a silver Porsche Cayenne that Melody suspected Eddie bought because it gave him the chance to say, "It's a Cayenne, hot stuff, right?" to anyone who showed the slightest interest in the car, was not in the driveway. This was to be expected. It was the middle of the afternoon and Eddie would be at work at the Marcus Bags headquarters in Manhattan, or walking the floor of the company's Paramus, New Jersey, factory. But when she pulled into the garage, which she could do now that the other spot was no longer reserved for Delia's red Audi, there was the Cayenne. Maybe Eddie wasn't at work, after all.

"Dad!" she called, walking into the house through the basement rec room. She stopped to listen, absently running a hand across the mahogany bar that Delia's antiques dealer claimed was from a speakeasy frequented by Al Capone. Nothing. The house was so quiet she could hear the hum of the refrigerator one floor above. "Dad!" she tried again, louder this time, climbing the stairs. "Dad!" She was suddenly afraid of what she might find. She'd heard about people—and they were mostly men, weren't they?—who couldn't bear to live without their spouse and willfully followed them into the dark. Eddie was devoted to Delia—that was irrefutable. But he was devoted to Melody, too, wasn't he? He wouldn't just leave her to be on her own, would he? Or was it all too much—dead wife, single parenthood? One thing

Melody remembered from the suicide unit in health class was that some large percentage of people who try to kill themselves do it on the spur of the moment, and of those who failed, most said they were glad to be alive after all. "Hey, Dad!" she yelled in the direction of her parents' bedroom when she got to the top landing. She proceeded cautiously, expecting to see the door closed—and then what? But it wasn't. At the threshold Melody took a quick inventory, found nothing unusual in her line of sight, then kept going. No one was in the bathroom or the closet. She sat on the king-size bed, then lay back to let her racing heart calm down. She stretched out and closed her eyes.

How long had she been there? She didn't know. The clock on Delia's nightstand had been unplugged—was this like covering the mirrors when someone died?—and Melody's phone was still in her bag, which she'd dropped in the basement, and the last time she wore a watch was in fifth grade (a yellow analog Swatch with daisies on its first and second hands), but it didn't really matter. She got up, exhaled a sigh, and made her way down to the kitchen. Opening the fridge, she saw the five remaining blocks of cheddar from the Harry & David gift baskets that kept arriving long after the funeral. It was like a wave cheer: one Marcus Bags client told another client about Delia's ("horrific" "awful" "untimely" "gruesome") "accident," who told an assistant whose job it was to send an appropriate gift to Eddie. Was there some algorithm that determined that the ideal "gift for grieving family whose wife/mother/daughter/aunt/partner was killed by a massive boulder" was a three-tier tower, cheese on the bottom, "fresh" fruit on top, and dried fruit in the middle, cradled in wicker, wrapped in green cellophane, and tied with a black bow? After the seventh one of these arrived, Melody began to wonder how Harry or David decided that sharp cheddar and not pepper jack or smoked Gouda would be best for mourners? Was it by consensus, or did they fight over the figs, or were yogurt-covered raisins the concession when David rejected dates (too sticky), or was that Harry? As she stood there, head halfway into the fridge, she heard the front door open, then shut loudly.

"Dad!" she called out, letting the refrigerator door close. Silence. "Hello!" she tried again. It sounded like whoever was in the house had put down a bag and gone into another room. Clearly they had no idea she was there, which was odd, since she had been shouting. Were there deaf robbers? It seemed unlikely. Not sure what to do—call Lily on the other side of the country, or Karolina, who was probably at volleyball practice, or her father, wherever he was?—she remembered she didn't have her phone, and then said, out loud, "Fuck it, what do I have to lose?" and walked out of the kitchen in the direction of whoever it was, doing whatever they were doing. The toilet flushed and, after a beat, a faucet turned on. Whoever it was had good hygiene, at least. Odd behavior for a robber, but even so, Melody decided it was too soon to rule out that they could be after the small safe in Delia's closet where she kept the jewelry that wasn't in a vault at the bank. Her "cheap stuff," she called it.

When Melody was little, she would ask Delia to open the safe and tell her the story of each piece: the diamond bracelet that was smuggled out of Nazi-occupied Belgium in the hem of a great-aunt's cloth coat ("they only had eyes for her mink stole"), the Tiffany heart Eddie had given Delia not long after they'd met, and a locket with pictures of her newborn self on one side and baby Delia on the other that she loved to look at. (When she was older she realized it could not have been her, though Delia continued to insist it was.)

"Oh, Dios mío!" their housekeeper, Maria, shouted, slapping her right hand on her chest as she walked out of the bathroom and into Melody, who was shouting herself. "Miss Melody," Maria said, taking a step backward and pulling off a pair of headphones. "You scared me! I did not expect you to be here."

"Me, too!" Melody said loudly. And then, catching her breath, said, "Sorry. I totally forgot." It was a strange thing to forget. Maria had been coming to the house every Thursday afternoon for as long as Melody could remember. She knew that.

What she'd forgotten was not that Maria came on Thursdays, but what day it was. Since Delia died it felt like she was living out of time: the days merged, weeks vanished, and the planet kept turning, no matter what.

"I didn't expect you to be here," Maria said again. "Your car was not in the driveway." Melody nodded. It was an understandable mistake. In the before times, Melody would still be at school at this hour. In the before times, there would not have been room in the garage for her car.

"Come," the housekeeper said, gesturing for Melody to follow her into the kitchen. "Sit," she said, pointing to one of the chairs in the breakfast nook. "You look"—she screwed up her face for a second—"your cheeks." She ran her fingers down her own face, poking at her cheeks. "It is written on your face. You are missing your mama's cooking."

She supposed she was. Delia considered her state-of-the-art kitchen (Wolf range, classic Aga stove, Sub-Zero refrigerator, All-Clad pots and pans, hand-forged Japanese knives) to be an annex of America's Test Kitchen, trying out competing recipes for gnocchi and buttermilk fried chicken and whatever new method for deglazing a pan was touted in that month's *Cook's Illustrated*. Then, because she worried she was consigning her family to a life of clogged arteries, she had a trainer come in twice a week so she and Eddie could sweat out the toxins circulating in their middle-aged bodies. Melody was exempt because her school required phys ed, which was the only good thing about gym class, as far as she could tell.

"There's nothing in there," Melody said when Maria opened the refrigerator. She couldn't remember the last time anyone had gone food shopping. Condolence casseroles went a long way.

Maria took out a slab of cheddar and found a couple of eggs and half a stick of butter, and in a matter of minutes slid a fork, knife, and napkin across the granite counter, followed by an omelet oozing cheese. It smelled heavenly. Melody hadn't realized how hungry she was, or that an omelet had a scent.

"This may be the best thing I've ever eaten," she said between mouthfuls, as Maria, arms folded across her chest, watched intently.

"Thank you so much," Melody said when the plate was empty. "It was so good. I inhaled it." She put down the fork and wiped her mouth. Maria reached for the plate, but Melody put her hand on it. "I can do this. You don't need to clean up after me." But that, in fact, was what Maria had been doing for fourteen of her seventeen years. She wondered how Danny would handle this. Would he tell her that it was demeaning to Maria not to let her do her job? Or would he lecture her on class and inequality and capitalism and colonialism? And don't forget about cultural appropriation. Also, why was she thinking about him at all?

"By the way," Melody said, "have you heard from my dad?"

As far as Melody could tell, Eddie had been gone as long as she had. The notes they'd been leaving for each other were exactly where they'd been when she decided, on the fly, to skip school and visit Danny at Wesleyan. The coffee carousel with the refillable stainless-steel pods looked untouched, and Eddie was a faithful Nespresso kind of guy who could get grumpy without his morning fix. Same with Delia, who had the beans shipped directly from a coffee plantation in the Dominican Republic. ("It says 'plantation,'" Delia explained, "but it's fair trade," when her eleven-year-old daughter asked if the beans were picked by slaves.) The trash bag under the sink was all but empty. Eddie must not have been home for days.

Maria was shaking her head. "No," she said. "Mr. Marcus, no. I thought maybe you knew." And then, more quietly, looking away from Melody, "I was hoping he'd left a check for me. It was your mother—" her voice trailed off. "But that is not the responsibility of the child," she said after a bit.

"Oh God!" Melody said, jumping out of her chair. "That's awful." She pulled open the top drawer to the right of the refrigerator where Delia kept the checkbook. It wasn't there, which meant it was probably in the small box of personal effects the police had dropped off three weeks after the accident, which Eddie had shoved to the back of the hall closet.

"No," Maria said. "Third one down." She must have watched Delia do this so many times.

"Right," Melody said. She retrieved the checkbook and flipped through the register. The last check her mom had written was to the electric company, more than two months ago. For a moment she worried that they were in danger of having the lights shut off, and made a mental note to tell Eddie, whenever he bothered to show up, to switch to auto-pay.

"When was the last time she—we—paid you?" Melody said, flipping through the pages.

Maria shrugged uncomfortably. "I can wait," she said.

"No!" Melody said, more harshly than she intended. "It's not fair. How much do we owe you?"

Maria reached into the back pocket of her jeans and took out a small notebook. "Twelve sixteen," she said shyly.

"Twelve dollars and sixteen—Oh," she said, catching her

mistake. "I mean, is that all? What about all the time you were here after—"

Maria waved her away. "Twelve sixteen," she said again.

Now it was Melody's turn to feel uncomfortable, and she wondered why. People got paid for their work all the time. That was the point. Danny—who seemed to have taken up residence in her head—would probably say that it had to do with the power dynamic, having this grown woman at her service. As she thought about this, Maria's phone rang, and she stepped away to answer it, speaking rapidly in Spanish. Melody focused on forging her mother's signature, then stopped. Wouldn't the bank manager know that Delia was dead? She tore up the check and started over. This time she'd pretend she was Eddie, whose signature was an indecipherable mess of loops.

She looked up and saw that Maria was smiling broadly. "I will be a grandmother," she said proudly. "My Alicia. In June."

"That's so great!" Melody said, though lately she'd been wondering how smart it was to bring a child into a world that was going to collapse because of climate change. Her earth science teacher said that by 2050 Manhattan would be underwater and there wouldn't be any more polar bears or koalas. "Beanie Babies are probably going to have a whole line of extinct animals wearing tutus and party hats," she whispered to Karolina when the teacher had turned his back and was drawing a graph on the whiteboard that correlated sea-level rise, rising temperatures, and hurricanes.

"It is very good timing," Maria said. "She will get her doctorate and her baby the same month. Her husband, he was my son Manu's roommate at Princeton."

"Princeton," Melody said.

"Yes," Maria said. "Manu is a very smart boy. He's studying to be a doctor. At Weill Cornell, in the city. Alicia is very smart, too.

She studies blood. At the Johns Hopkins University. In Baltimore. A terrible city."

"But they will be able to leave soon, no?" Melody said. "Once she graduates?"

Maria shook her head. "No, no. Her husband, he is in medical school there."

"Wow," Melody said, and meant it. A daughter at Hopkins, a son studying to be a doctor at Weill Cornell. Another doctor for a son-in-law. How many of her parents' friends would shell out wads of cash to be able to put Princeton, Hopkins, and Weill Cornell decals on the back windows of their prestige vehicles? (How many of them would complain to each other how diversity quotas and affirmative action were shutting out deserving—they'd never say wealthy and white—kids with leadership extracurriculars and excellent test scores?) (Danny had definitely commandeered her brain.)

"Here you go," Melody said, folding the check in half, as if she were passing a note in class. Maria thanked her, and though she didn't look at the amount, she made a note in her little book. Then, just as she was sliding it back into her jeans, they heard the distinct sound of a key unlocking the front door and the door opening.

"Maybe it is Mr. Marcus," Maria said. But before Melody could call out to her father, she heard a woman's voice, an unmistakable voice.

"Anyone home? Mel?" It was Marcia, Danny's mother. "I have a key," Marcia said, stating the obvious as she glided into the kitchen. She was a puffy woman who, despite the best efforts of her personal trainers—she'd gone through many—was unable to lose the extra pounds that had settled around her middle. She was fond of oversize sweaters and wool ponchos that actually made her look fat, instead of just a little chubby, which no one, not even

Delia, had the heart to tell her. Her hair was a shade not found in nature, tawny, with a strange pink cast to it. She was wearing, Melody noticed, a pair of turquoise earrings—Delia's earrings—that Melody remembered from her mother's Native American phase, when she'd go to trunk shows in SoHo to meet the artists and come back with spirit animals and fetish birds and try to get Melody and Eddie interested in their provenance.

"Your dad gave these to me," Marcia said, fingering the earrings, when she noticed Melody staring at them. Melody's heart skipped a beat. Was Eddie "seeing" Marcia? Was it because they were now members, as Danny said to her, of the same club?

Before Melody could fully wrap her head around this, Marcia said, "I mean, he told me I could pick one piece of hers. As a memento."

When? Melody wondered. And where was she when this transaction took place?

"It was that second week, I think," Marcia said, as if reading her mind. And then, when Melody said nothing, added, "I will give them back, of course, if you'd like to keep them yourself."

"No, it's fine," she said. "I'm sure she'd want you to have them." Was this true? Melody didn't know and at that moment did not care. The real question was: Why was Marcia there, in her house?

"Daniel told me you'd probably be home by now," Marcia said. It was uncanny, Melody thought, how this woman kept anticipating her questions. It was also uncanny how quietly Maria had slipped out of the room and begun vacuuming upstairs.

"Danny," Melody said. It was more statement than question. He hadn't been in his room when she stopped by to pick up her duffel, and the note she left for him was polite and vague.

Thanks for hosting. See you

She couldn't decide between an exclamation mark and a comma, but settled on a comma, because it was neutral and the only thing that could be read into it was that it wasn't an exclamation mark, which Lily once told her was the Labrador retriever of punctuation—

, M.

See him where? No place, probably, unless his mom was getting together with her dad, the thought of which made her ill.

"How did he seem to you?" Marcia said. She was making herself at home, opening the mullioned cabinet to the left of the range, taking a glass, and filling it from the five-gallon Polar dispenser, though the tap water was perfectly fine, as Eddie sometimes pointed out to Delia, who then reminded him of the time some college kids dumped a cow carcass in the reservoir and half of Westchester was under a boil-water order. And global warming, she would add, explaining how storm surges were going to compromise the water supply. Eddie knew better than to argue.

"Danny?" Melody repeated. "He seemed fine. Happy." Truth be told, "happy" was not the first word she'd use to describe Danny Yandel. It wasn't that he seemed unhappy, either. And what was happiness, anyway? Was it being boisterous and giddy, or was it something quieter, like acceptance and contentment? But couldn't people be content without being happy? It struck her that when she went to college, if she went to college, she'd major in philosophy. Maybe other people had already figured these things out.

"That's good to hear," Marcia was saying. She took a long gulp, as if she hadn't had anything to drink in ages. "Parents always want their children to be happy." She took another long drink. "It's this new diet," she said. "It's water based. So tell me about your visit." *Translation*, Melody thought, *tell me about my son, the boy genius.*

"It was pretty short. I got there on Wednesday, around noon, and luckily Danny was in his room," careful not to reveal he'd been asleep. "He took me to lunch, and when he went to his afternoon class, I took a tour and didn't see Danny till much later."

Marcia, who had drained the glass, was refilling it. "Did you meet his roommate, Benjy?" (Translation: Where did you sleep? Did you sleep with my son? This was a trick question if Marcia was trying to sniff out whether her son was gay or not.)

"Benjy basically lives with his girlfriend," Melody said. "So I slept in his bed. Danny had to stay up late to work on a paper." This was a bald-faced lie, but it threaded the sexuality needle and also seemed like the sort of thing a parent would like to hear. He was in college, after all. But not, apparently, Marcia.

"He's not working too hard, is he?" she said.

Did smoking weed count? Melody wondered. "I mean, I wasn't there long, but I don't think so," she said.

"Good, good," Marcia said. "I worry about that boy."

"Of course," Melody said, and considered mentioning her other son, the Hasid, who studied Torah day and night in some outpost near the Negev Desert while his wife popped out grandchildren she'd never meet, but thought better of it. Danny was really all she had, she'd heard Eddie tell Delia when she complained about her friend's obsession with her younger son. "Melody is all I have, but you don't hear me bragging about every little thing she does."

"What am I," Eddie said, "chopped liver?" And they laughed and moved on. But it made Melody wonder: Did Delia ever brag about her? Did she have anything to brag about?

"So," Marcia said in a strangely conspiratorial way, "now that you've seen it, are you thinking of applying to Wesleyan? You know it's very hard to get into."

Melody considered this question. Obviously, it was about Danny. It would probably shatter her if Melody applied and got in.

"Haven't decided," Melody lied. "I did like the philosophy class I visited." (Marcia didn't have to know it wasn't a philosophy class.) "But I'm not sure how strong the philosophy department is there." She made sure to look genuinely concerned.

"I'm sure it's very good. Very good," Marcia said. Clearly this wasn't the answer Marcia was expecting. She took another long drink, made sure to swallow the last drop, opened the dishwasher to load the glass, then recoiled. "When was the last time anyone ran this?" she said, and began opening cabinets, looking for dishwasher soap.

"No idea," Melody said.

"No idea," Marcia repeated contemptuously. "What about Eddie?"

"What about him?"

"Where is he?"

"He's at work," Melody said, still confused about his car. Did he walk to the train station? Was this the new, improved Eddie? "He probably just forgot to run it. It's not a big deal." It occurred to her again that Marcia might be scheming to insert herself into their lives. Well, into Eddie's, now that he was a rich widower with no obvious health problems and a teenage daughter who was almost out of the house. He was a good catch—as if he was a fish that any number of women would be angling to get their hook into. And Marcia, as Delia's best friend and a member of the dead spouse club, already had a head start. It made Melody sick. What if her sweet father, in his grief and loneliness, let her reel him in?

Marcia's phone was ringing. They could hear it now that

Maria had turned off the vacuum and was probably dusting the photographs hanging on the long wall between Melody's bathroom and her parents' bedroom. They were family portraits taken at two-year intervals and blown up to "in-your-face size." She had walked by them so many times they were imprinted in her brain. Melody at three, sitting at the top of the playset slide flanked by her much younger parents, back when what was left of Eddie's hair was black and curly and Delia was painfully thin, and two years later, in the same place, with Melody clutching her favorite stuffed animal, a bucktoothed beaver she called Baby, Delia no longer skeletal, Eddie beaming, her parents holding hands across the slide, resting them on Melody's ankles. Did the photographer pose them this way? It might have seemed so, but it also seemed to Melody that her parents were always holding hands. When she was small, she would pretend that their clasped hands were a rope and her hands were an axe and she'd sever them and insert herself between them.

"You're lucky," Lily once told her. "My parents don't have time to hold hands."

"But holding hands doesn't take any time," protested Melody, who was about eleven then.

"That's my point," Lily said, which confused her.

Marcia, with her back to Melody, was speaking loudly and gesturing with her free hand. "No, no, no," she said (*peremptorily*, Melody thought, and then: *See, Mom, I did study for the SAT*).

"No-oh-oh-oh," Marcia said until it seemed as though there was no more air in her lungs. Standing nearby, Melody studied the way Marcia moved, the way she spoke. Objectively, there was nothing wrong with her. She wore nice clothes, read the newspaper, drove a Prius. And she was familiar. But ultimately, she couldn't imagine Eddie with anyone other than Delia. Every year at Thanksgiving—Thanksgiving, oh God, was coming right up—

when they went around the table saying things they were thankful for, Eddie would always say "Delia," and Delia would say "Eddie," and then, together—holding hands, of course—they would look at Melody and say, in unison, "You!" Of course her parents were supposed to be together. The repetition made it seem inevitable. But when Melody got older, she sometimes wondered how Delia had fallen for Eddie, a chubby guy with thinning hair who could not care less about his appearance. Yes, he was on his way to becoming a very rich man, but he wasn't there yet, and Delia, who towered over Eddie when she wore heels, who had outgrown her overalls phase and cared deeply about her appearance, was out of his league. She couldn't have married him for his money, since it did not yet exist in piles—but could she have married him betting that he, they, would become fabulously wealthy? Melody doubted it, because even after they did become wealthy and acquired all the accoutrements of wealth—the big house, the fancy cars, the housekeeper, the expensive vacations, the exclusive country club, the charitable donations—Delia was always saying how grateful she was to have Eddie in her life. How he was one of the good guys. And it wasn't just words. That was the thing: she showed it, in ways small and large. True, it could have felt like a rebuke when she tossed out his frayed khakis and took him to Paul Stuart for clothes that fit his (short, mildly squat) frame, but he knew she did it out of love (and because, she heard Delia tell Eddie, he had a cute butt and should show it off). Apropos of nothing, it seemed, Delia would come up behind Eddie when he was reading the paper at breakfast or talking on the phone and kiss the back of his head or massage his shoulders. She didn't have to do that.

Didn't have to whisper whatever she whispered into his ear that made him smile so hard his back molars were on display. It wasn't for show. It was real. "You spoil me," Eddie would say sometimes, which to an outsider might have seemed precisely the opposite: Delia was a woman of leisure who could easily drop a few thousand dollars at Bergdorf's, money that came from her husband's long hours at the office. But Eddie didn't care about money. Not in the usual ways. He liked to work, and it made him happy to make Delia happy. With Delia gone—evaporated from their lives—Melody understood those words, "you spoil me," in a new way. Eddie was right. Delia did spoil him. Like milk spoils and becomes undrinkable. How could another woman love him the way she did? The simple answer was that they could not. Any woman who tried would fail. Eddie was spoiled for the rest of his life.

Marcia hung up the phone and put it back in her purse. "That was crazy," she said. "I ordered a twelve-pound organic turkey from a farm in the Hudson Valley." Melody looked at her, counting silently the seconds before Marcia mentioned her beloved son. She hadn't gotten to five when the older woman said, "It was Danny's idea. For Thanksgiving. He insisted. Sent me these disgusting pictures of factory farms. I mean, I would have done it anyway because it's the right thing to do, but it turns out that they don't have any twelve-pound turkeys. The smallest ones they have weigh twenty-two pounds because, apparently, the turkeys live the good life before they're slaughtered. So I asked the woman who called if they have any young ones, and you should have heard her go off on me. Like I was a serial killer or something. I mean, they butcher calves for veal, so what's the big deal about young turkeys? A twenty-two-pound turkey for two people. Ninety-three dollars. I kid you not." Melody flashed her a smile. It was pretty clear that Marcia was not kidding.

Then, suddenly, Marcia raised her right hand and bopped herself on her head. "You know what?" she said. "You and your dad should come. You have to. That's the silver lining. You don't have plans."

This was a statement, not a question, and though she was

probably right, Melody didn't want to concede. Sitting opposite a tearful Eddie on the holiday Delia liked best, pretending there was something to be thankful for, was preferable to spending the day with the Yandels and their twenty-two pound, ninety-three-dollar organic bird, while Marcia was flirty and Danny was high.

"That is very kind," Melody said solicitously, "but Dad and I do have plans."

"What plans?" Marcia said. Her tone was skeptical, accusatory, and hurt all at once.

Melody was just about to invent a trip to Eddie's cousin's house in the Poconos, where she hadn't been since she was nine and broke her arm falling off the trampoline, or maybe to Lily's, where one of the doctors was always on call and the other one ordered takeout from the Chinese restaurant. (They said it was to honor her cultural legacy, Lily told Melody, but it was really because her fellow countrymen were willing to deliver.) And then, like a charm, or divine intervention, Melody's phone rang and it was Lily herself. Melody held the phone up. "Thanks for coming over," she said to Marcia. "I need to take this. I'll tell my dad you stopped by," and she walked out of the kitchen and upstairs to her room and plopped down on the bed. The newly laundered sheets smelled like lavender, she told Lily.

"Lavender is supposed to impart a sense of peace and calm," Lily said. "How are you?"

"Peaceful and calm, now that I think Marcia is gone. What's up?"

"What was she doing there?"

"I don't know. Checking up on Danny. Making a play for Eddie?"

"Eeww," Lily said. "Isn't it a bit early?"

"I guess. Yes. She wants us to go to Thanksgiving at her house. I told her we had plans. I mean I was about to tell her we were going to your house, but then you called and basically saved me from lying."

"How was Wesleyan?"

"Fine, I guess. Some professor thought I was smart."

"You are smart, you dummy," Lily said, and laughed. There was noise in the background, and what sounded like a person talking over a PA system.

"Where are you?" Melody said.

"At SFO. I'm meeting up with my parents in Hawaii. The Big Island. They got invited to some medical society conference and are taking me. Break starts next week, but I finished all my work."

"Cool," Melody said. "No House of Chang."

"Nope. Apparently there is a Thanksgiving luau at the hotel. Strike that. At the resort."

"Cool," Melody said again. "Eddie and my mom went to Hawaii on their wedding anniversary, and as far as I can tell, they spent a lot of time swimming with sea turtles."

"That's what they said," Lily said. "Probably a euphemism."

"Maybe," Melody said, "but they came home with this sea turtle garden gnome and said it was our family's spirit animal. 'Slow and steady wins the race,' Eddie said, but when I asked him if we were in a race, he just laughed and said, 'The human race.'"

"Cute," Lily said, obviously distracted. "There's a sunset welcome cruise tonight where all the doctors get loaded and sing karaoke. I think the whole purpose of this trip is to get me excited about going to med school. You know, look at all the fun you'll have if you spend the next fifteen years never sleeping. Oh shoot, I think they're calling my boarding group." Melody heard her friend asking someone nearby if they'd called boarding group four, heard her say "steerage." "False alarm," she said to Melody. "My bad. Oh, I forgot to say that there is going to be hula dancing at the Thanksgiving shindig. How insane is that?"

Later, when Melody thought about it, it didn't sound insane at all. What was insane was Thanksgiving without her mother, whose favorite holiday it was, who always went all out and made the pies herself (with a little help from the frozen crusts at Whole Foods), and everything else, too, starting at least a week before, even if some years it was just the three of them. And it was Delia who made them say the things they were grateful for, and Melody would get impatient and complain that they always said the same thing, and one or the other of them would tell her it was because what they said was true. "What are you thankful for?" Eddie would ask, and when she was little she'd say things like, "I'm grateful that Josefina and Felicity"—her American Girl dolls— "are getting along" and "I'm grateful that the pool at Grandma Syl's house got fixed." (The "house" was really an apartment at Delia's mother's assisted living facility; she didn't live long after she moved in. "Forgot how to breathe," Melody overheard Delia say about her mother to someone on the phone. Melody was eight. Could she forget to breathe, too? How many nights of sleep did she miss, worrying about this? And how had it eventually slipped her mind?) When she got older, she wondered if saying what they were thankful for was an exercise to get her to say that she was grateful her parents had chosen her, had bestowed this life of privilege on her. She could do it. She could say it. They were only words, after all, but she wouldn't. She didn't know why. Just that it felt wrong. Coerced. She regretted it now, and added it to the list of things that, in the wake of Delia's death, she regretted. What did she and Eddie have to be grateful for this year? Would they even bother?

"Oh shit!" Lily said. "They really are calling my boarding group. Gotta go—"

"Wait!" Melody said. "When are you coming home?"

"Christmas," Lily said. Melody heard her reach down, pick

up her backpack, and slip an arm under the strap. "This line is very long. You should apply to Stanford. Think of all the fun we could have."

"I'm thinking of not applying. I mean not going to college. At least, not next year. I met this boy, Connor—"

"You met a boy!" Lily said. "Tell me. Oops. Gotta go, for real this time. Love you." And she was gone.

Melody lay on her bed, staring at her phone. Through two accidents of birth, she and Lily were best friends. She couldn't imagine that not being true. But she couldn't imagine life without Delia, either. Or rather, she corrected herself, had not imagined life without her. She and Lily were so different. Lily was going to become a doctor. She'd probably marry a doctor. She'd give birth to little wunderkinds, three of them, maybe four, and never skip a beat in her career. They would still talk, occasionally, and pretend they had more in common than not knowing their birth parents.

There were voices downstairs. Was Marcia still in the house? Was she talking to Maria? Why was Marcia still there? Melody sat up and walked into the hall. It was definitely Marcia's voice, but the person she was talking to was not Maria—it was her father. She raced down the stairs and into the kitchen. "Daddy!" she said, calling him by a name she hadn't used in years but that Delia always did. As in, "Daddy and I are going to . . ." "Daddy and I decided . . ." "Daddy is in . . ." Melody gave him a big hug, then stood close to him as Marcia prattled on about Thanksgiving. Clearly, a twenty-two-pound organic bird was in their future.

"I'll be on my way, then," Marcia said at last. "So glad you'll be joining us. Don't feel like you have to bring anything." She flashed a smile at Melody. If Eddie thought it was a friendly smile, Melody knew better. This was a look of triumph. She had bested Melody, and wanted to make sure the girl knew it.

CHAPTER TEN

Tom Nicholson did come for the dog. He arrived shortly after eleven, just as Candace, Paul, and Noah were finishing breakfast. Winston had taken up residence on the ottoman nearest the woodstove and did not seem at all disconcerted to be in Candace's house, though this might have been because Paul had filled a bowl with leftover turkey, which the retriever scarfed down, and then Noah, not knowing this, did the same, and now the dog was probably drunk on L-tryptophan. In less than a day, Winston had become a congenial addition to the household, thumping his tail approvingly whenever one of them walked by, or when he heard his name, or for no discernable reason at all. For a brief moment, Candace wondered why she didn't have a dog, a faithful companion who would be happy to see her at the end of the day, and who might share her bed, and improve her fitness by demanding she go for walks even when she didn't want to. But then she remembered that she had a job, and as nice as it might be to share space with a sentient being whose needs were manageable, her "lifestyle," such as it was, wouldn't allow it. Even so, not long before Tom knocked on the door, Winston sighed and stretched and lay his blocky, handsome head on his front paws, and Candace decided that if Tom never came to fetch him, it would be all right. She'd find a doggy daycare, the kind where the van came every morning, and she'd wave goodbye as if he was going off to school, and then she'd get on with her day. She didn't love the name Winston, which reminded her of the cigarettes her mother had insisted on smoking—it was the one thing dementia hadn't taken away—and wondered if it was possible to change the name of a two- or three- or four-year-old dog. But there was Tom, in one of those waxed canvas barn jackets she'd admired in the Orvis catalog, standing on the porch, a bottle of wine under his left arm, a bouquet of irises in his right hand, and an expression on his face that seemed to be some combination of concerned, eager, contrite, and curious.

Noah got to the door first and opened it, and all at once Tom's face wore a look of recognition. "You're the guy," he began, nearly shoving the wine and flowers into Noah's hands, but the doctor cut him off.

"Come on in," he said. "How are you feeling? Any residual effects from your swim?"

"Swim!" Tom said and laughed ruefully.

"He's a doctor," Paul explained.

Just then, Winston came ambling up, and Tom said, "There's the culprit!" and kneeled down and buried his face in the dog's ruff.

"Come on in," Paul said, though Tom was already inside the house.

Tom looked up. "We don't want to impose any more than we have already. Do we?" he said to the dog. To Noah he said, "You have a beautiful home."

"Oh, it's not mine," Noah said. "I'm just a guest."

"Me, too," Paul said.

"Are you a guest, too?" Tom said to Candace, who had come in behind her friends.

"She's the lady of the house," Paul said before she could set the record straight. "By which I mean, the house is hers. Noah and I are just freeloaders. Take off your jacket and have some pie."

He had a nice face, Candace decided. Not so handsome that he'd be arrogant about it, but pleasant and angular, though it was covered in a scrim of stubble. "I came as soon as I could. They kept me overnight, which was crazy," he said, as if he knew she was evaluating his unshaven face. He was absently petting the dog's head as he said this. "I hope that was okay."

"Of course," Candace said. "Winston was a perfect house-guest." And Winston thumped his tail.

Somehow, there were still six kinds of pie. Paul cut a slice of cranberry hazelnut and another of pumpkin and motioned for Tom to take a seat at the kitchen table. "We want to hear the whole story, start to finish," he said. "How you and Winston happened to be at the pond, and the ER and the ambulance, all of it."

Tom, who was shoveling pie into his mouth like he hadn't eaten in days, held up the index finger of his right hand to signal he'd get to it in a minute. His left hand, Candace realized all at once, was not there. She'd just imagined—assumed—it was. Per-ception was such a strange phenomenon. She knew this. Knew that you often saw what you assumed you were seeing. Maybe Paul was right. When she looked in the mirror, for instance, she didn't look her age but rather the age she felt she was. Tom's age, she guessed, was somewhere between fifty and sixty. The side-burns of his otherwise light-brown hair were graying, and there were crow's-feet etched around hazel eyes. But where was his hand? Not that she was about to ask him.

Tom's story took seconds of pie, and a turkey sandwich Noah made and put in front of him without Tom asking. It began three days before the holiday, he told them, when his only child, a daughter in her late twenties, almost thirty, whose house he was supposed to be going to for Thanksgiving, called to say that her mother-in-law in Scotland had taken a bad fall and was in the

ICU or whatever they called it over there, so she and her husband were going to Glasgow and could he come to the house anyway and take care of the dog. "Yes, she married a Scotsman," he said, answering a question no one asked. "Like William and Kate, they met at Saint Andrews," he added, as if they were all on a first-name basis with the future king of England and his wife.

"Anyway, what was I going to say? Her mother, my former partner—we were never married—lives in Taos, with her husband."

This story raised so many questions in Candace's mind—had he ever been married? Had he wanted to marry the mother of his child? Why was he at the pond? How did he know where she lived? Who was he?—all of which went unasked.

"So you don't really live here, and Winston is not really your dog," she said.

"Guilty as charged," Tom said, taking a long drink of coffee that, like the sandwich, had been put in front of him. "Winston is not my dog, which is why I panicked when he ventured out onto the ice. I had visions of having to call Izzy—Isabella—and tell her that her dog, who might as well be her child, died on my watch. I'm staying in her house, which used to be my house, my summer house. They've winterized it. It's on the other side of the pond. I've got a place in the city."

The New York City real estate questions then commenced. Where was it? Condo or co-op or rental? How long had he been there? What about those new, soulless buildings on the West Side? Which gym? Tom fielded them as they came, told them that he owned a loft in the Meatpacking District, swam at Chelsea Piers, kept his Volvo on the street and his pickup at Pier 40, tried to walk the High Line every day, frequented the Greenmarket at Union Square even though it was a schlep, had seen *Hamilton* at the Public Theater before it got to Broadway.

"What kind of work do you do?" Paul asked. "If you don't mind me asking?"

Candace listened to this back-and-forth as if it was a play. All these men, in her house, talking, while she said nothing, silenced by the strangeness of it, and feeling out of sorts. It was one thing to walk around her own house in sweats and a DataStream hoodie, no bra, when it was just Paul, and now Noah, but the longer Tom stayed, the more self-conscious she became. She considered excusing herself to get dressed, but worried it would make her seem desperate and trying too hard in front of this good-looking man, even if he wasn't her type. (Too L.L.Bean catalog, she'd decided.) But she stayed where she was, leaning against the kitchen counter, pretending all these thoughts were not going through her head.

"DataStream," Tom said suddenly, as if he'd been trying to work out what it was and just remembered. "That's that shower kid!" he said to Candace.

She smiled and said, "That's the one."

To Paul, he said simply "consulting," and took another long drink of his coffee, which Noah had topped off during the interrogation.

"I never know what that means," Noah said. "I can't tell you how many of my college classmates went into consulting, and I can't tell you what they did except, it seemed, mint money."

Candace grimaced. She'd been a consultant once upon a time, but Noah didn't know this.

And then, realizing Tom might take this the wrong way—though it was actually the way he'd meant it, because when they were pulling in six-figure salaries, he was pulling all-nighters in med school and then in his internship and then in his residency—he said, "Sorry. You're looking at someone who is still paying off student loans."

"No worries," Tom said. "I get that a lot. It's an engineering consultancy. And the reason I don't have any student loans to pay off is that I didn't go to college."

"What?" Paul said, incredulous. "Why didn't someone tell me that I could have a loft in the Meatpacking District if I didn't go to college!"

Tom laughed. "I come from a long line of academics. So I joined the navy. Which I hated and loved in equal measure." And he told them about working as a nuclear electronics tech, and getting sent to nuclear power school, and how he was in a classroom for nearly two years before getting assigned to the USS *Dwight D. Eisenhower* out of Norfolk.

"The joke was on me," Tom said, "because Uncle Sam gave me college credit for all my training, and then they sent me to MIT for graduate work."

"So you did go to college," Paul said, and seemed relieved.

"Technically, yes," Tom conceded. "Anyway, I became a warrant officer, eventually transitioned out, took my honorable, and then started a small engineering firm with some of my navy buddies, mostly doing work for the government that I'm not allowed to talk about. We sold it to a big defense contractor and the three of us, the partners, made the kind of money that people play the lottery to win. By then I'd met Carrie—Are you sure you want to hear all this?"

"Go on," Paul said. This was his kind of saga, one that he would pick over once Tom was gone.

"I'd met her right before we sold the firm, and we had a kid, and I suddenly had enough money to do whatever I wanted. But I still thought of myself as a navy man, and what do navy men do? They buy boats. So I bought a beautiful Beneteau Oceanis and outfitted it myself, and we lived on it when Izzy was little, going wherever the wind would take us. The joke was always that I single-handedly sailed around the world." He smiled, held up his left arm, and looked at them to see if they were smiling, too, and then went on. "It was great—until it wasn't. It was like one of those rogue waves that come out of nowhere. Izzy got sick, then my father got sick, and then one of my former partners was arrested for passing secrets to Iran, which cast suspicion on me, especially because I didn't have a fixed address. We came back to the States for Izzy's treatments, and my dad died, and my former business partner went to jail and I had to testify against him, and there were doctors' fees and lawyers' fees, and Carrie said it was all too much, and she needed to quote, unquote take a breather. I don't know. Maybe it was. But it turned out that she had started an 'internet affair' with an old boyfriend of hers, which she later claimed was not cheating because we weren't married, and then they got together for real and one day she tells me they've quote, unquote made it legal."

"That's the worst story I've ever heard," Paul said sympathetically.

"It gets worse," Tom said. "First, she wants me to pay her alimony, and when her lawyer tells her that the only way she'll get any money out of me is to sue for custody, she sues for custody. This is while Izzy is in treatment. Unbelievable. And the only thing that finally saves me—and Izzy—is that the husband decides that he doesn't want to be 'saddled'—his word—with a kid that's not his, and to seal the deal they move to New Mexico, and basically drop out of our lives. It was just me and Izzy since she was eight. But now it's Izzy and Fergus and Winston."

"How's her health?" Noah asked.

On brand, Candace thought.

"Very good," Tom said. "There was a problem with her thyroid. She's fine now."

Candace, who had not moved, felt uncharacteristically touched by his story and said, "You two must be very close."

"I like to think so," Tom said. "She was my life for so many years. It was harder than you'd imagine—or I'd imagined—watching her fall in love and get married and begin to create her own life, where I was at the margins. Good for dog-sitting and a place to stay in the city."

Candace nodded as if she knew. "Yeah," she said.

"What about the mother?" Noah asked. As Candace spent more time with him, she was beginning to understand that Noah was a linear thinker—not in a bad way, in a way that made him look at a problem and assume there was an answer and also assume the answer was his to find. Of course he'd jumped into a freezing-cold pond.

"She's living her best life, apparently. Izzy didn't invite her to the wedding. She's very protective of me. Anyway, more than you wanted to know." He put down the mug he'd been holding, though he had drained it somewhere between the sailboat story and the wedding.

Noah took it—another thing about him, Candace noticed: he was very tidy—gave it a quick rinse and turned it upside down on the drying rack. "I would have gone after you yesterday, no matter what, but now I'm even more glad that I did," he said, turning around. "We did." He looked over at Paul, and then Candace, pulling them into his orbit with his radiant eyes.

"What about you?" Tom asked, nodding in Paul's direction. "I'm guessing lawyer?"

Candace would have loved to know what about Paul made Tom think he was an attorney. His expensive haircut? The BMW parked out front? Or possibly nothing. Just an easy, uncontroversial guess.

Paul laughed. "Uh, no. Personal trainer."

"Cool," Tom said. Candace knew that though her friend loved

his work and was good at it, and was making plenty of money, he was sometimes embarrassed not to have a more conventional, suit-wearing career, like financial adviser or corporate vice president of this or that. "Anyhow, once the noncompete agreement with the company that bought my company ran out, I started another consulting firm—you can see a pattern here—but not doing defense work. Mostly we help governments, corporations, and NGOs solve problems, like building small hydro dams in Nicaragua and bringing electrification to villages in Africa."

"Like the Peace Corps!" Paul said.

"That's one way of looking at it," Tom said. "We just designed a logistics system for a big trucking company, a mill to recycle paper in Fortaleza, and new runways for an airport in Dubai, so maybe not exactly like the Peace Corps. We only take on projects I think will be challenging or fun or—"

"Lucrative?" Candace said. It came out more aggressively than she wanted. She didn't even know why she said it. No, that wasn't exactly true. She didn't want Paul to lionize this man and badger her to go after him. Which was, her logical brain knew, putting the cart before the horse. But she could already see how this was going to play out, now that Paul had Noah.

Tom chuckled. "Well, we have to pay the bills. But we do have scruples. Some, anyway." He laughed again. "I—we"—he looked at Winston, who was snoozing under the table—"really should be going. I'm sure this was not how you were planning on spending your day."

"Sorry," Candace said. "It's just that my company, DataStream, is in the process of hiring one of those consulting firms that parachutes into a workplace to streamline operations, probably in the hopes of an acquisition, and when they're done half the people who used to work there have been escorted out of the building carrying their family photos and lumbar pillow and coffee cup in a cardboard box while the consultants sit in a conference room tallying their billable hours."

"Um," Paul ventured. "Didn't you work for one of those firms?"

Candace nodded her head yes. "It's how I know how this goes."

"I take your point," said Tom. "But that's not what we do. We build things, not tear them down. Though"—he beamed a smile at Candace—"every once in a while we get to blow stuff up, which is actually a lot of fun."

"I can see that," Noah said, which caused Paul to raise his eyebrows, though he said nothing.

"So," Tom said, "I owe my life to a doctor, a personal trainer, and an employee of DataStream. Not to put too fine a point on it." He laughed.

"Well, there were others, but feel free," Paul said, putting an arm around Noah. "Saving lives is what this one does. I followed him into the water because"—he hesitated, sighed, and for a second Candace was sure he was going to declare his love again—"just because. And Candace called 911 because she was the only one of us with cell service. Turns out that T-Mobile doesn't work in the hinterlands."

"Right," Tom said. Winston, meanwhile, got up from the floor where he'd been resting on Candace's feet, took a sloppy, desultory drink of water, and plopped down by Candace again.

"He likes you," Tom said. "Though to be fair, he likes pretty much everyone." To Winston, he said, "We'd better get going, young man. We've overstayed our welcome." He stood up and Candace noticed, again, the missing hand, which might have been, she decided, the most interesting thing about him.

Paul gave Candace a look she knew was meant to encourage her, but when she said nothing, he asked Tom how long he would be in the neighborhood. Candace knew he was scheming to get them together and flashed him a dirty "cut it out" look that he ignored.

"Not sure," Tom said. "Depends on what happens across the pond." (Across the pond. She hated it when people said that.)

Paul scanned the room and when he didn't see what he wanted, said, "Wait here," left, and came back quickly with a scrap of paper and a pen. He wrote something, then handed it to Tom. "Candace's number," he said. "In case you need anything."

"Though I'm usually at work," Candace said, embarrassed.

"Thanks," he said to Paul. "I'd put it in my phone, but my phone is at the bottom of Dead Man's. A name that almost became too accurate."

As soon as they heard the tires rolling over the gravel driveway, Paul nearly jumped out of his chair. "OMG," he shouted. "This is perfect!"

Candace scowled.

Noah turned to her. "As you no doubt know, our mutual friend is an inveterate romantic. He's called me at work to read me the Vows column from *The Times*." She must have grimaced, and Noah must have seen it, because he smiled and said, "After he's read them with you, of course."

Paul walked over and kissed Candace on the cheek. "Don't worry," he said. "It's still our thing." But was it? Wasn't this how your friends moved on—by co-opting your rituals and repurposing them with someone else? He looked concerned for a second, but only that. "Don't you see?" he said, brightening. "Here you are, stuck out here in the middle of nowhere, perfecting your role as, I don't know, Miss Havisham, and along comes this fine-looking, *rich* Prince Charming who is unattached, lonely, and lives nearby."

Candace groaned. "First of all, Miss Havisham was left at the altar, so it's a terrible analogy. Second—"

"Sorry, relying on eighth-grade English. But OK, some spinster, to put it crudely."

Candace winced but went on. "Second," she said again, "he didn't say he was lonely or unattached. Third, I am happy with my life. Fourth, I don't like dogs."

"That's not true!" Paul said. "I've seen you pet dogs. You were fine with Winston. And doesn't your friend Angela have a dog? Ben Franklin?"

"Abe Lincoln, and I don't live with Angela."

"Whoa, hold your horses, cowgirl. Nobody said anything about you living with Tom. Anyway, Winston isn't even his dog."

Noah, who had been scrolling through his phone during this exchange, looked up. "Found him," he said. "Or rather, his firm." The other two crowded around and watched him swipe through photos of floating bridges, children pumping clean water, metal fabrications none of them could identify, a government building in Abu Dhabi whose roof was shingled with solar panels. "Interesting guy," Noah said.

"And not a serial killer," Paul added.

"You don't know that," Candace snapped, then softened. "But yeah, you're probably right." No one brought up Tom's missing hand. Could she have imagined it? No—he made a joke about it. Their omission, she decided, was actually an admission that they didn't want her to think that this guy was anything other than perfect. Those two really were on the same wavelength—she had to give them that.

Paul and Noah left on Saturday, after the rental company had moved the table and chairs and dirty dishes off the porch, and after the last of the pies had been eaten and there was barely a trace that two days before, the house had been full of life and everything that came with it—the buzz, the smells, the blur of bodies moving through space.

"This was lovely," Noah said as he and Candace stood outside and Paul loaded the cooler into the car. He drew her into a hug.

"Paul has a big heart," she said, quiet enough so that her friend couldn't hear. Even she didn't know if this was a description or an inchoate expression of love or a warning to Noah to tread lightly.

"Agreed," Noah said as Paul walked back toward them.

"Don't forget to call your future husband," Paul said and grinned.

"Very funny," Candace said. "Anyway, he has my number and no phone, and I don't have his, but if I did and called it, I don't think the snapping turtles burrowed in the mud of Dedam Pond will pick up."

"Snapping turtles," Paul said. "Now you tell me."

"You could always call his office," Noah offered.

Candace turned to him. "You, too?" she said. "Geesh. You guys need to leave now." And off they went, waving as they took off down the driveway, and Candace waving back till the car receded and the quiet was audible.

Candace walked back inside and lay down on the sofa, exhausted. If she was honest with herself, she'd liked having all those people in her house. But if she was honest with herself, she was also relieved they were all gone, even Paul and the lovely—and brave—surgeon. She hoped he wouldn't get bored with her friend.

Tom called on Sunday. "Hello, this is the guy whose life you saved," he said by way of introduction.

"You must have the wrong number," she said. "You must be thinking of someone else."

"Don't think so," Tom said. Was he flirting? She thought so. "Anyway, I was hoping to take you to dinner to thank you."

"You already thanked me," Candace said. She was making this more difficult than necessary and wasn't sure why.

"Okay," he said, unperturbed. "I won't thank you, but I'd still like to take you to dinner. You looked hungry. Nothing fancy. I just had a hankering for New Haven pizza, and since my near-death experience on Thursday, I've decided to live each day as if it could be my last." And then he laughed, a deep belly laugh, and she could imagine him at the other end, his smile pushing up his cheeks and the skin around his eyes crinkling. "Just kidding. I have a craving. That stuff is like crack. Not that I know what crack is like, though maybe crackheads say things like 'this stuff is like New Haven thin-crust pizza." He laughed again, though nervously this time. Candace could hear it. He was nervous, and despite herself, she found it endearing.

"New Haven is far," she said.

"I know. We'll have to bring Winston. How about if I come over at five. We can take him for a walk before he has to spend the evening in the car."

"5:30," she said firmly. "And no dog walk—I mean, for me." She felt like a dog herself, marking territory. She'd go with him, but on her own terms.

"Noted," he said.

At 5 p.m., not 5:30, Candace heard a car rolling down her driveway, and when she looked out her bedroom window saw the silver Volvo approaching the house, and it made her angry. They had agreed on 5:30, she'd specifically said no to 5, and here he was anyway. It spoke volumes to her about his character—clearly, he was not a man of his word—and she was considering calling the whole thing off as she watched Tom emerge from the car and walk around to the back and the hatch rise. He was wearing hiking boots, she noticed, a black fleece jacket, and an orange knit beanie. Was it hunting season already? Tom leaned into the car, fiddled with something, and then stood back. He glanced over at the house, and she thought he was looking to see if he was being observed, and she was glad she was upstairs, watching between the slats of her wooden shutters. He turned his attention to the car again, and she could see that he was saying something. Then he closed the hatch and bent down, out of sight, and she imagined he was talking to the dog. Soon after, the two of them took off down the driveway, Winston attached to a leash that wrapped around Tom's waist. The dog was wearing an orange vest. It was definitely hunting season. She watched them disappear around an elbow bend and a stand of conifers (she should really figure out which kind) and found herself smiling and didn't know why.

They reemerged twenty-five minutes later. Candace just happened to be passing by a window when she saw them, Winston in the lead, with no slack in the umbilical cord connecting him to Tom. She saw Tom check his watch, and reflexively, she checked hers. She was dressed—jeans, a gray cashmere turtleneck, and a small pair of hoop earrings, gold, which she'd swapped out for the pair of pearl studs she'd put in first, then rejected because she decided they looked too Martha Stewart-y. She considered calling out to him to come in, or just grabbing a jacket and purse and heading out to meet him, but she was curious what he would do. What he did was check his watch again, put Winston back in the car, and check his watch once more. It was 5:27. Tom opened the passenger-side door and sat down at the edge of the seat, his boots resting on the driveway. From this vantage, she could get a good look at the man. She felt a little guilty for spying, but not too guilty. As Angela was always telling her, you couldn't be too sure, though she wasn't sure what she needed to be sure about. 5:28. A minute later she watched him stand up, close the car door, sweep dog hair from his fleece with his hand, and walk toward her front door. She opened it before he could knock.

"Hi," he said, clearly caught off guard, his face reddening. And then, recovering, said, "All set for the pizza express?"

He was so not suave, she found it charming, which confused her. "I have to warn you, no pepperoni and no anchovies."

"How do you feel about pineapple?" he said as they walked to the car.

"In general, or on pizza?" He opened the car door for her and she slid in. It was a nice, old-fashioned gesture and it pleased her. That confused her, too.

"Both," he said. She considered this for a minute—or, at least, pretended to consider it. He started the car and turned it around.

"Yes," she said, "and no. Not on pizza. Not my thing."

"So what is your thing?" he said after a while.

"What do you mean?"

"I mean, what do you like to do?" They were merging onto the highway. Most of the traffic was going in the opposite direction, back to the city after the holiday. He pulled out next to an eighteen-wheeler. Winston, who had relocated from the way back to the seat behind Candace, let out an audible harrumph, like he was clearing his throat. Candace looked to see what he was seeing: there was a small dog, maybe a Jack Russell, with his head poking out of the window of a cab.

"Cool it, Winston," Tom said, accelerating.

"What do I like to do?" she repeated. "I used to like running, but I gave that up. I don't know. I like watching surfing videos."

"That's so funny!" he said, and as soon as he did, she bristled.

"Women can like surfing, too," she said curtly.

"Of course. Some of the best surfers in the world are women. Maya Gabeira. Bethany Hamilton."

"Then what's so funny?" She wasn't annoyed anymore, just curious.

"What's funny is that I do, too. I also like to surf. I think it's why I thought I'd be okay going after Winston on the ice. I'm a strong swimmer, despite, you know"—he raised his left arm for a second, and she realized he was wearing (was that the right word?) a prosthetic—"and I'm used to cold water. Though usually when I'm in cold water, I'm wearing a wetsuit."

Suddenly, it clicked. "Bethany Hamilton," she said. "Is that what happened to your hand?"

"The woman whose arm was bitten off by a shark? I wish. I mean, I wish it was as dramatic as that. No, it was really stupid. Let's just say I tangled with a propeller. Do you surf?"

"Oh God, no. I just like the videos. I find them relaxing."

"Do you want to learn? I could teach you."

"No thanks," Candace said. "When I worked at the consulting firm, some sadistic partner decided that all the first-year associates should take a surfing lesson together, out at Brighton Beach, at the end of October. Said it was a bonding experience, but the scuttlebutt was that our bonuses depended on showing our mettle, or some such thing. It was brutal. Someone actually got hit in the head by a board and ended up with a traumatic brain injury and never came back to work. Though we never found out if it was because he could no longer work or if he didn't have to work after the firm's insurance company settled before the case went to trial. Depending on which rumor you believe, he either got fifteen million or fifty million, and an NDA."

"That sounds bad. I guess," he said, was about to go on, and stopped.

"What?"

"No. It's inappropriate."

"What?" she insisted.

"OK," he said. "I was going to say that I bet there wasn't a lot of bonding that day."

Candace shook her head. "Actually, there was. It was all we talked about for months. It accomplished what the partner wanted, just not in the way he planned."

"Can I say another inappropriate thing?" he said, smiling nervously. "It's a question, actually."

What could this be? She braced herself for the inevitable—some variation on "why aren't you married?" as if that was anyone's business. But when you were in your forties, and a woman, and unmarried, it was as standard a question as asking a pregnant stranger when their baby was due. So Candace had worked out a standard answer to a standard question, one that was bound to end the discussion before it could begin: "no reason." Still, it wasn't like she didn't ask herself the same question, and it wasn't like she didn't know the actual answer. Those that forget history are doomed to repeat it. The last thing she wanted was to replicate the only marriage she'd observed up close. That was her inheritance. That's what her parents had bequeathed her.

Still, turnabout being fair play, it wasn't like she couldn't ask him the same thing—not that she would. Better to think he was an outlier rather than damaged goods.

Tom cleared his throat. "Umm," he started as a smile worked its way across his face, "I mean, we hardly know each other, and I think we need to establish this before things get, you know." He paused and looked over at his passenger, who was staring straight ahead, her hands gripping her knees, as if braced for impact. "Okay, here goes." His face became serious again. He waited a few beats. "What," he said at last, "is your favorite flavor of ice cream? I'll go first. Rum raisin."

"Yuck," she said.

"I know, I know," he said. "I just had to get that out of the way. Now you?"

Candace relaxed and pretended to be contemplating a response. "Hmmm," she said. "This is probably heresy, but I hate ice cream that's loaded with stuff, especially cookie dough. What monster thought it was a good idea to add raw frozen dough?"

"I think it was Ben, though it could have been Jerry. But that's what you hate. Tell me what you love? Don't be embarrassed if it's vanilla."

"What do you mean?"

"You know, plain vanilla. Boring."

"A good vanilla is hard to find," she said. Would he get the Flannery O'Connor reference?

"Very funny," he said. "So is it really vanilla?"

"Sort of. Vanilla fudge." She looked over to see his reaction. Not—she told herself—that it really mattered.

"Retro, like rum raisin," he said. "Cool."

They were passing through Bridgeport, the city's smokestacks smudging the otherwise brilliant blue sky. The Long Island Sound, empty of vessels, stretched eastward.

"When Izzy was little, we'd sometimes stand on the beach near here and say we could see France, but it was just some part of Long Island, though I never told her," he said.

Winston had moved forward so his chin was resting on the back of Candace's seat and his snout was alongside her ear.

"He really likes you."

"So you said."

"No, I mean it."

"Thanks, Winston," she said, reaching behind and patting his snout. "I'm not much of a dog person." Was that a hint of a frown crossing his face? Did she care? "I mean, not to the extent that I'd risk my life for a dog."

He grimaced. "I was doing it for my daughter."

"I know," she said, chagrined. It had been a joke, but not a funny one, she saw now. They drove in silence then, the sound of Winston's gentle snoring marking time like a metronome.

After a while he said, "So what would you risk your life for?"

"Isn't that one of those beery, late-night questions we asked each other sophomore year?" she said.

"I wouldn't know," he said, easing the car onto the exit. "But it's a legit question. At least it is for me. Maybe it's a military thing. I don't know. But look at Noah. He risked his life for me. A perfect stranger."

"Perfect," she said, trying to lighten the mood.

"You know what I mean," he said. And she did. When she saw Noah start running, she was amazed at how reflexive it was, running toward danger. True, he was in the business of saving lives, but not like that.

"Do you think you would have done it if the situation was reversed?" she asked.

"I hope so," he said. "I've been asking myself that question almost since it happened. I want to believe I would. I mean, I guess we all want to think of ourselves as heroic. But I just don't know."

They were in the city now, dodging pedestrians and bike riders who seemed to find stop signs and traffic lights optional.

"You went after Winston, and whether you did it because you love your daughter or because you are a dog person, or both—it doesn't matter. You did it. That should tell you something."

"I don't know," he said again.

They were stopped at a red light. A young man on a beat-up

road bike pulled alongside them and inched ahead. Just as the light turned green, he stuck out his left hand to turn, crossing directly in front of them. Tom slammed on the brakes and they all jerked forward and backward, Winston yelping as he was thrown against the front seat.

"Jesus! It's like that guy has a death wish," Tom said, and pulled over. "Feel my heart," he said, and grabbed her hand and placed it on his chest and held it there with his own. Then, just as suddenly, he relaxed his grip. "Sorry," he said. "I probably shouldn't have done that."

"No worries," Candace said. "It was scary."

"Too many scary things," Tom said as Winston tried to climb into the driver's seat. "You're not scary," Tom said, and she couldn't tell if he meant her or the dog.

CHAPTER ELEVEN

MELODY: Thanksgiving was not half bad. Fun, actually,

Melody texted Lily, who was stuck in an open-air pavilion with ocean views, listening to an endocrinologist from UCSF talk about his cutting-edge research into hirsutism because her parents thought it would be useful when she interviewed for medical school there.

"This whole trip is a trap," Lily said when they finally talked on the phone. It was six in the morning for her, and Lily was walking along the beach because it was the only time of the day when her parents didn't have her scheduled. "All the orthopods are out here going for a run," she said. "Apparently, you can't be an orthopedist unless you were a varsity athlete in college. JV athletes probably become podiatrists. But I wouldn't know because they don't get invited to these VIP confabs."

Melody was still in bed, though it was noon. She could hear Eddie pottering around downstairs. Once golfing season was over, he grew restless and a little out of sorts, and Melody worried that without the ballast of Delia, he'd sink back into a funk. He seemed to have a good time at the Yandels'; it was good that they hadn't stayed home—too many memories of Thanksgivings past. Marcia made sure to ask him to carve the turkey, which gave

Eddie the opportunity to try out his annual roster of silly Thanksgiving jokes on a new and unsuspecting audience.

"Do not give away the answers," he warned Melody. "Not even a hint," he said, pointing Marcia's twelve-inch sujihiki carving knife at her before launching in. "Okay, then," he said, sawing the breast from the bone, "what's the official dance of Thanksgiving?" "Why did the turkey say no to dessert?" "What was the turkey arrested for?" Everyone was shouting the answers—"The turkey trot," "he was stuffed," "fowl play"—and laughing and groaning, and it made Melody happy to see the old Eddie, the goofy, unself-conscious Eddie, the Eddie she'd been missing. He was the hit of the party, and it was a party.

Danny had brought home some stray kids who couldn't get home or had no place to go. One was from Ghana, a freshman Danny had befriended when he heard him say he was from Accra, and an ethereal vegan girl who couldn't eat the turkey, or the mashed potatoes, or the candied yams, or the stuffing (butter) but seemed content with a plate of steamed green beans and a rectangle of braised tofu she'd brought with her, and Lark, who brought a pumpkin pie she'd baked in the toaster oven in her dorm. From what Melody could tell, Danny had a crush on her, and because of that it seemed that Marcia had been warned off commenting on her pierced eyebrow. Also, she was premed.

"Honestly, I was kind of proud of Marcia because the thing looked like she'd stuck a pin through her forehead, which I guess she had," Melody told Lily.

The other guest was Connor. "I almost didn't recognize him," Melody said. "He cut his hair and he was wearing a collared shirt. Oh, and glasses."

"Wait!" Lily said. "I thought he and Danny weren't friends."

"Apparently they are in a band together now. It's called Skatch Tape. They play ska music."

"Clever," Lily said. "FYI, I'm rolling my eyes."

Waves were crashing in the background, and Melody could imagine the water running over the tops of Lily's feet and quickly disappearing underneath as the tide pulled it back to sea. Melody looked out her window. The leaves were gone. The sky was steel gray. It had been a long fall; it was going to be an even longer winter.

"It's better than Tone Def, which was the other name they were kicking around."

"Oh, the irony," Lily said. "Is safety-pin girl in the band, too?"

"No. But it was pretty clear that Danny wants her to become their groupie. Well, his groupie."

"What about Connor?"

"I don't think he cares. Anyway, he looks like a junior banker now. Very respectable. He says he's still going to WWOOF, maybe at this farm in Italy, where they don't just feed you, they also teach you Italian and take you to the opera and you learn to make pasta from scratch, but if he doesn't get in, he'll work at this other place in Vermont. It's really competitive. The Italy one."

Lily laughed. "If he doesn't get in? Like they want to know his SAT score? That's insane."

"I'm thinking of doing it, too, Lil. The Vermont one. For the summer and maybe the fall, if I like it. They let you stay for six months."

"Oh shit!" Lily said. "Never turn your back to the ocean. I just got splashed by a big one and it looks like I wet my pants. Okay. Okay. I'm okay," Melody heard her say to someone. "Okay," she said again. "Sorry. The fall? What about Northwestern or Tufts or Hudson Valley Community College?"

"I'm definitely not applying." It was the first time she said it out loud like that, and it sounded strange, like someone else was talking.

Lily was walking away from the ocean, its rumble fading as she walked up the beach toward the resort. "Let me get this straight," she said. "You want to be a lady farmer? Like Old MacDonald's wife? Do I need to remind you that you are from the suburbs, born and raised? Or at least raised? Your parents have a gardener!"

"It's a lawn service," Melody corrected her.

"Whatever. Do you even know what one of those little hand shovels are called?"

"Not unless it is on my SAT vocab list."

"Very funny. I hate to sound like my parents, but have you lost your mind?"

"Maybe," Melody said. "I'm just done with school. Fini, fidi, fici."

Lily laughed. "Pro tip: don't take the Latin AP exam. I don't think it will go well. But seriously, if you're tired of school, why don't you go on one of those fancy gap year programs to some exotic land. My biochem partner climbed Kilimanjaro and then lived with a host family in Tanzania for two weeks and said it was transformative. He's kind of a jerk, though, so I don't know what kind of transformation it was."

Melody sighed and ran a hand through her hair and wondered for a second if she should cut it all off, get tonsured. Now there was an SAT word! Were there gap year programs to monasteries, where you didn't have to talk to anyone or explain yourself, even to your best friend? "I don't want to climb mountains. I just want to get off this express train."

"I hear you," Lily said. "I really do. I mean, look at me. After breakfast I'm supposed to go to some continuing medical education class, and I haven't even gone to med school and I don't even know if I want to be a doctor, or if I think I should be a doctor so I won't disappoint my parents. Shoot. They're waving to me from the front of the buffet line. Gotta go. Love you."

Melody was just about to hang up when she heard Lily say, "Wait. Wait, Mel, have you told Eddie?"

"Working on it," Melody said.

The truth was, she wasn't working on it. She wasn't scared what Eddie would say. What could he say? It wasn't like there was a law that said you had to go to college, and it was not as if it was going to cost him money for her not to go. She could try the "I'm saving you money" argument, but when had Eddie Marcus not liked to spend money? And she knew him well enough that he would counter her argument with some back-of-the-envelope calculation that showed if she simply postponed the inevitable four-year excursion to some country club that also required its select members to read Wittgenstein and study ancient history, it would actually cost him an additional sixty-five thousand dollars. Of course, if he did want her to go back to school at some point, he might not want to bring that up. The truth was that she wasn't working on it because, as her mother might have said, "it wasn't his department." Delia was the one who found the Montessori preschool, and the one who found the tutor when it became clear that the sweet, sweet teachers at her Waldorf school were never going to teach her how to read or do long division, and the one who decided that the public school was the better option, and the one encouraging her to study for the SAT the morning of the accident. Car is to rock as mom is to death—who could have imagined that being the correct analogy? The truth was, now that she thought about it, her mother, who professed to be a feminist, who dutifully contributed to Planned Parenthood every year, who could make a compelling argument why it was antifeminist to argue that feminists shouldn't, or couldn't, wear heels, had been living the most cliché gender role. She was the one who made all of Melody's doctor and dentist visits—did Eddie even know the name of her pediatrician? It was Delia who arranged for her driving lessons, researched summer camps, made sure she took her vitamins, read her homework. It was Delia who ran the household, hired the help, and made sure they got paid. She had traded the life of a high-powered lawyer for the life of a suburban mom. *No judgment*, Melody told herself. What was privilege but being able to choose your own path? She hoped it had been the right one, and that Delia had been happy or content or not full of regret.

Melody kicked off the covers and got out of bed. She considered going downstairs and telling Eddie right then, but when she looked in the mirror and saw the bed wrinkles on her cheek and hair corkscrewing out of her head like a hundred limp Slinkys, she decided it might be better if it didn't look like a decision she'd made on the spur of the moment.

Eddie was still in the kitchen when she went downstairs, his face obscured by the newspaper he was reading.

"Morning," Melody said, though morning had come and gone.

"Morning," Eddie said absently. And then, dropping *The Times* enough to peer over it, said, "You look nice. Are you going somewhere?"

This was a big difference between her parents. Delia would have taken note of the hint of blush on her cheeks and the discreet frame of eyeliner, the freshly washed hair, the raw-hemmed jeans, and would have said, "Where are you planning on going?" or even, "Where do you think you're going?" She was more direct, and for better or for worse had a sixth sense when her daughter was going to do something sketchy, like take the train into the city when she said she was spending the day with Karolina. Technically it wasn't a lie, because she would be spending the day with her friend—a defense that Delia the lawyer found mildly winning, and Delia the mother shot down instantly. "Two thirteen-year-old girls are not getting on that train without me," she said, which put an end to that particular adventure. Eddie, on the other hand, was less discerning. Or maybe he just trusted her more.

"I'm not going anywhere," Melody said reflexively, defensively, and then immediately amended the statement. "Actually, I'll probably go over to the Yandels' later. They're doing a post-Thanksgiving leftovers thing."

"That's nice, dear," Eddie said, and turned back to the newspaper.

Melody didn't move. She stood there for a bit, watching the top of his head move from side to side as he read. "Dad," she said finally, and when he lowered the paper again, she noticed that his glasses were clouded with fingerprints, something Delia would have pointed out and then, in a gesture that was either loving or censorious, taken them from him and sprayed them with lens cleaner. *Not my department*, Melody said to herself. To Eddie she said, "There's something I want to talk to you about." She stopped herself from saying "to tell you," to at least suggest that this was a discussion, not a done deal.

He lowered the newspaper and seemed to see her for the first time. "My God!" he said suddenly, "you look more like her every day!" Melody was embarrassed. She felt sorry for him. Eddie was seeing what he wanted to see—was delusional, really.

Melody twirled a finger around one of her curls, winding it up like a toy. Delia's hair was straight. So perfectly straight that other women sometimes asked her which flat iron she used. Her eyes were so brown they were black, and could be arresting if she trained them on you with intention, as Melody knew too well. Her own eyes were a muddy khaki—not quite green and not quite brown, unless she had been crying. Then they were a bright, crystalline green, as if they'd been washed and polished by her tears. Eddie was seeing things. If she resembled Delia at all, it was in the same way that dog owners start looking like their dogs.

"Dad!" Melody said sharply, to snap him out of his reverie. Eddie looked at her for a second, uncomprehending. For a brief moment she worried that he was in the beginning stages of Alzheimer's disease—didn't people with dementia sometimes confuse their children with their spouse? Or was it that they thought their wife was their mother? She couldn't remember. Maybe both.

"Sorry," he said. "What is it, sweetheart? Don't you want to sit down?" He pointed to a chair catercorner to his and pushed away the plate he'd parked there when he finished one of the blueberry corn muffins that he bought fresh from the bakery and stored in the freezer, a guilty pleasure that Delia had campaigned against and lost, until it became a running joke and she'd praise him for choosing a breakfast high in antioxidants.

Melody did not sit down. "I'm not going to college," she said, and shoved her hands into the pockets of her jeans to keep them from shaking.

"Ever?" Eddie said, which was such an Eddie thing to say.

"I don't think I can answer that right now," she said—which was totally a Delia thing to say.

He folded *The Times* and pushed it to the far end of the table. "Do you want a muffin?" he asked.

Clearly he was nervous now, too. A muffin? Melody shook her head.

Eddie rested his elbows on the table, cupped his chin in his left hand, and drummed the table with the fingers on his right hand. "What would your mother say?" he asked after a while.

She couldn't tell if it was a genuine question, like he was coaching himself, or if it was meant to weaken her resolve, because, of course, Delia would be appalled. Wasn't the whole point to go to a "good" college and get a "good" job and have a "good" career and "do well" in life?

"I think we both know she wouldn't like it," Melody said. "And maybe I wouldn't have made this decision if she was still alive. But she's not, and if what happened to Mom taught me anything, it's that things can change in an instant." She paused and looked at Eddie and tried to make out the expression behind his cloudy glasses. "I know it's a cliché, but life is short. Or can be." She didn't think she needed to add the next part and paraphrase Joseph Campbell, who she'd read in honors English the year before, and point out that that's why people should "follow their bliss," though it wasn't as if pulling weeds and spreading manure was her bliss. It might turn out to be, but right now, her bliss was about what she would not be doing.

"No," Eddie said flatly. "No," he said again, with more resolve.

"No, what?"

"No, you can't," he said.

This was not at all what Melody had expected. Eddie was the pushover parent, the yes man to Delia's more finely tuned fact-finding inquiries that typically ended with a "we'll revisit this at a later date." Law school had served her well.

Melody felt herself getting defensive. "There's no law that says I have to go to college. I mean, you can't make me. I'll be eighteen."

Eddie, who prided himself on his rationality—a habit of mind he developed in reaction to, and as a way of dealing with, his brother's delusions—looked incensed. His hands were balled into fists and his mouth was pinched but ready to discharge, like a cocked gun. Melody had rarely seen him angry, and it scared her. But it also deepened her resolve. It was her life, after all. Why couldn't he see that?

Then, just as suddenly as it appeared, the storm within Eddie seemed to recede. His fingers unfurled from his palms, and he took off his glasses, polished them with the hem of his shirt, noticed they were still dirty, and did it again, as Melody stood there, her own anger mounting. When he spoke, his voice was calm and measured.

"OK," he said. "You can work for the company—start on the factory floor, work your way up. It's a union shop. You'd probably start at eleven dollars an hour. Not bad for someone without a college degree."

Was he goading her? She thought maybe.

"I'm not going to work for Marcus Bags. I'm going to WWOOF," she said.

"You're going to what?"

"Work on an organic farm. Probably in Vermont. Connor—you met him yesterday, he goes to Wesleyan with Danny—that's what he's going to do, and he will have a college degree, ultimately. He's the one who told me about it."

"Let me get this straight," Eddie said. "You have decided not to go to college so you can follow this boy to a farm somewhere—"

"Vermont," she interjected. He ignored her.

"—so you can pick beetles off potato plants or something?"

"I'm not following him. But aside from that, yes," she said.

"I sure hope it pays well," Eddie said.

"It doesn't pay anything," she said. "Room and board."

"And then what? Become a milkmaid?"

"Very funny."

"How will you pay your car insurance?" he asked. It sounded like a reasonable question, but Melody heard it as a get.

"I'll sell the car," she said, not trying to hide her insolence. "I won't need it on the farm."

"And after?"

She shrugged. "No one knows what the future holds," she said.

That, of course, was not completely true. She knew that she'd be going to the Yandels' later in the day. She knew that she'd be texting Lily about this conversation. She knew that she'd tell Connor that if the potato beetle job didn't go well, she could always work at the paper bag factory, and she knew that he probably would say something positive like "cool" or "awesome." As long as a large rock didn't crush her on the way to Danny's house.

"Actually, Danny says that WWOOFing will look good on a college application," Melody said, trying to salvage the conversation.

"I'm confused," Eddie said. "You started this by telling me you weren't going to college."

"Yet," she said, hoping this would appease him. It didn't.

"No," he said. "Just no."

She was about to remind him, again, that he was not—or soon would not be—the boss of her, when he said, as much to himself as to her, "You are dishonoring her."

Melody felt the anger grip her like a vise. "How can I dishonor her when she's dead," she said. It was cruel. She knew it was cruel. That's why she said it.

Eddie recoiled, closed his eyes for a second, and when he opened them, they were wet and shiny. "Her memory," he said quietly. "You are dishonoring her memory."

"I don't get why this is such a big deal," Melody said. "It's not like Mom did anything with her fancy education."

Eddie pushed his chair away from the table and stood up. "You don't know anything about what your mother did with her education," he said, and walked out of the room.

CHAPTER TWELVE

The pink slips showed up on Monday morning, only they weren't pink and they weren't slips of paper. Instead, there was an email marked Private and Confidential that would have been cryptic if Candace wasn't already on the lookout after Banerjee hired the thousand-dollar-a-day consultants to "rationalize" the business while he was sailing from Newport to Saint Barth, where he planned to be "for the duration." The scuttlebutt on the seventh floor, where Angela worked, was that he'd hired the sailing crew that had worked for DiCaprio the year before, so they'd take him to all the cool, secret places celebrities hang out.

"Which would you rather be, rational or crazy?" Banerjee's enigmatic deputy, Rodney Nguyen Smythe, had asked during a companywide videoconference months earlier, to alert them to the imminent arrival of the consultants. "It's the same for DataStream," he said, assuming everyone chose rational, though they were all strategically muted. "You'll know who they are because they dress better than we do," he said, which may have been a joke. It was hard to tell. He rarely smiled. RNS, as he wanted to be called, with each initial sounded out, like FBI or NSA—or "Rinse," as the rank and file called him—made it a point to be inscrutable, even in his choice of clothes. He wore the same outfit every day: jeans (the ostentatiously overpriced Saint Laurent kind), a gray mock turtleneck (merino wool in winter, organic cotton otherwise, a nod to Steve Jobs), and any number of

DataStream hoodies (sort of like Zuckerberg). Angela said there were people in her department who were certain they could tell what mood RNS was in by the color of his sweatshirt, but to Candace his mood was always the same—cloudy. The maintenance staff had a weekly betting pool: whoever correctly guessed on Monday which hoodie he'd wear every day that week won the pot. "Frosted Flakes are on the floor" was shorthand for Nguyen Smythe's sudden appearance: he liked to wander through the warren of cubicles, quiet as a tiger on the prowl, hands deep in his pockets, saying nothing.

"It's a way to increase productivity," he told Candace, the time she mentioned that she'd been hearing from supervisors that their teams found it creepy. "It's called the 'keep 'em guessing' approach." *If only he knew*, she thought. "Probably the most useful thing I learned at HBS." HBS, everyone in the firm was supposed to know, stood for Harvard Business School, where RNS had not matriculated. He'd taken an online course and printed out the certificate, had it framed, and hung it on the wall of his office, next to a locked case of his esports trophies, positioned directly across from his desk where he could see them through the channel between the two computer monitors that dominated it. The walls were key-lime green because RNS was a believer in feng shui, and green with undertones of yellow projected both prosperity and balance. He'd had a queen-size Murphy bed installed for the nights when he didn't feel like driving back to the city, where he still had roommates, and an electric piano that he played throughout the day, though no one ever heard him because he always wore headphones and had a light touch. It was a large space, airy with high ceilings, much of it taken up by an octagonal conference table with eight small Zen gardens and eight small hand rakes in front of each ergo chair, though no one could remember the last time eight or even five staff members had been invited to sit there together, or at all. An audience with RNS was typically one-on-one, by summons. Like today. MY OFFICE. NOON, the email said, and then the names of six of the company's eight departments and the words twenty-five percent.

How did Nguyen Smythe, the offspring of a woman who had fled Vietnam in a rubber raft and a British businessman who met her at the Vegas casino where she was running the craps table, ascend to this august position? Also by chance: by connecting with Banerjee on a *Mortal Kombat* Internet Relay Chat forum when they were both in high school. This was part of the DataStream origin story. A guy Banerjee knew only as "cousin suntzu" became employee number one the day cousin suntzu graduated from Berklee College of Music, where he went to study jazz, got sidetracked by emo, learned to build and program his own synths, and toured one summer with Weezer.

On his résumé, which Candace skimmed when she first got to the company and was still interested in the backstories of the people she was going to be working with, this bullet point was called "glorified roadie." Banerjee brought him on to write the code that executed the vision he'd had all those years before. And because Nguyen Smythe was the first DataStreamer, with a long relationship with the owner and founder, he simply self-appointed himself chief executive when Banerjee got bored with the whole thing. (Though not with its money.) He was the boss by fiat.

Candace stared at the email as if she didn't know what it meant. But of course she did. The consultants had spoken, and it would be up to her to separate what they considered chaff from what they believed was wheat, an analogy that let them pretend that these weren't people, with families and mortgages and medical bills and car payments and college tuitions. She texted Angela.

> **CANDACE**: Rinse cycle. Can't do lunch. Sorry.
> **ANGELA**: Full report,

Angela texted back, unaware that her department was one of the six about to be threshed.

Candace knocked on Nguyen Smythe's door at 11:59. A minute later he called, "Enter." He was wearing what for him would pass as formal wear: a blazer instead of a hoodie and blue-light blocking computer glasses. She suspected the look he was going for was gravitas, but the result was more like cosplay. He was a short, elfin man with long hair worn in a bun atop his head that gave him another two inches but made it look like he was trying too hard. He had a soul patch, and a single onyx stud in his left earlobe the same color as his eyes.

"Damian," he said, summoning his assistant, who did have an MBA from HBS, "get Candace a Fiji water."

"I'm fine," Candace said, but Nguyen Smythe rejected her rejection.

"It's important to stay hydrated," he said. "It waters the brain." Candace suppressed a smile. She was imagining a bed of flowers poking through her gray matter. Or palm trees, since it was Fiji water.

Nguyen Smythe was serious. He was always serious.

"Damian, lunch," he said, and in an instant, the young man appeared with a burrito bowl from Chipotle and a ginger kombucha that off-gassed an odor of decaying organic matter when the young assistant opened it. (Did she see him make a face?)

"I would have ordered something for you, if I knew you would be here now," RNS said.

Candace decided not to state the obvious: she was sitting across from him, at noon, watching him eat, because he had commanded her to be there. But she knew this game. He was asserting his dominance by creating his own version of the truth. She stared at him and said nothing. The burrito bowl did look good. She willed her stomach not to growl. Downstairs, in the minifridge next to her desk, was a single piece of pizza in a Styrofoam box, a souvenir from the trip to New Haven with Tom, who took the other leftover pieces, one for him, one for Winston. She couldn't help herself: she smiled, thinking of the trip, of Winston resting his snout on her shoulder and going to sleep there, and the warm rhythmic puffs of his breath on her neck. Was she falling for . . . a dog?

"Why are you here?" Nguyen Smythe said, by which he did not mean why was she sitting there. This was his rhetorical style—ask the question that the person on the other side of the table might ask, and then answer it as if he was the smartest guy in the room, the only one who could answer it—which in this case was not true. She knew why she was there.

"We'll be implementing bullet point sixteen from the consultants' report," he said between bites. "The report is confidential, so you'll have to trust me that this is the best course of action."

"Which is?" Candace said. She wanted him to say out loud that he was ordering her to fire something like sixty people.

"We need to do some serious trimming around here," he said. He had hot sauce dribbling down his cheek. She expected Damian to appear any second now and dab it with a cloth napkin.

"Trim?" she said.

"Trim," he said.

Was this something else they taught at online HBS: how to talk about firing employees as if you were clipping hedges? "When?" she said.

"ASAP," he said, taking a swig of the kombucha. She watched him try not to burp.

"I understand the need to trim the staff," she began. Truly, she did not, but without the consultants' report there was no way for her to argue the point, and in her experience, people liked to be agreed with, feel validated, which helped soften the coming blow. "But we're weeks from Christmas and—"

He cut her off. "Better to pull the bandage off fast than bit by bit," he said, and in her mind she could hear adhesive ripping away from skin and taking chunks of epidermis with it.

Candace sat up straight in her chair. She was at least four inches taller than Nguyen Smythe (sans bun) and had nearly ten years on him—a decade more of learning to read people, but this guy was insoluble. He was neither nice nor not nice; was supremely confident or his supreme confidence masked a deep insecurity; had perfected the poker face or had no affect at all. Candace was used to dealing with difficult people. Her mother was difficult. Her father was difficult. She went into personnel because she was good at dealing with difficult people. It was probably a mistake, if she thought about it, but she tried not to. Running HR was a job, not a calling. The pay was good and she was good at it and what else was she going to do at this point in her life?

"Twenty-five percent in each of these departments," she said slowly, pretending to be giving this order some thought. "We'll have to be strategic. Last one in, first one out won't cut it. I mean, we'll need to assess each department and figure out where we can lose a position without losing quality or productivity." She was buying time—a review like this could take months.

"Nope," Nguyen Smythe said, "the Bridgewater boys beat you to it." (At least half of the Bridgewater boys were women, but no matter.) He reached into his desk, pulled out a spiral-bound book the color of money, and pushed it in her direction.

There was no title across the front, only two logos,

DataStream's and Bridgewater's. Those in the know would know. "It's all in here," he said, then pulled it back as she reached for it. "Damian has copied the relevant pages." As if pulled by an invisible string—though more likely, he'd been standing just outside the door—Damian appeared with a file folder and handed it to her.

"So old school," Candace said.

"Email isn't safe," Nguyen Smythe said. "It could get into the wrong hands."

"Is the company getting sold?"

His silence sounded like a yes to her. She opened the folder and leafed through the pages. They were full of names, top to bottom.

"This needs to happen pronto," he said. "Pronto" was one of his favorite words.

"It's three weeks to Christmas," she tried again.

Nguyen Smythe threw up his hands. "I don't care about Christmas. Or Hanukkah. Or Kwanzaa. Don't give a flying fuck!" He said this quietly, evenly, with what preschool teachers would have called his "indoor voice," but his indoor voice, coldly absent of anger or annoyance or any human emotion, was worse than if he'd been yelling.

What kind of messed-up childhood did he have, Candace wondered, then made herself focus. "Look," she said, "on the off chance that we're being sold, or we're going public, or whatever front-facing activity is prompting this" (the one activity she steered clear of mentioning was the possibility that Banerjee simply wanted to squeeze as much money out of the place as possible to fund his fabulous lifestyle), "I think we"—by which she meant Nguyen Smythe—"need to take into account the PR implications of mass layoffs right before the new year."

"Go on," he said, suddenly paying attention.

"First of all, it's bad optics. Makes you look like Scrooge." Would he even know who Scrooge was? Or Dickens, for that matter? "Second, we'll get terrible reviews on Glassdoor and those kinds of sites. I realize you might not care about bad optics or getting bad reviews on a site that rates workplaces, but anyone considering buying this place—I know we're talking hypothetically here, but if there is such a person or entity—they will care because it will make it difficult to hire the best people in the future."

Nguyen Smythe pointed to the clock on the wall. "I have another meeting," he said. "Don't let that folder out of your sight." Had the bullet been dodged? She couldn't tell.

"I'll look forward to hearing from you about this," Candace said, pretending and hoping that it was not over.

Though she was alone in the elevator, Candace squeezed into the corner, out of sight of the security camera, and opened the folder. She was looking for one thing, hoping she wouldn't find it, and said "dammit" out loud when she did. Nobody liked Christmas more than Angela. She was on a first-name basis with the salesclerks at the Christmas Tree Shops in Paramus, Woodland Park, and Cherry Hill. This was not good. It was going to be hard enough, and bad enough, to lay off people who she'd hired over the years, and "let them go" as if they were balloons or animals released back into the wild. But Angela? That was personal. How do you tell your friend to put her family photos and Garfield mug and sit-bone pillow in a trash bag and vacate the premises? Candace needed to get back to her office, shut the door, and get her thoughts in order. The elevator opened on seven, and Teresa from marketing got on and nodded to Candace. Before she could make small talk, Candace rushed off and headed for the stairs.

The stairwell was empty, and her heels echoed on the concrete as she made her way down. She heard people chatting and laughing somewhere below her. On six, she decided she'd tell Angela the truth because that's what a true friend would do. On five, she thought, *No, that would be cruel.* Angela had gotten Nick a sit ski ("cost an arm and a leg," she joked) and booked a family vacation at a ski resort in New Hampshire. Why cast a pall over it? On four, her floor, she was back to where she'd been in the elevator—confused and concerned and clueless about what to do with what she knew. It wasn't like Angela was the only one. It wasn't like this sort of purge didn't happen every day at companies all over the country—the world, really. It wasn't like this wasn't what Candace did for a living. Hiring, firing, and everything in between, except this firing—as if calling it downsizing was supposed to lessen the blow—wasn't about poor job performance, it was about ROI, the finance guys' euphemism for greed.

Candace pushed open the stairwell door and rushed down the hall to her office. "To tell or not to tell, that is the question," she said under her breath.

"What did you say?"

Candace took a step back, startled. There was Angela, in a lime-green pantsuit with a 9/11 commemorative pin attached to the lapel, sitting on her office sofa, drinking a Diet Coke through a straw.

"The door was open, so I let myself in," she said, stating the obvious. "Nice flowers, by the way. Secret admirer?" she said and laughed and pointed to a vase of red-and-yellow tulips on her coffee table.

The card was one of those small ones with a preprinted greeting embossed on the front. "With thanks to you," Angela read out loud. "Who is Noah?" Angela said, reading the other side. "Great name. Conjures up images of animals. And couples, you know, walking two by two. Very promising." Angela's right foot was shaking up and down. That was her tell. She always did it when she was anxious or excited or both.

"What? Oh. He's Paul's boyfriend. He came for Thanksgiving and stayed for the weekend. Nice guy. A neurosurgeon."

"Good for Paul!" Angela said, as if he'd won a five-figure payout on a scratch card, then frowned. "Maybe you should, I don't know, branch out"—she hesitated—"spend more time with straight guys."

"Angela! Jeesh!"

Angela stood her ground. "You know what I mean."

"I love Paul," Candace said. "You know that."

"Of course," Angela said with either real or pretend empathy, Candace couldn't tell which. "What can I say? I'm old-fashioned. I want you to meet your own neurosurgeon."

"Thank you," Candace said, walking over to her desk and shuffling the folder Nguyen Smythe had given her among the other folders on her desk, hoping her friend would not ask what she'd been doing upstairs. And then, she wasn't sure why, she said, "I did meet a guy on Thanksgiving. He was taking care of this dog. Winston."

"You met a guy named for a brand of cigarettes?"

"No, his dog. Well, not his. His daughter's dog."

"How old?"

"I don't know. Six. Two. It's hard to tell."

"You met a man who is either six or two?"

"Very funny. The dog. Tom is—actually, I have no idea how old Tom is. Fifty-three? Fifty-eight? I didn't ask."

"Well, don't just stand there," Angela said. "Sit down. Details, please," just as the phone started ringing.

"Gotta take this," Candace said. "Just wait a minute," she said and picked up the receiver. "You've reached human resources, how may I help you?" She made a face. When the company got rid of administrative assistants (except in the C-suite) back in 2009, everyone was instructed to answer the phone as if they worked in customer service, even if they did not.

The person on the other end of the line did not identify himself or answer her question. "January fifteenth," he said.

"That's good news," Candace replied, but he hung up before she got all the words out.

"What's good news?" Angela said, leaning forward.

"Rinse is not going to make any announcements about. . . about restructuring the company—you know, because our dear leader seems to have gone rogue—until after the holidays."

"How generous of him," Angela said, rolling her eyes. "Rinse, I mean."

"I guess," Candace said. It was like the doctor saying you had three weeks to live and then revising it to a month. That extra week would be precious, but still.

"Okay, dish," Angela said, rubbing her hands together as if she was about to tuck into a big juicy steak.

Candace considered this. To her surprise, she had an unnatural desire to talk about Tom, which was butting up against her natural reticence. Their time together had not been especially romantic, not at all. Instead—and this surprised her, too—it had been comfortable, and she wanted to savor that feeling the way she had savored the taste of tomato and char on her fingers at Sally's Apizza, and the way she loved the nearly scientific way Tom dissected what made Sally's pie better than Pepe's, though admittedly she wasn't really listening, just watching the way his lips moved, and how far back his ears traveled when he was smiling.

"You liked him," Angela said, preempting her. "Like," she said, correcting herself. "You like him."

"He's a nice man," Candace said.

Angela slapped her knee. "You are impossible," she said. "He's a nice man," she mocked. "Come on!"

"We got pizza," she said. "In New Haven. New Haven pizza." She was tongue-tied. This was new. She almost liked it. And it was odd. She hadn't been tongue-tied with Tom. Quite the opposite, which she wanted to savor, too.

"Okay, before I have to go," Angela said, checking her watch, "will there be a second date?"

Candace bristled. "It wasn't a date," she protested.

"Hmm," Angela said, standing up and smoothing her blazer, "I believe if you look it up in the dictionary, or online, when two people make a plan to go out to dinner, it's called a date."

"Fine. We talked about going to that other pizza place in New Haven. Well, he did. He said I should make up my own mind about which was better."

"So, more New Haven pizza in New Haven." She was walking out of the room now. And then, as if she had forgotten something, turned and said, "When?"

Candace felt herself blush. This was new, too. "Friday," she said.

Angela smiled at her enigmatically.

"What?" Candace said.

"When someone makes plans to see you on a Friday, it's because they are leaving room for the possibility of seeing you on Saturday," she said, stepping into the hall and disappearing. "New Haven pizza in New Haven," Candace heard her say. "Classic."

CHAPTER THIRTEEN

For the first time ever, Melody was glad her family didn't celebrate Christmas. When she was little, she'd cried about this, knowing her classmates would return from vacation bragging about the toys that came all at once, in a big heap. Hanukkah—or, as her fourth-grade teacher called it, "Jewish Christmas"—was a pale imitation, even though it wasn't supposed to be an imitation at all. In school they sang the obligatory dreidel song, then memorized all four verses of "Joy to the World" and decorated the classroom with tinsel and strings of popcorn and cranberries that mice nibbled at once the school was emptied of students. When she was nine, one of the synagogues in town—there were two—objected to all this religious stuff in the public schools, while the other one urged its members to keep their heads down and not rock the boat. But the boat was already listing. The town newspaper devoted an entire page to letters complaining that this was a war on Christmas, and the school board approved a resolution decreeing Christmas to be a secular, all-American holiday, which they somehow seemed to believe would satisfy all involved. Delia said that it was an indefensible argument, that the Constitution had something called the establishment clause, and Melody wanted to know if that clause was related to Santa Claus. It was the third night of Hanukkah, Melody remembered, because in her mind's eye she could see the four candles illuminating the smile on her mother's face, and she was just about to taste the potato latkes

Maria made before she took the bus back to Mount Vernon to wrap Christmas presents for her two kids. Before Melody could feel silly for asking, Eddie proclaimed that she would make a fabulous lawyer someday, just like her mother, which confused her. As far as she could tell, Delia was not a lawyer; her profession was stay-at-home mom. If only she had stayed at home *that* day.

But now Melody was grateful that she and Eddie didn't have to feel Delia's absence when they hung ornaments that told the story of their family, didn't have to pretend that they were getting back to normal, as people seemed to want and expect them to. For years, they'd driven into Manhattan on Christmas Day, watched the skaters glide across the ice at Rockefeller Center, had a meal at Shun Lee Palace, and went to the Big Apple Circus or *The Nutcracker*. But then she turned thirteen and wanted no part of it. She knew it made Eddie sad, because she heard Delia tell him that she'd been the same way at that age. "Give it time and she'll come around," she told him, assuming that time was on their side.

Eddie was watching a Knicks game on TV with the sound off, and barely looked up when Melody walked into the den. He called it his "man cave," but Delia had decorated it, found the perfect leather sectional, and had the electrician mount the largest television she could find on the opposite wall so it felt like you were standing on the greens with Tiger or in the Garden with Carmelo Anthony. Melody stood beside him and watched for a few minutes, too. The Knicks were losing badly; they were never going to recover.

"What's the point of watching when you know they are going to lose," she said as the Knicks' coach called a time-out. Eddie shrugged. They had all but stopped talking to each other. He was hurt and angry; she was stubborn. Though it was someone else's holiday, Melody was hoping she might cajole her father into a

Christmas Day truce that would lead to a lasting détente. What she wanted to say was how much Delia would have hated what they'd become: cohabitators who traded polite monosyllables, if they spoke at all. Instead, she retreated to her room and put on headphones to drown out the oppressive quiet of the house. But even with Dr. Dre injected directly into her head, she could hear it. When it got too loud, she grabbed her car keys, called out a perfunctory goodbye to Eddie, who may or may not have heard her, and left.

Melody drove around for a while, then parked on a street where the houses were close together and she could see into the well-lit living rooms as if they were dioramas at the natural history museum. TVs cast a blue light, blinking Christmas tree LEDs stuttered like strobes, families floated in and out of view like flotsam and jetsam.

Someone was knocking on the driver's side window. Startled, Melody turned her head and saw a state trooper standing there. He was wearing a black knit watch cap under his officer's hat, and when he spoke, steam preceded his words. "Open the window, miss," he said fogging it. "Are you all right?"

Melody reached into the glove compartment and pulled out the car registration. "No, no," he said. "I don't need that. You weren't speeding." Melody rolled down the window. "Some of the neighbors were concerned. Not a lot of Lexuses in this part of town." She remembered seeing a Neighborhood Watch sign nailed to a telephone pole. Apparently, someone had been watching.

"Got it," she said.

It hit them at the same time. They had met before. "You're . . ." he began.

"Yup," she cut him off. She waited to see if he'd say something about it.

"Well, have a good holiday," he said, tipping his hat. "I mean, if you celebrate."

"You're sure it was the same cop," Lily was saying as she sawed a piece of bread from what sounded like a stale loaf. It was two days after Christmas, and Lily was home on break and wearing pajamas even though it was late afternoon.

"Positive," Melody said. "It was awkward."

"I can see it now," Lily said, spreading a thick layer of peanut butter across her bread. "It's the perfect setup for those rom-coms you like so much. Young cop breaks the worst news of her life to our hero, and some time later he pulls her over during a routine traffic stop, maybe she's had a little too much to drink, he sits with her and sobers her up, and a year later they are married and with child."

"Very funny. I think you should stick to science."

Lily's house was big like hers, but messy, because the Drs. Shapiro and Horowitz shared a habit of leaving half-read medical journals and books and coffee cups scattered about, as if they'd been suddenly called away to attend to an emergency but were planning on coming back any minute and finishing the article, the novel, the cold French roast. Unlike their neighbors, they didn't have a housekeeper, didn't think it was right to have some-one poorer than themselves cleaning up after them, made sure to donate to charities that supported migrant families and efforts to stop human trafficking, all the while failing to recognize, or acknowledge if they did, that their casual attitude to clutter drove their innately orderly daughter nuts. When it got overwhelming, Lily would gather up the half-empty mugs and relocate the medical journals to her parents' study and add to the piles of books on the floor of their bedroom. But with her away at school, it was starting to look like her parents were hoarders.

"You want to know something crazy," Lily said, taking two Diet Cokes from the fridge and sliding one to Melody. Lily was short, with jet-black hair that she wore in a high ponytail, and had chunky glasses, also black, that would have made her look studious if she wasn't already. "I think Nina and Peter may have become naturists."

"What's so crazy about that," Melody said. "Lots of people like nature."

"No, not naturalists. Naturists. Aka nudists." Lily shook her head in disapproval.

Melody tried not to spit out her drink. "Are you sure? What's your evidence?" Knowing Lily, there had to be evidence.

"I know, right?" Lily said. "They left the name of the place where they're spending their little weekend getaway and I looked it up and if you read the not-so-fine-print like I did, you'd see that it is a clothing-optional resort. Also, they left me, their only child, behind. I rest my case."

"Nice work, Sherlock." Melody took another drink. "This stuff is disgusting, by the way."

"Yes, but it's diet, so we can eat these," Lily said, taking a bag of Mint Milanos out of the cupboard nearest her and tearing it open. "It's all about the math, baby!"

Later, as the sun was setting and wisps of snow began to skitter and whorl, they stripped down to their underwear, wrapped themselves in towels, and stepped onto the deck and into the hot tub the doctors had gifted themselves when Lily went to Stanford. The water felt scalding at first, but soon it was up to their shoulders, and cool flakes of snow landed on their warm faces and ran like tears along their cheeks. The neighbors' lights came on sporadically, as if they were waking to the night, and the sizzle of cars on wet pavement drifted up from the parkway.

Melody closed her eyes and tried to visualize the line across her shoulders between water and air, between earth and heaven, and felt her body relax and seem to wander away.

"So you're set on this farming thing?" Lily said after a while.

"Yup."

"And Eddie is cool with it?"

"I wouldn't say that. He's barely talking to me. He thinks I am dishonoring the memory of my mother. I kind of can't wait to graduate and get out of there."

Lily considered this for a bit, staring down at her legs through the water. "Sometimes I think that the thing I'm most afraid of is dishonoring my parents," she said.

"You don't have to go to med school, you know, Lil. Nina and Peter will get over it if you don't. Especially when you win the Nobel Prize."

"Very funny, but that does not help. I love my parents, and I'm grateful to them for all that they've given me, but sometimes I worry that they wanted a little Chinese baby because they had visions of her becoming the Chinese Midori and the Chinese Marie Curie and going to Harvard and Harvard Medical School and following in their footsteps. Like they chose me because I was a sure bet, the model model minority." She let out a long sigh and reached over and turned on the jets, and the water bubbled and churned and she sank down lower till it touched her chin.

"Well, you showed them, Lil," Melody said. "You went to Stanford, not Harvard."

"You're hysterical. I'm serious."

"Wasn't it your dad who coached the counselors at adoption camp to reassure all of us that we wouldn't be sent back to wherever we came from if we weren't perfect?"

"But that's the thing," Lily said. "I mean, I'm not worried they will send me back to the orphanage, I'm worried that I will be a disappointment. I know that they are proud of me, but I kind of hate that they are proud of me. That's why I'm scared for you, jumping off the train. But I also admire you for jumping off the train. I couldn't do it. Not in a million, trillion years."

"If I'm being honest, I don't think I would have if Delia was still alive. But maybe if she was, I wouldn't want to, or it wouldn't have crossed my mind. I don't know."

"Yeah," Lily said, and turned off the jets. An owl hooted and Lily said "barred," as much to herself as to her friend. "I hate to channel my shrink dad, but do you think maybe you're angry at your mom? Like this is a way to get back at her, you know, a big eff-you for dying."

Melody considered this for a moment, then shook her head. "It's not as if she knows. How can I get back at her when she's not here?"

"I don't think these things are rational."

"Said the most rational person on the planet."

And then, as they were getting out of the hot tub and standing barefoot on the deck letting the snow cool them down, she said, "Maybe. Maybe I am angry. I don't know. Danny said it was like becoming an orphan again. I mean, Eddie is there, but he's checked out."

"How is Danny?"

"No idea. We haven't spoken since Thanksgiving. He is in Israel, visiting his Hasidic brother, which has to have Marcia tearing out her hair. Talk about jumping off the train. Seth left Penn to study Hebrew at a yeshiva junior year and never came back. He was the original Yandel boy genius."

"That has to be rough."

"Marcia says he joined a cult because of what happened to his father. That he needed ballast after his father got sick and, you know, hovered between life and death and then died, something to steady him, or something like that. That's what she told Delia, anyway. And Delia said she understood because of her brother, who followed his guru to India."

They were in the upstairs bathroom peeling off their wet underclothes when Lily said, "Peter says that trauma is written into the body because it changes your gene expression. The mind can do a good job of blocking things out, but the body doesn't forget."

"That's profound, Lily," Melody said sarcastically, but she suspected her friend was right. She could not remember a time when she wasn't Melody Marcus, daughter of Delia and Eddie Marcus, but that time existed, and love was provisional, and maybe her body had absorbed the knowledge that she was nobody's, without her mind knowing it had.

"Tell me about that boy Connor," Lily said when they'd changed into sweats and were lying on her queen-size bed. This was their safe space, the place where, over the years, they'd traded secrets and gossip and made forts and watched movies and complained about their parents and wondered aloud about their other family, the one that was absent, which they couldn't do anywhere else.

"Okay, but first tell me about junior year. What's going on?"

Lily cracked her knuckles. "It's pretty cool. Everyone but me, I think, is planning on working in the Valley. No, let me rephrase that. Everyone but me is planning on disrupting pretty much anything they can think of. Light bulbs, doorbells, refrigerators. It's crazy. This one kid showed his pitch deck for smart sneakers to some VC guys and came back to school driving a Ferrari."

"What's a pitch deck and what's a VC guy?"

Lily laughed. "I didn't know, either, when I got there. VC stands for venture capital. Those are the guys with the money. The pitch deck is like the business plan. There's a whole class devoted to developing and creating your deck. It's even more popular than intro to CS. Oh, sorry, computer science."

"What else?"

"So," Lily said, "I did shots for the first time. My lab—by which I mean the lab where I do all the scut work—got an eight-million-dollar grant, and the bigwigs took us all to this fancy restaurant in the Bay Area that cost over a thousand dollars. Which they probably expensed, by the way. And I finally got around to joining the Chinese students' association and met three other Lilys who had been adopted from the mainland. It was like all the parents got the same memo."

"Can we rewind?" Melody said. "You did shots? You?"

"Peer pressure," Lily said. "It was the night we went to that restaurant. Phil, the principal investigator, the one who recruited me to the lab—we call him Dr. Phil—said we should all pregame the celebration, and we went to a bar, and I ordered my usual—"

"Diet Coke with lemon," Melody interjected.

"Of course," Lily said, "and they all made fun of me, and I got shamed, I guess, into taking a shot."

Melody feigned outrage. "A shot? A single shot? Who does a single shot? Did you even go to high school? Or college, for that matter?"

Lily shrugged. "All I could think about afterward was my parents explaining how the prefrontal cortex is not fully formed until the end of your twenties, and before that alcohol can impair brain development. They even had slides."

"Pitch decks!" Melody said and laughed at her own joke. "Anyway, they were just trying to scare you into not drinking excessively. I'm sure they won't love you less for doing a shot. Or even two."

Lily colored. "I did three."

"Okay, three."

"You don't know that," Lily said.

But Melody did. A rock falling out of the blue and killing your mother could be clarifying, because when she thought of all the times she'd annoyed Delia on purpose over the years, testing her patience with eye rolls and snarky comments, Delia never stopped letting her know that her love was stronger than whatever unpleasantness Melody threw at her. Would Delia approve of the farm plan? For sure not. But would she stop loving her daughter because of it? Also no.

"But enough about me. Connor?"

"He just donated his hair to Locks of Love. He hadn't cut it in like ten years. Turns out he is an Eagle Scout. It's probably a red flag."

"A red flag for what?"

Melody shrugged. Her first real boyfriend, Scotty Refrew, who was so sweet in sixth grade, became a jerk in seventh. Her ninth-grade crush, Rory Stine, was never particularly nice to her, which may have been why she liked him. Then he catfished an overweight boy who'd never had a date and got expelled and had to transfer to another school, and she never saw him again. She'd had sex, once, to get it over with, with a boy named Matthew, who was homeschooled by his evangelical mother but was on Melody's high school's swim team and came to practice just as her gym class was ending, which is how they met, he in a butt-hugging Speedo, she in the pilled, school-issued but suggestive one-piece. It was his first time, too, and he cried about it, and sent her flowers, and when his parents saw the charge on their credit card bill, they questioned him, and he confessed, and they made him quit the team and apologize to her parents, which was mortifying for all of them. Delia was cool about it, though, and took her to the doctor, who prescribed birth control pills, which Melody didn't take because she heard they made you fat and she was pretty sure she was never going to have sex again, which so far had turned out to be true.

"I don't know," she said after a while. "He's a good guy, almost too good, honestly. I think he thinks of me as damaged goods and, like, a new do-gooder project now that he's cut his hair and doesn't need any more merit badges."

Back in the kitchen they tore into a pint of Cherry Garcia, chatting between spoonfuls. Lily described the pimply aspiring engineers in her dorm who spent meals tossing out P/E ratios and the latest Andreessen Horowitz investments and were so boring she agreed to go on a date with the plumber who came to fix a broken radiator. But he, too, had a pitch deck and an idea for an app that he wanted to run by her, as if because she was at Stanford she had a direct line into Silicon Valley. She loved Stanford, and she hated it, she told Melody, which proved it was true that you could hold two diametrically opposed thoughts at once and your head would not explode.

Melody watched her friend root around the ice cream container and pull out a frozen cherry bit. "Gotta get our five fruits and veg," Lily said, dropping it on her tongue. It reminded Melody of the time Eddie took them fishing in Harriman State Park when they were eight, and Melody was content to let her bobber float on top of the water, and Lily decided it was too passive and kept reeling in the line and tossing it out again, until she snagged what turned out to be a man's soggy dress shoe, which she brought home as a prize. Every time Melody saw it, sitting on a shelf in Lily's bedroom next to her science fair ribbons, she was reminded how different they really were. Lily had always been ambitious and committed to taking matters into her own hands, while she was content to sit back and wait for the universe to reveal its plan for her. But maybe that was changing. Not for Lily, but for her. Sometimes she wondered if they'd be friends if they hadn't met when they were so young, but they were friends, sisters born of circumstance. There were things about their lives that they shared and would always share, especially the not-knowing.

"Remember that time when you turned out to be allergic to shellfish, just like your mom, and she said it was learned behavior?" Melody said. "Or when you asked for a real stethoscope for your third birthday, and then wore it like a necklace, which everyone thought was so cute?"

For years they'd turned nature versus nurture into a game, trying to guess which of their attributes had been imprinted by their adoptive parents and which were inherited and inevitable. Some of the time it was so obvious it didn't bear acknowledging. The only physical feature Lily shared with Peter and Nina was their tendency to put on weight, which was a hundred percent nurture, since her parents were foodies before there was a name for it. Melody didn't look like either of her parents, no matter what Eddie said, but she looked more like them than Lily ever would with hers, which meant that it was easier for her parents to attribute everything to their influence, genetic or not. "She got that from me," Eddie crowed when Melody started playing the cello in fourth grade, because he'd played the trumpet in his middle school band and apparently had a lock on her musical abilities, which in both cases turned out to be none at all.

"You know what would be weird," Lily was saying. "What would be weird is if nothing is nurture. Like nurture is just some invention, and it's all nature from the get-go."

"Says the girl who was found in a box on a bridge, thousands of miles from here."

"I know, I know," Lily said as she scraped her spoon along the side of the carton, as if the calories would count less if they were delivered that way. "But maybe I'd be the same person, just living a different life."

"We need chocolate sauce," Melody said, opening the fridge and rooting around until she found the Ghirardelli. "But seriously, Lil, even I, a potential college dropout, if you can be a dropout before you actually go to college, know that that can't be true."

"I don't know," Lily said. "What about all those twin studies where babies are separated at birth and live these completely separate lives, but end up getting married on the same day to someone with the same name and work the same job and both sing baritone in their church choir? I mean, maybe we both have a twin floating around out there, living a parallel life. Have you ever considered that?"

Melody squirted the chocolate into the ice cream container and dug in. "Brain freeze," she said, making a face. And then, "No, I haven't. Anyway, they say that twins who were separated at birth always know or feel that something is missing, and I don't."

"OK, then what about a sibling? Don't you wonder sometimes?"

Melody was about to say no—then stopped herself. When she was younger, she imagined she had an older brother named Toby. Delia called him her imaginary friend, but Melody insisted that he was real. She talked to him, set aside half her sandwich for him, blamed him whenever it was convenient. Melody didn't remember outgrowing him, but she must have. And there was something else, something Melody found when she was looking through Delia's desk for a padded envelope: a report from the therapist she vaguely remembered visiting once in those early years. The woman had a box of toys she encouraged Melody to play with, so she built a small house out of Legos, where she said Toby lived. SUMMARY EVALUATION, it said at the top, and her name, and something about her imaginary brother being a coping mechanism to deal with her abandonment issues. Reading that, so many years later, it seemed stupid to her. It still did. She knew she'd been adopted, but she'd been with Delia and Eddie from before she could remember. How could she have abandonment issues if she didn't remember being abandoned? The truth was, being adopted was as much a part of her as her curly hair and size-eight feet—a feature, not a bug, was how Lily once put it. What had Delia told her when she was seven and came home from school crying because a boy in her class announced that her real mother took one look at her ugly face when she was born and decided she was too disgusting to bring home? "Nonsense!" Delia consoled her. "That boy is a—well, that boy doesn't know what he's talking about. Your real mother thinks you're beautiful and always has and loves you to the moon and back!" Melody remembered that Delia had tears in her eyes, and hugged her so hard she said "ouch" and wiggled out of her mother's embrace.

They finished the ice cream and washed off their spoons, and then Lily turned to her with a strange expression on her face. "So," she started. "I need you to help me with a study my lab is working on."

"Me, the person whose lowest grade was biology," Melody said skeptically.

"That doesn't matter. Just say you'll do it."

CHAPTER FOURTEEN

The power must have gone out while they were asleep. Noah had arrived at the cabin around 10, after a snowy, white-knuckle drive up from the city, and there was still power then. But here was Paul, sitting in the dark kitchen in the morning, unsure what to do.

This was not in the plan when he pitched the idea of heading upstate to wait out those miserable days of forced good cheer between Christmas and New Year's to Candace and Noah. He had left Noah, exhausted from an unusual rush of preholiday glioblastomas, passed out under the covers, planning to make French toast and squeeze oranges for juice and present it to his boyfriend in bed.

"Nice bathrobe," Candace said, rubbing her eyes at the lack of light as she walked into the room, "what I can see of it."

"Very funny," he said. "I didn't like *Little House on the Prairie* when I was a kid, and I don't like it now."

"Well, I loved it. I made my mother buy pints of cream so I could jump up and down to make butter."

He perked up. "Did it work?"

"Of course it worked. I think the only reason my mother went along with it was that it kept me occupied for a very long time. I had a lot of energy. Unlike now," she said, yawning. "Anyway, the one thing I know is that we have to stir the coals in the fireplace so we can revive the fire. We don't want the pipes to freeze."

"Or us," Paul said, following her out of the kitchen like a duckling.

The cabin was owned by one of Paul's clients from his time at Equinox, an investor who had winter homes in Aspen and Punta Gorda, and used this one now and again, though from what they could tell, it was neither "now" nor "again." "Cabin" was one of those words rich people use to signal how rich they are, Paul explained to Candace, like when they call a yacht a boat. And he was right. The place was palatial, with a sauna and companion plunge pool and a massive stone hearth that had some connection to the Battle of Saratoga, though Paul could not remember what it was.

Candace poked the coals and tossed pieces of fatwood on the embers until they caught, sending flames shooting up the chimney. She added kindling, then some larger logs, and before long the fire had settled in and was casting an orange glow that was reflected in their eyes as they stared into it as if it was about to tell them something.

"Noah still asleep?" Candace said after a while, though the answer was so obvious Paul didn't reply. Noah—sweet, low-key Noah—looked ragged the night before and went straight to bed, with Paul trailing behind. From a far corner of the house, she could hear a rumble of voices, punctuated by an occasional laugh, and it seemed to come from an alien universe. Candace stayed up, fed the fire, and read a piece in a years-old New Yorker about a ballerina who had lost a leg in a terrorist attack. For the first two thousand words she identified with the woman without the leg, but when the woman started dancing again and said she was happier without her leg than she'd been when she'd had it, it seemed like the story had abruptly veered from fact to fiction. But then she thought about Banerjee, whose storybook life was headed for the big screen, and Tom—Tom!—who seemed perfectly content to have a prosthetic hand or no hand at all. "Disability is a word invented by people who are scared of the human body, their own body, especially," the dancer in the story said.

Was she, Candace, afraid of her own body? Possibly. Was she afraid of someone else laying claim to her body? Definitely.

"I've been thinking," Paul said.

"Uh-oh."

"No, seriously. There's something I was thinking I wanted to talk to you about—"

She felt her heart skip a beat. "You're getting married."

"What? No. I mean, maybe someday. But I don't think we should rule it out." He looked at her expectantly.

"We," she repeated.

"Yeah."

Candace burst out laughing. "Paul, sweetheart, are you asking me to marry you?" She looked around the room before settling her gaze on his face. "Where's the flash mob doing that cute Bruno Mars song?"

"Very funny," he said. "You know that's not what I mean. We're not getting any younger, and there's that whole in-sickness-and-in-health thing, and coming home to an empty house—"

"I like coming home to an empty house."

"Do you? Really? I know for me—"

"But I'm not you."

"And a good thing, that," he said.

"Wait a minute," Candace said, suddenly serious. "Are you breaking up with me?"

"Of course not. I'm saying this as your dearest friend. I mean, you're my dearest friend, and I only want good things for you."

"So you are breaking up with me." They had promised each other, years before, that if neither was in a serious relationship by the time they both hit fifty, they'd get married and have one of those sexless companionate unions that so many heterosexual couples seemed to settle into after decades of state-sanctioned coupledom. It had been a running joke between them that no longer seemed especially funny.

"You're not listening to me."

"I think I am. You want me out of the way so you and Noah—"

"Can go on double dates. Hi, babe," Paul said as Noah walked into the room.

Candace turned to look at Noah, who was wearing the same black watch flannel robe that Paul had on. "His-and-his robes," she said flatly, not quite to herself. What better confirmation that she was the odd one out? No wonder Paul wanted her to find a partner. It wasn't about her happiness, it was about his.

"Babe, did you remember?" Paul said to Noah.

"I was tired, but I wasn't that tired," Noah said. She marveled again at his perfect teeth and his tawny, unblemished skin, and had the sudden urge to go back to bed and wait for the storm to pass so she could leave.

"Don't go," Paul said as she stood up. It sounded like an order, and she didn't like it, but she sat down again as he rushed past her, holding up his index finger, saying, "Just wait a minute." She heard him zip up his jacket over his bathrobe and step into his boots. "It's still snowing," he called from the hallway as he opened the door.

"It's unlocked," Noah called to him. She sat there uncomfortably, shrugging when Noah tried to engage her, asking when she thought the power might be restored.

"No idea," she said as the front door opened again, and they heard Paul wiping his boots on the mat before he came back into the living room, carrying a big box.

"This is from us," he said, handing it to her. "Merry whatever. And we have one more thing for you, but it hasn't gotten here yet."

"Here?" she said, trying to hide her discomfort. "I didn't realize Rudolph would be stymied by a snowstorm."

Paul and Noah exchanged glances. "All in good time," Noah said.

The box was wrapped neatly with gold-flecked paper and tied with a green-and-gold ribbon. She held it tentatively, still out of sorts but feeling her edges soften despite herself.

"Go on," Paul urged, "open it."

"Who wrapped this? Not you," she said, looking at Paul, who laughed. Usually, he put presents in gift bags stuffed with tissue paper and that was that.

"I would like to claim credit, but I'm afraid it was the good people of Macy's," Noah said. His arm was holding on to Paul's shoulder as Paul perched on the arm of a midcentury calfskin sofa that was so smooth he kept sliding down. "I—we—hope you like it."

"Just rip it off," Paul said as she was carefully peeling back the tape.

"You know me," she said (did he?) and took her time, unwrapping the package, then folding the paper and putting it on the coffee table before, finally, shaking the bottom of the box loose from the top.

"Do you like it?" Paul asked anxiously. "I mean, we're loving it."

She reached in and pulled out a black watch flannel bathrobe.

"His and his . . . and hers," Noah said. "Let me help you put it on."

"It's like our team uniform," Paul said, as she cinched the belt and did a clumsy pirouette. "We need a selfie," and pulled out his phone.

So they stood in a line with their arms around each other, framed by the stone hearth, and no one looking at the photograph later would have guessed that the woman on the left was planning to crop herself out of it.

It was hard to move away from the fire, but they decided to get dressed and venture outside. Snow was still falling, but lightly, and it was sticking to the needles of the tamaracks, so the whole world was a bright gauzy white even though the sun was sequestered behind a thin curtain of clouds. After venturing around the property, following fresh deer tracks to the edge of the woods, then doubling back, Noah suggested that they cut a couple of small switches from a poplar tree so they could roast the kielbasa he'd brought over the open fire. He pulled a Swiss Army knife from his pocket. "A Boy Scout is always prepared," he said.

"You were a Boy Scout," Candace said. It was more a statement than a question.

"Honestly, no," Noah admitted, "but I did scout boys."

"Very funny." She watched him slice into a branch and took it when he handed it to her. The cut was clean. Then he did it again. "I guess you really are a surgeon," she said.

"Speaking of that," he said, tugging at another branch, which let loose a small avalanche on both their heads. "You know we talked to Tom about a hand transplant." He took off his hat and shook off the snow and turned to face her.

There were so many things wrong with that sentence, Candace didn't know where to begin. "We?" Who was that? And no, Tom did not tell her this, so why was Noah? What about doctor-patient confidentiality?

As if reading her mind, he said, "My team. We've been working on some new procedures for nerve conduction and Tom might have been an excellent candidate. I thought he had told you. He said he was going to talk it over with his daughter and his friends. Anyway," he continued, obviously embarrassed for Candace that she wasn't one of those friends, "he probably didn't mention it because he decided against it. Thought it wasn't worth it at his age, especially given the chance of rejection."

"Oh," she said. She'd only seen Tom once since their second trip to New Haven, which was a near repeat of the first one, even the way she rushed out of the car when he dropped her off, before he could jump out and open the door for her, which allowed her to duck the awkward handshake, hug, or kiss dilemma, though Winston was having none of it and licked her face when she leaned into the car to say thanks. Tom was back in the city but invited her to an opening at a gallery in Ridgefield, then begged off dinner because he was leaving for Dubai the next night.

He said he'd call when he got back to the States, and that was the last she'd heard from him. It was probably her own fault, if it was a fault at all. She didn't know how to go on a proper date. A proper date, if it went well, was supposed to lead to another, and then another, and another. But "another and another and another," with their expectations and obligations, was what she had always avoided. How strange to find herself wanting more.

"I mean, Tom seems fine with one hand," Candace said, picking up the conversation. What had the dancer in *The New Yorker* article said? "Disability is a word invented by people who are scared of the human body," Candace offered.

"Maybe," Noah said tentatively, but it was clear he didn't believe it.

"Maybe what?" Paul said, trotting up to them. He'd been scavenging for sticks on his own but had come back empty-handed. "Maybe this!" he said and gathered up snow in his gloved hands and dropped it on Candace's head.

The snowball fight was still going on when a utility truck

skidded up the driveway. "Oh, hooray," Paul said as a large man in a head-to-toe down suit jumped out.

"Just checking to see if you've got power," he said, and looked at them, three adults with wet hair and wet jackets and sheepish grins on their faces.

"I'll go," Noah said, starting to make his way back to the house ahead of them. "All good!" he called when he got near enough to see that the lights were on. Candace and Paul thanked the utility worker, then burst out laughing when he was out of sight.

"Michelin Man!" they said simultaneously, and without thinking, she slipped her hand through his arm as they made their way across the snowy field to the house. She really did love him.

"Thanks for the bathrobe. That was sweet," she said. "Truly, I don't need anything else." She knew if she used the word "want," it would hurt his feelings. He just smiled and ran a gloved finger across his closed lips.

"Be that way," she said, and laughed. She knew how hard it was for him—the guy who invariably yelled "Surprise!" before the guests jumped out of their hiding places—to keep a secret. "But I call first shower now that we have hot water."

"No problem," Paul said, and then reminded her that the house had so many bathrooms they could invite the neighbors to bathe, if there were neighbors, which there were not.

Candace stood in the shower and let the water crash down on her body. Eyes closed, she replayed the strange, out-of-context conversation when Paul brought up marriage. No, that wasn't quite right. She'd brought it up, but he'd flipped the script and made it about her. Was he preparing her for the inevitable, when his allegiance to her would diminish? How had she not known that adult relationships were no more fixed than childhood ones, which were almost always fleeting? Who was still friends with their best friend from third grade, no matter how many playground pinky swears were made promising to always be as devoted to each other? Somehow, she had tricked herself into believing that her friendship with Paul was inviolable. The whole chosen family thing. Somehow, she skipped over the part where the root of "chosen" was "choice." She opened her eyes, reached for the shower handle, and turned up the pressure, then the temperature, and let the water bore into her. It was her own fault for buying into this fantasy despite knowing better. If she was being honest, it was because he was gay and fated to be single in the eyes of the law, and as allergic to social convention as she because of it. But now that there was gay marriage, all bets were off. For all she knew, while she was railing against marriage (too confining; the patriarchy; blah blah blah), he was secretly pining for it.

Candace stepped out of the shower, shook her head from side to side like a soggy dog, then pulled a towel from the warming rack and dried herself off. She was tired. Not sleepy tired, but bone tired, a concept that made no sense until they were your bones. As soon as her hair was dry, she climbed back into bed and burrowed under the covers. One more day and it would be New Year's Eve. Two more days and it would be a whole new year. When she was a child, she ticked off each year as if it were a notch in her belt. The goal was to get older, to not be a child, to not be treated like a child. Somewhere that had changed, and she felt each new year as a subtraction—not making her younger, but taking away time itself. Of course, that was not true: Time was indifferent. It would march on whether or not she was in lockstep. She looked up at the broad beams overhead, wondering how old they had been when they were cut down and milled so the man with the money could add this house to his Instagram-worthy real estate portfolio. But that wasn't fair. People built houses.

People drove cars. People picked flowers. People ate steak.

People were complicated. How did that saying go? Candace thought back to her sophomore politics seminar and the arguments that broke out around the table: If you foreswore driving and were self-righteous about it, what about flying home to California? If you demanded fair-trade coffee in the dining halls, why were you wearing clothes made by child laborers in some third-world country? It was so easy to take a random, everyday activity and turn it into a crusade. And it was even easier to turn that around and expose the hypocrisy. The professor, an older man with a sonorous but indistinguishable pan-European accent and pictures of Sartre and Nietzsche on his office wall where his diplomas might have been ("But aren't they the same?" he was rumored to have said to the department chair), listened and clapped when the debates got heated.

"What you need to understand," he would say, "is that the only completely consistent people are dead." It was her third semester at a school where, she was convinced, everyone was smarter than she was, but this seemed, if not dumb then too glib and too easy.

"Shouldn't we, instead, try to become more consistent?" she blurted out. "Like eating lower on the food chain, or carpooling, or wearing recycled clothes?" As if her classmates were willing to wear clothes that someone else had discarded, unless they were vintage, or ironic.

"Yes, yes," the professor said impatiently. "That is admirable. But it is really for your own benefit. The world will not care." A few weeks later, the professor put a gun in his mouth and pulled the trigger but lived. She'd see him around campus sometimes, leaning on the arm of one of his caretakers, vacant and smiling, a shuffling embodiment of the nihilism he'd been trying to impart.

She awoke sometime later when the front door slammed shut and an unintelligible mélange of voices wafted upstairs. They were male voices—she was pretty sure of that—punctuated by a hearty laugh that she knew was Paul's, she'd heard it so often over the years. And then it was quiet again, and Candace rolled over and stared at the bedroom door, trying to decide if she wanted to stay wrapped in the nest she'd made or go downstairs and investigate. As if he had read her mind, there was a tentative knock on the door, and there was Paul, just his head, urging her to come downstairs. Candace yawned and stretched and before she could ask him what was going on, he closed the door and was gone.

It took a while, but she threw off the blanket, put on jeans and a bulky brown sweater, ran her fingers through her curls, and stepped into the hall, as ready as she'd ever be to confront the surprise waiting for her downstairs.

"Ahh," she shouted. "Whaaa—" She took a step back and looked at the stranger she'd just about tripped over, who looked just as surprised as she. He was not much taller than she was, balding, maybe sixty, maybe forty-five, dragging a roller bag behind him like a recalcitrant child.

"You okay?" a voice from downstairs called, and Candace was unsure which "you" he meant. It was a familiar voice, and within seconds there was Tom, bounding up the stairs, then stopping short to survey the scene.

"What are you doing here?" Candace said, turning to him.

Despite the unmistakable annoyance in her voice, Tom laughed. "And Merry Christmas to you, too." Then Paul appeared, and behind him, Noah.

"Surprise!" Paul said, though from the look on his face, it was clear that he was suddenly reconsidering the plan he'd hatched with Noah, to bring Tom into their not-so-little idyll. And who was this somewhat squat, bespectacled man glancing from one to the other, clearly confused and saying nothing?

"I see you've met," Tom said.

"Not really," Candace said.

"Well," Tom said, "let me rectify that. Candace, Wardo. Wardo, Candace. Wardo is an old friend. And Candace is a new one," he said, as if that explained anything. "We're here to crash your party."

"Here, let me show you where you're staying," Noah said, stepping between Candace and the stranger. "It's a big house, kind of confusing." He started down the corridor, with Wardo behind him, followed by Tom. When they had turned the corner and were out of sight, Paul grabbed Candace's arm and nearly pushed her back into her bedroom, shutting the door behind them.

"Do you know who that is?" he whispered excitedly, and before she could answer said, "He's that guy!" He looked at her expectantly. She looked at him blankly.

"The guy whose wife was in that accident!"

"What accident," she began, and then it dawned on her. "The one with the rock? Are you sure?"

He nodded vigorously.

"How do you know?"

"I put two and two together. Also, Tom told me."

"What's he doing here?"

Paul shrugged. "I don't really know."

Later, when they were sitting by the hearth and Paul had made a random comment about the provenance of its masonry—while admitting that he might have gotten the Battle of Saratoga story confused with some other battle in some other place during a different war, because it was something to say, and that's what he did when he was nervous—Candace turned to Wardo. "So how do you two know each other," she said.

Wardo looked at Tom, waiting for him to answer, and when he didn't, said, "Tom was at MIT with my brother."

"Oh, cool," Paul said. "Is he an engineer, too?" Paul was in his full overeager, manic "we're in the presence of a celebrity" mode, and it was making Candace uncomfortable. No one there knew Paul as well as she did, not even Noah, so she was hopeful that they would attribute his excitement to a mix of standard-issue curiosity and a desire to be inclusive—to make sure that this newcomer wasn't ignored.

Wardo swirled the old-fashioned that he hadn't actually been drinking, and before he could answer, Tom said, "No, though he was a talented computer scientist. Brilliant." He smiled at Wardo, who continued to stare into his drink.

"He was schizophrenic," Wardo said. "He didn't make it," and then looked at each of them with such intensity, Candace felt his gaze slice through her, as if he was searching for a genuine reaction.

"That must have been awful," Paul said.

"It was," Wardo said. "It was a long time ago."

"Even so," Noah began, and was about to finish his sentence, but didn't. Candace felt as if it was her turn, as if they were all waiting for her to say something anodyne, because what else was there to say—"I'm sorry"? She never understood those words. Sorry for what? Sorry that Wardo's brother had been sick. Sorry that he'd died. Yes, of course, but it was a sentiment that muddled the object: Who were you sorry for? The deceased, the living, yourself?

"How old was he?" Candace asked gently. Paul shot daggers in her direction—a warning, she supposed, that he thought she'd overstepped.

But Wardo brightened and said, "He'd just turned thirty-two."

"He got his doctorate at twenty-three," Tom interjected. "That's how we met. He was the TA in a course I was taking on quantum engineering. He was a crackerjack teacher. I mean, that stuff is so arcane, but he was able to convey it to a dumb navy guy like me. Granted, I was the most faithful attendee at his study sessions and office hours."

"When he got sick"—Wardo said, picking up where Tom left off—"I mean, he was probably sick before, but we just attributed his quirks to his brilliance. When someone is that precocious, it's easy to miss the signs, until they become billboards. But what happens, or what happened here, is that as his strange behavior became harder to avoid, the people in his life began to avoid him. But not Tom. He stuck with Alan until the end."

"Just to close the circle here," Tom said, clearly addressing the three friends, who had been watching the other two intently, "after Alan died, Wardo set up a foundation in his name to provide mental health services to people who can't afford it and asked me to be on the board. But I didn't know that, because I was sailing around the world. I didn't know anything about it till I was back on terra firma, and, of course, I said yes."

Noah, who had been sitting quietly, observing this exchange, said, "Excuse me if this is rude, but is Wardo your, uh, given name?" Candace had been wondering this, too, thinking that it would have stuck out to her during the endless rounds of news reports about the accident, and it hadn't.

Wardo smiled sadly. "It was his nickname for me. Alan's. Short for Eduardo, after some Venezuelan baseball player. My little brother was one of those kids who could reel off the stats of every player, even the obscure ones. Everyone else calls me Eddie."

"But I didn't know that," Tom continued. "I thought it was his actual name. I don't think I found out it wasn't until I got the invitation to join the board, but by then it was too late. He was Wardo to me."

There are many ways to pass on a legacy, Candace thought, but held back from saying so. Who was she to presume anything about someone else's sorrow.

"Who needs their drink freshened?" Paul said, popping up suddenly like a jack-in-the-box and causing them to turn and look at him, and just as suddenly the mood in the room shifted, and they all held out their glasses, which he topped off with the words "and one for you, and one for you," as if he were passing out snacks to toddlers. When he was done, Noah began talking about the nerve conduction study his team was working on, which made Candace uncomfortable, knowing that Tom had declined to participate. But that wasn't it—or maybe it was just part of it. No, the real reason was that Noah was bringing attention to Tom's disability. Not that Tom thought about it that way. If she was being honest, it was her discomfort, not his. Like the dancer in the *New Yorker* article said.

". . . and Tom has signed on as one of our advisers," Noah was saying. "For which we have Winston to thank." He raised his glass, and reflexively, the others raised theirs. "To Winston," he said.

"To Winston," they repeated, even Eddie.

"I miss Winston," Candace said unbidden, the words just falling out of her mouth. Paul exchanged a knowing look with Noah, but Candace herself was confused. Why did she say that? Did she really miss the dog?

"He misses you, too," Tom said, and before she could dismiss this out of hand because obviously it was a throwaway line, he went on, "Of course, he would miss anyone who asks for a doggie bag at a pizza joint and gives it to the dog."

Everyone laughed, even Candace, who colored and said, "Not all of it. We each got a piece."

"I rest my case," Tom said, and they all laughed again.

Candace woke early, her head pounding from the flight of whiskeys and bourbons Tom brought, which they drank blind, seeing if they could distinguish the pricey ones from the rotgut. Her favorite, if she could call it that, turned out to be the Yamazaki, from Japan, and because it was the most expensive, the four men praised her palate, even though she picked it because it burned in the least incendiary way going down her throat. She didn't dare turn on the bathroom light, just bathed her face in cold water, popped two Advil, and, when she felt less fuzzy, made her way down the stairs in the near-dark to the kitchen, eagerly anticipating whatever clarity would come from her first cup of coffee. She was so single-minded in her pursuit, it took a few seconds for her to register that Eddie was in the room, sitting at the kitchen table, pencil in hand, working on the *Times* crossword.

"Oh, hey," she said, suppressing a yawn. "Where did you get a newspaper? I thought we were in a news desert here? Blessedly," she added.

"Not to worry," he said, looking up at her and smiling sympathetically. "It's yesterday's news."

Of course, it was always yesterday's news, but that didn't stop her from reading the newspaper obsessively, a habit she picked up at the consulting firm. "If a tree falls in the forest of Borneo, why should we care?" a partner asked at one of the fancy restaurant meals where the summer associates were being judged through every course—did they use the correct spoon for soup, did they know the Brazilian-real-to-US-dollar conversion rate that day, would they chew the oysters? Candace did not care about the tree in Borneo, but she knew that was the wrong answer. She also knew that if she looked down and concentrated on the curl of endive left on her salad plate, the partner was likely to call on her, but that turned out not to matter because one of the Yale boys answered quickly, as if they were on a game show and he had pressed the buzzer first.

"The economy is an ecosystem, so that if that tree falls, it is going to affect biodiversity, and if biodiversity is compromised, so are food systems, and before long prices rise globally and so does inflation, and it is up to us," he said grandly, "to anticipate its effect on markets." In his zeal, he had picked up a spear of asparagus with his fingers and was waving it around the table, as if he were anointing each one of them. Candace wondered if this would get him some demerits, but the partner nodded and said, "Very good. And?"

Someone called out "taxes," and someone else "regulation," and the partner beamed. It didn't take long for Candace to realize that the correct answer always entailed their firm's twin nemeses, taxes and regulation.

"How is the puzzle going?" Candace asked after taking one long swallow of coffee, and then another, and letting out a grateful sigh.

"Oh, I'm not very good at it," Eddie said. "What do the kids say? I'm a noob. I only started doing the crossword after Delia—my wife—died. It's a way to trick my brain into thinking about something else, unless there is a clue that reminds me of her. Which happens more than you might imagine." He said this brightly, but Candace could see that it was forced. She wondered what she should say, decided she should say nothing, then decided that would make his comment more awkward.

"Thanks for making the coffee," she said, which came out all wrong, or maybe was all wrong, since it was neither here nor there and left his acknowledgment of his dead wife hanging.

He must have sensed her discomfort, because he said, "Twenty-four across, five letters, pen name."

She thought about it for a minute, then said, "Alias."

"Bingo!" he said. "You're good at this."

"Beginner's luck," she said and sat down beside him, and they pored over the clues in silence. "I'm not a puzzle person," she said apologetically.

"What kind of person are you, then?" he asked.

"Oh, oh, I know that one," she said, dodging his question. "Thirty-five down. It's C-O-S. You know. For 'cosine.' Thank you, Mrs. Shiffman. She was my high school calculus teacher."

"When my daughter was taking calculus, she asked me what the point of it was. I should have told her it was so she'd know the answer to a *New York Times* crossword puzzle clue twenty years from then." He looked happy, almost gleeful, but it didn't last. "If she ever asks me anything again."

"How old is your daughter?" Candace was pretty sure she knew the answer because it had been repeated endlessly during the wall-to-wall coverage of Delia's death, but it was something to say.

"Seventeen," Eddie said. "Eighteen in May."

"That must be hard," Candace said. "Losing her mother at that age."

"I'm not sure age has much to do with it," Eddie said sadly. "It's always going to be terrible."

Candace knew she could argue with him: when her own mother died after years of declining health, it was a relief. Instead, she changed the subject. "She must be a senior, then. I sometimes do alumnae interviews for my college, if she'd be interested. I'm happy to talk to her, extol its virtues."

Eddie shook his head. "She's not going. She's decided to become a farmer. Not that she knows anything about farming. She's from Westchester, where we harvest at Whole Foods."

"Manual labor is probably a good thing for a kid from the suburbs," Candace said. "She'll be more than ready to hang up her overalls for some ripped jeans from Madewell. Also, I think thirty-nine down is Imelda. First lady with a foot fetish. You know, from the Philippines."

"Oh, right. I should have known that. My company gets a lot of pulp wood from there." He penciled it in. "The thing is," Eddie said, "Delia, my wife, would not like it. I know she wouldn't, and Melody knows it, and she's doing it anyway."

"What's the worst thing that could happen? That she finds out she likes farming? The world needs more farmers," Candace said, trying to sound breezy. "My best guess, though, after years in HR, is that these things have a way of working themselves out." It was a lie—a gentle lie, but a lie nonetheless. A career in HR gave her no more insight into the mind and motivation of a teenage girl than he had, maybe less. "My mother didn't want me to go to Williams, but I went anyway and did OK." She didn't tell him that her mother never got over it, forever accused her of becoming hoity-toity, but that was a different story.

"She's a good kid, but I feel like we're not connecting. No, strike that. We're definitely not connecting. And now I wonder if we ever were. I mean, I thought we were. I was always the good cop, if you know what I mean. I don't know. I'm rambling. Sorry. Tell me about you. Have you always worked in HR?"

"Pretty much. I kind of fell into it. I was working at a consulting firm, and the company I had been advising for a couple of years asked me to come on board to help with HR. Did that for a while, got recruited to work at another firm, and that firm got swallowed up by DataStream, and the rest is history. I didn't plan it. It just sort of happened."

"And you're good at it," Eddie said. It was a statement, not a question.

"Apparently," she said.

The front door opened and closed, and in seconds Tom was standing in the doorway, ruddy-faced and sweating. "I'm so glad

I brought my cross-country skis," he announced. "I just did a lap of this property and saw lots of deer and rabbit tracks. The trails are—"

"Oh, no!" Candace interrupted. For some reason, just as Tom began to speak, she'd glanced over at the business section, at the far end of the table. The story was a small one, not more than a few hundred words, but they were above the fold. "Precocious tech entrepreneur to sell company," and even before she read the story, she knew that the precocious entrepreneur was Vivek Banerjee and the company was hers.

CHAPTER FIFTEEN

"Marcia brings dinner over, like, once a week," Melody was telling Lily, whose parents were still out of town. "If she's making a play for my dad, she's definitely playing a long game. When she's there, Dad and I have to pretend everything is fine." The TV was on with the sound off. It was New Year's Eve and they were half watching the crowd gathering in Times Square.

"If they eventually get together, Danny Yandel will be your brother."

"Stepbrother. So will Seth, or whatever his name is now, and I'll be step-aunt to his ever-expanding family. Apparently, his wife just had number six."

"Can you imagine how floppy her vagina is?" Lily said.

Melody reached over and playfully punched her friend's arm. "Truly, Lily, I would rather not. Marcia invited Dad to spend New Year's with her, but he already had plans to go upstate with his friend Tom. Tom only has one arm. Actually, hand."

"And that is relevant how?" Lily said.

"It's just a data point. He went to MIT with my uncle Alan. The one who convinced Eddie never to have bio children."

"Speaking of which," Lily said breezily as she walked out of the room with Melody trailing behind.

"Speaking of which, what?" Melody said to Lily's back.

"You'll see."

Lily slid open the coat closet door and pulled her school backpack off the hook where she'd hung it the week before, when she declared the house to be a "no-school zone." She dug around the bottom and retrieved a padded envelope with no markings on it. "I almost forgot," Lily said, and took a small box out of the envelope and handed it to Melody. "My study. I know I said no school, but this is more than school. It's an opportunity to advance science, and all you have to do is spit into the six test tubes in the box. Remember I told you about Dr. Phil? In my lab? Well, technically it's not my lab, but anyway, Phil is developing this new autosomal genetics protocol."

"Dr. Phil who got you to do shots?" She raised her eyebrows. "Do I detect a budding romance?"

"Oh God, no. He's married. What you detect is the junior member of the lab following orders."

"Go on," Melody said. She was suspicious. Anything to do with genetics or, more specifically, her genes made her uncomfortable. She was happy to believe that she just appeared in the world without biological parents. She knew it wasn't true, but she wanted it to be true, and why complicate her life?

"Phil says that with just a small amount of saliva, a milliliter, he will be able to construct an entire family tree and medical predispositions. It's breakthrough stuff."

Melody handed the test tube back to her friend. "First of all, isn't that what Ancestry and 23andMe do already? And second, as you of all people know, I have no interest in knowing that I come from a long line of axe murderers with, I don't know, macular degeneration."

"Macular degeneration? Where did you get that from?"

"I don't know, Lil. I probably saw an ad for some drug on TV. Or in *People*. You know how they have all those drug ads next to stories about Jen and Brad and Angelina."

Lily laughed. "So your ancestors murdered their victims before they lost their sight?"

"Very funny. You know what I mean. I am happy not knowing. Eddie and Delia are my parents. They've been my parents for as long as I can remember, and that's enough for me. And to tell you the truth, it feels kind of creepy, like disrespectful to Delia, to go searching for my birth mother right now. Like I'd be trying to erase her from the picture."

They were both quiet and then Lily said, "You wouldn't be erasing her. That's not what this is about."

"But that's how it feels to me. You want to find the people who left you on that bridge. I mean, you study genetics because it's personal to you. There's probably a deep psychological reason why I could barely wrap my head around meiosis in bio class. I just don't want to know what it is."

Lily looked thoughtful. "I know we're different that way. I get it. But this is not just for me, it's for science. The data is all anonymized, unless the results show a predisposition for a disease that would benefit from an intervention. It's a numbers game. We have to get a statistically significant sample size to test the efficacy of Phil's methodology."

"You're sure it's anonymous?"

"It's science, so yes. We couldn't get the IRB otherwise."

"English, please."

"Institutional review board. The people at the university who have to approve experiments that involve humans."

Melody twirled a clump of hair around her index finger and tugged on it, saying nothing. She let go, rubbed her chin, closed her eyes, and scrunched up her face, thinking. This was something she'd never do on her own, at least so far, but it wasn't like she was doing it for herself. "I will do this on one condition," Melody said finally, opening her eyes and looking at her friend.

"Anything."

She pulled out the first stopper. "That you promise to take me as your date to Oslo, for the Nobel ceremony."

"Stockholm," Lily said.

"What?"

"The Peace Prize is in Oslo. Everything else is in Stockholm."

"Cool. Stockholm."

"Done," Lily said.

"Done," Melody said when she finished spitting into each test tube. "Can we please go back to watching the ball drop?"

Ten minutes later, they were settled on the living room couch, a bowl of popcorn between them. On the screen, people were standing shoulder to shoulder, blowing on horns and not bothering to hide their cans of beer in paper bags. For a second, the camera zoomed in on what looked like a cigar but was actually an overstuffed blunt being passed from stranger to stranger, then it cut away when the camera operator realized what it was.

"Why do people do that?" Lily asked.

"Do what? Smoke weed?"

"No. Why do they spend hours in the cold in a massive crowd of people, waiting for the ball to drop. I mean, it's not like it's not inevitable. Everyone knows how it's going to go."

"Jeez, Lil. Have you ever watched a movie or read Jane Austen? I finally finished *Middlemarch*, by the way. The inevitable is the point."

"I guess," Lily said, but Melody wasn't listening. Not to her friend. Not to the TV. Delia's voice had come into her head unbidden, as it did sometimes. Delia, explaining that romantic comedies were not fantasies, they were expressions of hope. "Things do sometimes work out the way we hope they will," she said, squeezing Melody's shoulder. The subtext, of course, was that a lot of the time they don't.

Melody knew that now better than she should. A dead mother could still be teaching her things, even if they were things she'd rather not know. A dead mother could still be talking to her, even though she was the only one who could hear her.

Melody and twenty assorted high school juniors were sitting in the study hall as the proctor droned on about the three-hour test that, for many of them, would determine their fate: Dartmouth or SUNY Albany, Bowdoin or Bucknell, scholarship or debt. Melody, in contrast, was free of expectation. She was taking this test because she could not rid herself of her mother's voice telling her to keep her options open. This was the makeup for the test she had been scheduled to take months earlier, in the before times, when she promised Delia that if she didn't do well (which, they both knew, meant well enough to put her in contention for one of her "reach" schools) studying on her own, she'd take a review course. In the after times, that test had come and gone because what was the point? This morning, sitting here with four sharp number-two pencils lined up at the top of the desk and a test booklet full of tricky questions, was her way of keeping at least part of the promise to her mom. The proctor was pointing to the clock on the wall, and Melody could almost hear the silent countdown of everyone around her, and when there was a perfect ninety-degree angle—nine o'clock—the proctor raised his arm and lowered it in what looked like a karate chop, said "Go!," and to a person, they reached for their pencils and got to work.

Unencumbered by expectations, Melody breezed through, carried along by the realization that she knew more than she'd given herself credit for. Either that or she was deluded, and the random pattern of carefully filled bubbles on her answer sheet was not the expression of knowledge—if knowing was the same as knowledge—just a reflection of how well she had absorbed the lessons in the thick review book Delia had given her. She glanced over at the boy next to her, who was bent over his desk with what looked to Melody like fierce determination. For a second, maybe two, Melody wished she had the same degree of focus and resolve, and in those few seconds noticed that the student diagonally in front of her had a cheat sheet taped to her wrist that was hidden most of the time by her sweater. Melody considered alerting the proctor, but then thought better of it. Cheating was not fair, but if there was one thing she'd learned in the past few months, nothing was.

The results arrived two weeks later, and they embarrassed her. Her scores were so high, they put her in the top 1 percent of everyone who had taken the test that day. "Across the whole country," Perry, the guidance counselor, said when he pulled her out of world history to talk to her about it. "You will certainly have your choice of top institutions now," he said with such glee, she felt like she should be congratulating him. Perry—he insisted that the students call him by his first name because, he told parents at the welcome assembly every year, it broke down the barrier between students and the administration and instead built a foundation of trust, and didn't seem to know that the students called him "Pervy" behind his back because of his habit of oversharing information about his divorce and postdivorce, Tinder-y dating life—was nearly vibrating. It took her a few minutes to understand the real reason for his joy: she now held the prospect of boosting the school's reputation, and his.

Where students landed after high school mattered very much to the administration. It mattered to the administration because it mattered to the parents, and it mattered to the parents long after their children had graduated because it mattered to their property values. A lot was riding on her and her impressive test scores—the whole infrastructure of their town, it felt like.

"Applications were due weeks ago," she reminded him. Why was she telling him? Wasn't that his job?

Perry winked. "I have my ways," he said. "I know a guy. Actually a gal. Actually a lot of gals. College admissions tends to attract recent female graduates." He looked at her knowingly. The word "salacious" came to mind. It had been on the SAT, in a reading comprehension passage about the discovery of King Tut's tomb in 1922, but it was a red herring. The right answer was "polytheism."

"Look," he said, adopting a more serious tone. "I've been at this a long time, and a lot of these schools make exceptions. Do you think if Emma Watson missed the deadline, Brown was going to turn her down? I don't think so."

Melody didn't think it made sense to remind him that she, unlike Emma Watson, wasn't the most well-known film star of her generation who was also a model, worth a bazillion dollars, and a Gryffindor. "I'm going to work on an organic farm. It's called WWOOFing," Melody said, cutting him off before he could go any further. She imagined that this would cause Perry to back off, but if anything, his excitement grew, and he seemed to be on the verge of clapping with delight.

"A gap year!" he exclaimed. "That's just wonderful. Colleges love older students. It's like it adds fifty points to your score." He raised his arms as if she'd just made a goal. "Not that you need it, I may add. Now, dear," he said, dropping his voice to a conspiratorial near-whisper—Melody made a mental note to tell Karolina that Pervy called her "dear," which was gross—"the best course of action is to apply now and then defer so you can go do the barking thing—"

"WWOOFing," Melody corrected him. "But if I apply now and then defer, how do I get those fifty extra points for taking a gap year?"

Perry frowned. It was clear he hadn't thought of this. "Well, it's still a good idea," he said without missing a beat. "And if you don't get into Cornell or Columbia or wherever you're ultimately planning on going this time around, you can reapply next year, which is when you'll need those extra fifty points." He folded his arms across his chest and looked pleased with himself. "We don't have much time left," he said, rifling through a folder on his desk. "I see that you haven't turned in your application essay yet." He shuffled other papers on his desk. It was obvious to Melody that he was thinking he had misplaced it.

"I haven't written one," Melody said. "Because I'm not going." She said this, she thought, definitively, but the guidance counselor didn't seem to hear it that way.

"Melody," he said slowly, adopting a compassionate tone, "I understand the desire to take time away from academics. I really do. I mean, it's completely understandable, given"—he paused—"given all that you've been dealing with. But these scores and, well, your personal story, which of course is quite, um"—he paused again, clearly searching for the right word and finally landing on "compelling"—"should compensate for any deficiencies in your record, not that there are many. Which makes you a top prospect." She imagined that the deficiencies he was referring to were the suboptimal grade she got in tenth-grade biology, or the fact that she hadn't traveled to a third-world backwater to dig latrines like so many of her classmates.

The bell rang, and Melody stood up to leave. "I'm glad my story is compelling," she said, and walked out before he could respond.

For a minute, standing in the corridor, buffeted by the crush of students rushing to class, Melody felt triumphant. She had made it clear that she would not be swayed from her decision. She had won. But by the time she got to the door of the physics lab, where she knew Karolina would be waiting to hear what happened in Perry's office, she was hit with a wave of sadness that caught her by surprise. So, her "story," which was a pathetic synonym for her life, was "compelling." What did that even mean? That Delia's death was a net gain? Or was he referring to Melody's trajectory, from foster kid to motherless child to world-class test taker? Pretty damn compelling. Hallmark-channel compelling. "He wants me to exploit her death," was all she said to her friend as they put on their lab coats. "It was gross."

All around her, Melody's classmates were getting ready for the next stage of their lives, waiting on college acceptances, showing up for classes but only half attending, like people at a party looking over the shoulder of the person they're talking with in case someone more interesting or well known was there. Everyone knew that once you knew where you'd be spending the next year or four, you were done with high school. What leverage did your teachers have over you anymore? Melody had never been an indifferent student, though now that she was not swept along in the school-to-college pipeline, she had begun to wonder what she would have been like if she hadn't been adopted by the Marcuses and injected into a community where overachieving parents were driven by the fear that their children would not "do as well" as they had. Delia had not been immune; she just assumed that Melody was bound for good and great things. In the contest between nature and nurture, Delia seemed to believe that nurture was the stronger force. No child of hers was ever going to be average if she had anything to do with it, and she had everything to do with it.

CHAPTER SIXTEEN

Something must have happened to Eddie over New Year's. Melody had become a barometer of her father's emotional state, and she could sense that something had changed. He was a little lighter, less distant. Some woman he met at a party, who runs a big company, told him that if she saw WWOOFing on a résumé, she would automatically add five points to their score, and now he wants to know how the whole thing works, she wrote to Connor in an email. Truth be told, that wasn't exactly what Eddie had said, but it did seem like he was less opposed, and she was hoping to enlist Connor to convince her father that she wasn't throwing her life away.

What's the scale? What are the metrics?, Connor wanted to know, and she couldn't tell him since she'd made it up.

Not important, she wrote. I think he wants to talk to you. This was only prospectively true: she figured that Eddie *would* want to talk to Connor. And if she was right about being Connor's latest do-gooder project, he would want to talk to Eddie, too.

Connor showed up a few days later, on a Thursday afternoon, when Melody was still at school and Eddie was in Jersey at the factory. Maria welcomed him and fed him and checked him out in case anyone wanted her opinion, which she was going to share whether Melody or Eddie asked for it. By the time Melody got home, Connor and Maria were chatting away in Spanish, and Connor was following the housekeeper from room to room, hauling her mop and bucket and emptying the soapy water when it got too dirty. Melody heard them as soon as she stepped into the house, bantering and laughing, and was struck by the sound, which was so unlike the dull hush that had settled there.

"Oh, hey!" Connor said as he came bounding down the stairs with a bag of trash. "I almost didn't see you there. Maria—she's great. She's been helping me." Leave it to Connor to turn helping their housekeeper into her helping him. "Algo por algo," he said, noticing her confusion. "I've got a Spanish test coming up." To Maria, he shouted that Melody was "en la casa," and within minutes the three of them were in the kitchen, where it became clear that Maria either did not know or did not remember Connor's name or had decided to forgo it and call him "chico dulce," which even Melody knew meant "sweet boy." Clearly, Maria approved.

Maria pulled a tin of Danish butter cookies from the cupboard, and without asking began to heat up milk for hot cocoa. Connor jumped up to help, nearly knocking over his chair, but Maria gestured for him to sit.

"Maria's been telling me about her kids," Connor said. "They sound amazing. Tan logrado," he said in Maria's direction.

"Y lograda," Maria added, beaming.

"I said that her son was so accomplished, and she corrected me and added the feminine because of her daughter," he explained to Melody. "It's a very gendered language. I'm having a little trouble with that."

Maria delivered two mugs of steaming cocoa, then stood nearby, arms folded over her chest, watching them.

"He says you will become farmers," Maria said after a while, aiming her words at Melody. Her words were neutral, but the look on her face was not. "My people were trabajadores migrantes," she said.

"Migrant workers," Connor translated, though Melody had figured that out herself.

"All we wanted to do," Maria continued, "was to leave that life behind. I do not understand why you rich kids want to get your hands so dirty when you have all of the opportunities."

It wasn't exactly the speech Delia would have given, but it was close enough, and Connor looked stricken. "I can see how it may look like we are playing at being poor, but that's not what this is about," he said. "I mean, we in the first world don't understand where our food comes from or what it takes to grow it or harvest it. We just go to the supermarket and toss things into our cart without understanding what it took for it to get there. The human cost. The environmental cost. Maybe we'd be less wasteful, you know, if we did."

Maria, however, was not buying it. "Dios mío!" she said and shook her head sadly. "You should be happy not to know such things." She held up a fat red tomato. "You should be happy not to know."

What she didn't say, because it should have been obvious, was that their sojourn on an organic farm was not likely to teach them this, either. It would teach them some things, but not this.

Undeterred, Connor pressed on. "Espero no tener las manos blandas," he said, and held up his hands. Melody, who was now lost, looked at Maria, whose hands were on her hips, and watched her stern expression melt away.

"Come work with me if you don't want soft hands," she said to Connor in English, who was oblivious to the fact that she was making fun of him, and it occurred to Melody, who did know, that when she was calling Connor "chico dulce," she might as well have been calling him a child.

Maria was not wrong. Connor's innocent good nature was both endearing and confusing. What had Danny called him? A "player." As if Connor's entire persona was an act.

"It's unnatural," Danny said. "You'll see." But so far, she hadn't.

"Do you want to watch a movie?" Melody said after Maria had gone home and she and Connor were alone and she realized that she had no idea how to entertain a boy—a college boy—and, as she was suddenly aware, a very cute college boy, with a spray of freckles across the top of his nose and hair that he kept pushing away from his eyes, which were big and credulous and bright behind his glasses. Lily and Karolina had accused her of liking him "that way," and she'd laughed them off. Now she wondered if they had known something that she hadn't.

"Actually, I have to study," Connor said. He was digging through his knapsack when he said this, so she could not see his expression, and she wondered if he didn't want to look at her because he felt that way, too. No, that was crazy.

"Me, too," she said, just in case. And that's how Eddie found them when he got home. The two of them sitting at opposite ends of the dining room table, staring at their laptops.

"You must be the young man who convinced my daughter to forgo higher education in favor of weeding someone's garden. For free," Eddie said, holding out his hand.

"Dad!" Melody said, embarrassed, but also curious how Connor would react.

"I'm Connor," he said, jumping up and taking Eddie's hand.

"You met Connor at Thanksgiving. At the Yandels'. Connor is a friend of Danny's," Melody said, though calling them friends was probably pushing it. "They're in a band together."

"Right, right, of course," Eddie said, though Melody could not tell if he meant it. Did he even remember Thanksgiving? "Nice to see you again," he said. So far, so good.

"You know my daughter is still in high school," Eddie said to Connor, as they were eating Chinese takeout.

"I do know that. Of course," Connor said, dumping a pile of fried rice on his plate.

"And you know that she knows nothing about farms or farming?"

"Well, I mean, that's why people do this. To learn," he said between bites.

"So you're saying this is farm school," Eddie pressed.

"Yes, exactly!" Connor said, beaming. "That's such a good way of saying it!"

"And then what?" Eddie said.

"And then what, what?"

"Then what does Melody do?"

"I mean, she doesn't have to do it for just a year," Connor said. "The longer she does it, the more she learns."

"Uh, hello—I'm right here," Melody said to them both. They ignored her.

"So you're saying she could—"

"Dad, stop!" Melody said. "Connor has no idea what I'm going to do with my life."

"It's okay," Connor said. "I get it. You just want to make sure she's not driving over a cliff."

For a second that felt like a minute, they were all quiet. Delia hadn't driven over a cliff. A cliff had driven over her. "Oh, sorry," Connor said, coloring. "My bad. I didn't mean to . . ."

Melody snuck a look at her father, wondering how badly he was reacting, and was surprised to see that he wasn't. Was he smiling? Eddie? Weird.

"No worries," Eddie said. "I've heard worse. I cannot tell you how many people have shared stories of almost getting killed by boulders and downed trees and power lines. The first few times I was offended, but now I find it almost amusing. Apparently there are more near misses than I ever imagined."

"Oh, wow," Connor said.

"I know, right? Who knew?" Eddie picked up a shrimp with his chopsticks and delivered it to his mouth. Melody could not stop staring at her father. Was morose, incensed, withholding Eddie really gone, or was this just a reprieve?

For the rest of the meal Eddie fired off questions at Connor, who answered them until Melody reminded her father that this was not *Law & Order*, they were not in court, and he was not a prosecutor.

"I don't mind," Connor said to Melody. "He's being a good dad."

"Thank you," Eddie said, looking at his daughter.

"Fine," she said, and sat back in her chair and watched the two of them settle into a more amiable conversation once Eddie changed tacks and asked Connor about his time at Wesleyan, which she knew was for her benefit, so she would see that playing Ultimate Frisbee and learning African dance was more fun than digging in the dirt. But Connor, sweet and oblivious, didn't get that, and without meaning to subvert her father, declared that his favorite activity of all was working in the college garden. So the conversation came full circle, and Eddie gave up, but in a good way, carried along by Connor's enthusiasm.

"You are a first-rate ambassador for American agriculture!" Eddie said when he got up from the table, and Connor said thank you, because it never would have occurred to him that Eddie was being even a little bit ironic.

"Whelp," Connor said as Melody was packing up the leftovers for him to take back to school, "it looks like my work here is done." He flashed her a goofy smile, and she found herself unexpectedly drawn to him, which caught her off guard. It was like a fever that comes on suddenly. One minute she was fine, the next she was burning up. Her body was thrumming and her mind was struggling to keep up. It was confusing. But thrilling, in its way.

"Let me walk you out," Melody said, wondering if he could feel it, too. "Don't let Rufus get the goods," she said, nodding at the plastic bag with the takeout containers.

Outside, the night sky was clear, and before he got into the car, Connor pointed out Venus and Betelgeuse and a satellite moving in a straight line, as if the world really was flat. He told her how the Hubble Space Telescope orbited the earth fifteen times a day, and in his astronomy class they got to see into a black hole it had discovered, and possibly the origin of the universe. She tried to think of questions to ask him so he'd stand there with her a little longer, but when he saw her shivering, he urged her to go inside.

"Thanks for coming. It was good of you," Melody said when she could not stall him any longer.

"Hey, that's what friends are for," he said, grabbing her shoulders for a hug, and as he did, she reached up to kiss him.

"Oh," he said, pulling away. "Not what I was expecting."

She was embarrassed. Mortified. "Sorry," she said as he ducked into the car, a silver Subaru Outback with a Rye Beach sticker on the side window. "Hey, is this—"

"Danny's car," he said, finishing her sentence. "He let me borrow it to come here."

Melody watched the car recede down Cornell Drive. Maybe she was wrong. Maybe Connor and Danny really had become friends. Clearly, she knew nothing. Clearly, she was an idiot.

"He seems like a very nice young man," Eddie said when she went back inside. He was in the kitchen pouring himself a drink, waiting for her.

"Yeah," Melody said, and turned to go upstairs to her room.

What did it matter what kind of young man Connor was? She hoped she would never see him again. It would be too embarrassing.

"Uh, before you go, there's something I want to talk to you about." He took a long drink from his glass, put it down on the counter, changed his mind, and swallowed the rest.

"Now?" Melody said. "I'm really tired." She feigned a yawn.

"It will only take a minute," he said, fingering the empty glass. So," he said, and stopped. "So," he said again, "I'm thinking of putting the house on the market." He let this sink in for a few seconds. "Marcia says—"

"Marcia? What does Marcia have to do with this?" Melody hoped he could hear the disdain in her voice. Marcia had made her move, and Eddie had fallen for it.

"She says that it's a seller's market and the house should go almost as soon as we list it."

"No," she said, fighting back tears. "You can't." Until this very moment, she didn't have a feeling about the house, one way or the other. It was just where they lived.

"Well, honey," he said gently, "it just doesn't make sense to hold on to it. I mean, it was your mother's idea to live here because of the schools, and she wanted you to have a yard to run around in, but you're graduating and leaving and then it will just be me in this big old place, surrounded by nothing but memories. It just doesn't make sense."

She knew he was right, but it still felt wrong. "What about me?" The tears spilled over and ran down her cheeks and she didn't care. She wanted him to feel as bad as she did. "Where am I supposed to go?"

"Sweetheart," Eddie cooed. "Honey." Eddie leaned forward and put a hand on her elbow. "Marcia says that once we sell this, we'll have our pick of a place in the city."

She pulled away from his hand. "You and Marcia Yandel?"

Eddie pulled back himself. "What? No. We. You and me. This is our house, and that will be our apartment."

"If it's our house, then how come only you get to decide?"

He looked perplexed. If Delia were alive, this would be the moment when she intervened and reminded Melody how much she loved the city, but Delia wasn't there, and this new place would be Eddie's apartment, not the Marcus family home, if there even was a Marcus family.

"I'm thinking Chelsea. Not too far from Chelsea Piers, remember, where we took you and Lily skating once."

"And that guy ran into us and knocked Lily to the ground and we had to call her parents and ask them if they wanted us to bring her to the ER? Worst birthday ever."

"Well," he said weakly, "there's also swimming."

Her phone was vibrating before she reached her bedroom. It would be Connor, saying something that was bound to make her feel worse. The best thing about Eddie laying the big news about the house on her was that for ten minutes she didn't have to remember the failed kiss, didn't have to feel humiliated. She lay face down on her bed and let the tears come. No house, and now this stop-the-world-I-want-to-get-off farm plan of hers no longer seemed like a plan at all. Really, what had she been thinking? Eddie was right: she knew nothing about farming. She'd just been tagging along on Connor's fantasy, pretending it was hers, too, while the whole time, like Lily said, it might have been a fuck-you to Delia, who had set her off on one path—live in a neighborhood of Ivy League street names, internalize the quest to go to one of those colleges, and live happily ever after—and then disappeared.

Eddie was knocking on the door. "Melly," he said cracking open the door and holding something out. "Danny Yandel is on the landline. He said he'd been trying your cell but you weren't picking up."

"Can you tell him I'll call him later?"

Danny must have heard her. "He says it is very important," Eddie said, stepping into the room holding out the phone in front of him like a shield and noticing her puffy face and red-rimmed eyes. He dropped the phone at the end of her bed, waited a minute, and then walked out. It was official: he was now the bad cop, the one who was uprooting her from the only home she knew.

"What do you want?" Melody said when she finally picked up the handset, hoping to hear a dial tone but instead hearing Danny's fingers drumming on his desk and the Ramones playing in the background.

"Nothing," Danny said. "Nada. Look," he said, "Connor asked me to call."

"Are you guys besties now?" she said.

"Very funny. He feels bad," Danny said. Melody said nothing. She knew he wanted her to respond, but she wouldn't give him the satisfaction.

"Here's the thing," Danny continued. "He feels like he led you on."

"He didn't lead me on," she said.

"He thinks maybe he did," Danny said.

"Well, this is fantastic," Melody said. "My old babysitter is telling me that his new BFF led me on," she said bitterly. "I don't know why I am surprised. I mean, you told me he was a player the very first time I met him."

"I guess I did," Danny conceded. "But I don't think I meant it like this."

"And how did you mean it?"

"I don't know. Like he's overly friendly with everyone, but it's not like he can be friends with everyone."

"So you're saying that Connor doesn't want to be my friend."

"No," Danny said. "I'm saying that he's so friendly, especially at first, that people think he's super into them. I mean, he may like them, but—oh, fuck it. I don't know what I'm saying."

"You're saying that I read too much into Connor's attention and then I kind of piggybacked onto his WWOOFing plan, and he was too nice or something to tell me to come up with my own plan—even though he was the one pitching it to me."

"The thing is," Danny said, "I mean, he does like you."

"But?"

"And he really wants you to do the WWOOFing thing."

"But?"

"You're in high school."

"For like another two minutes. And anyway, so what? It's not like we're those people in that novel."

"What people in what novel?"

"You know. The one with the old guy and the young girl. They took it off the senior English reading list because somebody decided the old guy was a pedophile. Oh, forget it. It's not like Connor is so much older than me."

"I," Danny said.

"What?"

"You said 'me.' But it's 'I.'"

"Jeez, Danny. What are you, the grammar police?"

"Here's the thing," Danny said. "Maybe if Connor was a freshman and you were the girlfriend he left behind, but college guys who go out with high school girls are . . ." He didn't finish the sentence.

"What are we?"

"No, not you. Them. People think they're losers."

"People?"

"Other guys. In college."

"That is stupid and pathetic."

"Don't shoot the messenger," Danny said. "Anyway, so what? So you tried to kiss the guy. It's no big deal."

This conversation was not making her feel any better. She hated that Danny was now in the middle of this—"this" being her total humiliation—which reminded her that if Eddie and Marcia got together, his big brotherliness would become official.

Not only that, Danny Yandel would be correcting her grammar in perpetuity.

"Me is hanging up now," she said, and pressed "off." Melody rolled over and stared at the glow-in-the-dark stars arrayed on the ceiling that the next family would probably remove when they took up residence on Cornell Drive, where they would have moved because of the school system and the promise it held, which she knew now to be a joke, because promises were just wishes, and wishes were words broadcast into thin air. This was all Delia's fault. Remove Delia from the Jenga stack of their family, and everything fell to pieces.

CHAPTER SEVENTEEN

The only good thing about DataStream's sale was that Angela was about to come into a lot of money.

"A boatload," she told Candace. "I mean I can buy a boat, too, just like Vivek. Not that I would, of course. But the boys can go to whatever college they get into, assuming they don't kill one another first, and we can pay off Nick's medical debt, and Abe Lincoln can finally go to the canine dentist to get her teeth cleaned so her breath won't be so god-awful, and I won't have to work for a while, or maybe ever again, though work has always been my happy place. I don't know, and I don't have to know, because in a very short time—assuming the sale goes through, and I can't see why it won't—I am going to be rich. Very."

They were talking on the phone, but Candace could picture her friend dancing around her house, picking up stray socks and feeding day-old pizza crusts to the dog as she delivered this monologue, and Candace was happy for her. If anyone deserved to win the equity sale lottery, it was Angela. As for herself, she knew what was coming next: a few weeks or months getting the new crew up to speed, then the axe. She wondered if she'd have to fire herself—call security to take her DataStream badge and escort her out of the building—or if it would be her replacement, if there was even going to be a vice president of human resources. From what she could get out of RNS—who was talking about starting an esports training league with some of the large pile of money he, too, was going to get—the new bosses thought HR was an artifact of an earlier age and were keen to outsource their "people division" to an algorithm because it was so much less messy.

"Data is neutral," Nguyen Smythe told her, but they both knew that was not true.

"Data appears to be neutral," Candace corrected him, and he even smiled a little bit.

"Looks like I'm going to be replaced by a computer program," Candace told Paul the next Sunday, when he arrived with bagels and a passel of cream cheese because he thought it might cheer her up.

"When has cream cheese ever cheered anyone up?" Candace teased him, but she was touched by the gesture.

"In my line of work, we get replaced by ripped pretty young things all the time. I mean, have you ever seen a gray-haired, fifty-year-old personal trainer? Or one that hasn't had calf lifts and Botox and monthly dermabrasions?" He smeared a dollop of blueberry cream cheese on half a bagel and took a big bite. "There," he said with his mouth full. "I am planting the seeds of my own destruction."

"Wait—you can have dermabrasion every month? Wouldn't that sand off your face or something?"

"I knew this guy who went to this clinic down in Mexico every two months for 'work,' and then he died."

"From getting his face sanded?"

Paul took another bite, then shrugged. "Don't know. He was also taking lots of drugs and supplements. He looked good, though. Not a day over forty-five. By the way, speaking of travel, Noah got invited on some junket to Iceland and I'm going to go with him."

"Junket?"

"Aka medical conference. Apparently when the docs are having their meetings, the spouses go to the Blue Lagoon for spa day."

"Sounds nice."

"You should meet me there. We could have a couple's mud bath."

"That's sweet, but I have to stick around here to get fired."

No one was getting fired for the time being. Everything, especially work itself, was on hold until the sale went through. Every time Candace walked by the copier room, someone else was printing out their résumé, and her new job seemed to be looking them over and suggesting changes and tweaks that might make them more attractive to a new employer. Not that she really knew what other employers were looking for these days. Younger people, for sure, but there were only a few ways to tweak a résumé to lop years off someone's life without being obvious. Experience counted, but only to a point. After that, someone was overqualified, a euphemism for "too old" or "too expensive" or "just go away." She imagined—no, knew for certain—that would be her fate, too, but she didn't have time to think much about it now that everyone around her was freaking out about their next move.

"There's something almost liberating about knowing I'm about to be put out to pasture," Candace told Tom when they were dining in the city—his treat, he said, because of her impending status as a victim of capitalism or, as he teased her, a VOC.

"Also known as 'very old Candace,'" she said, but didn't protest when he told her he was paying. "Next time I'll pick a more expensive place," she said. "Like Per Se."

"Try me," he countered. This was their sixth date, if falling into the pond and showing up upstate at the cabin both counted. And against her better judgment, she continued to like him. He was smart and independent and had kind eyes. All his clothes seemed to have come out of the Patagonia catalog, with a hint of J. Press, and he wore them well. Paul called him a "keeper," and Candace wondered aloud what that made her, a woman clearly past her sell-by date.

"Way to be sexist, ageist, and self defeating all at once," Paul said. "You are a gem. I mean, come on, isn't it obvious that the gods want you and Tom to be together? Look at me and Noah. If the line at Jamba Juice that day had been as long as it usually was, I wouldn't have seen him doing those pathetic little crunches that would probably give him neck pain for the rest of his life. That line was short for a reason."

Tom cleared his throat. "Um, earth to Candace, come in please."

"What? Oh, sorry. I was just thinking—"

"About?"

"Paul keeps telling me that everything happens for a reason, and that the universe—whatever that is—is pulling the strings and that fate is real. So does my friend Angela, now that I think of it."

"What do you think?"

"I think that it only looks that way if you want to see it that way. I'm too rational, I think, to believe in fate."

"Maybe fate is what we make of circumstance." He held up his left arm. "I can't imagine why the universe wanted me to lose my hand, but I suspect that losing my hand made me a more empathetic person, which made me a better father, yada yada yada."

They chatted aimlessly for a while, he telling her what it was like to live underwater in a metal tube for ninety days at a time, only knowing it was morning because there were pancakes in the mess or evening because there was spaghetti, and she telling him how Paul's mother made up the story that he was a Jewish son of Argentina's Dirty War to appease his bigoted father. They finished a bottle of pinot noir and moved on to a shared crème brûlée that was torched at their table by a server named Anson, who invited them to his open mic set at a Chelsea comedy club later that night as he lit the propane and aimed its flame at their dessert. They ate it slowly, breaking through the candied crust, which Tom said reminded him of the ice that day at Dedam Pond, "but sweeter, of course," he said, smiling at her. When they finally put down their spoons, Candace checked her watch and apologized and said she should be catching the 10:08 back to Connecticut. It was an opening for Tom to ask her if she wanted to stay over, but he didn't, just thanked Anson, who was hovering nearby, and said he'd think about going to his show.

"So there's something I want to ask you," Tom said, when they were waiting for Anson to return Tom's credit card. Candace felt her heart skip a beat. This was it, she told herself. This is where he asked her to stay over, or for them to become a couple, or both, and this was where she would break with tradition and say yes.

"Of course," she said, hoping that her nervousness was not apparent.

"I have to go back to Abu Dhabi for about a month, maybe longer, for this project I've been working on, and I'm wondering if, while I'm gone, you will meet up with my friend Wardo."

"Wardo?"

"My friend from New Year's."

"Yes, I know. Eddie Marcus. Whose wife died."

"Exactly. He told me he'd like to see you."

"He's a grown-up—he could ask me himself," she said. Did she sound annoyed? She wanted him to hear her annoyance.

"I'm sure he would. I'm just expediting," Tom said as he fiddled with the bill, calculating the tip.

Candace did little to hide her disappointment. "Tell him to be in touch," she said in her best dispassionate corporate HR voice.

In the cab to the train station, Candace tried to put the puzzle together: If Paul was right about the universe, and Tom fell into the pond so Candace could meet him, and Eddie's wife died so he could meet her because Tom fell into the pond, how did that work? It was crazy and it made no sense.

She leaned forward and tapped on the plastic shield that separated the front and back seats. "Change of plans," she said, and gave him Paul's address. The odd thing was, she was angry with Paul.

Candace rang the buzzer. No one answered. It hadn't occurred to her that he wouldn't be home, but he was probably at Noah's. She rang again—nothing. Finally, as she was about to leave—she'd already missed her train, which made her angrier—he pressed the intercom and said, "If this is a prank, fuck off."

"Hey," she said, "it's me."

"You need to be more specific," Paul said.

"It's Candace."

"Oh," he said, brightening, "why didn't you say so."

"Christof and I were watching *Top Chef*," he explained when she reached his door.

It crossed her mind that maybe that was not all they were doing, but she'd had one romantic bubble burst that night and was not in the mood for another.

"I was just leaving," Christof said, gathering up his jacket and scarf and putting on his shoes.

"You know each other from Thanksgiving," Paul said, as if that explained everything, and then, when he was gone, said "Noah is on call," as if that did, too.

"What's up," Paul said when they were settled on his sofa, she at one end, he at the other, their feet touching in the middle. "You seem, I don't know, out of sorts." He had poured her a glass of wine, then thought better of it and took out a nearly empty bottle of Jack Daniel's and handed it to her.

"What am I supposed to do with this?" she said.

"Sometimes it's best to drink it straight from the bottle."

"What's up is that I just had dinner with Tom," she said.

"Great," he said brightly. "Where did you go?"

She opened the bottle and took a swig and relished the burn. "Doesn't matter," she said.

"And?"

"It was all going well until he told me he was leaving for a month or so and asked me to go out with his friend Eddie."

Paul yawned, frowned, and ran a hand across his chin. "What's so bad about that? It's like he was offering Eddie as a placeholder till he came back."

"I don't think so," she said.

"You like him," Paul said. "I knew it."

"That's not the point."

"If that's not the point, then what is?"

Candace took another drink. She couldn't believe he was being so obtuse. "The point is, he wants me to go out with Eddie. You know, date him. Could he have been more obvious that he's not interested in me? I mean, come on. I mean, when we said goodbye tonight, he hugged me. It was our sixth date. Well, fourth, depending on how—oh, never mind." She tipped her head back and finished off the bottle. "This stuff is horrid, by the way."

"You're welcome," he said, just as his phone rang. "Also, sweetheart, it's the twenty-first century. Women have been liberated. You can go for it."

"Noah," he said, pointing at the phone, getting up from the

sofa, and walking into his bedroom. "Hi, hon," she heard him say. "Candace is here. Boy trouble."

"He says hi," Paul said when the call was over. "It's a slow night and he's bored. It's like the third time he's called tonight."

"Maybe he's checking up on you," she said. She was being mean. She could feel it.

"He knew Christof was here, if that's what you mean," he said. He could feel it, too. "Maybe Tom doesn't know you like him, you know, like that," he said after a while.

"I came into the city to have dinner with him," Candace said.

"Friends do that," Paul said. "He probably doesn't know."

"Yeah, and now he never will because he is leaving and has handed me off to his friend whose wife just died and who I wouldn't be attracted to even if that wasn't the case. It's messed up."

"You could tell him," Paul said.

"Why would I do that?" she said. She was sulking, and a little drunk.

"Maybe it was a setup," he reasoned.

"Of course it was a setup! With Eddie Marcus." She was close to shouting now and, against type, close to tears.

"No, hon," Paul said in his best "calm the client" voice. "Maybe it was a setup so you'd give him a sign, if not just come straight out and tell him how you feel."

"Well, I didn't," she said. "End of story."

"Sweetheart, it's not the end. It's the beginning. Or at least the middle. It's the part in the story where everything goes to hell so that everything can be even better in the end."

"Oh God, listen to you," she said, and closed her eyes. She was very tired. Her head hurt.

"Life is short and you're being ridiculous. Did it ever occur to you that Tom is shy? Or that you scare him—"

"Scare him? Why would I scare him?"

"Oh, let me count the ways," he said. "One, you're an attractive woman. Two, you're an attractive woman with a high-powered job—"

"Not for long," she interjected.

He continued: "Three, you're an attractive woman with a high-powered job who lives by herself in the middle of nowhere and appears to need no one or want anyone intruding on what appears to be her perfectly curated life. Should I go on?"

"It is not perfectly curated," she protested. "I don't even know what that means."

"I didn't say it was perfectly curated."

"Yes, you did."

"I did not. I said that it appears to be perfectly curated. Maybe Tom assumes that there is no room in Candace-world for another person."

She thought about this for a second. "That's dumb," she said.

"It may be dumb. It may also be true." He looked at her triumphantly, like he'd just returned an unhittable backhand.

Candace ran her hands through her hair. There was no point arguing with him. He was probably right. But then what?

"You need to go there," Paul said, and when she looked confused he clarified, "To Tom's place. Right now. You need to go there and tell him how you feel."

"Can't I send him an email? Or a text?" she said.

Paul threw up his hands. "Of course not! In what movie do our star-crossed lovers profess their undying love for each other in an email?"

"Well, there's *You've Got Mail* and—"

Paul shook his head. "That was a rhetorical question. You're wasting time."

As if on cue, they both looked at their wrists. "It's almost eleven," Candace said. "If I go over there now, don't you think I'll look desperate?"

Paul considered this for a moment, nervously tapping the fingers of his right hand against his thigh. "You may be right," he said after a while. "New thought: send him a message asking him if he's free for breakfast before you go back to the godforsaken suburbs."

"They're not godforsaken. I'm sorry you feel that way," she said, feigning hurt. "Also, he thinks I went home."

"Candace! Focus! Just give me your phone." He held out his hand. She hesitated, then put it in his palm and watched his thumbs fly over the keyboard.

"There," he said, handing it back. She read what he'd written: Hey Tom, I ended up staying over in the city. Any chance you're free for coffee tomorrow before I head to work? I'd love to see you.

"I hate messages that begin 'hey!'" she said. "Reminds me of my mother saying 'hay is for horses, not for people.'"

"Then change it," Paul said. He sounded exasperated. He was exasperated. She pushed send instead. "There. Happy?"

"I am if you are," he said. "There's an extra toothbrush in the bathroom. Go wash up and I'll get the sofa bed made up for you. But first, give me a hug and thank your old friend Paul for saving you from yourself." He opened his arms to envelop her.

"Pecs of steel," she said, leaning her head on his chest. "Impressive."

Candace had forgotten how noisy the city could be. Car alarms, sirens, the groan of the garbage truck—if it was not one, it was the others, all night long. She would have slept fitfully anyway, waiting to see what, if anything, Tom would say, but she had grown accustomed to the quiet that blanketed her home every night.

"I don't know how you do it," she said to Paul early the next morning. The sun—as much as she could see from the apartment—was just rising.

"Earplugs, baby," he said. "And a white noise machine. And exercise." He was dancing around his narrow kitchen as he said this, tossing kale and spinach and a banana and yogurt and blueberries and chia seeds and flax seeds into a Vitamix.

"You are in a better mood than anyone deserves to be at this hour," she said, leaning against the refrigerator.

"Well, when you were getting your beauty rest—which I'm not sure worked, by the way. Just kidding—I was meditating, doing my stretches, booking tickets to Reykjavik, and reading about float therapy at the Blue Lagoon. Want some?" He held out the blender container filled to the brim with viscous, dark-green liquid.

"Eww—no. That stuff looks disgusting."

He poured some into a tumbler. "Never judge a book by its cover," he said.

"I'll remember that the next time someone offers me a book to drink."

"Ha ha," Paul said. "This stuff is the fountain of youth."

"More reason not to drink it," she said. "Youth was bad enough the first time around."

"Suit yourself." He tilted back his head and took a long swallow. "Ahhh. I can feel it going to work already." He put down the drink and flexed his left bicep. "But enough about me. What did Tom say?"

She smiled shyly. "He said that I should come over for breakfast if I have the time."

"Girl!" Paul said.

CHAPTER EIGHTEEN

Candace stood on the street, staring at the two black doors, side by side, with the same street number. There was 935A and 935B, and she didn't know which intercom button to press. It was a squat, three-story brick structure with no distinguishing features, dwarfed by the buildings on either side of it. She took a guess and pressed B, and when there was no response, pressed A, and then waited. She considered pressing both again, worried that she'd seem pushy if she did, and was checking her phone to make sure she had the right address when, suddenly, there was Tom, opening the door to B.

"Bet you didn't know I lived in a doorman building," he said, warmly. He was in Levi's and a worn, mostly unbuttoned green corduroy shirt over a gray Saint Andrews tee. "Isabella went there," he reminded her when he saw her trying to make out the letters.

"Right," she said. He guided her down a dark hallway to what looked like an ancient cage elevator.

"Don't worry. It's old, but it's safe," he said. "It was just inspected."

"What's in 935A?" she asked as Tom slid open the metal accordion door and they stepped inside.

"That's the office. It takes up the first two floors. The living space is on three. Also four, if you count the roof. I've got a little garden up there." He closed the door and the elevator lurched upward. "The whole building used to be a hat factory. It's kind of nuts, but until the seventies, there were something like three hundred hat manufacturers in New York. Now there are like three. I just made up that number, by the way."

He was talking fast. Was he nervous? Candace couldn't tell. *She* was nervous and trying hard to pretend otherwise.

The elevator groaned and stopped abruptly. "We're home!" Tom said, sliding back the door and holding it open for Candace. There was no transition, no door between the elevator and the apartment.

"Oh, wow!" she said, stepping into the loft. The original tinned ceiling, painted robin's-egg blue, must have been fourteen feet high, and the windows half that. "This place should be in *Dwell*!" she said, surveying the main room. A long table made from repurposed barn wood surrounded by six artfully mismatched spindle chairs was off to one side, and an assortment of playful living room furniture that might have come from the MoMA design catalog took up the rest of the space. An enormous rya rug, with orange and yellow maple leaves scattered on a shaggy light-gray background, gave the place a cheery autumnal look. Morning light filled the room.

Tom shoved his hand into the pocket of his jeans. "Actually, it was," he said sheepishly. "About four years ago. As a favor to the photographer son of a client."

Candace was moving around, taking it all in. To the right was an open kitchen with four diner stools, their seats upholstered in a shiny red vinyl and tucked under a long, stainless-steel counter.

"Found the stools in a salvage yard and got them reupholstered," he said when he saw her eyeing them. "The junk man—that's not politically correct, is it?—anyway, the guy at the salvage yard said they came from a diner in Philly. And a friend who owns a company that fabricates airplane parts made the counter for me."

Past the kitchen, also on the right, were a couple of doors—bedrooms and bathrooms, she figured—and between the doors were nearly life-size architectural renderings of boats, and then a long wall of photographs, mostly of Isabella through the years, but a few of Tom, younger and tanned and two-handed and almost always on a boat.

"She's beautiful," Candace said, pointing to a picture of a woman in yellow shorts and a white shirt knotted at the waist, her long legs dangling over the side of a sailboat, with Tom standing behind her and Isabella on his shoulders. They looked like they were laughing.

"Izzy's mother," Tom said. "I hung it there to remind Isabella that at one point in time we were a happy family. I know it sounds counterintuitive. At least, it did to me. But the therapist said—we saw a counselor after Carrie left—it would help with attachments later on. After Izzy got married, I thought about taking it down—I mean, I guess it worked—but I decided it was a good reminder for me, too. You know, for the same reason." She didn't know but nodded anyway. He seemed to be telling her something important—intimate—about himself, but she wasn't sure if it was that he had trouble with attachments (like her, if she was being honest), or that he was looking for attachment. (Like her? She thought maybe?)

"Anyway, enough about me. What can I get you? Name your poison. Cappuccino? Mocha latte? Macchiato?" He put his hand on her shoulder and turned her back in the direction of the kitchen and pointed to a copper espresso machine perched on the back counter. He had touched her before—the hugs goodbye, the time he put her hand on his chest—but this was different.

Unbidden, she uttered the word "electric." Did he feel it, too?

Probably not, because he looked confused and said, "It is, but I had to change the plug because it was shipped over from Italy. I'm impressed that you knew that."

She didn't, but why let him know.

"It was a great indulgence," he continued. "But I did do the math once and figured that if I spent six dollars a day at Starbucks, the machine would pay for itself in a year and a half. Anyway, what will it be?"

"A macchiato sounds great," she said. "I could use the caffeine. I'd forgotten how hard it is to sleep in this town. The sirens and the car horns—"

"And don't forget the backup alarms," he added.

She sat down on one of the stools and spun around so her back was to him. "What's that rope over there?" she asked, noticing for the first time a braided rope hooked to the ceiling at one end that appeared to disappear through a hole in the floor.

"Oh, that. It goes down to my office. I wanted Izzy to have a way to get there without having to take the elevator. It's a trapdoor that opens when you pull on it from up here and push on it from down there, with a small hole that the rope is threaded through. A boatbuilder friend of mine came up with it."

"But isn't it dangerous, anyway? I mean, the ceilings are so high. What if she fell?"

"I did think of that," he said, sliding a coffee cup in her direction. "So the way it works is that it goes down to a landing in my office, a platform—it's padded, just in case—with a railing. We call it the 'poop deck,' like on an old schooner. It's got a ladder underneath, so she can climb down or up. That's what happens when your dad is an engineer and a sailor. Your macchiato has been delivered, by the way."

Candace turned around and picked up her drink just as a timer went off and, given her state of mind, startled her. "Oh," she said, nearly spilling the coffee.

Tom walked over to a wall oven, opened the door, and looked in. "I think it's done," he decided after jiggling the pan. He took it out and set it down on the counter. "Careful, it's hot," he said, grabbing two plates and a spatula. "I call this the kitchen sink frittata. It's got whatever was left in the larder. Asparagus, red peppers, a purple potato, three kinds of cheese. A specialty of the house."

"It's beautiful," she said. "But you shouldn't have. If I had known you were going to go to all this trouble, especially—"

He cut her off. "My pleasure," he said. "Also, it was a good way to use up what was lying around, since I'll be away for a while." He cut a slice for her and one for him and plated them. "Dig in. Bon appétit."

They had covered all the basics at dinner the night before—their work, his trip, his daughter, Winston, country living versus city living, whether the country was ready for a female president, the nightmare of air travel—and now she didn't know what to talk about. The only thing that had happened between then and now was that she found herself in the unusual and uncomfortable position of wanting more from this man, of having *feelings* for him. She was used to pushing people away, not inviting them in.

"So," he said, "the last time I saw you"—he made a point of checking his watch—"ten hours ago, you were rushing off to Grand Central. Did you end up missing your train?" He ground some pepper on his frittata and slid the grinder over to her. "Could use a little more oomph," he said. "I've also got this great small-batch hot sauce if you really want to kick it up. It's made with ghost peppers. It will really wake you up."

"That's okay," she said, barely getting the words out. She was tongue-tied. That's what it felt like. She could think of words, but she couldn't say them.

"Was there construction? Con Ed sometimes does that at night. You know, so it doesn't interfere with rush hour, which in this city seems to cover all hours anyway."

Was she going to say something? Take her shot? Confess her feelings? Over a plate of eggs? When she'd rehearsed the scene in her head, this was not the way it went.

"I don't know. I mean, no. I guess you could say that I had a change of heart." Would he get her meaning? Why would he? She was being obtuse. She could hear Paul in the background, berating her.

"I get it," Tom said. "Sometimes it's no fun getting home late at night. I mean, what—it would have been close to midnight."

They lapsed into what appeared to be a peaceable silence, but inside she was roiling. The odd thing was, he didn't seem to question why she was there or wanted to see him.

"What's up with your friend Wardo? Eddie?" she asked after a while.

"What do you mean, what's up with him?" She could sense him tense up. This was not good.

"I mean, I was surprised you wanted me to go out with him." There, she'd said it.

He looked at her quizzically. "No, I didn't."

"You asked me to go out with him when you're away. You said he liked talking to me when we were upstate."

Tom looked like he was about to burst out laughing, then composed himself. "To be clear, I said he'd like to meet *with* you. And he did like talking with you."

"I think you said 'meet up' with me. Which sounded like, you know, a date."

He shook his head. "Oh boy! I am so sorry. He's a bit over-whelmed these days, you know—business stuff, and the accident, and suddenly being a single parent—and he's worried about his daughter, and I think you calmed him down about the whole working-on-a-farm thing. Like you have some insight into teenage girls."

"I really don't know anything about teenage girls," she said.

"Well, you were one once," Tom said.

"If that's the criterion, every woman over the age of nineteen is qualified," she said. She tried to sound offended, but it was a feint. She was relieved. He wasn't setting her up with Eddie Marcus after all. Candace finished the last bite of the frittata, pushed the plate away.

"Dollar for your thoughts," Tom said when she had been quiet a while.

"Dollar?"

"Inflation," he said, and flashed her an impish smile and spun around on his stool so he was facing away from the kitchen and from her.

She took a deep breath and closed her eyes. When she was nine, a boy she knew from school dared her to jump off the high dive at the municipal pool, promising he'd give her half his ice cream sandwich if she did. Ice cream sandwiches were an indul-gence her mother did not abide, so it was tempting. But the diving board was so high up, and the water such a long way down. When she thought about this episode when she was older, she recog-nized that it was a textbook risk-and-reward scenario, the sort of dilemma they discussed at the consulting firm, but at the time it just felt scary. And then she was flying through the air, propelled by her own hubris, an object in motion that would soon be slowed and swallowed by an external force.

She was feeling good about herself as she floated up through the water, and then, just after her head breached the surface, the boy squeezed the chocolate cookie pieces together so the vanilla ice cream oozed out and made a show of licking the entire perimeter. "Still want it now, sucker?" he asked, walking away before she could answer. She had been a sucker, she had to give him that, but the upshot was that she was no longer afraid of going off the high dive. And now?

"I stayed because I wanted to see you," Candace said in a rush. "Before you took off." She couldn't see his face. Maybe that was better.

Tom said nothing. And then, without warning, he spun her stool and his own, so they were facing each other.

"Because I like you," Candace said, quietly, so maybe it wouldn't land so hard.

"Well, I like you, too," Tom said. "Obviously." Was he mocking her? She couldn't tell.

"I mean I like you, like you," she said. (Did anyone ever get past the awkwardness of junior high?)

Tom reached over and pried apart her hands, which she hadn't even noticed were folded defensively across her chest. "I like you, like you, too," he said. "I really do."

"But—" she said, anticipating what was coming next.

"No buts," he said. "No, that's not true. You're a bit of an enigma. You seem so self-sufficient. A regular Henry David Thoreau out there in the woods. I didn't want to intrude, didn't want to assume you wanted to be more than friends and screw that up."

He squeezed her hand, and she squeezed his back. "Well, I do," she said.

There. She'd done it. She'd taken the leap and was flying through the air, scared and exhilarated. But still, she couldn't look him in the eye. Instead she was focused on her shoes, a pair of ballet flats that she noticed could use a good shine.

Tom stood up without letting go of her hand and pulled her to her feet. When she was standing, he let go and put his hand under her chin and raised her head. "Would it be okay if I—" he started, and before he'd gotten all the words out, someone's phone started ringing. They ignored it.

It was a long, slow, exploratory kiss. A kiss that she knew, even in the midst of it, would be memorable. The phone started ringing again. They ignored it again.

Whoever was calling gave up. Her eyes were closed. The phone rang again. She opened them and saw him looking at her, the skin around his eyes folded upward in a smile. The ringing stopped. It started again. "You should get that," Candace said, making herself break away. "In case it's the airline. Or your daughter."

But it wasn't his phone, it was hers, and it was Angela.

"Where are you?" Angela said when she picked up.

"Doesn't matter."

"It matters to me. Didn't you see the email from Vivek?"

"I've been busy," she said, smiling broadly at Tom, who was leaning over and kissing her neck. "Tickles," she said.

"What?" Angela said impatiently. "Look, just read the email and get over here ASAP."

"Everything okay?" Tom asked when she hung up.

He looked over her shoulder as she read the email, and there it was, with the subject line All Hands on Deck! The guy had really bought into the whole nautical theme. The message was brief: Staff meeting at 11:45 a.m. Everyone is required to attend.

She put the phone down and reached up and stroked the side of his face.

"I'm guessing you have to go," he said.

"Sadly," she said.

Ten minutes later they were back in the elevator, holding hands and grinning like they'd gotten away with something. "Epic," he said. At the front door, he ran his fingers through her curls and kissed her again. "To be continued," he said as she climbed into a taxi.

Angela was waiting for her in the lobby, which was otherwise deserted. Candace could see her through the plate glass windows, pacing. She was wearing a velour tracksuit circa 1986 and orange Vans her son Liam had outgrown—either she didn't care anymore about workplace decorum or this was the new look of a soon-to-be very wealthy woman.

"Where were you?" Angela demanded as Candace emerged from the revolving door. She slipped her hand through Candace's arm and guided them both to the bank of elevators.

Feeling suddenly shy, Candace just smiled and said nothing.

"Wait a minute!" Angela said. "You were having dinner with Tom last night. You didn't sleep over, did you?"

The elevator door opened, and Angela pulled her in. "No," Candace said. "I mean, yes. Not with Tom. At Paul's."

Angela studied her friend. "Spill it," she said. "You're blushing."

"I had breakfast. At Tom's. His loft is amazing."

"You're holding out on me," Angela said. "Details, please."

"If you must know, you interrupted one of the world's greatest kisses."

Angela clapped her hands and looked upward. "Praise God," she said as the doors opened to the ninth-floor cafeteria, where Vivek would be beamed in from somewhere in the Caribbean.

"It's over, by the way," Angela said as they walked into the mostly empty room.

"But it's just after eleven."

"No, silly, I mean the company. DataStream is over. At least in its current incarnation."

The cafeteria had been closed for weeks and the cafeteria workers, who were contractors, hadn't cleaned out the pantry, so when Candace and Angela got there, a random assortment of crackers and cookies and pickles and whatever else could be scavenged was arrayed on a table. A couple of the engineers had rigged up speakers and were blasting "Party in the USA" on repeat, and welcoming everyone who came in to DataStream's Day of the Dead celebration. Someone had strung twinkly lights and paper garlands made from years of DataStream newsletters, and people who might only have known each other from the elevator or the restroom chatted like old friends, and old friends huddled together for what was likely the last time, knowing that once the doors were shuttered their friendships would end, too. Maybe not right away, but eventually.

"Come," Angela said, and led Candace to a far corner of the room where it was marginally quieter. "Tell me everything! Spill it."

Candace shrugged. "Like I said, we kissed."

"And?"

"And he's leaving town in six hours."

Candace was torn. She wanted to share all the details, dissect them, even, with her friend. But she also wanted to hold them close, as if they would float away if she said them out loud.

And then the music stopped, and a screen dropped down from the ceiling. The two of them and everyone else turned toward it, and there was Vivek, pixelated. Maybe the color tone was off or maybe he had stayed too long in the sun, but there was a reddish cast to his skin, and his jet-black hair had blue highlights that were refracted through the Oakleys perched atop his head.

"Greetings, friends," Vivek said brightly. He was sitting in a nook at what looked to be the back of his boat, the turquoise expanse of the ocean behind him. "Welcome to my world!"

"'Friends'? Fuck you," someone behind Candace yelled, and

there was an outbreak of foot stomping that drowned out his next sentence, though it was obvious from the way he moved his hands that he was extolling the beautiful scenery around him.

"So," he was saying, "as you all know, DataStream has been my baby. And I hope that for all of you, it has been yours, too."

"He needs a better speechwriter," Angela whispered to Candace. "Also, I'm getting seasick, looking at him."

Vivek's boat was rocking side to side, and so was the camera, and so was he. For a second, his left side was higher than his right, then his right was, back and forth with no discernable pattern. And then the screen went dark.

"Sorry," he said. "Technical difficulties." But they weren't so difficult or technical that the people in the room could not still hear him swearing at whoever was behind the camera, until a woman's voice informed him that the mic was hot. People started leaving the room, lobbing obscenities at the black screen as they went. Before long, it was just Angela, Candace, what was left of the legal team, and a bunch of the tech bros, who were passing around a vape pen because who was going to stop them. Nguyen Smythe hadn't bothered to show, and Damian, his assistant, hadn't been seen in days.

"Sorry," the CEO said again. "I'll be brief. As you know, DataStream has been my baby. And I hope that for all of you, it has been yours, too."

"Either this was prerecorded, or it's Groundhog Day," one of the lawyers said. "Or he's really bad at this and is reading from a teleprompter like he's the fucking president of the United States."

"He can't be president because he wasn't born in this country," Angela said.

"I don't think anyone was suggesting he was president," Candace said.

"Oh. Well, he can't."

Vivek cleared his throat. "As you may have heard, we have entered into an agreement to sell the company to a global multinational that will be better able to fulfill the mission I set out to accomplish all those years ago."

"Global multinational?" Angela said to no one.

"Pretty sure it's illegal to sell your baby," one of the very high engineers said loudly. "Isn't it?" He clapped the padded shoulder of one of the lawyers. The lawyers were the last employees to come to work dressed for work.

Vivek took a deep breath and exhaled even longer. Finally he said, "I wanted you all to know, before it was reported in *The Wall Street Journal* and in the other papers, that—"

And then his microphone cut out, too.

CHAPTER NINETEEN

The Club Car in Old Greenwich was the kind of place where men—they were mostly men, Candace noticed—stopped in for a drink after disembarking from the 6:21 from Grand Central Station. Jackets off and ties loosened at the neck, they crowded the bar in twos and threes, chatting loudly, and laughing loudly, and drinking loudly. Heads turned as Candace made her way to where Eddie stood, waving her over, and she couldn't tell if those men were checking her out or wondering what lucky bastard she was there to meet, or if they were just surprised to see a woman in a place that was so decidedly their domain. In his well-tailored suit, blue with white-and-gray pinstripes and a yellow power tie, Eddie seemed to fit right in. The last time she'd seen him, he was wearing flannel lounge pants and a bulky fleece pullover and it was hard to picture him as a master of the universe, even if that universe was paper bags. Not anymore.

"I feel like an interloper," she said when she reached Eddie, who pulled out a chair so she could face the wall, not the men at the bar. "This place is like a Cheever novel."

"Never read him. Should I?" Eddie asked when they were both seated. "Though reading for me is mostly listening to audiobooks when I drive to Jersey."

Candace shook her head and waved her arm in the direction of the men at the bar. "I think it might be redundant for you," she said. "Sorry I'm a little late. A work thing."

That was not precisely true, since the work thing was her sitting at her desk, reading and rereading her own résumé, which, to her trained eye, looked pretty thin. Did anyone still get rewarded for doing the same thing every day for years? She had been fielding calls from headhunters interested in the company's roster of software developers, data scientists, and lawyers, but when she inquired if anyone was looking for an experienced human resources professional, no one was.

"I am like a flip phone. Nobody wants one, even though they're perfectly serviceable," she told Angela, who still came to the office every day as she waited for her big payout.

"Tom Cruise is really short," Angela would say, apropos of nothing, plopping herself down on Candace's office couch, or "Nick's cousin Arabella just came back from Malta—the country, not the town upstate—and said the beaches were gorgeous and I said, 'Sign me up.' But seriously, should I get a place on the Jersey Shore?"

"How is DataStream? What's happening with the sale?" Eddie asked, pushing a menu across the table to her.

She skimmed it quickly. "Oh, you know," Candace said. "Everyone who doesn't want to take up the offer to move to South Dakota, where the new mother ship is setting up shop, are waiting to be fired so they can collect unemployment."

"And you?"

"Let's just say that I'm not interested in living in a place that's called 'the Badlands.'"

A waiter appeared to take their drinks order—a mustang for her, the double IPA on tap for him. "Makes sense," Eddie said. "I mean, I'd move my operations team out of the northeast if I could—it's so expensive—but I'd lose my best people. But look at me, I'm actually moving into the belly of the beast."

When she looked at him quizzically, he said, "I'm selling my house and getting a place in the city."

"That's big," she said.

"Tell me about it. My daughter has basically stopped talking to me. All of a sudden, she loves the place. But I can't wait to get out of there. Too many memories."

Their drinks came, and Eddie raised his pint glass and said "cheers," but sadly, Candace thought, and took a long swallow.

"Maybe that's the reason she wants to stay," Candace ventured. "Like she would lose those memories if you sold the house."

"It's not like I want to erase Delia from our lives," he said, hanging his head.

Candace sipped her drink slowly to give him a moment. Raucous laughter and chatter swirled behind them, but it was like an offshore wind that would never reach them.

"The thing is, my whole world was based on the assumption that my wife would always be by my side. That we'd grow old together. That Monday would segue into Tuesday and Tuesday into Wednesday and so on. My whole world was built on that assumption, and it turned out not to be true."

"But what's the alternative?"

"Exactly," Eddie said. "The alternative is not to take anything for granted, but how do you do that? We all crave stability. So we tell ourselves and each other that tomorrow will be like today and today will be like yesterday. It's a necessary lie, and then, I don't know, it feels like a betrayal when it turns out not to be true. The house—the house reminds me of that every day. Every day," he repeated. "I'm sorry. This is what I'm like now. I just cycle through emotions, up and down, up and down, and down and down. I try to put on a good face, but that's all it is. No one wants to be a burden. The truth is, I can't stop thinking about it. I go to bed thinking that when I wake up she'll be right next to me. Every day it's the same disappointment, the same awful realization, but I can't seem to stop. And I'm angry, but who am I supposed to be angry at? A rock? I can have a good day, or a good hour, and then something happens, something nobody else would notice, and it sets me off on this endless loop of what-ifs. Stupid stuff—at least I know it's stupid—like what if I convinced her to come with me to the club. She was a decent tennis player, you know. What if she hadn't stopped for gas. And the biggest what-if—what if she never met me? If she never met me, she'd still be alive." He cradled his head with his left hand for a second, then repositioned it so his chin was resting in the heel of his palm. *Like that Rodin sculpture*, she thought, but instead of thinking, he seemed to be waiting for her to say something.

Candace shifted uneasily in her chair. What she really wanted to say was, "Why are you telling me this when we hardly know each other," but that would be unkind. She imagined that it was easier talking to someone who didn't know him and didn't know Delia, someone who was a blank and detached slate. If her years of listening to other people's problems had taught her anything, it was that the only sensible thing to do when someone was hurting was to validate their feelings.

"I can see why you feel that way," Candace said slowly. This was her gimme line. The I'm-on-your-side line. "Of course you're going to blame yourself. It's only natural."

Eddie scrunched up his face. He seemed to be considering this. "Maybe," he said. "Maybe." And then, after a while: "What's the worst thing that's ever happened to you?"

"I mean, nothing like what happened to you," Candace said. This was new. Usually, people in distress only wanted to—or only could—talk about themselves.

"It's not a competition," Eddie said. "Everyone has something."

Candace bypassed the cocktail straw and took a hard slug of her drink. She reminded herself that this was Tom's friend, and anything she said to him might get back to Tom. But it wasn't like she wouldn't tell Tom himself if he asked—and maybe, even, if he didn't. "Well," she said, "there was my father, who liked his liquor too much. And my mother, who yelled too much. A match made in heaven."

"Is that it?" Eddie said.

"Isn't that enough?" She downed the last of her drink, then stuck her fingers in the glass and swirled the ice cubes.

"A wise person once told me that we bury the high-hanging fruit," Eddie said, smiling. It was a knowing smile, not a happy one.

"Your wise person likes mixed metaphors."

"Liked. Delia. My wife. So?" he said, not letting go.

"The worst thing that ever happened to me?" she said and couldn't believe she was going to tell him. "Like I said, my father drank too much. My parents fought a lot. It was just after my tenth birthday, which I remember because in fourth grade chorus they'd just sung happy birthday to me. Mom and Dad were in their bedroom arguing, and the door was open a crack, but they didn't know I was there." Candace took a long, deep breath, then exhaled into a sigh before continuing. "I couldn't see what was in my father's hand, but I could hear him threatening to kill himself."

"That's horrifying," Eddie said.

"That's not the worst of it," she said. "The worst of it was that she laughed. She laughed and told him he was a fool, and if he wanted to do that, he could be her guest. It was an unusual thing to say, 'be my guest,' which is why I remembered it. And the sound of my mother laughing."

"You were just a kid," Eddie said, leaning forward across the table and shaking his head slowly. "It must have been awful."

She closed her eyes for a second and shook her head, remembering. It felt strange to be sitting in this noisy commuter bar, speaking of things she hadn't thought of in years. No, that wasn't accurate. Thinking of things she hadn't spoken of in years, and then only to herself.

"The thing is," she continued, "after that, I could never look at my father as anything but a weak man. A coward. Someone not worthy of respect. I guess you could say that I completely bought into my mother's narrative. Not that I would have been able to understand that then."

Eddie reached over and squeezed her hand. "Like I said, you were a kid," he said.

"Thanks," she said, withdrawing it. "But I don't think that cuts it."

The waiter came back to ask the obligatory "is everything all right here?" and it struck them as such an absurd question, they both suppressed a laugh.

"Just great," Eddie managed to say.

The dark mood had been broken.

"So what do you hear from Tom?" Eddie said.

Candace felt herself blush. What did Eddie know? That they kissed? Did grown men tell each other things like that? "I've gotten a few emails from him," she said. (Untrue. They'd been writing every day and also playing a very slow game of Scrabble online, what with the nine-hour time difference. Would Eddie know that, too?) "He thinks he'll be back in two weeks."

"Glad to hear it," Eddie said. "You know, I've known Tom for a very long time. Great guy. I never could understand why he never married after Carrie left, you know?" (No, she did not know.) "But I get it now," he went on, "because losing someone so central to your life, to your identity, really, maybe you just don't get over it." (Did he realize who he was talking to, she wondered, or was he really just talking to himself?) "The funny thing is—I mean it's not really funny at all—is that I thought the worst thing had already happened to me when my brother, Alan, died. Like everyone gets one terrible catastrophe in their life. I thought I was done."

Candace felt dizzy. Not room-spinning, vertigo dizzy, but dizzy from the roller coaster of Eddie Marcus's emotions and her own.

"I used to wonder if it was because of his hand," Eddie said.

"What?" Candace was confused. "Oh," she said, comprehending. "Tom. I doubt it. He seems comfortable in his skin."

"Yeah," Eddie said. "I guess. But I don't know him the way you do."

"I barely know him," Candace said, but she knew what he meant.

"I suspect that might change," Eddie said, and smiled at her. For the first time all evening, he seemed lighthearted, a little impish.

The bar had cleared out for the most part, and only the heavy drinkers, the ones who didn't want to go home or had no reason to, were still on their stools.

The waiter came back and asked if they wanted anything else, and just as Candace said "no," Eddie ordered a plate of sliders.

"Sorry. If my daughter were here, she'd be accusing me of mansplaining or manspreading or man-something like that. But it's dinnertime, and it would be rude of me to keep you here without feeding you."

Candace laughed. She liked this guy. He was a mess, but in her line of work, she was used to messes. Eddie Marcus seemed to know that about her already.

"So," he said, "you're probably wondering why I wanted to meet you here. I mean, not here, specifically, but with you." He looked at her intently.

"I can't say I wasn't wondering," Candace said.

"Look," he said. "I'm a good CEO. My employees like me—unless they're just lying. But I think they do. I'm fair. Our suppliers like me, probably because we pay our bills on time. Our buyers like me because we make a good product. Do you know how many paper bags are used in this country every year?"

Candace shook her head.

"Ten billion," he said proudly. "I ask that question to everyone who interviews for a job with me."

"Paper or plastic?" Candace said. Was she interviewing for a job without knowing it?

"A question with only one right answer. Everyone thinks paper bags are boring—I mean, not everyone, I don't, obviously, but most people. Anyway, like I said, I'm a good CEO because I'm a hands-on guy, but my hands only stretch so far." He looked to see if she was following him. "Why am I telling you this?" Eddie said, when it was clear she was not.

"Now there's a question," Candace said, trying to keep the mood light.

"Remember when we were upstate, and Tom and I told you about the Alan Marcus Foundation? It's been this very small foundation that I've been able to run pretty much on my own, with help from Tom and the other board member. But there's going to be a settlement from the state over Delia's death, many millions of dollars, and in all honesty, I do not want that money. So I am going to donate it to the foundation, but once I do, the mission will have to expand. To start, we're changing the name to the Alan and Delia Marcus Foundation. But that's just paperwork. We're going to need more oversight, more input. That sort of thing." He seemed anxious, a bit unsure of himself.

"And?" Candace said.

"And we're going to expand the board. It's really small right now, just me, Tom, and an old MIT colleague of Alan's, and I'd like you to join it."

"Why me?"

"Well, to start, you're good people. Tom likes you. It was his idea, actually."

So they *were* talking about her. Was it before the kiss or after? It had to be before, she decided, and wondered if that would change anything. But if this was Tom's idea, why hadn't he warned her? Did he put Eddie up to it so they'd spend more time together, have more in common? Maybe Eddie was just doing him a favor.

". . . for the purposes of the foundation, you're a people person," Eddie was saying. "I mean, given what you do—"

"Which I may not be doing for much longer," she interrupted him.

"Right," he said absently. "Anyway, given what you do, I think you'd be really good at helping us figure out which potential grantees are worthy of our support and which aren't. Also, as Tom reminded me, you used to work for that consulting firm. Which was it, Bain? McKinsey?"

"Lucentum."

"Right, Lucentum. So I imagine you know how to evaluate an organization, even a nonprofit one."

"That was a long time ago," Candace said.

"Muscle memory," Eddie countered. "Look, you don't have to decide now. In the past we met four times a year—so not a huge time commitment. I'm also going to ask Melody to join as soon as she turns eighteen. I'm sure Delia would want her involved. By rights this is her money, too. I'd love for you to meet her."

Their food came, and when it did, they realized they were the only ones left in the Club Car who weren't on a liquid diet. "That's a whole other reason I want to move to the city," Eddie said, waving his arms toward the bar. "Those guys have no reason to go home. I don't want to be like them. I mean, I have my golfing buddies, and Marcia is always around—"

Candace raised her eyebrows. "Marcia? I thought your daughter's name was Melody."

"No. No. I mean, yes, my daughter is Melody. Marcia was Delia's good friend, and I guess I sort of inherited her. She lost her husband years ago, so she thinks she knows the ropes, so to speak. Melody thinks she's a buttinsky."

"A what?"

"You know, someone who is always sticking their nose in someone else's business. Honestly, she's been incredibly helpful, but between you and me"—his voice dropped to a whisper—"I won't mind having a home that she doesn't have a key to."

Later, when they were getting ready to leave and Eddie was thanking her for meeting with him and for considering joining the foundation board, Candace wondered if she should bring up the question that had been on her mind since Eddie asked her.

"Um," she began, "Eddie. There is one potential wrinkle if I do join the board. I mean, what if Tom and I don't—"

"Candace," he said, taking both of her hands in his, "it does no good to anticipate the worst. It's a waste of time and energy. If bad things are going to happen, they're going to happen. No use expecting them, since the ones you're expecting are probably not the ones that will happen." Coming from anyone else, she thought as she drove home, this would hardly be a vote of confidence. But coming from a man whose wife was killed by a rock that came out of nowhere, it seemed to be.

CHAPTER TWENTY

"We've been summoned," Tom said.

"I know. I was copied on that email from Eddie—Wardo—too," Candace reminded him. They were talking over Skype, and the connection was bad, as it often was, but she could see that he was tired from his late night out with one set of clients and his early mornings with other ones. She was a little ragged herself since she'd taken up running again—a sure sign, Paul told her, that she was in love.

"I don't really understand brunch," Tom was saying. "I mean, if it's too late for breakfast—though in my estimation it's never too late for breakfast. When Izzy was growing up, one of our favorite meals was breakfast for dinner. But if you're the kind of person who thinks it's too late in the morning for breakfast, why not just call it lunch?"

"Marketing," she said. "Also, when is there a better opportunity to have Vivaldi's *Four Seasons* on repeat?"

Tom laughed. Talking at a distance behind a fuzzy screen suited them. "Your brunches sound a lot fancier than mine," Tom teased. "Mine featured waffles smothered in whipped cream, strawberries, and an astronomical insulin spike on the side that required a nap for me and a trip to the playground for Izzy. We'd go to the park and I'd nod off. I'm sure the other parents thought I was a vagrant."

"I would have liked to have seen that," she said.

"Be glad you didn't," he said. "It wasn't pretty. Anyway, brunch with Wardo when I get back. I may not be a fan of not-breakfast-not-lunch, but I am a fan of yours."

"Cut it out," she said, but they both knew she didn't mean it.

Sixteen days later they were in her car, on their way to Cornell Drive to meet Eddie and Melody, who seemed to be talking to her father again. Candace's hand was resting on Tom's thigh and every so often he'd take his right hand off the steering wheel and squeeze it. He had downloaded *The Four Seasons* on his phone—"to get us in the mood," he said—and it was playing loudly through the car stereo. Neither of them felt the need to talk.

Less than forty-eight hours earlier, Tom—not long off the airplane—had showed up at her office, uninvited, near the end of the workday. It was a Friday, and Candace was at her desk preparing for the corporate transition, and Angela was on the couch, flipping through a copy of *Self*. The door was ajar enough that Angela could see Tom approach, though she didn't know it was Tom until he stopped in the hallway and put his fingers to his lips so Candace wouldn't know he was there. He was about to knock when Candace looked up from her work and said, "I wonder when I'll see Tom?"

Angela, who was in the middle of an article about self-actualization, said, "Maybe you should manifest him."

"Very funny," Candace said, and then Tom walked in, and Angela yelled, "Yes!" so loudly that it drowned out his "special delivery," as he dropped a small box on her desk.

"What are you doing here?" she said, dumbfounded.

"Go ahead, open it," he said, not bothering to answer.

She untied the ribbon, tore off the wrapping paper, and opened the box. Inside was a single bar of soap. She looked up at Tom, confused. "Thanks," she said. "It's soap?"

"Do you like it? My driver told me that all the ladies love the smell. It's made from camel's milk."

Candace put it up to her nose. "It's lovely," she said.

"They had these gorgeous Persian rugs, but they would not have fit in the overhead compartment."

"Adorable," Angela announced and picked herself off the couch, said "adieu," and walked out, shutting the door.

As soon as it was closed, Candace got up from her desk and Tom opened his arms and wrapped them around her.

"Seriously, what are you doing here?" she said.

"Um, what does it look like," he said. "Let's blow this pop stand? There's something I want to show you."

Ten minutes later they were on the highway in her car, heading south, and then they were on spur roads, following signs to City Island, but Tom wouldn't say where exactly they were going. There were signs for boat access and beach food and fishing charters. "Are we going for fried clams?" she guessed.

"We could be," he said, then took a sharp right, just before a weathered sign that said NEW REHOBOTH YACHT CLUB.

"Isn't Rehoboth in Delaware?"

"It could be," he said, and laughed. "I used to think it was a joke, but it turns out that it is a family name." They were out of the car, walking toward a white two-story clapboard house that did not look at all new, and beyond it, a series of docks where sailboats and pleasure boats were moored. Tom led the way, eventually stopping in front of a sailboat called *Jack's Sprat*.

"Kinda fishy," he said when he saw her puzzling over it. "But what do you think?"

"What's a sprat?"

"That's the joke. It's a kind of fish," he said. "But what do you think? Isn't she a beaut?"

Candace looked at the craft. "I don't know anything about boats, but it's pretty, yes," she conceded.

"I'd been searching for one of these for months. My boat broker found it when I was away."

"You have a boat broker?" She didn't know how she felt about this. No, that wasn't true. She thought it was a little . . . rich.

"Well, I wasn't going to buy a boat off Craigslist."

"You bought this?"

"Not yet," he said. "I wanted to show it to you first."

This was not good. They had known each other for what, four months? And one of those months was over Skype and most of the other three they'd danced around each other—and now he was making big life choices based on her opinion? "You should do what you want to do," she said coolly.

He looked surprised, and a little wounded. "So you don't like it."

"I didn't say that," she said. Were they having their first fight? "I just said that you should do what you want to do. What's best for you," she amended.

Tom considered this for a second. "I want to do what's best for us," he said, and jumped aboard before he could see her reaction.

Her reaction was—confused. Flattered, in a way, but scared and annoyed. She was so used to making her own decisions and being solely responsible for those decisions, and here he was, roping her into making a big financial decision with him—though, granted, it wasn't her money. If it didn't work out—the relationship, not the boat—no big deal. He could go sailing into the sunset. But if it did work out, this boat could turn into an albatross for them both. She remembered Vivek bragging that "a boat is a hole in the water you throw money into"; for him, the true sign of wealth was having so much money that it was worth almost nothing to him.

"Here," Tom said, holding out his hand. "Actually, you may want to take those shoes off first."

Candace stepped out of her heels, left them on the dock, and took his outstretched hand. Once onboard, she began to pull her hand away, but Tom gripped it tighter. "Come on," he said. "Let me show you around."

It was a gorgeous craft—she had to give him that. Mahogany wainscoting top to bottom, a master cabin outfitted with a bed built into the bow, and a galley with sea-green Corian counter-tops and a four-burner stove. "It's like an RV for the open ocean," Tom said. "Check this out." He dropped her hand, opened a cabinet in the saloon, and unfolded a tabletop with a Scrabble board lam-inated to it. "Isn't it perfect? It's what really sold me. I mean, we both like to play, so this seemed like a good sign."

"How do the pieces stay on the board when the boat rocks or tips?" She knew the word was "heel." She'd heard Vivek use it many times, but for some reason she didn't want to use it herself. It felt like a concession.

Tom's eyes lit up. "That's why it's ingenious!" he said. "There's a very thin magnetic sheet under the board, must have been Dremeled in. All the pieces are magnetic, too."

Candace looked at his face and thought she could see back through the years to when he was a little boy. His expression re-minded her of a child on Christmas morning—happy, excited, ex-pectant, and a little worried that his hopes were about to be dashed.

"I think you definitely should get it," she said suddenly, and more emphatically than she intended.

"You do?"

"Yeah. I mean, when does life present you with something that makes you so purely happy?"

"It presented me with you," Tom said, and leaned down and kissed her.

She let him drive her home that night. She let him stay over. She let herself believe that it wasn't a choice, that it just happened. It was late, he was there. She could have dropped him off at his daughter's house; he even offered to go there. Or, he said, "we could watch surfing videos," which they did for a while, the whole time Candace wondering if watching surfing videos was actually code for having sex and wondering, too, if she wanted it to be. Close to midnight, when it was clear he was not leaving, though she hadn't invited him to stay but hadn't not invited him, it got awkward. "Do you want to stay over," she asked finally, and as soon as she did, she felt uneasy, worried that the rule she'd set for herself—that she'd never bring a man back to her home—would go by the wayside, and then where would she be? It was not lost on her that this house, this structure, was the frame she so carefully built around herself. And now, with a few words, she was dismantling it. No—blowing it up. (He did say that blowing things up was fun, so there was that.)

They were lying together on the couch when she asked. "But you don't have to," she said when he didn't answer right away.

"There's something I should tell you," he began, and before he could say what it was, she was already filling in the blanks: he'd met someone else (in business class, on the fourteen-hour flight); he wasn't ready for a relationship (well, neither was she, really); he had an STD (it seemed, statistically, given his age, to be within the margin of error). She shifted her weight and started to sit up. "Where are you going?" he asked, putting his hand on her waist to keep her from leaving. "You just need to know that I take my prosthesis off at night."

"What? Are you joking?" she said and immediately wanted to pull the words back into her mouth. "I mean, is that all? That's what you needed to tell me?" She was almost laughing, she was so relieved.

"I didn't want to freak you out. Like if you wake up in the middle of the night, go into the bathroom, and there is this disembodied hand sitting on the vanity."

Now she did laugh. "First of all, you can't freak me out any more than I can freak myself out. Second, maybe don't leave it in the bathroom."

Neither had heard the crunch of tires on the driveway, though it was Tom who said, "I think there's someone in the house," as much to himself as to Candace, who lay on her side, half asleep, the movie of the past thirty-six hours playing in her head. If it was projected on a screen and she was watching with someone else, even Tom (the film's star), it would have made her blush—or leave the theater.

"Oh!" she said, fully awake now. "It's Sunday. I lost track," and grabbed at the clothes strewn on the floor and stumbled into the kitchen, where Paul had set the table for three.

"If I'd known we were going to have company"—he raised his eyebrows—"I would have gotten more bagels and actual lox, not just the spread"—he paused for effect—"to celebrate."

"Very funny," she said. And then, suddenly self-conscious, "I must look like the dog dragged me in."

"Is the dog's name Tom, by any chance? Actually, sweetheart, you look fabulous. Glowing." He passed her a cup of coffee. They heard the shower turn on. "Okay," Paul said in a conspiratorial whisper, "tell me everything!"

Candace slathered a sesame bagel with cream cheese and took a big bite. "Mmm," she said. "I am ravenous." She took another bite.

"You're stalling," Paul said. "Speak."

Candace shrugged. "What can I say? We went to look at a boat, a catamaran, *Jack's Sprat*, that Tom is probably going to buy, and then we came here. Did you know that a sprat is a kind of fish?" She didn't tell him that they saw the boat on Friday.

"And," he said, trolling for details.

"And," she said, "use your own overactive imagination.

He stood up and walked to her side of the table. "I hate you," he said, leaning down to give her a hug. "And I'm proud of you."

They heard the shower turn off, and a few minutes later Tom appeared, his hair still wet, his face cleanly shaven and look-ing, Candace thought, ridiculously attractive. Even the little bit of shaving cream in his ear was appealing. "I thought I heard someone," he said, pouring himself a cup of coffee. As he did, he happened to glance at the Audubon calendar tacked to the wall.

"It's Sunday," he said, stating the obvious. The other two stared at him.

"Yes, we established that," Candace said, chiding him.

"No, I mean, today's the day we're supposed to have brunch with Wardo," he said, reminding Paul who he meant.

"Well, kids," Paul was saying, "I can't stay long anyway. I've got a client."

Candace knew this could not be true—Paul never worked on Sundays—and she loved him for wanting to give them their space. But it scared her, too. She and Tom were seeing each other in daylight, with the shutters open and the shades up for the first time since they had collapsed on her bed. These were the critical hours, when it would become clear if this union was just a happy coincidence of desire and opportunity—her specialty—or if it was something more.

Candace removed her hand from Tom's thigh and pointed. "There," she said as they drove down Cornell Drive. She recognized the house from that week of newscasts, when the camera trucks were lined up along the road, as if there was something to be learned about the woman who'd been killed by focusing on the house where she no longer lived.

"Yup," he said. "Last time I was here was the funeral. Awful day. She was a good woman, Delia. Wardo was gutted. Just gutted. It's why I asked him to come upstate with me. Change of scenery. And because I knew you'd be there."

Candace, who had been unable to suppress the image of Eddie torn apart, stem to stern, with his entrails exposed, from infiltrating her mind, snapped to attention. "Me? What did I have to do with it?" But she knew. Defense. Diversion. And she smiled. That was her playbook. But was it still?

Eddie met them at the door, ushering them into a grand foyer like, she thought, the concierge at the Plaza. Even though he was in his own home, he seemed more formal than the other times Candace had seen him, but so did she, she realized—something about not being on neutral ground.

"I love the tile work," Candace said as Eddie took her jacket. "It's stunning."

And before he could respond, a disembodied voice said, "My mother found it in a church in Italy." The voice soon merged with the figure of a teenager in Carhartt's and a Keith Haring graphic T-shirt, with hair as wild and crazy as her own, coming down the stairs. She sounded oddly possessive when she said this. Candace wondered how long she had been standing there, looking down at them.

"You must be Melody," Candace said, holding out her hand when the girl got closer. "I'm Candace."

"You remember Tom," Eddie said.

A timer went off just as Eddie guided them into the kitchen. "Perfect," he said. The table was set for four, with a bottle of Prosecco off to one side chilling in a silver ice bucket and an assortment of pastries in the middle.

"Sit, sit," Eddie commanded as Melody pulled a pan from the top oven. "It's the Marcus house specialty," Eddie said to his guests.

"What he means," Melody said, "is that this is one of the few things that Dad and I can cook. It's our everything frittata."

"Oh my goodness," Candace said, and both she and Tom burst out laughing.

Melody looked mortified. "What? Did I say the wrong thing?"

"No, no, no," Tom said, shaking his head. "It's just that right before I left on my trip—I've been in Abu Dhabi—I invited Candace over for breakfast and made her my house specialty: the kitchen sink frittata."

"Oh," she said. "Cool."

"Obviously, great minds think alike," Eddie said with false cheer. "Who wants Prosecco?"

"Mom called that 'grown ups' soda pop,'" Melody said as Eddie filled the glasses.

"There's something to that," Candace agreed. "My dentist told me that it's actually worse for your teeth than Coke. I didn't believe him, so I looked it up, and it turns out that there is something called Prosecco mouth."

Eddie looked stricken, and Tom nudged her under the table.

"The thing is," she added, "orange juice is even worse."

"So the moral of the story is, when in doubt, drink Coke," Tom said, and they all laughed. "But do you want to hear something crazy? The government in Abu Dhabi was considering banning the sale of Coke and Pepsi because they found trace amounts of alcohol in them."

"Please tell that to the principal of my school," Melody said. "They finally put a Coke machine in our cafeteria, and now the boys keep having these burping contests. It's disgusting."

The rest of the meal was pleasant, just a lot of back-and-forth about Melody's school, Eddie's company, Tom's work in the Middle East, and the DataStream sale. Every so often, Tom would put down his fork or his coffee cup, reach under the table, and squeeze Candace's thigh, and each time he did it, it reminded her that this was the first time they were out in public as a couple, if they were a couple, or maybe she was putting the cart—sex—before the horse—coupledom. Eddie wanted to talk about the foundation, and they did that for a while, though Candace reminded him that she hadn't yet agreed to join the board.

"I'm just not sure what I have to offer," she said.

"That's silly," Tom said, but in a loving way.

But Eddie, who had been watching her closely, said, "What's really holding you back, Candace?" and that question, or the way he said her name, cut right through her.

She hesitated. "I guess," she began. They were all looking at her intently, Melody especially. "I guess," she said again, "because I'd be the only person on the board who didn't know either Alan or Delia. Seems like a liability. I mean, if the point is to honor their memories, it seems to me that it would be best to know what they'd want this money to support." She braced herself for Eddie to echo Tom and tell her she was being nonsensical, but he didn't.

He was quiet for a moment—they were all looking at him. "I can see where you're coming from," he said, "but I think it's a strength, not a weakness. Do I wish you'd known Delia or my brother? Of course. Do I wish this foundation didn't have a reason to exist? Of course I do." He threw up his hands and let them fall to the table. "But these are the cards I was dealt—we were dealt"—he looked at Melody, who was looking down at her plate—"and I am committed to doing right by my wife and my brother, and this is the best way I know, at least right now." His voice, which had become strident, softened. "I don't mean to pressure you," Eddie said to Candace. "Well, maybe that's not true. All I can say is that I—we," he again amended, "could use your help."

Later, when Candace and Melody were cleaning up and Tom and Eddie were in the den, talking, Melody said, "If you don't do it, it will just be me and a bunch of old guys. Sorry, not Tom. Tom doesn't seem that old."

"I get it. Everyone seems old when you're seventeen, even people two or three years ahead of you in school, let alone the rest of us."

"Yeah, and everyone who is older thinks seventeen is really young." She couldn't help but think about Connor. "It's so annoying."

"I can see that," Candace said, rinsing a plate and handing it to Melody to dry, all the while trying to make out the snippets of conversation coming from the other room. "Doing better." (Eddie. About his work? His daughter? Himself? His relationship with his daughter?) ". . . will ask her." (That was Tom. Was she the "her"? If so, what was the question?)

"So you're going to go work on a farm," Candace said, to distract herself.

"That's the plan. Was the plan. I'm not really sure."

"Oh?"

"It's complicated. But boy, if you want to get a rise out of people around here, just tell them you're going to work on a farm instead of going to college. Works every time."

"I can imagine," Candace said. She wanted this girl to like her.

"Dad wants me to work at Marcus Bags instead," she said. "In the factory. Like it will, you know, teach me a lesson."

"He does?"

"I mean, he suggested it, but I think it was his way of trying to get me to apply to college. Like I could break my back working on an assembly line for eleven dollars an hour, or I could go to college and, I don't know, read books, smoke weed, and meet boys at the climbing wall and get an allowance from the college fund my parents set up even before I knew how to read."

"You do know that you could read books, smoke weed, and meet boys at the climbing wall even if you did work on an assembly line," Candace said. Then, realizing that she sounded like she was endorsing this idea, said, "But you'd probably be way too tired. Tell me about this farm that you may or may not be working on."

"I don't know much. It's north of the Berkshires, just over the border with Vermont. I've only seen pictures. I applied and they took me right away, so I didn't have to apply to a safety farm." She laughed at her own joke, then looked at Candace to see if she got it. (She'd have to remember to tell Lily.) But Candace didn't seem to hear her.

"Wait a second!" Candace said. "It's not New Moon, is it?"

"You know it?"

"I do. It's not far from Williams, where I went to college. At least when I was there, they had this huge harvest festival in the fall. Lots of us would go to help with the picking, and then there'd be this big communal meal outdoors at night, with music and a bonfire. And in the spring, they'd pay students to sleep in the barn when the lambs were being born. I never did it, but lots of kids did. I mean, that was a long time ago, but if they still have sheep, they probably still do that.

"New Moon," she said wistfully. "Think of that."

CHAPTER TWENTY-ONE

The worst thing about being a high school senior who has not applied to college is not being able to slack off second semester like everyone else. "Colleges are going to look especially hard at your last set of grades," Perry, the guidance counselor, had warned Melody, thinking that it would scare her into submitting at least a couple of applications before it really was too late. "Remember, you can always defer," he said, but Melody had been adamant—if the idea was to jump off the train that she and everyone she knew had been riding since preschool, submitting an application would be like hopping a boxcar and hoping no one noticed. Thanks, but no thanks. On the other hand, the best thing about being a high school senior who has not applied to college was that everyone else was slacking off, and since grades were distributed on a curve, she was rising in class rank like a hot air balloon that had slipped its tether.

"Not that I care about class rank," she told Lily when they spoke on the phone.

"That's admirable, I guess," Lily said, "but actually, that's the sort of thing admissions officers care about. That, and if your parents are going to pay for the new library. Actually, this dude who doesn't even have kids here just gave a gazillion dollars for an esports complex."

"That's brilliant," Melody said. "Expend your capital costs now, assuming the price will go up by the time your so-far-nonexistent

child is old enough to apply to college, knowing that your goodwill will be honored, wink wink, by the university. Really, that
guy has figured out how to game the system. I'm taking AP Econ,
by the way. I like it. Who knew?"

"Noted," Lily said. "Should help you when you're tending the
compost pile on your organic farm."

"Ha ha, very funny. And like I told you, I'm not sure about the
whole WWOOFing thing because, you know, the whole Connor
thing."

The whole Connor thing was not going away. It was living
rent free in her head. Where had she gotten the idea that all boys
thought about when they were not thinking about tossing around
a ball or stuffing their faces with pizza and beer was sex? Probably health class, when their no-nonsense sex ed teacher, Ms.
Romano, told the girls that it was scientifically proven that men
thought about sex every seven seconds. If that was really true,
then going in for that kiss should have been like hitting a bull's-
eye blindfolded. So, either her timing was off and she tried to kiss
Connor in one of the few seconds when he wasn't thinking about
sex, or—and this was the most humiliating part—her timing was
precise.

Melody was enough of her feminist mother's daughter to
know that a woman shouldn't do something just to please a man
or because of a man, and a woman shouldn't let a man dictate her
behavior or compromise her desires, but the honest truth was that
until Connor mentioned the whole farm thing, her only desire
was not to do the thing that Delia wanted most for her, because
she was angry, though she didn't know she was angry. And what
could be worse in Delia's estimation than to skip college to be a
farmhand? But what was she supposed to do now? Be more like
Lily, whose path to greatness, or at least to a solid career, had
been ordained somewhere between being found in a box on a

Chinese bridge and living in the Westchester home of two promi-
nent American doctors, who gave her a real stethoscope, not a toy
one, when she was three? Medicine was Lily's calling, no matter
how much she pretended it was all her parents' idea. Genetics
would be where she would make her mark. She wouldn't be the
kind of geneticist who delivers bad news to prospective parents—
she'd be the kind that discovers new ways of treating the diseases
that all prospective parents fear. And maybe, in the process, she'd
find her way back to the people who had swaddled her in a blanket and left her on that bridge. But unlike her friend, Melody
had no clue what she was going to do with her life, and no clue
how she was going to figure it out. Grown-ups were always telling
children that they could be anything they wanted to be if they
worked hard enough, but what happened when they didn't know
what they wanted? What happened to those kids?

Lily was going to Cancún with her parents over spring
break—another medical continuing education scam, she'd told
Melody, five hours of lectures on innovations in electronic medical records and fifty hours of drinking and scuba and hot tubbing
and learning to tango. So why was Lily texting her now, saying
they should meet up at the Starbucks on Woodhaven at 3:30.
Melody checked the date. Sometimes messages got lost and re-
appeared months later, as if they'd gotten hung up in the cloud
before finally drifting back down to earth, but this one was from
today, and there was an earlier one that she'd missed when she
was at New Moon for a weekend orientation—encouraged by Eddie, who figured that a couple of days of digging in the dirt would
disabuse her of her desire to spend more days digging in the dirt.
The text was a cryptic couple of words: "I'm out." Melody was still
basking in the glow of two days in the spring sunshine, learning
to drive a tractor and planting the corn and tomatoes that in three
months' time she'd be not only harvesting but eating. Her back

hurt and her nails were broken, but there had been something so elemental and sweet about tucking a tiny sprout into the warm earth and knowing she would be around to watch it grow that it didn't matter. Melody tried calling Lily, but it went to voicemail. She waited fifteen minutes, then tried again. "Pick up," she said, but Lily didn't. She checked the time, tried calling once more, then got in her car, perplexed but happy to have her friend home for a few days, eager to tell her about the farm's resident five-hundred-pound pig named Wilbur, who loved spaghetti, and the kitten called Charlotte who followed him everywhere, and how wrong Eddie was. She loved it there.

The Woodhaven Starbucks was almost always empty and a little forlorn, unlike the one near the high school. That one was always jammed, even during school hours, since seniors were allowed off campus when they didn't have class, and everyone else knew it was the easiest place to score weed and Adderall. Woodhaven mostly served women rushing between yoga and their kids' soccer practices, and UPS drivers coming off their shifts or loading up on caffeine before the next one began. Melody pushed open the door just as Lily was ordering her usual, a venti caramel steamer.

"Can you make that two," she called to the barista, who looked to Lily, who nodded before turning around to greet her.

"Oh my God," Melody said. "You cut your hair!" For as long as they had known each other, Lily's perfectly straight black hair was cinched in a ponytail, and she claimed to be envious of Melody's curls, which Melody could never understand. Curls were impossible. They had a mind of their own. When she gathered them behind her head and secured them with a scrunchie, they looked like overcooked fusilli. She had always envied Lily's hair—the way it never frizzed in the summer or lost its shine in the winter. But now the silky ponytail was gone, and what remained of her hair was bowl-shaped, with a fringe of short bangs, as if Lily had gone to the salon and asked for the medieval monk look. "I almost didn't recognize you. What are you doing back here? I thought you were in Mexico, living the good life."

Lily grimaced. "Go grab a table, and I'll wait for the drinks," she said.

"How are you?" Melody said, but Lily, walking toward the pickup counter, pretended not to hear. Or maybe she didn't hear. Lily could be that way: so in her head, working out some quadratic equation or memorizing a formula. Still, this felt different. Something was off.

"So, did Nina and Peter ditch you so they could go to one of their naturalist retreats?" Melody said when Lily sat down. This was her father's playbook: when in doubt, make a dumb joke.

"Naturist," Lily corrected her. "No."

"Did something happen?" Obviously something had happened, that much was clear, since Lily was here, in this mostly deserted Starbucks, with a bad haircut, being distant and weird and not in Cancún, swimming with dolphins (if that was a thing there) and chatting up potential mentors.

Lily was silent, and it took a minute for Melody to realize that she was crying.

"Your caramel steamer is turning into a salted caramel steamer," Melody said, trying again to channel Eddie, because what else was there to do? Lily was her sane, rational friend. She was tough-minded and unsentimental and did not cry, not even during *Titanic* or *Love Actually*, both of which made her laugh out loud at what everyone else thought of as the sad parts. But here she was, head bent, shoulders shaking, quietly sobbing in Starbucks.

"I have to get out of here," Lily said, rising suddenly, grabbing her jacket from the back of her chair.

"Wait, Lil," Melody said, "I'm coming with you," and rushed

out the door two steps behind her friend, leaving their drinks on the table. "What is going on?"

Lily didn't turn around. When she got to her car, she unlocked the doors and Melody slid in and waited for Lily to say something, but she didn't, and she didn't start the engine, either. Instead, she rested her head on the steering wheel like a child napping with her head on her desk.

"Talk to me," Melody said after she counted fifty-two vehicles go by.

Instead of answering, Lily put the car in gear and pulled out into traffic, still saying nothing.

"Where are you going, Lil?"

"Don't know."

"Do you want to go to my house?"

"Not really."

"Yours?"

"No."

"Can you please tell me what's going on?"

Lily, staring intently ahead, accelerated suddenly, and both their heads slammed into the backs of their seats.

"Jeez, Lily, you are going to get us both killed."

"So?"

"So? I don't know if you remember this, but my mother died in a car not that long ago, so could you please slow down. At least long enough to let me out."

"Can't," she said.

"Can't what?"

"Can't let you out."

"First of all, you can, and second of all, you are scaring me. So please slow down and pull over, otherwise I am going to call 911 or your parents or both."

"There's no shoulder."

Melody let out an audible sigh. "That's the most sane thing you've said all afternoon. Just take the next right and we'll find a place to stop.

"There," Melody said when she spied a gas station. "Pull in there," and Lily obeyed.

"Turn off the motor," Melody said. "Good. Now will you please let me know what the heck is going on?"

Lily closed her eyes and took deep, regular breaths, the kind that they teach in meditation class. Her hands were still holding the steering wheel tightly. Her knuckles were white from the pressure.

"I'm not going back to school," she said.

"You don't have to go back. You're on break."

"After break. I'm not going back. I can't."

"What do you mean, you can't? Did someone do something to you? Did someone hurt you?"

Lily started to cry again. "I wish," she said.

"You wish someone had hurt you?" Melody said. "What are you talking about?"

"If I tell you, you are going to hate me," Lily said.

"I am not, one hundred percent, going to hate you. I love you, Lily. You know that. Can you please tell me what's going on."

"What's going on is that I can't go back to Stanford."

"I know. I mean, that's what you said. But why?"

"You are going to hate me."

"You said that, too, but I told you I wouldn't."

"Promise?"

"I promise. Yes."

"Should I believe you?"

"Lily. Stop."

"What they said was that I could finish the semester at home. It's just a couple of papers, but I have to drop chemistry because I won't be able to do the labs."

"You can always do chemistry over the summer. I bet Columbia has a summer session. Or NYU. Or Pace. Is that what you meant when you said 'it's over'? I doubt that is going to prevent you from going to med school."

Lily ran her hand through what was left of her hair. "That's not it. I can't go back because our lab is under investigation for academic fraud."

"But you're the lowest person on the totem pole. You're an undergrad."

"You don't get it. My name was on the paper we wrote. And because my name was on the paper, I'm implicated. It's that simple."

"OK, they'll investigate, find out that you were just washing beakers or something, and you'll be back there next fall. Or you could come with me and we can both pull weeds and feed the chickens."

"I'm a failure," Lily groaned. "End of story."

Melody knew enough not to argue with her friend. Among her many accomplishments, Lily had been a champion high school debater. No matter what Melody said, she'd parry it away and leave Melody without an angle of attack. Best to let Lily say whatever crazy thing she was thinking. Maybe then it would make sense.

"You are a good person, Lil," Melody said.

"Not really."

"I'm not going to argue with you, but you are."

"I lied to you. That's the thing. I lied to you."

"What are you talking about? And what's with the hair?"

"I cut it."

"I can see that. But why?"

"Atonement."

"You're Jewish, Lil. Jews only atone one day a year. Today is not that day."

The old Lily, the Lily before today, would have pounced on this obvious contradiction, a logical fallacy—of course you could atone on more than one day, since she was doing it right now. But this Lily only grunted.

Melody had to pee. Could she trust Lily not to drive away and strand her there if she went inside? "Give me your keys, I have to use the bathroom," she said, and Lily handed them over without comment. Melody didn't even ask if she wanted anything, but before she headed back to the car she bought a king-size bag of peanut M&M's, Lily's favorite, and a pack of Twizzlers, hoping to appeal to her friend's sweet tooth.

"Here," she said, tossing the M&M's into Lily's lap. "Now will you please tell me what's going on? I'm not giving you back your keys until you tell me."

Lily tore open the bag and poured the candy into her mouth till her cheeks ballooned like a chipmunk's. "I may lose my scholarship," she said after a while.

Lily's scholarship was prestigious. It came with a full ride to college and even had a stipend for books and research materials, but for Lily, it wasn't about money: Peter and Nina could afford to send her to Stanford and to medical school and still live a plush life. For Lily it was about being seen, about being recognized and singled out. The list of Cardinal scholars was long and impressive: professors of this and that; a gaggle of Nobels; the Fields Medal, twice; cabinet secretaries, senators, and a Supreme Court justice; a vice president. Lily's hard work in high school had paid off and would continue to pay off. The grown-ups were right: Lily Horowitz-Shapiro would grow up to be whatever she wanted to be.

"Did someone tell you that you were going to lose the Cardinal," Melody said.

Lily shrugged. "They didn't have to." She dumped the rest of the M&M's into her mouth. Melody had seen stress eating before. For weeks after Delia died, all she wanted were chicken McNuggets from McDonald's, the food of her childhood (much to her mother's chagrin), even though people she'd never heard of kept leaving casseroles on their doorstep. She'd gone to the McDonald's drive-through enough times that all the cashiers knew her name. She'd get to the microphone and place her order, and the person on the other end would say, "Melody, is that you?" or "Hi, Melody," until one day, as she was leaving the high school parking lot on her way to McDonald's, she turned around and drove the car back into the student lot, because suddenly she couldn't stand the sight or smell of chicken McNuggets. In science class she had learned that people who were bitten by a particular kind of tick were disgusted by red meat ever after. This was something like that.

"Give me the keys and I'll tell you," Lily said, holding out her palm, which, like her tongue, was stained blue from the candy.

"No funny business," Melody said, though to her ears, her voice and her choice of words could have been Delia's.

Lily told the story in fits and starts. How she was tapped by Dr. Phil to work on his project in the lab within days of getting back to school junior year, because he had been a Cardinal scholar himself, and Cardinals helped Cardinals. At the same time, Cardinal scholars were perpetually overachieving because no one wanted to be the Cardinal who didn't have a named chair or a Pulitzer or whatever the next prize was.

The pressure—not just to succeed, but to prevail—was intense, and Phil felt it acutely. At least, that's what Lily deduced when his deception was discovered. And most shameful to him, it was discovered by one of the no-name computational biologists who were reviewing their paper—"a nobody," Phil called him.

"I don't understand what that has to do with you, or with me, for that matter," Melody said. They had been driving down one cul-de-sac after another, and the houses were getting bigger and increasingly baronial, with gates across their driveways and NO TRESPASSING signs warning that security cameras were placed strategically on the property.

"I'm getting to that," Lily said. "This is hard for me."

Melody handed her a Twizzler. "It's all right," Melody said, but was it? It was almost five and Lily had been stonewalling for over an hour.

"The reason I can't go back is because I think I knew the algorithm was junk, that it was all junk science, and I let him put my name on the paper anyway." She started crying again, and Melody reached over and rubbed her arm.

"Thinking you knew and actually knowing are not the same thing. You had doubts, I get that. But you were in no position to challenge your boss. That's why they call it a hierarchy."

Lily let out a small laugh even as her tears fell. "I don't think that's why they call it a hierarchy."

"OK, fine, but you know what I mean."

"I did bring it up with Phil, and he reminded me that I was a college junior who hadn't even taken an upper-level systems bio class, which was true."

Melody slapped her thigh. "See, what did I tell you. You were in no position to blow the whistle."

Lily looked pained. "Actually, I was. I could have gone to the head of the department. I could have asked to withdraw my name from the paper. I'm just as bad as Phil. I wanted to be known as the youngest person ever to get a citation in *Nature Genetics*. I wanted to be that girl."

"So you were ambitious. Is that so bad?"

"It's bad when your success is predicated on lies and deceptions."

"I get that, but it's not your lies or deceptions. They were Phil's. Your supervisor. What did your parents say? Were they pissed?"

"Peter did his shrink thing and reminded me that just because I was adopted, I didn't have anything to prove and they loved me no matter what—that whole speech. And Nina was livid, but not at me. She said that she and my dad would sue the entire university administration if they didn't let me back in, and maybe they'd sue them for defamation even if they did. Lots of talk about lawsuits. I mean, I hope they don't sue anyone, but it felt good to have them in my corner."

Lily's face was puffy and her eyes were bloodshot, but she had stopped crying and had a look of determination that Melody remembered from the first time they'd gone to the indoor climbing wall when she was nine because Lily wanted to conquer her fear of heights. "The thing is, it wasn't just ambition. I wanted to be known as the girl who was left on the bridge who grew up to make an important scientific discovery, because maybe then the people who left me there would come forward to claim me."

Melody reached over to console her friend, but Lily jammed herself against the driver-side door. "Jeez, Lily," Melody said. "I get why you're upset. I do. I get it. It's messed up. But this whole thing is just a big misunderstanding. They'll figure it out and realize you didn't have anything to do with it and fix it. You'll still be able to go to med school. You'll still get your Nobel Prize—"

Suddenly, out of nowhere, Lily let out a cry so primitive and shrill, not unlike the coyotes Melody sometimes heard at night roaming the neighborhood, that she stopped talking and looked at her friend, whose face was contorted and wrenched.

"Lily," she started.

"Stop," Lily said. "Just stop. You don't get it." And then, more to herself than to Melody, "Why would you get it."

"Lily," Melody tried again.

"You don't understand," Lily said, her voice now drained of affect.

"Then explain it to me," Melody said, unable to hide her exasperation.

Lily chewed on her lower lip. Finally, she said, "The reason I figured out Phil was cheating was because of you. Instead of finding my biological family, I'm pretty sure I found yours."

CHAPTER TWENTY-TWO

The year she took biology, Melody could barely master the vo-cabulary, let alone the concepts, and here was Lily using words like "mitochondrial DNA" and "organelles" and "polypeptides" to explain her finding, and Melody was thoroughly lost. "Lily," she said, interrupting her friend, "this is not science class. I don't care how you figured this out."

Lily took her left hand off the steering wheel and put her thumb in her mouth and began to chew on the nail. "Sorry," she said. "I just thought I should explain how it happened."

"I don't care how it happened."

"You should."

"It feels like you're holding out on me because I come from a family of famous psychopaths. Just tell me."

Lily dangled a red Twizzler from her lips as if it were a ciga-rette. "Remember how you had to spit into six different test tubes? Phil said the reason was that he wanted to test his results against those of the commercial DNA companies. He also said that all of the samples would be anonymous. But that's not what he did. He did give everyone fake names, but they were the same fake names for every company. Then he wrote an algorithm that incorporated all the data he—we—gathered from those companies, to make it seem like his method of DNA analysis was more comprehensive than any of the others." Lily looked over at her friend. "Are you with me so far?"

"I think so."

"Anyway, it was easy to figure out which were your samples because I found his cheat sheet, where he matched every sample to the person who had collected it. I'd gotten five of them, including mine and my parents', and I knew that we were LHS 1 through 3, and number 3 was my dad's because he was the only male among the first three, so LHS 1 and 2 were me and my mom. That left my next two, you and my father's mechanic, a male and female, which meant you were LHS 4 and that guy was five. I looked at my results, and they weren't surprising in any way. But when I looked at yours, I saw there was a match for someone who was probably a second cousin. In genetics terms, that's not so unusual. It means that that person and you share a great-grandparent, but still, it seemed like a big deal to me."

"Okay, so you found out that I have a second cousin out there somewhere? I mean, aren't we all cousins if you go way back?"

"Maybe, but I did some digging, which I should not have done, and found out that your second cousin is related to someone I found on Ancestry.com who is into genealogy and had built out a family tree. And in that family tree, the surname of one of the great-grandparents was Danziger."

"Danziger." Melody closed her eyes. Her body was buzzing. "I don't get it," she said quietly. "That makes no sense. It's got to be some kind of mistake, or fluke. You're sure?"

"I mean, not a hundred percent. It could be a coincidence. I mean, I guess Danziger could be a popular surname."

"Oh God," Melody said. "Do you think Delia's brother got someone pregnant eighteen years ago and left the country and when Delia found out there was a baby—me—she decided to adopt me?"

"Sounds plausible," Lily said.

"Do you think they didn't tell me because they didn't want me to know that my father was, like, a strange cult member?"

"Maybe he doesn't even know Delia and Eddie adopted you," Lily reasoned. "I mean, maybe they thought if he did know, he'd try to claim you and take you back to India and make you join his cult."

"I guess," Melody said.

"Don't be mad at me for digging into this without telling you."

"I'm not mad at you."

"Then what are you?"

It was getting dark, and they had just crossed into Connecticut, and Melody was numb. She had spent so long trying not to care about her biological family, convincing herself that they had not been in a position to take care of her, rather than the alternative: that she was unwanted. But now she was sure. He clearly did not want her. And what if her biological mother was some poor, unsuspecting follower who he dropped as soon as he found out she was pregnant? Or what if she ran away from the group because she didn't want her child to be born into it? If that was true, then Melody could feel grateful to her.

"I'd rather study for the SAT," she said suddenly.

"What?"

"I was just thinking that I would rather have grown up here, you know, as a suburban kid, than in an ashram where my mother was probably part of a harem. What a nightmare." She was suddenly grateful to Delia and Eddie in a way she hadn't been before. Not only had they gotten her out of foster care, they had saved her from a life of hardship and weirdness, though maybe it would not have seemed weird if that's where she'd grown up. Whatever she had imagined her life might have been if she hadn't ended up with Delia and Eddie had coalesced into this. She pulled out her phone and began to type quickly and there he was, Krish (née

Carl) Danziger. True to form, he was wearing a long flowing robe, and his hair, not quite as curly as hers, reached his shoulders. He looked like Jesus. Not Jesus on the cross, but Jesus in that famous painting *The Last Supper*.

"Makes sense," Lily said. She had made a U-turn a few miles back, and they were heading in what looked like the right direction, back toward Woodhaven and Melody's car.

"God, this is bad. My father is my uncle. Or, put another way, my father is my mother's brother. Do you think that's why they didn't tell me?"

"Maybe. They must have had their reasons, right?"

But Melody was only half listening. Instead, she was rehearsing what she would say to Eddie when she got home.

And then she was home, walking through the basement door, still unsure what words to use, looking at the pool table and the carpet on the stairs and the coats hanging in the closet as if she'd never seen them before, thinking about what might have been if not for Delia and Eddie and this home they had made for her. She was grateful, but her gratitude was tinged with resentment: how could they have kept this from her?

Eddie was in the kitchen, padding around, when she walked in. "There you are. I'm thinking of ordering Thai, from that place on Broadway, Garden Thai. How does that sound?"

There was something about his voice—so unencumbered, so normal—that she was gripped by a ferocious, uncontrollable, boiling anger. "I can't believe it. I can't believe you!" she cried out. The timbre of her voice, the unconstrained contempt, startled him.

"I mean, it doesn't have to be Thai," he said slowly, unsure what was happening. As far as he knew, she loved Thai. "Bantam Sushi is always reliable, and you really like their dragon rolls. Or we could go out. Tortellini is probably not too crowded at this hour. You know the suburbs. Everything shuts down by nine."

Was it nine already? Melody looked over at the wall clock. No, it was just after seven. She had been with Lily for nearly four hours, but when she thought back, she could barely remember the first three because the last one canceled them out, canceled out every single thing she thought she knew about her life. All of it, gone.

"Why didn't you tell me!" she demanded.

"But I just did, sweetheart," Eddie said, blindsided by her sudden vehemence.

"About him," she said.

Eddie, who had recently convinced himself that they had reached a workable détente—he making peace with her gap year or gap forever plan, and also withdrawing his intention to sell the house after reading in a used copy of *A Field Guide to Grieving* that it was a mistake to make big life decisions in the first year after a consequential death—was confused. He remembered how volatile she had been just a few years back, but her anger and snark had always been directed at Delia; he remained neutral to both sides of the conflict, like Switzerland.

Now, in the absence of his wife, he was the object of Melody's ire. That much made sense, but it was all that made sense.

"About who?" he said. It occurred to him for one brief second that maybe she was on drugs. He'd heard that drugs could make someone aggressive, then remembered those were steroids taken by athletes with thick necks. She didn't care about sports. Her neck was normal. "What did I do?" His voice was plaintive, submissive. "I don't understand."

"That's rich," Melody said, and stormed out of the room and up the stairs, each footstep meant to sound like an exclamation point and, she hoped, a definitive "fuck you."

Eddie sat alone in the kitchen, picking at the pad Thai he'd ordered because it was Melody's favorite. He'd called up to her, knocked on her door, tried the knob—it was locked—even dialed her number, to tell her that the food had been delivered, but she refused to respond. As he ate, he flipped through the grief hand-book, looking for all the passages about anger. There were a lot of them, but only one about incendiary anger that seemed to come out of nowhere "like a Santa Ana wind," the book said, though it didn't offer any actionable advice beyond sitting it out, the way he imagined the people in California did when they were about to be blasted by gales of desert air. What else could he do? Clearly, he was out of his depth. He tried to channel Delia, but it was hopeless. He waited till midnight, thinking Melody might come down if she got hungry, but finally gave up and went up to bed, knocking on her door again, this time quietly, in case she had fallen asleep, but there was no response.

In her room, Melody rooted around the internet, looking for anything she could dig up about Krish Danziger's cult, or reli-gion, spiritual practice, whatever it was. There wasn't much—the group didn't have a Facebook page or any kind of presence on social media; the few things she found were from parents claiming that their kids had been hoodwinked into handing over their trust funds, or former members explaining why they left. (Three out of the five found the long days of meditation too gru-eling. "Who would have guessed that doing nothing would be so hard," one of them wrote, but praised the food, and the other two liked it well enough but seemed to have gotten bored.) It did not appear to be one of those groups that branded its members, not with hot pokers, anyway—a plus—though Melody wondered if they were branded more subtly, like in their minds. From what Melody could piece together, it seemed as though Krish had risen through the ranks, from a lowly mendicant to the group's business manager and finance chief, obtaining a new name along the way.

MELODY: Putting his Wharton MBA to good use,

Melody texted Lily, who was doing her own research in between apologizing to Melody for wrecking her life.

MELODY: Looks like you took us both down,

Melody typed after the third apology, then thought better of it and deleted the text. Things were bad enough in Lily's world: she didn't need Melody to pile on, too. And was her own life wrecked? She wasn't sure yet. Her origin story was now more colorful, so there was that. And it was not like she had demanded to know who her father was.

Was Krish a good guy? It was hard to tell. Had business school pushed him in the opposite direction of his classmates, who by now were running hedge funds and banks and Fortune 500 companies? But had he really gone rogue if he was now, essentially, the chief financial officer of a multimillion-dollar enterprise—though unlike those other guys, with their Hamptons beach "shacks" and Jaguar XFs, all he had to show for it, she imagined, was an ability to sit in silence for days at a time.

What she was looking for, too, was evidence of a wife and children, her half siblings, but there was nothing. The cult seemed to be one of the ones where everyone was married to everyone else and the children belonged to no one.

The phone rang, and it was Lily. "My thumbs got tired," she said. "So did you confirm with Eddie?"

"We're not talking," Melody said. "Actually, I'm not talking to him."

"My shrink dad would say you're practicing avoidance," Lily said.

"No offense to your dad, but isn't that what not talking to

someone is? Isn't calling not talking to someone 'avoidance' a—
what's that vocab word—tautology?"

"Maybe you should email him?" Lily said.

"My da—Eddie?"

"No. Carl. Krish."

"And what? Say, 'Hi, it's the daughter you abandoned eighteen
years ago'? Or, 'Hi, I'm the child you know nothing about'?"

"Did it ever occur to you that maybe this was planned all
along? Like maybe it was his idea to give you to Delia?"

"Give me?" Melody felt her anger beginning to bubble up.
"Like I was a box of chocolates?"

"Sorry. Sorry," Lily said. "My bad. I knew I shouldn't have
told you."

"Great. And then you'd be just like them."

Melody fell asleep with her laptop on her bed, open to a picture
of Carl Danziger from his pre-India days, when he was a blue-
blazer-wearing business school student with neatly shorn hair and
wire-rimmed glasses. In the morning it was gone, and the black
screen broadcast her own reflection. Weirdly, it seemed to her,
she was no longer angry. The weight she had been carrying the
night before had lifted; she felt lighter. Her bio dad was some not-
exactly-rando guy who ran an ashram in India, which was kind
of interesting, cool even. Cooler than a guy who ran a paper bag
company. It was Sunday, which meant that Eddie would be at the
club, playing golf if the greens were up to it, talking golf if they
weren't. But when she entered the kitchen, there he was, hunched
over his coffee instead of the newspaper, and staring into the cup.
He braced himself for her next onslaught, but it didn't come.

"Where's the paper?" she said. "Did the guy leave it at the end
of the driveway again?"

"Not sure," Eddie said. "I haven't looked yet."

"Would you like me to?" Melody said. She realized that she was suddenly feeling sorry for Eddie for not being her birth father, since every time he looked at her, he was seeing evidence that there was another father out there with a greater claim to her. Why had it never occurred to her before? On the other hand, she told herself, any time she did something he didn't like, he could always chalk it up to that guy's genes. She toasted a piece of seven grain and slathered it with Nutella, thinking how Lily would reason that the sugar in the Nutella would be offset by the whole grains in the bread.

"Can I ask you a question," Melody said, sitting catercorner to Eddie, who was consoled by her temperate tone but a little suspicious, too. It was as if the night before hadn't happened. But it had. A gaggle of chickadees suddenly descended on the feeder that Maria had been filling for years. "Bird TV," Delia called it.

"Where are the finches?" Melody said.

"That's what you want to ask me?" Eddie said. "I think you'd be better off asking the internet."

"No, no. That wasn't the question. I mean, it was a question, but not the one I wanted to ask you. I bet the finches aren't here because of climate change." Her leg was shaking under the table. She took a bite of her toast.

"Maybe," Eddie said. "We've seen some evidence of that with our wood pulp suppliers."

Melody steeled herself. What did they always say in those inspirational sports movies? It was go time. "Why didn't you tell me about him?" she said.

"Who, sweetheart?"

"My father."

"But I'm your father." Reflexively, he put his hand on his chest.

"I mean my"—she stopped herself from saying "real"—"birth

dad." And then, before Eddie could answer, she said, "I know who he is," and quickly explained the Danziger connection Lily had found in her research, and what she herself had discovered about Carl. "Was it that you didn't want me reaching out to him, or were afraid his beliefs would infect me and make all this stuff"—she waved her hands in the direction of the Aga stove and the All-Clad pans hanging from the ceiling rack in height order—"seem wrong?" She was talking fast, her anger reasserting itself and snowballing with each word as it tumbled out of her mouth. "Does this have something to do with that strange woman from his sect who came to the house?"

"What strange woman?" Eddie said.

"With the hair halfway down her back."

He looked at her blankly.

"Doesn't matter. Did you guys fight him for me, is that why I was in foster care? Or didn't he care about me?"

Eddie closed his eyes and tried to remember the breathing techniques for something the grief book called "centering," but found himself hyperventilating instead. He stood up abruptly and took a lap around the prep island, running his fingers along the demi-bullnose edges as he did. Those edges were Delia's idea, of course, because she did her homework and found that they'd show off the grain of the granite more dramatically than a standard bullnose, and he smiled because he remembered that conversation and where they were standing when they had it.

"Why are you laughing?" Melody demanded.

"I'm not laughing."

"Yes, you are!" she said petulantly.

"Well, if it looked that way, I'm sorry," he said. "We didn't tell you because it is not true."

"Then explain Lily's research. Which got her kicked out of Stanford, by the way."

"I'm sorry to hear that," Eddie said. His voice was measured, calm, but his heart was racing and he could feel his throat begin to thicken and his chest felt like someone was standing on it. Was this a heart attack? He thought maybe, and then a fleeting thought: he hoped so. He leaned over, gripping the side of the island to steady himself. The room was spinning. No—he was.

"Are you okay," Melody said.

Sweat was beading on Eddie's forehead and his hands were clammy, and for the first time since Delia's death, anger was rising up in him in a way it hadn't before. It had been so much easier being angry at a rock than at his dead wife, who had left him here, on his own, to do this, but now he was infuriated with her.

Eddie let go, got a glass, and filled it with water from the cooler. "Why do we still have this thing?" he said, more to himself than to Melody, who was so unnerved by her father's behavior that she tried to say something funny—"The cows in the reservoir, remember?"—but as soon as the words were out of her mouth, she realized they sounded like she was making fun of Delia.

Eddie hardly noticed. "Right," he said. "Dead cows," and took a long gulp of water, put the glass down on the countertop, thought better of it, and took another swig. As the cold water ran down his throat, he felt his anger cool, but not the sense of abandonment and not the feeling that he was fundamentally, irretrievably alone.

"I'm OK," he said, though it was obvious that he was not. "I should sit down." But he didn't.

"The genes," Melody prodded him. "The genes don't lie."

"No," he said. "I guess they don't."

CHAPTER TWENTY-THREE

Melody's phone buzzed. She pulled it out of her pocket and read the text. It was from Lily.

> **LILY**: Still sorry. Any news?
> **MELODY**: Getting deets now.

Deets? Does anyone still say that? she wondered after she'd hit send. *Did they ever?*

"Did I ever tell you how your mother and I met?" Eddie said.

"You're procrastinating," Melody said.

"I'm not," he said. "It's relevant," and launched into his story before she had a chance to shut it down. "Shirley Cooperstein," he said. "She made sure everyone knew it was pronounced 'stine,' not 'steen.' She was a friend of Grandma Syl, but she also knew my mother, and I guess she considered herself something of a matchmaker."

Melody was intrigued. "Like it was her side hustle?"

"I guess," he said. "Anyway, one day she calls up my mom and says, 'I know who Eddie should marry,' and tells her about her friend's hotshot-lawyer daughter who was single and between jobs and not seeing anyone."

"Mom was out of work?" This was new.

"She'd left her job," he said.

"So did you call her up?"

"I did," he smiled, remembering how nervous he'd felt. And how silly, calling a woman out of the blue because Shirley Cooperstein thought he and Delia would make a nice couple.

"And then you lived happily ever after until—" Melody blanched at her own words.

"Not at all," Eddie said. "Delia told me she wasn't dating and wouldn't be for the foreseeable future. Honestly, I was relieved. Took the pressure off. We actually had a nice conversation once we got that out of the way. I think she was lonely. So I asked her if I could just call her now and then, and she didn't object, so I did. I'd call and we'd just talk and she laughed at my jokes and after about a month she relented and agreed to meet me for a walk. I had no idea what she looked like, and I was gobsmacked when I finally saw her. Definitely out of my league. But by then I'd hooked her on my charm." He laughed. "Not really. I think she felt safe with me. Not a creep." He chuckled. "It was a low bar. We invited Mrs. Cooperstein to the wedding. She gave a toast."

"What did she say?"

"It was something like, 'I've got five words for you: when you know, you know.' And then she wagged a finger at us, and everyone clapped." He paused, then added, "It was a small wedding."

They were both quiet then, and Eddie, cosseted by these memories, felt his heart revert to its usual steady rhythm. Delia had always been beautiful to him. In the beginning he was certain that someone so lovely would wake up and see him for who he was: a balding Mr. Nice Guy, the sort of man a woman like her might decide was too nice, too bald, too unlikely to be her date (retrospectively) to the senior prom. It took him a while to realize that Delia didn't see herself as she really was, didn't believe that she was beautiful. Maybe at one time she did, but he hadn't known her then, and whenever he told her she was, Delia would screw up her face or shake her head and tell him he needed new glasses. Sometimes she'd accuse him of being interested in her only because she was pretty—"not because I am pretty," she'd say, "but because *you think* I'm pretty." He'd protest but realized that there was a kernel of truth to it. It made him feel good about himself to step out with her on his arm, so sometimes, when she said this, he would envision her at forty or fifty years old, gray haired, no longer svelte, with crepey skin—the "will you still love me tomorrow" test, and realized that yes, he would.

"Dad," Melody said. "Did you even hear me?"

Eddie looked in her direction and was surprised to see his beautiful daughter, not his beautiful wife. "What? No. Sorry. What did you say, sweetheart?"

"I said that I'm still confused. If Mom's brother is not my father, are there other Danzigers that I don't know about? Someone in prison. Or like a complete loser black sheep?"

Eddie appeared to consider this. "Not that I know of. I mean, I suppose it's possible."

Was he going to lie? Take the easy way out?

"But wouldn't you know? I mean, how much of a coincidence would it be—I mean, what are the odds that you and Mom just happened to adopt a child who is genetically related?" She was standing now herself, with her hands on her hips and an expression on her face that was either curious or accusatory—Eddie couldn't tell which, but knew it didn't matter.

"Let's go for a drive," he said. This was Delia's trick in those eye-rolling years when it was so hard to get their moody teenager to communicate. Maybe it was the calming motion of the car, as if she was a baby with colic, but more likely it was because they were locked in a small space with nowhere to go.

"No," Melody said. "I'm tired of being in the car. I spent hours driving around with Lily yesterday."

"Yes," Eddie said absently. "Do you want another piece of toast?"

"Dad!"

Eddie sighed, defeated. "Come," he said, and walked out of the kitchen and into his den. Melody followed and flopped down on the couch. Her father was acting strange—so strange. She didn't know what to make of it—or him—but his strange behavior was infecting her. That's what it felt like. Like he had a communicable disease that he was passing on to her, a sickness they would share.

Eddie sat down next to her. "Give me your hand," he said. It wasn't an order, it was a plea, and she wasn't having it.

"Why?" Melody said.

He said nothing, just held his own hand out, and reluctantly she slipped hers into the familiar pocket of his flesh. When she was little, when they had first met, he'd held out his hand and she grabbed onto his thumb—he could still remember how strong her grip was and how attached he felt, and how he knew then that this day, this instant, was inevitable. And then he put it out of his mind, telling himself that it was Delia's story to tell, that he was just a bit player, which was not untrue, up to a point. Of all the things she'd left behind, this was the one thing he couldn't donate to Goodwill or give her friends or deposit in the bank.

"Sit down," Eddie said.

"I am sitting down," Melody said. "You are sitting next to me. We are holding hands."

"Right," he said. "Sorry." He took two deep breaths, exhaling slowly after each one. "I always imagined that this would be a conversation between you and your mother," he began. He was choosing his words carefully, and wondered if the possessive, the "your," had registered with her, but if it had, she didn't let on. He took another long drink of air, yawning on the exhale. If he could, he'd go back to bed right now. "It starts a long time ago, before I knew her." He was squeezing Melody's hand with such force she tried to wrest it away from him.

"You're hurting me," she said.

"Sorry," he said and let go.

"Your mother," he tried again. "You mother was a lawyer."

"Yada yada yada. Columbia Law School. Top of her class. Law Review. The next Ruth Bader Ginsburg. I know all this."

"She was hired right out of school by Karp, Silverstone, and Thorpe, one of the best corporate firms in the city. She'd worked there for two summers, they loved her, put her on the fast track for partner. Her plan was to work there for a couple of years, then clerk for a district court judge, then RBG if all went well, and then decide what she wanted to do with her life. She was a star, or a rising star. Those places are incredibly competitive, and you know her, she thrived in a competitive environment. Remember that tennis tournament—"

"Dad!"

"OK, sorry. I was just remembering the time she trounced that braggart at the club who started calling her Billie Jean King after she walloped him. Anyway, she was so good at her job that they gave her a lot of responsibility, which meant she was working all the time and didn't have much of a life outside of the firm. One of the senior partners took her under his wing, an older guy who'd already had a storied career—he did clerk for RBG, but when she was on the Court of Appeals—and was incredibly well connected. He made sure she got good assignments and made her second chair for a lot of his cases, which meant they were spending a lot of time together, and I guess one thing led to another and—do you know what I'm saying?" He looked at his daughter, who was ever-so-slightly shaking her head.

"I'm not dumb," she said.

"What your mom told me was that she fell under his spell and—"

"Oh, come on! That is so lame."

"I'm just telling you what she told me," he said. "She thought she was in love with him and saw a future together, except that he was married, and when he wasn't at work he had a whole married life. No kids, though. Not his thing, he told her. He also told her that he was going to leave his wife, that they'd grown apart, had different interests, that whole thing."

She remembered Delia telling her that rom-coms were about hope, since they had reliably happy endings, and her affection for even the dopiest, unlikely ones suddenly made so much sense.

"They talked about opening their own firm one day or transferring to the Paris office and getting an apartment overlooking the Tuileries. She was twenty-nine, thirty, thirty-one. And then it all fell apart and she got fired."

"Seriously?" Melody said derisively. "I thought she was supposed to be so smart."

Eddie was relieved. Maybe this wasn't so hard after all. "So you get it, right?" He leaned back into the bolster and felt the muscles in his neck slacken and his head fall forward, as if he was praying, and in a way he was, to Delia, who, he was now certain, was guiding him.

"Earth to Eddie," Melody said to Eddie, who had spaced out again. "Look, I get that she had an affair with her married boss and it wrecked her career. Even I could have told her that it wouldn't end well."

"Yes, I'm sure you're right. But it wasn't all bad. I mean, she met me," he said, smiling at the memory, "and"—he girded himself—"you."

Now she was confused. "Me? What do I have to do with it?"

Eddie said nothing, just looked at his daughter, bracing himself.

Suddenly—it really was like a lightbulb turning on, he thought—her face seemed to rearrange itself in a way he'd never seen, as the muscles of knowing competed with those of disbelief. "No," she said. "No, no, no. Are you fucking kidding me? Are you fucking kidding me?" She pounded the couch with her fist. "Fuck you. And fuck her. Fuck her especially. You are fucking liars."

Eddie recoiled. "I don't think anyone explicitly lied to you," he said. "I mean, you always said you didn't want—"

She cut him off. Her body was overcome by an anger so lit she felt as though she was burning from the inside out. "You lied to me. She lied to me. My fucking life is one big fucking lie! You know what? I'm glad that she's dead. Maybe there is a God after all. She fucking deserved to die."

"Your mother loved you," Eddie said to her retreating back, as she ran out of the room and up the stairs.

"Well, she had a fucked-up way of showing it," Melody called down to him, and slammed the door to her bedroom.

Eddie, defeated, just sat there. And then he began to cry.

Even in her room, Melody could hear Eddie sobbing. Keening, really, and she wanted to open the door and tell him to shut up: this was her tragedy, not his. She flopped down on the bed and then, instead of crying herself, she began to laugh.

How fucked up was this? Her mother was . . . her mother. Now what? She wanted to interrogate Delia. She wanted to shake her. Ask her what she was thinking. Ask her how she could let her own child live in limbo when the truth was right there. But there was no one to ask, no one to shake. This person, this stranger who had given her life, was nowhere and everywhere. And for the first time since Delia had died, she began to weep violently, the tears coming from a well deep inside her that had been waiting to be tapped all along. They were tears of loss, but that was not how they felt. They were the tears of a toddler, thwarted and frustrated not to have the words to express how she was feeling, because those words did not exist.

She must have fallen asleep, still in her clothes. The phone in her pocket was vibrating. She looked. It was a text from Lily.

LILY: Meet up later?

Melody turned off the phone and rolled over and put a pillow over her head. It was dark out. The house was quiet. She imagined Eddie was still in the den, feeling sorry for himself, and she wanted to drop some books, make some noise, so he would come upstairs and she could tell him to go away. But she was exhausted and slipped off her jeans and crawled under the covers and waited for the world to fall away. In the extracurricular Wednesday-night Intro to Philosophy class for Westchester high achievers that Delia had signed her up for in her junior year because it was taught by a professor from SUNY Purchase and she'd get college credit, they learned that Kant thought reality was unknowable, and now she wished it was true. When some boy, who made it a point to wear his father's faded Princeton T-shirt to class each week, proclaimed that there was no way to disprove Kant's assertion, the professor removed his suit jacket, rolled up his left sleeve, and read off the numbers etched crudely into his skin. That was the image in her mind as she drifted off.

It was still dark out when she heard Eddie knocking, and before she could tell him to go away, he was in her room, backlit from the hall light.

"You need to leave," she said, but he didn't.

"Mellie," he began, but she cut him off.

"I don't want you here," she said. It was odd. She could hear herself talking, but the words sounded far away, and the voice was unrecognizable. For a second she wondered if she was dreaming, if this whole thing was a dream, but then he reached out and touched her foot through the blanket and she knew it was not.

"I came to apologize," he said softly.

"That's rich," Melody said. "Or should I say 'wealthy'?"

"Look," he said. "I understand that you are angry and upset. I *know* why you are angry and upset. It wasn't my idea—"

"What wasn't your idea? Lying to me? Also, way to go, blaming a dead person. How convenient."

"The thing is, was," he went on, "it was your mom's story to tell. It's mine now, obviously, and I wish more than anything that it wasn't, but I'll tell it to you whenever you are ready." He turned and quickly left the room before she could reject the offer. She jumped up and locked the door.

The problem was that as curious as she was about her origins—not left on a bridge on the other side of the world like Lily, but the product of a cliché—she didn't want to give her father, who now felt more like her "real" father than Delia felt like her "real" mother, the satisfaction. She needed him to know—actually, she didn't know what she needed him to know. That her life was one big, fat lie? Obviously he knew that already, and had always known it. And so had Delia. Melody had never been more furious with her. No—furious was too mild. How she wished Delia was there so she could say all the hateful things to her. How she wished to make her mother feel so bad she'd want to be crushed by a rock. It wasn't fair. It wasn't fair *to her* that Delia was not there. And as that thought crossed her mind, she realized that she missed her mother. Maybe she had always missed her mother. And that thought pierced her anger and let loose another torrent of tears.

CHAPTER TWENTY-FOUR

She must have fallen asleep again, because a sound she couldn't quite identify roused her. It was like hammering, but not quite hammering, and seemed to be coming from the hall. And then, suddenly, her bedroom door was being lifted from the hinges, and there was Marcia Yandel, striding into her room and pulling up the window shades.

"Don't ask," Marcia said. "When you live with boys, you learn all the tricks. Okay, missy, sit up, sit up."

Melody went to pull the covers over her head, but Marcia was quicker. "All the tricks," she said, grabbing the blanket, which she didn't let go as she sat down on the edge of the bed.

"What do you want?" Melody said.

"What do I want?" Marcia repeated. "I want you to sit up."

"Why?" Melody said petulantly.

"Why? What are you, three years old?"

Actually, she did feel like she was three years old, and the world was confusing and scary. "Wait a minute," Melody said, as it suddenly dawned on her. "Did you know, too? Did Danny? Was I the last person to know?" She groaned and turned over. This whole thing was getting worse.

"For the record, I did not know until last night when your father called, and no, Daniel does not know."

"Why did Eddie call you?" Melody said into her pillow.

"You'll have to ask him."

"I'm not talking to him."

"So I gathered," Marcia said.

"Go away. Just go away."

"All in good time," Marcia said.

"He's not going to marry you," Melody said, turning on her side, with her back to Marcia.

"Who's not going to marry me?"

"Eddie Marcus, the paper bag king. He thinks you're bossy."

"First of all, I have no interest in marrying your father, and second of all, if I had to guess why he called me, it's because I *am* bossy. When you are a single woman raising two children, you have to be bossy. Goes with the territory.

"Look," Marcia said, her voice softening, "I am pretty hurt by your mother, too. I thought we were good enough friends that she would have confided in me. It made me wonder what I had done to make her distrust me. But when I was in the shower this morning"—Melody tried to rid herself of the image of a naked Marcia Yandel and what she imagined were copious folds of shar-pei-ish skin rolling down her belly and over her hips—"I realized that it probably had nothing to do with trust. What your dad told me was that she wanted to tell you before she told anyone else."

"But she didn't tell me," Melody said. "She lied to me. She lied," Melody repeated.

"Maybe," Marcia said. "I don't know if a sin of omission is worse than a sin of . . . what's it called?" Her voice trailed off.

"Commission," Melody said. This was another thing the SUNY professor talked about. His example of omission: ordinary Germans during the Holocaust who did nothing. "Doesn't matter," Melody said, remembering his lecture and paraphrasing it. "Omission, commission, they have the same effect."

"Be that as it may," Marcia said, and before she could finish her thought, Melody burst out crying again, and she didn't know if it was the thought of all those people, murdered because of their lineage, or because her own lineage had been denied to her. The cruelty felt unbearable. "Come here," Marcia commanded, and moved herself closer to the girl. "Just come here." Melody turned over and Marcia slid her hands under Melody's arms and lifted her up, and before she knew it, she was sobbing into Marcia Yandel's ample chest, and she didn't care. It felt safe to be there.

"I knew your mom for close to twenty years," Marcia was saying as she gently rocked back and forth. "She saw me through some pretty dark times. If there is one thing I knew about her and still do, it's that she was a very good person who loved you with every fiber in her being. She wasn't perfect, who is?"—reflexively, between sobs, Melody thought *Danny*—"but she never would have intentionally done something to hurt you. That wasn't who she was. My guess is that she let it get away from her, and the longer she didn't tell you, the harder it got."

"But it doesn't matter if she didn't mean to," Melody said plaintively. "She didn't tell me. Nothing else matters."

She expected Marcia to argue with her, to take Delia's side, but all she said was "OK," and for a long time they just sat with that thought—at least Melody did. Delia had withheld a crucial thing about her identity, and that was unconscionable, and the strange thing was, knowing more about herself meant knowing less about the woman who raised her. Who was she, really?

As if reading Melody's mind, Marcia, who still had Melody in her embrace, said, "Another thing, and this justifies nothing, but she was probably embarrassed. Parents want their kids to look up to them. They don't want their shortcomings exposed. They want to be the hero of the story, not the villain or even the putz. We all have secrets, every one of us. I doubt she would have kept this a secret forever, but then—"

"But then she died," Melody said, finishing Marcia's sentence. "So you're also saying 'blame it on the rock,' just like my father."

"Not at all. I'm saying that every parent makes mistakes. Some are small, some are huge. Someday, if you have children, you will know this and hope to God your children will forgive you for screwing up. It's your right to be angry at your mom for the rest of your life, and your dad, too. But what kind of life would that be?"

"Can I ask you something?" Melody said, wiping her face and blowing her nose with a tissue that had appeared magically in Marcia's hand.

"Of course."

"How did you get the door open?"

Marcia gave her an enigmatic smile. "Something else you'll learn when you're a parent. OK, it's time for you to get up and wash your face and brush your hair. I'll wait here. Then we are going to go downstairs, and you are going to talk to your father."

Melody knew better than to protest.

They found Eddie in the kitchen staring into space, a half-eaten muffin and a cup of coffee on the table in front of him. He was unshaven, and the circles under his eyes were so dark he looked like he had been punched. When he saw Melody walking in behind Marcia, he looked frightened, but gave a half smile and said nothing.

"Over there," Marcia said to Melody, and pointed to the chair opposite her father. "Hungry?"

She nodded yes. She was starved. So far, neither she nor Eddie had uttered a word.

"Speak," Marcia ordered. It reminded Melody of when she was trying to teach Rowdy to bark on command, which turned out to be a lost cause.

"I'm sorry," Eddie said softly.

"Good," Melody said stridently. And they lapsed back into silence.

"You need to go shopping," Marcia said, standing in front of the open refrigerator. She pulled out a nearly-empty carton of eggs, some butter, and the last rasher of bacon. They both watched her work, scrambling the eggs, frying the bacon, toasting two slices of bread.

"What is this, *Top Chef*?" Marcia said when she felt their eyes on her back. "Talk to each other. It's not that hard. Use your words."

But it was hard. Even Marcia had to know that. When the eggs were set, the bacon was crisp, and the toast had popped, she buttered the bread, put it all on a plate, and handed it to Melody, who had hardly finished saying "thanks" before she took the first bite. She couldn't remember the last time she had eaten.

"Okay, kids," Marcia said jauntily, putting the pans in the sink to soak. "My work here is done," and with that, she walked out the door, leaving the two of them alone, and in silence.

It was Eddie's move, Melody decided, and after a while he seemed to think so, too. "I'm sorry," he said.

"You said that already," Melody said. She was not going to make this easy for him.

"Right," Eddie said. "I suppose I will never be able to say it enough. I also suppose that maybe it doesn't mean much to you. My apology," he clarified.

Melody considered this as she chewed her toast. She did want him to be sorry. No—she wanted him to be more than sorry, but she wasn't sure what more than sorry was. Repentant? Self-flagellating?

"So, he was a jerk?" she said.

"Who?"

"My—" she hesitated and then said, "real father."

Eddie flinched. "I don't know. I mean, maybe. But your mother didn't think so. I mean, obviously."

"Until she did," Melody said. "Obviously."

"I guess so," Eddie said. He was trying to tread lightly, unsure where the traps lay that could set her off or make things worse. "Never met the guy."

"The guy," Melody repeated. "My father." But even she knew that just because a man contributed half her DNA, it didn't actually make him her "father." Something they emphasized at adoption camp.

"By the way, why did you send me to adoption camp if I wasn't really adopted?"

Eddie sighed. "The social worker suggested it. Because you had been in foster care. Delia—your mom—she'd been fighting for you for so long, but then when the court finally said we could bring you home, she—we—realized we had no idea what we were doing. We were new parents, but you weren't a new baby, and we figured the social worker knew more about this than we did. She thought it would be helpful, ease the transition. For all of us."

"That's dumb," Melody said. "Also, why was I in foster care in the first place? It makes no sense."

Eddie sighed again. Under the table his leg was shaking, and his left hand was resting on his right forearm, holding it steady. "So you want me to tell you the whole story," he said. It wasn't a question, it was more like a resignation.

Melody nodded. There was part of her that wasn't sure—the part that never wanted to know—but that part of her was overwhelmed by the other part, the part that had to. "Before you start, I mean, do I have any, you know, like, half siblings?"

"No," Eddie said. "That was part of it. He never wanted to have children."

"Didn't anyone tell him about vasectomy?" Melody said.

"You'd have to bring that up with him," Eddie said. "But you can't. He died seven or eight years ago. Heart attack, I think."

"Convenient," Melody said. "So now I'm an orphan."

"That is one hundred percent not true," Eddie said with a vehemence that surprised them both.

"Sorry," she said quietly. "I apologize. That was unfair."

"Accepted," he said. He broke off a small piece of muffin but didn't put it in his mouth. "Remember," he said, rolling it between his thumb and index finger, "this is secondhand. I met your mom after all this happened."

"I know," she said, though in fact, she didn't. That was the point. This was all new to her.

Eddie crumbled the muffin, fingered another bit, and made another little ball. He'd never smoked, but found himself craving a cigarette, just to have something to do with his hands. Melody was looking at him intently. An internal alarm was buzzing inside them both: the time had come.

"What she told me was that when she found out she was pregnant, she was thrilled. She assumed he would be, too," Eddie began. He wanted Melody to know, unequivocally, that she'd been wanted, no matter what. "He'd finalize the divorce that he'd told her many times he was going to get, and she'd have the baby, and they would live happily ever after. Except that when she told him she was pregnant, he told her to 'take care of it.'"

"Me," Melody said. "He meant me."

Eddie nodded. "Your mom was confused, and devastated, but remember, she was also a very talented litigator, and I guess she thought she could convince him to change his mind. But of course he was a much more seasoned litigator than she was, and when it became clear to him that she was not going to quote, unquote take care of it, she was summoned to the managing partner's office and told that if she signed an NDA—you know, a piece of paper that said if she never talked about her affair with the senior partner, who, it turned out, was not separated from his wife and not planning on getting a divorce—she'd get a generous severance. But if she didn't sign, she'd get nothing. The managing partner also told her that if she ever tried to contact the senior partner or any member of his family, she would be on the hook for the severance money. So she signed, and then they fired her. She left the firm and tried to get another job, but no one would hire her, either because she was pregnant or because her firm had blackballed her or both. She had the money they'd given her, so it wasn't like she was going to be homeless. But somewhere along the line she decided to have the baby, put it up for adoption, and move on with her life."

"Me," Melody said again. "We're still talking about me."

"Yes," Eddie confirmed, as if she had been asking a question. "I met Delia not long after you were born. As you know, she was the most beautiful woman I'd ever seen, and so, so smart. She told me what had happened right away. I think it was either to scare me away or see what kind of guy I was. She was depressed, but she was also on a mission. She wanted you back the second she met you. She realized she had made the biggest mistake of her life, agreeing to the adoption before she pushed you out into the world. The law was very strict, but it had a tiny amount of wiggle room. I had lost my brother not long before that, so I think I had some idea of how bereaved she was. I couldn't get him back, but I told Delia that I would help her get you. It took years. It was a fight, and the state put you into foster care while it was going on. You should have seen her in court. She was spectacular. The day we were finally able to get you home was the happiest day of our lives. She loved you so much, and by then, so did I."

"Then why didn't she tell me?"

"That she loved you? She told you all the time."

"No—that she was my real mother."

"Because she was your real mother either way."

Melody felt the anger rise in her again. It would be dormant for a minute or two, and then reignite and consume her, its embers fanned by Eddie's words. Eddie's ridiculous, self-serving words. "Really? That's it? That's all you've got? 'My mother was my mother either way'? Do you know how lame that sounds?"

Eddie closed his eyes and grimaced. "Now," he said quietly. "I do now." He pushed his glasses up his nose, and then, head bent, massaged his forehead. "I guess I believed, like she did, that love was enough." His voice was barely audible. Like he was talking to himself.

"No!" Melody said, shaking her head. "Just no!" Eddie raised his head and they locked eyes. It reminded her of the staring contests they'd had when she was little. But instead of waiting for him to blink, she was daring him not to look away. "Not what you believed. What you *wanted* to believe."

"I'm sure you're right," he said, hanging his head again. "But we didn't see it."

"Because you didn't want to," Melody said, not giving up.

"Probably not," he conceded, and then, unable to help himself, he looked up and smiled at his daughter. Her tenacity so reminded him of Delia. Delia could talk her way out of a paper bag—as he, the paper bag king, knew better than anyone.

"What?"

"It's nothing," he said, treading carefully. But it was not nothing. She may not have gotten her mother's hair or her eye color or her tendency to talk with her hands, but the way Melody was prosecuting this argument—that was all Delia. And he knew better than to tell her so. Maybe some other time, but not now.

He laced his fingers together and rested his chin on his knuckles, thinking. "Like I said," he began, "we didn't know anything. The social worker told us that you'd been through a trauma and that you were too young to understand and that it would confuse you and that what we needed to do was love you and establish that you were secure, and that you would tell us when you were ready to know. In retrospect that was terrible advice, because you told us that you didn't care or you didn't want to know, and the longer we didn't tell you, the more complicated it got. After a certain point there was never going to be a good time. And," he said, cutting her off before she could protest, "I know that is not a good excuse, or any excuse, really.

"The thing is," Eddie continued. "The thing is, your mom was a really good person. She didn't mean for this to happen. It just got away from her. From us. I don't want you to think she meant to hurt you. Quite the opposite."

"Omission," Melody said, thinking of her conversation with Marcia. "It was a sin of omission."

"She was a good person," he said again. What did the Christians say? Hate the sin, love the sinner. He had loved Delia so much. He took a deep breath and then another, exhaling slowly each time. "But I'm not so sure about myself."

"You?" Melody said. Everyone loved Eddie Marcus. He was a stand-up guy, a guy who gave twenty-dollar bills to homeless people on the street. He was the walking, talking definition of a good person. It was something Melody had always known about him.

He sighed and looked away. "I was a coward."

"A coward," she repeated. "What do you mean?"

"What I mean is," he said, then hesitated, not sure he wanted to say it out loud or admit it, even to himself. "What I mean is, I could have told you myself." He added after a beat, "But I didn't."

Melody was skeptical. "I thought you said it was her story to tell?"

"It was, but I could have told you anyway. What did you just call it? A sin of omission?"

She scrunched up her face. "And go against her wishes?" This was revisionist history. He was never going to go against Delia's wishes. And the reality was, he hadn't.

Eddie didn't seem to hear her. "I'm the bad person because—" he stopped talking.

"Because," she prompted him.

"Because it wasn't just that I didn't tell you. It's that, if I'm being honest, there was a part of me that didn't want you to know. Because if you knew, then you would think you had one real parent and one, I don't know, lesser parent. I was scared of that."

"But I'd never think that," Melody said.

"You don't know that," Eddie said.

"Neither do you," she countered. Melody looked at Eddie, this man who had always loved her, even before he knew her. Maybe he was right, maybe he was wrong. She hoped he was wrong. He had tears in his eyes, and without thinking, Melody reached across the table and put her hand over his.

"I'm still really angry," she said.

Eddie put his free hand on top of hers. "I know," he said. "You should be."

"I don't know when I won't be."

"Understood."

CHAPTER TWENTY-FIVE

Before Paul proposed to Noah, there was something he needed to do first. "I have to ask you something," he said to Candace, trying to sound casual and nonchalant as he stood at the toaster, his back to her. She was in her usual Sunday morning sweats, but he had dressed up in a button-down shirt and khakis, because this was serious. Noah was in the city—Candace was grateful that he never tried to insert himself into their Sunday morning ritual, though maybe he was happy to have some alone time—and Tom was at the marina, working on the boat. In a few weeks, after Candace walked out of DataStream for the last time and into a future that was largely uncertain, they were going to sail up the Saint Lawrence River and around New Brunswick so Candace could get her sea legs. If all went well, if she could master the knots and all the comings about, their next trip would be longer. A nautical map was spread out on Tom's dining room table, with unintelligible notes penciled in here and there. He wanted to sail to the Azores, and from there to Portugal, and finally to Scotland, where Izzy, Fergus, and Winston had relocated to help Fergus's mother. It would be a long trip, and probably a hard one, but Angela, ever hopeful, told her it would be a stress test for their relationship, "like what the cardiologist makes you do on the treadmill," after which, she predicted, they'd be finishing each other's sentences.

"Noah's okay," Candace said, blowing on her coffee. It was meant to be a question, but it came out sounding like a statement.

"I know," Paul said, just as the toast popped. "Tell me about it." And then, turning to face her, he said, "I'm going to ask him to marry me"—he put his hand up to stop her from speaking—"not for a while, but you may be gone when I do, and I want to ask you in advance for your blessing." He averted his eyes and started to butter his bagel with quick, stabbing strokes. "Like I said, it won't be anytime soon. First I need to be sure he'll say yes."

"He'll say yes."

"You don't know that."

"I know how he looks at you," Candace said. She broke into a wide grin. "Though maybe he's just ogling your hot body."

Paul groaned. "That's what worries me." He looked frightened, like he'd lit the fuse to a firecracker, but it had not yet exploded and was still in his hand. "So, will you?" Paul said.

Candace took the measure of her friend. Sometimes she forgot just how handsome he was. They had always made a good-looking couple, the two of them. She didn't even have to try—all eyes were always drawn to him. She'd miss that. He wasn't just asking her to give his blessing to the marriage, but also to the dissolution of their long-standing partnership. He needed her to tell him it was all right—good, even.

"You do realize that it is a little unusual, asking your straight female friend if you can marry your boyfriend."

"Not unusual," Paul said. "We're family."

Candace stood up, walked over, and pulled him into a tight hug. "Of course you have my blessing."

"Look at us," he said, holding her shoulders. "Me and Noah. You and Tom. It's like we've finally grown up."

"Speak for yourself. I'm a homeowner," she said. "I'm a certifiable adult."

"Certifiable, in any case," he said.

"Very funny. Maybe we're regressing"—Paul began to protest, but Candace shook her head—"Hear me out. It's not like we grew up in a war zone, but—"

"Speak for yourself, sister," he said. "You try growing up gay in the house of a raging homophobe."

"I get it," she conceded, "but maybe you are becoming the person you would have been if you didn't have to defend yourself all the time."

Paul considered this. In the war of wills he'd been born into, he had to be stronger and more tenacious than his father, but that fight was over. He had won. He was in love with Noah, and he wanted the whole wide world to know. "I guess so," he said.

"Not a guess," she said firmly. As for herself, she liked Tom despite herself.

"You need to get out of your own way," Angela had told her more than once, but it was not so easy. She was her parents' collateral damage and had spent years convinced that she was better off because of it—that it had made her tougher, self-reliant, invulnerable. But what if that was not true? What if a man, falling through the ice to rescue a dog, had already proved her wrong?

"I want to amend what I said," Candace said. Paul raised his eyebrows. "About my blessing. I mean, it's not a quid pro quo, but if I'm giving you my blessing, I would like to walk you down the aisle."

"I thought that was a given," Paul said, letting out a breath he hadn't realized he was holding. "But you know you won't be giving me away, right? You're stuck with me till death do us part and all that." He swallowed hard, bit the inside of his cheek, and squeezed the bridge of his nose, but the tears came anyway.

It was hard to hate Eddie Marcus. Even when Melody was resentful and enraged, even when her anger and resentment came on like a summer thunderstorm, she couldn't hate him. Delia, though, was another story. Delia had done something that felt unforgivable. But it was strange. All the adoption stories she'd ever heard were about children finding out that one of their parents wasn't their biological parent, or that the reason they felt uncomfortable in their family was because they were not related by blood, or that somewhere in the world was a twin who had been ripped away from them. Delia had turned the whole adoption narrative upside down. This might have made it easier to forgive her, but so far, after weeks of sitting with her betrayal, it hadn't. When Melody was little and someone did something hurtful, like cutting ahead of her in line or calling her names, her mother would always tell her that she could choose to use the experience as a lesson in how not to treat other people. At the time, it was only marginally consoling, though she got the whole "do unto others" point. But the only takeaway she was getting from Delia's deception was that trust is brittle; even if it could be repaired—which was doubtful—the cracks would always be visible.

"Who discovers that their adoptive mother is actually their birth mother?" Lily marveled when Melody told her. "You are a unicorn!"

"Why is that a good thing?" Melody said. "It doesn't feel that way." Her mind would wander to Delia, to images of her, to things they had said to each other, to the ways she had pushed Delia away, rejected her some of the time, even when they mirrored each other, finding the same things funny, liking the same dumb movies, and the times they had argued over clothes and school. The big looming question, the one that could reduce her to tears at any moment, was: Would she have treated Delia differently if she had known? The answer was unknowable, and when she thought of Delia now, her anger was tinged with remorse.

"It feels like I'm going through all those Kübler-Ross stages of grief all over again. Half the time I'm furious at my mother, and half the time I'm just so sad," she told Lily. "And I don't know if I'll ever accept it. And then I think that that doesn't even matter. It's not like I can go back in time."

"Maybe that's what acceptance is," Lily said quietly. She had gotten word that the university would be taking her back in the fall, that her scholarship was safe, and that what the dean was calling "this unfortunate incident" would not appear anywhere in her record. (Dr. Phil had been "relieved" of his appointment.) It would be like the whole thing hadn't happened. In a few weeks, she and her parents would be going to China, to the orphanage where they'd first met, and to the bridge in Chengdu where she'd been discovered. "I guess it's the season for parental apologies," Lily said. They were sitting on Melody's bed as Maria's husband, who sometimes did odd jobs for the Marcuses, was installing a new bedroom door. Marcia's "trick" had damaged the old one.

"Peter and Nina told me that they sort of felt responsible for what had happened to me at Stanford, and that they didn't realize the pressure I was under to, you know, excel. Which is a little strange, since Peter is this hotshot shrink and should have been on top of this. They said they thought they were following my lead, when in fact I was following theirs. They asked me if I wanted to take some time off from school, maybe go with you to the farm."

Melody perked up. "Do you? Would you?" Eddie had dug out a box full of Delia's overalls from college, which she thought was his way of giving the plan Delia's approval, and Tom and Candace told him to tell her that they'd stop by when they were driving to Canada to meet up with their boat hauler, but having Lily there would be a relief. "We can milk the cows together."

Lily laughed. "I love you, but not that much. I remain happy not to know where my food comes from."

"Fair," Melody said.

"Speaking of your career as a lady farmer, what do you hear from the boy?"

"Connor? He'll be at Danny's graduation party. It will be strange to see him, but I don't even feel like the same person I was the last time we were together. That's what I tell myself, anyway." The party was two weeks away, in the Yandels' backyard. Marcia had rented a tent and hired locavore caterers, and Danny's band was going to play while his girlfriend, Lark, the one with the safety pin through her eyebrow, freestyled. Lark had gotten into Harvard Medical School, which pleased Marcia almost as much as if Danny was going there. But Danny was going to Jamaica, Brazil, and Mali to study drumming cultures on a Watson Fellowship. The catch was that he couldn't come back to the United States for a year.

"A professional wandering Jew," Marcia called him, but seemed genuinely pleased that his genius had been recognized by a panel of experts.

"You know," Lily said, changing the subject, "I hope you realize that if your parents hadn't fucked up the whole big reveal, they probably would not have sent you to adoption camp, and we never would have met."

"Three cheers for parents fucking up," Melody said.

"I'm serious," Lily said. "You and I are the opposite of separated at birth. We're cathectic."

"That wasn't on my vocabulary list, sorry."

"It's like connected, but stronger," Lily said. "It's a Peter word. Wanna know something else?"

"Are we doing vocabulary drills? You know I did very well on my SAT, right?"

"No, no. It's about my dad. We were talking about the whole nature versus nurture debate, and he admitted that when they adopted me, they didn't really think it mattered that I was Chinese and they weren't. They just thought if they loved me and made sure I didn't want for anything, the fact that I looked different from them and from pretty much everyone else around me would just sort of melt away. Then—get this—my dad told me that he and I should do some research about the psychological effects of transnational adoptions and coauthor a paper."

"Oh boy," Melody said.

"I know, right? My mom told him he was incorrigible, and told me to ignore him. Then she handed me a long list of all the restaurants she wants us to visit when we're in Beijing and Shanghai and Hangzhou. She also signed us up for a mapo tofu cooking class while we're there. And she and Dad are doing an online Mandarin class during their commute. It's totally over the top."

"But sweet," Melody said. "They're trying."

"Not to go all Pollyanna on you, but maybe, in her way, your mom was trying, too."

Melody felt that current of anger, never too far from the surface, course through her. Had Delia been trying? Maybe, like Lily's parents, she believed love was enough. But was it? It didn't seem so. Not to her. Not right now. "I'll never know, will I," Melody said, as much to herself as to her friend.

"Maybe you don't have to know it," Lily said, reaching for her hand and gently uncurling the fist Melody didn't realize she was making. "Maybe you just have to believe it."

ACKNOWLEDGMENTS

So many thanks to my agent and friend, Kim Witherspoon, for her astute editorial guidance and encouragements, and to her insightful and patient associate at InkWell Management, Maria Whelan. The team at HarperCollins, led by the inimitable Sara Nelson, is nonpareil: Edie Astley, Suzette Lam, Julie Hersh, Lisa Erickson, Heather Drucker, Natalie Blachere, Robin Bilardello, and Virginia Stanley. The care they have taken with this book is apparent on every page as well as the beautiful cover. Thank you to my early readers: Sara Rimer and Jillian Medoff, and to Bill McKibben, my earliest reader and biggest cheerleader, always. This is a book about family. I am forever grateful for mine.

ABOUT THE AUTHOR

Sue Halpern is the author of eight books of fiction and nonfiction, most recently *Summer Hours at the Robbers Library*. Her writing has appeared in *The New Yorker*, *New York Times Magazine*, *New York Review of Books*, *Rolling Stone*, and *Condé Nast Traveler*. She lives in Vermont with her husband, the writer and environmental activist Bill McKibben, and is a scholar-in-residence at Middlebury College.